SUSAN GRANT

SUREBLOOD

HQN™

Recycling programs
for this product may
not exist in your area.

ISBN-13: 978-0-373-77466-1

SUREBLOOD

Copyright © 2010 by Susan Grant

This edition published by arrangement with Harlequin Books S.A.

For questions and comments about the quality of this book please contact us at Customer_eCare@Harlequin.ca.

® and TM are trademarks of the publisher. Trademarks indicated with ® are registered in the United States Patent and Trademark Office, the Canadian Trade Marks Office and in other countries.

www.HQNBooks.com

Printed in U.S.A.

Dear Reader,

On February 5, 2008, in Sacramento, California, a three-year-old girl was rushed to the hospital after being found unconscious. Medical personnel could not revive her, and she was pronounced dead. Her mother's boyfriend was charged with the murder. The tragic story of Valeeya Brazile haunted me, even more once I read that this three-foot, thirty-one-pound dynamo had such a joyous spirit, despite her violent home. So when it came time to name my female pirate captain, I knew there could be only one choice. Through *Sureblood*'s heroine, Valeeya Blue, a little girl lives on, strong, free and brave.

Fly high!

Susan Grant

ACKNOWLEDGMENTS

Huge thanks go out to Tara Parsons, Tracy Farrell, Ethan Ellenberg, Lisa Richmond, Pat Meyer, Cindy Feuerstein, Carolyn Curtice, Rae Monet, Linnea Sinclair and George Meyer. And I can't forget Sarah Calder, whose winning bid won her the namesake of a pirate clan, the proceeds of bidding going to charity.

To moms—
past, present and future.

CHAPTER ONE

THE CREW OF THE *Varagon* pursued their prey across a notorious region known as a graveyard to all but the pirates who lived there. Today there would be no escape for the old freighter trying to sneak away with a cargo full of stolen ore.

Blue clan's ore, Valeeya Blue thought and yanked her weapons belt snug around her hips. Trespassers *and* thieves, they were. This was her people's home, not theirs. With a swell of possessiveness, she took in the sight of a million suns glowing fiercely behind a swath of bleak and rocky worlds. The Channels. It was a breathtaking sight even now, years after she'd first taken to the stars as a teenage apprentice.

The mineral riches on the asteroids were what outsiders found so bloody attractive about the place, zelfen ore most of all, coveted by the galaxy's two warring factions to strengthen battleship hulls and other war machines. For the chance to thieve what they'd normally have to buy at sky-high market prices, these outsiders were willing to risk life and limb…and space pirates like Val.

"Eyes on me, Blues!" Her captain, Grizz, pushed through the crowd and stopped in the center of the bridge. His body armor and everyone else's was etched into an intricate, individual pattern. Tattooing the protective plates was considered good luck. The better the art, the better the luck. Whether the myth bore out over time, nobody wanted to say, but no one ever went out undecorated. As a newer raider, Val's was still a work in progress, only hinting at what she hoped it would someday be: a depiction of the wind—wild and free, like her.

Grizz thrust his hand at a magnified image of the freighter. "Look at that old crate, sailin' through our lands as simple as you please!" he bellowed over the sound of outraged yells. "Well, she miscalculated, thinkin' no one would come after all that zelfen she took without askin'." His eyes glimmered. "Nezerihm's gonna pay well when we hand it back to him."

"Ore stealers!" Val added her yells to those of the other raiders. With zelfen's value soaring, the mine owner had started paying out lucrative bounties for the return of plundered ore. In exchange, the pirates left Nezerihm's assets alone, unlike the old days when his family's riches were at their mercy. The days when the pirate clans were united and mighty, and the Nezerihms were not. Val couldn't imagine the clans holding sports tourneys and yearly gatherings, even intermarrying, but once upon a time they did. Clan elders like Grizz and Malta and even her parents recalled those times. These days, pirates didn't even trust each other let alone outsiders. They squabbled, jostled for power and practically stole food off each other's plates. Things had gotten so bad that Val wouldn't be surprised if a rival clan showed up today to crash their raid. Bring it on. The crew of the *Varagon* was ready. Aye, and she was ready. She gave her armor one last tug.

The raiders began to stomp their heavy boots, calling for the beginning of the raid. Grizz's eyes warmed but held on to a deadly glint as he took in the sight of his crew. "Blues! Are you ready to go a-raidin'?"

Battle cries and boot heels thundered in the confines of the ship. Val's blood thrummed with anticipation, and also a wee bit of fear. "You need some fear," her clan-leader father had always told her. "Some. Too much paralyzes you, and too little makes you reckless. *Arrogant*." Conn no longer went out on raids, having lost a hand years earlier, an injury through another raider's recklessness. As eager as Val was to leave the *Varagon* and help collect the booty, she rechecked her gear. Where the breather hose connected to her nitrox cylinder a disc was loose. She tightened it with an O-clamp. She didn't need something like suffocation distracting her from the pleasure of a good raid.

"Cap'n!" a deep, husky female voice cried out over the thunder. The noise ebbed a fraction as Grizz stalked to where Val's skiff commander, Malta, kept watch for other clans' jackals. The woman perched like an ornery, aging forest raptor in a chair on the bridge, her unflinching gaze on an array of screens. Her competence proved Val's belief that not all girls were content being dirt-bound back on Artoom tending the home fires. Like Malta, Val wanted to raid for her clan and have the best bloody time of her life doing it, too. "Looks like we got company," the woman told Grizz. "Calders, maybe. But my money's on them Surebloods."

Matching the woman scowl for scowl, Grizz swore as he drove a hand through his graying dark brown hair. It fell around his shoulders as he leaned over her muscled arm. "That's their way—the greedy bastards—hanging back like that. Using the asteroids as cover. Looking to steal what ain't theirs to take."

Boos and jeers told what the crew thought of that news. The pirates of the Sureblood clan were their chief rivals.

Malta enhanced the faint signatures. Then she nodded grimly. "It's them, all right. Surebloods."

"Raid crashers," the crowd roared.

"We were here first," Val muttered. The Surebloods had no right to the freighter. First come, first raid: it was one of the first laws of piracy. Once skiffs attached to a ship, any other comers were supposed to back off. No matter how contentious the relations between the clans, no one broke the rule.

Except, apparently, the Surebloods.

"First come, first raid is the way we pirates operate," Malta was grumbling. "But here they are, elbowing their way in. And they have the gall to accuse us Blues of doing the same to *their* raids." Malta shook her head. "You'd think the death of their clan leader would have mellowed them, but the son's set them on a path his sire never did."

Dake Sureblood. Stars above, did the man's arrogance have no limits? For someone not much older than she was, he'd sure gotten far in stirring things up.

Thanks to him, their two clans were ready to come to blows. He was a thug, like the rest of them Surebloods. Built huge like forest giants, they were barely literate and drank boar blood for breakfast! That was what she grew up hearing, transfixed by the stories Nezerihm confided on his visits to Artoom, especially when they plied the mine owner with moonshine.

Furious, Grizz pushed upright and faced his seething raiders. "They want this prize, but we're gonna beat them to it. Those good-for-nothin' Surebloods and their upstart boy captain were too slow this time. We got here first. There won't be anything left worth picking over by the time they show up. Blues! *Let's go a-raidin'!*"

The cheers were deafening as Grizz called out orders above the bedlam. "Launch the skiffs!"

A *thwump-thwump* sound signaled the first two boarding craft detaching from the *Varagon*. The skiffs looked tiny as they soared away across the void. When amongst the asteroids, skiffs were virtually undetectable. More would follow, a swarm of them. They'd hide until it was time to attack. Sneaking in from the rear, they would use the vessel's own openings to gain entry. They'd be inside before anyone raised the alarm.

Reeve, one of Val's skiff mates, stepped next to her as they waited their turn to launch. "Hope that old crate don't fall apart like a birthday pop-box when we bust through."

"She just might." Val grinned, remembering a long-ago birthday celebration: her with a wooden rod gripped in tiny hands and the thrill of sweet treats showering down from a shattered pop-box. "And if she does, we'll take their booty as easy as candy."

The rest of the raiders were just as vocal in their contempt of the broken-down hulk that dared steal their ore, adding their insults in language that got more and more colorful.

"Shut your traps!" Grizz glared at his rowdy crew. "She ain't a Coalition warbird, and don't look like much, but keep your eyes open and watch your backs— and your fellow raiders'. I'm of no mind to bring any of you fools home in bio-sacks." His scowl deepened. "Not everything that looks easy always is."

The warning sent a coil of unease spinning through Val. It wasn't so much what he saw out there, she realized, but what *he felt*.

Never argue with your gut. When skill can't carry you and your luck runs out, your gut keeps you alive. Grizz had told her that and so had her father. Whether her instincts were as good as theirs remained to be seen. She liked to think she had something of her sire in her besides his grin and golden eyes.

"Don't listen to the old man, Val. He's worried for nothing."

Val sighed against clenched teeth at the voice belonging to the one raider she tried to avoid: Ayl, the stupid sot. She heard the hushed clank of his armor and the scuff of his boots as he inserted himself between her and Reeve, who threw the man an annoyed glance before making room. "You'd be smart to mind him, Ayl. The captain's been busting hatches since before we were born."

"Maybe that's too long."

"Think you can do it better?" she challenged.

"Oh, I know I can." His sly, dark gaze crept over her armor as if looking for a way in. "The same goes for a lot of other things. You know that, Val."

His smile was brilliant, his posture confident with a bit of swagger. The clansman well knew his many charms and used them, notoriously, to his advantage, fooling even her. He'd cheated on her the eve they first slept together, hopping from her bed to Despa's *within hours?* The humiliation still stung.

Why out of all the ships did Ayl have to be reassigned to the *Varagon?* Before he arrived, she'd easily avoided both him and Despa on Artoom in between raiding sorties and all was well. Here, it was impossible. Yet, she knew the answer: at her father's behest Grizz trained the best and brightest, the future leaders of the clan. As the firstborn son of a high-ranking, respected clan captain, Ayl was on track to be one of them.

"Let's talk," he said at his smoothest. "You and me. Later."

"Like Grizz said, we'll be celebrating later in the bar. You can talk to me there."

"I meant just us."

"There's no 'us.' You made sure of that."

Sighing, Ayl scrubbed his glove over his face. Then he dropped his hand, looking as if he wanted to touch her arm, then seeing the look in her eyes decided wisely against it. "Despa seduced *me.* I told you. I didn't want to sleep with her."

Val snorted. "Same old story."

Even Reeve smirked at the lame excuse, coughing out a laugh.

Ayl looked as if he wanted to deck the raider but held back, his words to Val low and firm. "You're not just any clan female, Val. It's your duty to make a marriage alliance. Your duty as Conn's daughter."

"You're right about that. I'm not just any female." She shoved her dozer into her holster, securing it, tempting though it was to use it on Ayl to shut him up. "I'm a raider. My duty's here."

"So is ours," Reeve said pointedly. "She's getting ready to raid, Ayl. Leave her be."

"This, especially, isn't your business," Ayl hissed with an edge of contempt, making it obvious he hadn't forgotten that Reeve's parentage wasn't as impressive as his own. The clans had a hierarchy on and off ship. Only some like Ayl openly acted on it. A sign of his insecurity, Val thought.

"Aye, it's my business," Reeve argued. "It's my skiff mate you're distracting. She's supposed to watch my ass and me hers. And since when do I take orders from you, Ayl? You aren't my commander, and you aren't her man. I think she's made that pretty bloody clear. Or do you need me to help explain it?"

Val tapped Reeve's armored bicep and shook her head. Her skiff mate went silent, but with bitter reluctance. Like the Blues and the Surebloods, one of these days he and Ayl were going to come to blows. But it wouldn't be today if Val could help it, and not before a raid. The men needed to burn up their energy on thieving merchants, not each other.

Ayl turned to her. "I'll say one more thing, Val. Eventually you'll have to give up raiding."

"Like hells, I will."

"Even Conn said so."

She froze. "You talked to my father?" A few raiders glanced over at her appalled tone. In the back of her mind was ever the worry her father would disapprove of her being a raider. She wanted to give him no opportunities for second thoughts.

"I made my intentions known to him, aye."

"What—what did he say?"

Ayl cleared his throat. "That's between me and him. All I'm telling you is that it's time—past time, actually—that you thought of your future." He looked her up and down. "You're not getting any younger."

"And aging every second I waste talking to you about this."

"Val! Ayl! Get the bloody hells over here!" Grizz jerked his hand at them, a summons to the bridge, and turned away before Val could read his expression.

Busted. Swearing under her breath, she dropped her conversation with Ayl like a hot stone. How much had Grizz heard? Or Malta? Would they think her flighty and weak or a flirt and tell her father? A thundering heartbeat of acute embarrassment drummed in her ears. It was all her fault for letting Ayl pull her into a silly argument in the middle of prepping for a raid.

"You'll come around," Ayl murmured as she pushed past him.

She felt his smug, sideways gaze on her all the way to the bridge. There, Grizz's broad-shouldered form blocked the view of the departing skiffs. The tenseness in his back told her he was scowling. Val felt as small and unnoticeable as a skiff in the Channels as she waited to be acknowledged by her captain. Where was the protective shadow of one of those crater-pitted asteroids when she needed one? She was about to apologize for dallying with Ayl when instinct told her to just be quiet.

Grizz folded his arms over his chest as he faced them. Val wanted to squirm under the lens of his scrutiny, but didn't. That, too, would be a mistake. His menacing glare landed on Ayl first. "You're stayin' behind, boy."

Ayl started to protest, but seemed to think better of it. "Aye, Cap'n," he mumbled.

"I could use your help on the bridge, coordinating," Grizz said, softening the blow a bit. "Stow your gear and be back in five."

"Aye, Cap'n." Gone was Ayl's swagger; in its place were sagging shoulders.

Grizz then turned to Val. The man's jaw muscles twitched, a sure sign he was gritting his teeth. Dread gripped her. A dozen possible fates came to mind, from latrine cleaning to having to serve bridge duty with Ayl. She wasn't sure which would be worse.

"Skiff Six is yours," he told her.

"Cap'n?" Her pulse lurched, pounding hard under her armor, as she blinked at the unexpected good news. If it were true, it would be her first time in command, something she'd dreamed of, trained for. Lusted after.

"Aye, you heard me right. I'm puttin' you in charge of your own skiff."

"But Six? That's Malta's skiff."

"It *was* my skiff, girl." Malta leaned a shoulder against the nav console, arms folded over her ample bosom as she listened in. Val could hardly look her in the eye. The last thing she wanted was to usurp the pirate elder under her very nose.

"Malta's staying," Grizz said. "I need an extra set of experienced eyes here on the mother ship, with those greedy, no-good, raid-crashin' Sureblood thugs in the area. We've got ourselves a prime prize, and I ain't givin' it over to them. So, Malta's staying and you're going. Even though I've got half a mind to keep you here after seeing your lack of discipline." His eyes narrowed at her embarrassment. "You didn't initiate the conversation with Ayl, I'll give you that, but you let yourself be distracted by it. Hells, socializing during a briefing—" he shook his head "—I expect more of you than that, Valeeya. Your father does, too."

Her face burned. "I know he does." Worse than her embarrassment and disappointment in herself was imagining what her father would think. Her brother Sethen was supposed to be the family screwup, not her. She wanted to be the raider her father could depend on. "I'll prove myself worthy if you send me out. I know I will. You won't regret it."

"I blasted well better not. You're gonna shine, girl. I know it. I wouldn't be sending you out if I thought otherwise." At that, he soaked in her excitement. "Now quit wasting time and get your ass in that skiff."

"You heard your captain—go," Malta said. There was a smile behind her sternness.

"Aye, ma'am. Aye, aye, Cap'n." Number Six. *Six!* Malta's skiff. No, *hers*.

Then they all noticed Ayl lingering within earshot. He'd heard the entire conversation, she thought, seeing his sullen eyes and mulish pout. "Congratulations," he muttered.

It's your own fault, Ayl. But she kept her opinion to herself to soften the blow. Maybe he'd leave her alone from now on.

Grizz scowled at both of them. "About time you two newbies carried your weight around this ship. Get to work." Then he turned back to the displays.

It wasn't finished between them: Ayl's glare told her that.

Reeve called out to the other raiders. "Val's takin' Six out!"

"About freepin' time!" someone shouted.

"Six is gonna kick some ore-stealin' ass!" yelled another.

"Freepin' right," Val called back, grinning, feeling her confidence return.

Raiders congratulated her as she pushed through the crowd preceded by the news. Flashing what everyone called her father's grin, slanted and cocky, Val hurried belowdecks. She flew down the ladder to the bottom, landing in the cavernous lower bay. Leaky air locks hissed. It sounded like the *Varagon* could use some rest and relaxation—and repair—just like the rest of them once they returned home to Artoom. It had been a long hunt. They'd been out raiding and away from the clan for weeks. As much as she loved it out here, it was time to go home. And she'd return as a skiff commander, she thought with no small amount of pride.

She'd make Grizz glad of his decision to send her out.

They joined Hervor, their third skiff mate, who was already on board Six. Val dropped into her seat, bending her comm over her mouth. The band crushed her hair to her scalp. The scent of shampoo mingled with fuel and the faint, acrid odor of onboard components. "I'm leading us out today."

Hervor grinned. "Good on you, girl!"

"You got that right, *skiff commander,*" Reeve said and pulled the hatch closed.

Val's ears stuffed up, then cleared as the craft pressurized. She took the controls, just as she'd practiced—and imagined—so many times, and forced herself to run through all the preflight checks despite her mounting excitement.

"Six is ready," she told the *Varagon.* The docking hooks retracted and the skiff floated free. "Woo! Let's go, boys."

Others echoed her call over the private comm between the skiffs. The beginning of a raid never failed to make her heart pound with excitement. The adrenaline rush was almost addictive. She'd experienced nothing else like it back on Artoom. Pushing the throttles to max, she swung the skiff in the direction of the Channels, regretting only that she'd miss seeing

the disappointment on Dake Sureblood's face when
he found out the Blues had beat his gangsters to the
treasure.

DAKE SUREBLOOD LAUNCHED his big frame into his
skiff and yanked the restraints over his shoulders,
his focus never leaving the day's prize. Ah, she was
as sweet as they came: an aging Drakken cargo ship
bursting at the seams with pilfered zelfen. *That old
ore-cartin' crate is practically beggin' to be plundered.*
Aye, and he'd be happy to oblige.

Dake pushed the comm mic over his devilish grin.
"Are you ready to take her down, Surebloods?" he said,
expecting no less than the enthusiastic roars that answered his call to action. With the fly-stick gripped in
a gloved hand, he soared away from the *Tomark's Pride*
with the rest of his skiffs in trail.

"The Channels are dead ahead, boss," Yarmouth
said.

Dake nodded at his first mate's alert. *Dead* wasn't a
term used lightly in these parts. Some of the asteroids
were as big as moons, others the size of starships. The
tiniest of the asteroids, mere grains, hissed and sizzled
where they collided with the skiff's hardened fuselage.
If anything much larger hit, he'd not have a chance to
ponder his demise before he landed at the gates of the
Ever After. If there was one good thing to be said about
death-by-asteroid, it was quick.

A tumbling boulder streaked past the skiffs. Then
another. Dake didn't back off his breakneck speed.
Many would consider it suicide maintaining such high

velocity in one of the densest areas of the Channels. Dake was no exception. But this time he'd managed to flight-test a launch route and even more importantly an escape route thanks to an early heads-up on the freighter's course given by Nezerihm.

The wily mine owner had promised Dake a big haul today, and a larger-than-usual percentage of what they'd normally earn returning stolen ore for a bounty. It reeked a bit of privateer work, but, hells, Dake had a clan to feed. He anticipated spending the windfall on much-needed supplies, and maybe even a few luxuries for his cash-strapped clan. They'd suffered their share of hard times of late. His aim was to shove those dark days into the past and keep them there.

Even if it meant making deals with Nez, the slimy little creep. The man made his skin crawl.

"We ought to have an easy time of it today," Yarmouth remarked. "If those Blues don't show up and try to steal what's ours. Nezzie says they want to take it all for themselves. Not just from us, but from all the clans, squeezing everyone out but them. You heard him—those greedy muckers will undercut us all if we let 'em."

"I know what he says." As a rule Dake dismissed most of what Nezerihm babbled on about, but the man had a point about the Blue clan. Used to be, pirate honor meant something. Not to the Blues apparently. They thought they could take what they wanted, when they wanted. It threatened the very way of life in these Channels. Potentially, the Blues' aggression could cause other, weaker clans to go hungry. Yet Dake recalled his father admiring the Blue clan leader, Conn. The way the story went, the two met once as young men and discovered they shared similar hopes of uniting the clans. As leaders they followed through in keeping their clans from tearing out each other's throats. Then tensions began to rise, and the two called a meeting to address healing the rift between the clans once and for all. His father, Tomark, was killed in a starship crash before the meeting could happen, cut down in the prime of life in a senseless tragedy.

The Surebloods lost their leader. Dake lost his hero.

He locked his jaw. The twinge of grief he felt at the memory he could hardly grasp, much less accept, was a familiar spike in a constant undercurrent of sadness. Not even distraction in the form of women and drink or raiding quite erased it.

A tail thumped against his pilot seat. Merkury pushed his muzzle into Dake's hand. Intelligent brown eyes gazed up at Dake almost too perceptively. He often wondered what his dog could figure out, suspecting it was more than he or anyone could guess. It had been that way ever since he'd freed Merkury as a pup during a raid on a military scientific vessel. An intelligence augmentation lab it was, apparently. Well, Merkury may have had his education interrupted, but his natural canine abilities were put to good use on raids.

Dake ruffled the herding beast's black-and-white fur. "Women," he muttered to Merkury's laser-like stare. *As if I could remember what it's like sharing the bed with anyone but you.* He'd been living an out-and-out monk's life since taking over the clan, little to drink and no women. His youth had been wild all right, like any young raider's, but it had met an untimely end, coming head to head with responsibility. Not that he'd been reckless, but he'd had his fun. At his age he should have been looking forward to more of the same for a good many years to come. Tomark's passing had changed all that.

The responsibility of the clan weighed heavily, taking all of Dake's attention. Duty was his focus now. He'd do right by the Surebloods. He *had to*. He was all they had.

And they're all you have now as well. It had been just him and Tomark after losing his mother and sisters in a firestorm during one of Parramanta's annual wild-fires when he was a boy. Although his father eventually remarried and started a new, young family, Dake considered himself the last of his line. The Surebloods did, too. He wouldn't relax today no matter how easy of a raid it seemed. Not for one nanosecond. The clan's survival depended on being able to raid ships.

The clan's survival depended *on him*.

Yarmouth persisted, "But, boss, if those greedy bastards have their way, we'll be turning to farming to make a living."

Dake practically shuddered with the thought. "They ain't here. This freighter wasn't being tracked. The chance of the Blue clan knowing about it is remote."

Malizarr popped his head up from where he lay on his belly manning the plasma cannon. The gunner looked worried. "What about Kormanna Hollows last month? We didn't think they'd know about that one, either, but somehow they did."

Dake scrubbed a weary hand over his face, exposing his frustration with the situation. He hadn't stopped wondering about the events at Kormanna either, but he'd held his own counsel, not sharing his worries. Out of respect for his father's views he refrained from stirring up animosity for the other clans, even for the Blues. Deep down, he agreed with Tomark that the pirates, all of them, were in this together. United, they were a force to be reckoned with; separate, they were weak. Still, the Blue clan was starting to irritate him.

Dake frowned at the scope in front of him. Several swipes of his fingers across the forward display screen paraded views of the flight path ahead. He flipped through the images, cross-checking with what he could see out front until he'd assured himself the data were accurate. "Nothing but rocks out there. No Blues."

"Better not be. I'm itchin' for a fight." Yarmouth unbent from a crouched position and hunted around for a more comfortable place to store his long legs. Dake at least had the extra room afforded by the pilot's seat. The skiff was blasted cramped but the small size was necessary for stealth. The breadth of his shoulders nearly spanned the inner walls of the craft. Squib, Dake's third skiff mate, was no better off, hunched over as he peered out the starboard portholes waiting for a clear view of the freighter.

The Surebloods' physical size didn't exactly work in their favor when it came to this stage of a raid. But once inside the target ship, it served them well. More often the merchants they raided were too frightened by the sight of boarding Surebloods dressed to the chin in leathers and tattooed armor and carrying every portable weapon known to man to put up much resistance. The few times it came down to fighting in hand-to-hand combat, the clansmen's sheer size aided their victory.

Only Merkury seemed comfortable in the cramped skiff. Ears erect, shiny cold nose twitching, the dog's attention appeared riveted on Dake, waiting for every blasted word he uttered. "You keep me on the right path, Merk," Dake murmured. "Keep me doing the right thing."

It was difficult, at times, to know what the right thing was. Dake bore all the responsibility of leading the clan without any of the experience. If only Tomark was still around to advise him.

The asteroids thinned out, becoming farther and farther apart until they petered out altogether.

"There she is, boss." Squib peered down the sights of the cannon at the vessel. "She's far worse in person than she was onscreen."

"Why, it's a bloody museum piece," Yarmouth coughed out.

"So much for holding it for ransom," Malizarr added. "We'll be lucky to find someone willing to scrap the thing. How the hells did this piece of flarg think they'd get away?"

With zelfen. Madness it was. The region was as notorious for its piracy as it was for its mines. Either these illegal ore harvesters were lying to themselves about their chances of success, or they'd been driven to desperation by a war seemingly without end. For a thousand years the Drakken had battled the Coalition. There'd be times of relative calm, aye, but it was only to regroup and keep on going. How could there be peace when neither side was willing to accept anything less than absolute domination and utter annihilation of the other?

"Listen up, Surebloods." Dake briefed the skiff teams over the group comm. "First thing once we're aboard is to take the bridge. Even monsters of this size won't have more than twenty-five crewmen. About a third will be snoring in their bunks. A duty officer will be on the bridge along with a pilot. The engineer belowdecks won't be much use for helping protect the bridge. Same with the galley crew. That leaves only a few people to defend. Tokotay, you'll lead your teams forward, defuse the crew and take the bridge. I want this ship under our control as fast as possible!"

The answering thunder of the raiders blasted in his ear comm. He grinned. "All right, raiders. Here we go."

Gripping the fly-stick in his gloved hand, Dake spiraled down toward the freighter.

At last, the freedom of open space, he thought. *None too soon.* He didn't like tightly enclosed spaces for long, but what pirate did, no matter what their size? The stars were their seas, the skies their muse. They were a freedom-loving people. Clan was everything. Stories had come back of pirates caught by one side or the other to fight in the war against their will. They never survived for long without their freedom and their clan. A living death, he imagined, a chill washing over him despite sweating in his armor and leathers.

Merkury's chin landed on the top of his thigh. The dog sensed the turn in his thoughts. Who knew what the military's goal had been with their research, but times like this Dake swore the animal could read his mind. "It's all right, boy. That isn't ever going to happen to us." The short shelf life of pirate conscripts was known well enough. Likely it was why so few ships came to the Channels looking for recruits. That, or the freepin' cowards remembered the consequences of venturing into the Channels in the first place: their valuables confiscated, their ships and their own pitiful selves ransomed.

Then Merkury sat up straight and growled.

Dake narrowed his eyes outside, trying to figure out Merkury's cause of alarm. The gigantic, glinting mass of metal blotted out the stars ahead like an eclipse, growing in size as they neared it until it seemed the ship was all there in front of them. Few of the freighter's running lights were on. Of course, they were trying to sneak out of the system. Darkened like that, the massive ship was an eerie sight.

Merkury growled again, low and deep, then made a small whine. The hair on the back of Dake's neck prickled. What was out there?

Or what *else?*

Yarmouth and Squib must have shared his unease: they were silent, peering out from their stations, looking for the trouble.

Then Squib broke the silence. "There, boss. See that?"

A couple of beats of Dake's heart later, he saw what his third mate did: lights falling around the freighter from the stern, as if the stars themselves had dropped out of the sky to float free.

Dake strained against the seat harnesses. He blinked, then, disbelieving of the sight. "Those are bloody skiffs!"

Anger and shock ripped through him, clearing away his confusion like a Parramanta wildfire cut through forest in the yearly drought. He whipped his fingers across the screen, calling up the skiffs' unique signatures. What he saw he'd dreaded. He knew those identifiers by heart.

"Bloody, freepin' hells. Those raid-crashing louts." He crushed his hand into a fist to keep from punching out the scope. "It's Blue clan." And today they'd gone too far.

CHAPTER TWO

BLUE CLAN DESCENDED around the freighter like a flurry of celestial snowflakes. Up close, the ramshackle Drakken hulk was darker, craggier. A faint shiver slid down Val's spine at the sight. Everything about the Drakken Horde seemed to reek of evil, she thought, conjuring the monsters of childhood nightmares.

"Boogeyman," Reeve muttered as if reading her thoughts. He was crouched by the starboard portholes, his handsome face blank of emotion as Val cut the power to coast silently in the shadow of the huge ship.

"Can't help the way she looks, being Drakken," Hervor said. "Best not to wake her up early, though."

"Aye, I'm tiptoeing." Val took extra precautions to slip alongside the fuselage like a shadow. Drifting the last few clicks, she found her assigned hatch and settled over it.

Soundlessly, she and her team jumped into action. Masks fastened, safety ropes attached and raiding suits checked intact before creating an airtight seal between the two ships. Using plasma and zelfen blades, and centuries of technique, Hervor and Reeve turned the hatch into a temporary opening. On a gargantuan vessel like the freighter the intrusion would show up, at most, as a blip in the environmental systems status that could easily be attributed to a hundred unimportant anomalies. "Pressure's good," Val said, monitoring the stream of data on her cockpit display. "Holding steady."

Holding steady against the void. Sweat prickled on her temples as she tried not to be so acutely aware of the vastness of space outside. The absolute cold. The impossibility of surviving out there. Things went wrong on raids. It wasn't common, but it did happen. She'd seen a raider get sucked overboard her first month assigned to the *Varagon*. A ruptured passage port, and out he went. The scene replayed in her mind: his expression of surprise, his mask flailing uselessly, the way his fingers grasped vainly for something to hold on to, his mouth opening and closing like a landed fish trying to breathe on the bottom of a boat. It wasn't the kind of sight one forgot.

Perspiration beaded on her brow despite the frigid air now rushing in through the passage port connecting both vessels. Reeve aimed his tester. "The air's safe to breathe."

She tore off her breather—and wrinkled her nose. "Safe, aye, but it stinks." The hammocks Drakken space hands used—their "sleeping skins"—gave off a peculiar odor that reminded her of bad cheese. It was the only hint that the ship was inhabited. Its sheer size was to blame. But the crew was here; she had no doubt about that. Aye, and they'd kill her in a heartbeat if she gave them a chance.

She judged the opening she'd shimmied through,

then sized up her team. "Boarding time, raiders. Give your gear another check." She looked over her weapons and armor one last time. Just to be safe. You never knew what you might run into on someone else's ship.

Or who.

THE SHOUTS OF OUTRAGED raiders blasted in Dake's ear comm as the shock of the discovery spread through the Sureblood skiffs. By mere moments, the Blue clan had beaten them to the freighter. Now he was racing in on their tails. He had but seconds to decide a course of action. Everything depended on making the right choice.

Malizarr growled from his station. "Let me shoot them. Come on, boss. It'll teach them once and for all."

"Hold your fire," Dake said sharply to him and all the other raiders in the formation with eager trigger fingers.

Yarmouth spat out a curse. "You're not going to let them get away with this, are you, Cap'n? It's time we defended what's ours. Two raids in a row them Blues stole from us. No one wants to give them a third."

"Trust me, there won't be a third," Dake said, firm. But if he were to give in to emotion and attack the Blues instead of the freighter, his efforts would be expended on other pirates and not the ore-stealing merchants. The outsiders were their enemies, not their own kind. "I won't abandon the raid to freepin' either one of them, Blues or Horde." His raiders wouldn't return home humiliated. They'd seen enough bad times the past year. He wanted to give them reason to celebrate.

"Continue!" he bellowed, feeling better already for having said it. For not turning tail and going home. "The raid is a go."

Squib pushed up on his knees. The boy's surprise was obvious even with slashes of bright war paint across his face. "But, boss, what about first come, first raid?"

"That rule's been temporarily suspended," Dake snarled.

Everyone was shouting now as they blazed toward the freighter. Yarmouth and Malizarr laughed and whooped. Squib looked incredulous. Even Merkury tipped his head at Dake's order.

"We're the superior force," Dake explained. "We're better trained, better equipped. Even Nezerihm says so," he heard himself saying despite his aversion to quoting the man. "We can well handle those merchants at the same time as a gaggle of poorly trained, rangy Blues. Surebloods fight to win!"

"Not fight. Unite."

Dake spat out a curse. He could hear the voice of Tomark Sureblood warning against bloodshed. Urging him to choose a course of unity.

"It is my dream, son, to see the clans as one."

It was almost as if the old man were sitting beside him, offering advice like he used to do on Dake's first skiff flights. But his idealist father never had to deal with *this,* a rogue clan wanting to squeeze out all the others. If Conn Blue was allegedly so eager to get along, why in hells did he keep sending his raiders to steal from all the others?

No matter who thought they were right, neither clan would be willing to give up this prize to the other. Would it lead to a stalemate or bloodshed?

Or something else entirely? he thought as an idea hit him. Why settle for lose-lose when win-win was within their reach? Aye, they could split the prize between them. It was bloody well big enough. Problem was, those Blues didn't strike him as the kind who'd care to share. Well, he'd find out soon enough, he thought as the massive freighter speckled with Blue clan's skiffs filled his screen. *Here we come.*

HUGGING THE WALLS, weapons at the ready, Val and the men moved away from the skiff in a wary but steady lope. The endless corridor was cavernous and dimly lit. Cold, bone-chilling cold, making her glad for the all-clime suit under her armor. All the mining crates felt this way, operating without a specken of comfort. She couldn't imagine a life caged inside one of these ships, especially one so foul.

An odor wafted by, worse than the sleeping skins. "Flargin' nasty, that," she whispered to the men. "I don't want to know what's making that smell."

"Dinner." Hervor tipped his chin at a pair of double doors. "I think we found the galley." Sure enough, the cloying odor of Drakken food, *stale* Drakken food, seeped out from under those doors. There'd be no feasting today as part of the raiding. If this were a Coalition freighter, it'd be a different story. Those ships were prime for good eats. Her mouth watered thinking of all the delectable treats they'd stuffed into their mouths and pockets on previous raids and would have to go without today.

Hervor slowed at the doors. "Wanna see if there's any sweef? Drakken rotgut. Can't handle it straight up myself, but there's a mixed drink I had once—Hordish heartbreak, or something like that. We'll bring some back with us and force-feed it to Ayl."

With a snicker, Reeve offered, "I volunteer to help. Wouldn't want my buddy Ayl to go thirsty. Especially after a day stuck on bridge duty."

Val grinned, thinking she might join them in quenching Ayl's thirst. The men's banter was one reason she liked being assigned to Skiff Six so much. Malta's steady presence was the other. Today Malta wasn't here to keep them in line. That responsibility had fallen to Val. She had a lot on the line. "Forget it, Herv. No side trips today."

Laughing, he kicked open the doors anyway. A blur of movement from inside the galley. Then a crash. Weapons swinging around, Val and the men took aim.

A wrenching heartbeat later she lowered her weapon. Squeezed her eyes shut for half a second, then felt like kicking something, namely Hervor. "A box." A freepin' empty box. It had fallen off a shelf and cracked open, spilling some sort of gray slime. Shaking mad, she turned on Hervor. "It could easily have *not* been a box. It could have been a galley hand, and he might have called for help and given our foolish asses away. Or worse, he might have been armed and shot at us."

"Sorry, Val—"

"You'd better be glad fate's kind to you, because if it wasn't, you wouldn't have been sorry, Herv. You'd have *been dead*. When I give an order I mean for you to obey it. The same as you'd do with Malta. You got that?"

"Aye, Val. Same as Malta."

She turned, her long braid whipping around her shoulders. "Search the room. Make sure no one's hiding." She kicked over containers and threw open cabinets to peek inside, her dozer ready to fire and stun. This had almost gone bad—and still could. She so wanted to please Conn, the man who was everyone's hero, and especially hers. She wanted him to be proud he'd agreed to let his only daughter train as a raider, not ashamed. She wanted him to revel in the deeds of at least one of his offspring.

"Come on. Let's do what we came here to do. Let's gouge these outsider muckers," she told the men, stalking forward. Then they were back in the corridor, jogging to make up for lost time.

WITH HIS TEAMS ON THE WAY to take over the bridge, Dake and his handpicked few went hunting. The advancing Blues had started out as separate teams, then coalesced into larger groups. Dake doubled back to check for stragglers, while the bulk of his raiders formed a human blockade around the bridge. These

Blues may have gotten aboard, but he'd keep them from taking control of this ship.

It belonged to his clan and no other.

Silence…utter stealth… The Surebloods might be large of frame, but they were undetectable. Not only didn't Blue clan know they were about to be ambushed, but there was also no sign anyone else on the huge freighter was aware they were aboard. Aye, but they'd be woken up to that fact soon enough.

The sound of something falling brought Dake to a halt. The disturbance came from a room down the corridor. He held up a hand, stopping the raiders behind him. Merkury crouched down flat in that curious way of his breed. Sharp ears detected voices, hushed arguing, before silence enveloped them once again.

So, there seems to be some foot-dragger Blues fooling around in the galley. Sweet. Dake already had the advantage of surprise and numbers in his favor; now he'd take these stragglers hostage to negotiate with their raid leader.

He'd force a peaceful end to this debacle, even if it killed him. He wanted the wealth this freighter promised, not bloodshed. He couldn't afford to lose a single member of his clan. There had been too much death in recent years, too much loss. He'd made a silent vow with his father to turn the tide, and by the stars he would.

He'd escort the Blues to their skiffs and give them a push in the direction of their mother ship. If they cooperated, he'd even offer them a small share of the haul. Aye, a little grease on the skids of possible future teamwork. He'd take the high road, even if these greedy, mangy interlopers insisted on playing in the mud. He'd win either way.

Get ready. Dake flattened his hand, pushing it palm down. At the signal, his raiders melted into the shadows, prepared to act. In seconds, they were invisible. The old ship had more hiding places than termite-infested hack pine.

The Blues emerged from the galley. Dake assessed his prey. Two men, lean, compact, nowhere close to the size of the Sureblood raiders but of a size that gave them the advantage of quickness and agility. If he let them escape, he'd probably be hard-pressed to win a second chance to catch them. He had to make this work on the first attempt.

Then, a third Blue raider appeared, closing the galley door behind them. "Why, it's a wench," Yarmouth whispered very low near his ear.

Aye, that she was. Comely, too. He made a quick, instinctive assessment: all long legs and feline grace that he could detect even under layers of leather and armor; a braided hank of shiny brown hair reached halfway down her back. Her armor was far from fully etched, yet she acted with authority. It was a skiff team, and she was the one in charge. Until, that was, he relieved her of command.

Dake cocked a small smile. Her dawdling would cost her.

Yarmouth whispered, "A right pretty one, too. Forgive me for sayin' so."

"Nothing says a man can't appreciate the enemy."

"If that's what you call it, boss. I volunteer to handle her."

Dake gave his head a single shake. "We're sticking with the plan. The skiff commander's mine." With a trace of a grin lurking at the edges of his mouth, he lifted his hand and circled it. *Move out.*

CHAPTER THREE

VAL HADN'T GONE MORE than a few steps outside the galley when she sensed something was wrong. She froze, her hand coming up in warning to the men behind her.

"Hold it right there, little Blues. Weapons down."

Too late. Heart plunging, adrenaline spurting, she jolted at the unfamiliar male voice. Little Blues—it sure as freep wasn't something a Drakken ore hauler would say.

They weren't the only pirates on board this ship.

Her dozer tracked across what appeared to be nothing but shadows. Then she saw a wall of giants who until a moment ago were invisible, their weapons aimed at them.

War paint crisscrossed their faces, concealing their features. Their exposed skin was deeply suntanned, telling her that their homeworld wasn't cloud-covered like hers. Although they wore no breathers their armor was well fortified with zelfen and heavily tattooed.

"Keep your dozers aimed between their eyes," she hissed under her breath to Reeve and Hervor. As long as everyone was still aiming at the other, no one was in control and it would give her precious seconds to sort out who these men were.

The apparent leader stepped away from the group. "Your dillydallying cost you, Blue girl," he drawled, squinting down his dozer. "I thought you'd never come out of the galley. Did you find anything worth taking?"

"I wouldn't share with you even if we did." Her dozer remained pointed spot-on between his eyes, and his aimed at her forehead. So much paint streaked the raw angles of his face that only his piercing eyes set him apart from the others. Like opals, they were—green and blue-gray and brown—no color and yet all the colors. A dull glow from the ceiling slithered over the pattern on his armor, tracing the intricate design: a ferocious sea snake, winding over and around his muscled body. And standing at his side, a dog. Not just a camp dog, but one with eyes that almost looked human.

Her heart skipped a beat. That dog—she'd heard the rumors. Some said the animal had magic powers. With alarm, she absorbed the sight of her opponent's fully etched armor. Not a specken of space remained for anything more, marking this young raider a highly respected veteran. Bah, he was nothing more than a dirt-mucking thief, an insult to the pirate breed—*a Sureblood*. And, sweet blazin' hells, the mountain of muscle and armor aiming a dozer at her brains was none other than Dake Sureblood himself.

Amusement lit up his eyes as he noted her revelation. She wanted to blast that slow smirk right off his painted face.

Her grip on her weapon remained steady, but inside she felt as inept as an Artoom hearth hugger. She'd let her team walk right into a Sureblood trap. Now they were outnumbered three to one. With them as hostages, he could force Warrybrook to trade the freighter for Val and her team. That was what *she'd* do, if the roles were reversed. It was a damned brilliant move, this ambush. Nezerihm had always dismissed the Surebloods as dumb hooligans, lazy and boorish, and nothing to worry about. Clearly, he hadn't seen *these* Surebloods.

Suddenly Malta's boots seemed impossibly big. How would she ever fill them? What would Grizz say about her fumble? Her father? That question pained her most of all. She'd spent years trying not to be like Sethen, her brother, but hadn't she just proven she was no less of a disappointment than he was?

No. She'd not dishonor her clan and embarrass her father.

"I'm not going to hurt you, if you cooperate. Nice and easy now, drop your weapons."

"Like hells we will," Val said low and cold. "You jumped us, not the other way around."

Fully encircling her team, his gang of giants chuckled at that. Condescending bastards, underestimating the Blues. Anger boiled up. "This is our raid—our prize," she said. "Get your trespassing, raid-crashing clan off the ship before we blow you off."

"Your raid?" The leader coughed out a laugh. "Now I've heard it all."

"We drilled in first," she insisted, knowing she was right.

"Because you cut us off. Just like a dozen times before." The amusement in his eyes faded, replaced by resentment that was shockingly passionate. "But this time we didn't back down. The days of letting Blue clan steal from us are over."

"This freighter's ours, fair and square."

"We raided at Nezerihm's request. It's ours by rights."

"It's ours by timing and skill, and by operating *independently*. Not like you Surebloods, who go fetch when Nezerihm says so. Like dogs."

"Woof, woof," Reeve said under his breath.

The Sureblood's fingers tightened around his dozer, his focus on her and her alone. His strangely colored eyes searched her face, his golden-brown brows raised as if he were stunned that this "little Blue," would dare stand up to him. His voice was as smooth as pillow talk when he finally spoke. "I'm thinkin' that maybe my hearing's gone bad. Did you call us Nezerihm's *dogs?*"

"Aye," Val said perkily. "Nezzie's pet pirates."

Hervor bit back a snicker. Everyone glared at each other down their weapons, waiting for an excuse to use them. Tension crystallized in the air and threatened to shatter. All it would take was one itchy trigger finger and all that would be left of them would be a smoking pile of flesh pudding.

Clearly, Sureblood was used to generating fear and awe in others—especially other clans. Even his dog reacted to Val's contempt with a skeptical tip of its head. Ears flicking with curiosity, it started over to sniff her when the Sureblood commanded, "Merkury—*stay*."

What kind of raiders brought their pets along? The same kind of clan who'd stoop to the unspeakable, busting into a ship knowing another clan's raid was already under way.

The rest of the Surebloods swore, their weapons rattling. "Ain't ya gonna teach these Blues some respect, boss?" one of the hulks asked.

"Not with a dozer to his head, he ain't," Reeve told the rival raider.

"He's aimin' at her also, Blue, if ya hadn't noticed."

The Sureblood quieted his man with a sweep of his hand, his gaze flicking from Reeve to her, as if he were sorting out whether the man's defense of her was due to their being merely skiff mates or there was something more between them. "Well, well, Blue girl," he said finally. "It looks like we're going to have to come to an agreement on whose raid this is."

"I'm not agreeing to anything a Sureblood says."

"Actually, I predict that you will." His dozer shifted to Reeve. The arming light flickered. "Because I'll make it easy for you. Now, allow us Surebloods to escort you off this ship."

Val swallowed at the sight of the weapon aimed at Reeve. It was a bluff. Pirates took prisoners from other clans, yet rarely was there a killing. But then, when did two clans end up on the same ship? Did she take the chance he wouldn't shoot?

Don't give in because of me, Reeve urged with his eyes.

She hesitated.

"Too much fear paralyzes you, Valeeya," her father would have cautioned in that moment. *"But too little makes you reckless."*

Arrogant.

Risking a skiff mate's life for any reason was arrogant. She was a skiff leader, the one who called the shots for her team, literally. The responsibility was on her to end this without loss of life, and without dishonoring her clan. Feeling sick as she gave in, she started to lower her firing arm when a distant, resounding boom echoed down the long corridor.

The floor vibrated beneath their boots. Reacting with shocking similarity and speed, both groups flew back against the walls, in the shadows, their dozers tracking in both directions up and down the corridor. The vulnerability of being trapped on someone else's vessel knew no clan boundaries.

"What the hells was that?" a now-familiar, rich voice demanded.

Dake Sureblood had taken up a position next to her. Her senses filled with the sounds of unfamiliar armor, the smell of distinctly foreign leather and the faint tang of male sweat mingled with other, exotically unfamiliar scents that were not at all unpleasant. At this close range, she could see a lot of details she didn't want to know, like a small scar or two on his face, one bisecting his brow, the other a small nick on the outer corner of his mouth. Probably gotten while out raid crashin', she decided. *He's a Sureblood. You're a Blue.* She wasn't supposed to feel any awareness of him as a male. Not even a specken.

"I sure as freep don't know," she replied carefully, realizing his aim was no longer on Reeve, offering a window of opportunity to turn this ambush around—if the chance arose.

"Malizarr," he ordered one of his thugs. "Go see what the hells that was."

"Aye, boss." The man dashed off.

Dake Sureblood watched his man disappear down the corridor, his weapon steadied in two hands. He'd forgotten all about her. Or he trusted her. For an agonizing moment she was torn, feeling it was somehow wrong to take advantage of a man who cared more about their joint safety than his clan's glory, enough to turn his back to her. Then she whipped her dozer around and pressed it to the side of his head. "Surprise."

The Sureblood went still. Val could tell by the sounds around her that every one of his clansmen had swung their weapons back to her. "Did you forget about me?" she murmured, almost giddy to see his throat move with a hard swallow.

His gaze slid sideways, a mix of surprise, amusement and reluctant respect. "That's the last time I ever will, I reckon," he said.

They weighed each other's resolve and deadly intent. She was shaking inside. She wondered if he was.

Another explosion boomed, closer this time. They jolted. "Raider leader, this is Six," she said into her comm, trying to raise Warrybrook while she kept her weapon pressed against the Sureblood's skull. Her comm barked with static but no voice. "Blast it." *Warrybrook, where are you? I've got my hands full of Surebloods.*

The muzzle of her dozer remained buried in Dake Sureblood's sun-streaked brown hair. Even the spikes of his beard were touched by gold—where the bright paint hadn't obscured his jaw. "I'm not your enemy," he murmured.

"You haven't done much to convince me of that."

"Do you think these ore haulers care if our clans can agree on anything or not?" he snapped, finally losing his temper. "Our differences don't mean a thing. To outsiders we're pirates, period. We're all the same. You know I'm right."

An explosion rocked the freighter. They all ducked. Movement in her peripheral vision caught her attention. On the metal floor, bits of dirt and dust were crawling by.

The hair lifted on the back of her neck. "A breach," she said, knowing the others noticed what she did. Somewhere on the massive ship a section of the hull now gaped open to the vacuum of space. The freighter was losing pressure and air. She thought of the raider she'd seen get sucked overboard. Cursing, she lowered her dozer as their situation once more trumped the contest to see who would get the other to surrender.

Even the most terrifying Surebloods looked worried. Val pulled her breather over her face, a move mirrored by Hervor and Reeve. Oddly, the Surebloods had no masks. Why? It left them vulnerable to oxygen starvation. Maybe they'd pass out and make her job easier.

"Boss!" Malizarr, the Sureblood scout, had returned. Out of breath in the thin, cold air as he staggered to a stop. "It's the skiffs, boss. Someone's blowin' them up."

No skiffs meant there was no way home. Hopelessness spread amongst the two groups like camp cough in rainy season.

The raider bent over, his hands on his armored knees. His struggle to breathe wasn't a good sign, Val thought. Hypoxia would bring mental confusion, unconsciousness and death. With holes in the hull, the old ship's environmental system was working overtime to keep the cabin altitude at a survivable level. How many more passage ports punched open would it take until the freighter could no longer keep up? Even the breathers her team wore wouldn't help any then. Without spacesuits, they'd be just as dead as the Surebloods.

Again she tried to raise Warrybrook. "Raid leader, this is Six." More static and interference. *Tell me what to do, Warrybrook.* "Advise your orders. Advise your location." The comm was dead. Were the other Blues? Reeve's and Hervor's eyes found hers and reflected the dread she felt in the pit of her stomach.

The Sureblood called into his comm. "Tokotay. Do you read? Tokotay—report." Then he turned to her. "They could be jamming us. We've got to get to the bridge. From there we'll take control and fight off who's fighting us."

Us. The concept shook her. But what choice was

there? They faced an unknown enemy intent on killing them all. A glance at her skiff mates revealed their agreement.

She wondered if her clan elders would feel the same.

"Move out!" The Sureblood attached his dog to a leash with a sturdy harness and set out in a steady lope.

Another flash of energy outside turned the portholes on the starboard side of the ship into blinding disks. The explosion was deafening and set off wailing alarms.

They didn't slow. Slowing would only prolong their escape to safety. But running the corridor had turned into traversing a deadly gauntlet. Every time they lost a skiff, the ruptured drill hole would turn into a human-size vacuum.

Val blinked away the memory of the doomed raider: the dying man's gasping mouth and glassy-eyed surprise as he drifted away into space. It would be quick, as deaths went, but that horrific fraction of time before blacking out would seem an eternity.

She was aware of the Sureblood's regard. Under different circumstances, those eyes could easily ensure a more susceptible female. As if his absolute self-assurance wouldn't be enough enticement, or his impressive frame. Luckily, she was immune to all of it.

Hiding her fears, she'd show him that the "little Blues" were just as formidable as the hulking Surebloods. Today she'd bring honor to her clan.

She ran faster, taking the lead. In the misty, frigid

distance were the double doors leading to the bridge. She began to allow herself to believe that the worst that awaited them was shooting their way onto the protected bridge.

To her left, a fighter craft streaked past outside. *Too close.* "Get down!" she cried. A brilliant flash filled the corridor just as she screamed the warning.

The shock wave threw everyone like toy soldiers. As she sailed forward, her eardrums filled with pain, fleeting but agonizing. Mist steamed into the corridor, and the terrible, otherworldly shrieking of sucking air overwhelmed all other sound.

She was tumbling, spinning over the slippery floor, trying to grab hold of something to stop her slide. She heard a yell as the Sureblood lunged for her, realized the scream for help had come from her. The blast illuminated the etched sea snake on his armor, turning it into a mystical, avenging creature brought to life as he dived for her, arms outstretched, seemingly oblivious to his personal safety. "Got you," he gasped. "Hold me."

She clawed at his armor, the belt or sleeve, she couldn't tell, but her fingers began to slip as they hurtled toward a hole open to space. The roar of wind…bitter, bitter cold. Both of them spinning, locked together.

And then he let go.

No, you freepin' Sureblood bastard! The scream never left her lips, but it reverberated in every outraged cell in her body. She was too shocked to think about what would come next. Too angry. Hands grasping, fingers sliding, scraping over the floor, she plummeted toward oblivion.

CHAPTER FOUR

WARM...WET...SUPERHEATED BREATH...

Val woke, dazed and angry. *The roar of wind...tugging at her mask...bitter, bitter cold...* It was as if she'd been roused, punching mad, from a nightmare with one foot still caught in the netherworld.

Someone was licking her jaw and neck.

No. Some*thing*. She tore open her eyes to black-and-white fur. A smooth tongue lapped at her. Round brown eyes focused warmly, intently on her face, then the dog angled his head and tried to lick her again.

She moaned and moved to get up.

"Merkury—give her a chance to catch her breath."

Then the silky fur was gone, replaced by broad shoulders, unyielding armor, and another clan's scent. The Sureblood. His gloved fingers were as rough as sandpaper as they lifted her breather, but his touch was gentle as a rag was pressed to her nose. "Hold it there a minute to stop the bleeding. Merkury thinks he's a better nurse, and maybe he is, but if I used his techniques, your clan would lop off my head in a Parramanta second."

"Freepin' right," someone said.

Hervor? Her brain was so sluggish. The voices

around her were muffled as if coming through layers of cloth as she came up on her elbows. "Reeve?" If anything had happened to him, and on her watch—

"Still here." Reeve stepped into her field of view. He gripped his blaster rifle, his gaze scanning the corridor every few seconds. Other than a bloody nose, he looked no more shaken than when he lost a game of dice. "Val, that was freepin' close. I thought you were gone."

Fury ignited in her gut as the horror rushed back: Dake Sureblood's hands opening, her fingers slipping down, down, down his body, it played over and over. Except she hadn't been sucked to her death, her blood boiling as fast as it froze. Somehow she was still here with stuffy ears and pulsing anger.

"Hold the rag over your nose, I said."

She angrily did as the Sureblood said, but only because she could feel the warm blood. "You let go," she accused, sitting up.

"I did what needed to be done," he mumbled.

Hervor came down on one knee next to her. "Val, we were all on our way out that hole. If the Sureblood hadn't hit that control panel and closed the door, we'd all be dead."

The door he referred to was massive, yet she had no recollection of it slamming shut. A questioning glance at the Sureblood caught him frowning as he busily untangled some gauze from a med kit and Hervor finished the story.

"Lucky for us, he had the mind to grab hold of that coolant pipe, there, and it stopped him. For a second there, he had you *and* the pipe. But he couldn't hold you both. He had to make a choice, or he wouldn't have been able to activate the door."

Reeve nodded. "Val, it'd stick in my craw to call a Sureblood a hero if it weren't the bloody truth."

All the raiders nearby grumbled their agreement. Dake Sureblood made a dismissive sound in his throat and shrugged off the men's admiration, not even pausing to embellish the deed and turning it into the colorful kind of raiding tale camp minstrels loved to sing around the fire. Even around Sureblood fires, she was sure.

In an act of selfless courage, he'd likely kept all of them from going overboard. Val met his unsettling, multicolored gaze as the realization of his heroic deed sank in. "I didn't realize…"

"Of course you didn't. That's what it's come to, between our clans," the Sureblood said, packing up his treatment supplies and shoving the sack into his thigh pocket. "Expecting the worst of each other."

He was right. A day ago—hells, an hour ago—she'd have sworn a Sureblood would have helped her overboard, not stopped her. Her face burned with embarrassment. "Let me up." Reeve bent down to grab her upper arms and hoisted her the rest of the way to her feet. The Sureblood started to protest, seeing her sway dizzily, but her skiff mate was only helping preserve her honor. Raiders didn't lie on the floor unless they were dead.

"I owe you," she told the Sureblood.

"You owe me nothing," he argued brusquely. "I did what I'd have done for any raider on my team. Let's move out, raiders. They haven't stopped firing, and we're losing air." He turned away to check the condition of his clansmen, all bent in various positions trying to catch their breath. The masked Blues had the benefit of oxygenated air over the other clansmen, who were now clearly flagging.

She followed. "A life debt can't be refused."

His frown made for a fearsome image on his painted face. "Life debt?"

"You saved my life, now I've got to save yours in order to be released from the debt."

He coughed out a quick disbelieving laugh as he harnessed his dog. "Check your weapons and let's go."

"It's what we Blues believe," Reeve explained as they started toward the bridge again. "She can't be released from that debt until she saves your life."

The Sureblood threw her a glance. "You'll die of old age before that happens. Now, is that the fastest you can run? If they blow another hole, we may not get a second chance to plug it."

Stung, she glared at his back as he ran ahead. No one treated a life debt so cavalierly.

"We Surebloods don't look at it the same way you Blues do," one of the Surebloods confided as they jogged side by side. "We don't believe in basking in great deeds. Your giving thanks is like hurling an insult."

A prolonged rumble echoed through the freighter. The thing was creaking now, a hollow metallic moaning as if it would come apart. Dake Sureblood circled his gloved hand and pointed to the sealed pressure doors protecting the bridge. In an adjacent alcove, they took up new positions. So much for divisive words, as one group, as *one people*, they prepared for the next stage of the raid.

The next moments were going to either win her a permanent skiff commander slot or strip her of raider status forever. She remembered thinking this would be an easy raid, and then listening to Grizz say: *"Not everything that looks easy always is."* If only he hadn't been so bloody right.

CHAPTER FIVE

TWO RIVAL CLANS PLANNING an assault. *Together,* Dake told himself. Nothing like this had happened in a generation. Fate had handed him a potentially failed raid. He was going to turn it into something worth living for.

Dake pushed all musings of historical significance aside to focus on the job. He'd stormed bridges before, countless times, but never had it put him on edge like this. *Could be because it's your last chance.* If they failed to break through the doors, they'd be stuck out here and all but doomed. His raiders would die first. Fortified by the nitrox in their breathers, the Blues would have the delightful opportunity to ponder the Sureblood's corpses until they, too, succumbed.

Like hells if he'd let that happen.

Crouched head to head with the Blue leader, Val, he drew his plan with a gloved finger on the floor between them. It helped him think. "Your plasma grenades will melt that pressure door like butter, nice and quick." He drew a slash. "But we have to limit collateral damage. There's fragile equipment. Personnel." He traced a circle on the floor. "We'll make a passage port and cut our way in."

Her face was animated as she nodded, reflecting what he felt whenever a good plan came together. Things had thawed since the near-fatal encounter with the ruptured passage port, but her wariness was palpable. "Hatch bustin' is one thing we all know how to do," she said.

The next few moments were a burst of quiet, intense activity as they assigned raiders to provide cover for the two hatch busters, Squib from his clan and Reeve from hers.

"The rest of you will move through as soon as we've cracked her open, using hostile entry tactics," Dake said. He wouldn't waste time fighting with the crew. They had but one chance to cooperate. "Yarmouth, your team will round up the civvies and keep them out of the way."

"Aye, boss."

The hatch busters ran to the doors. Light flickered in the dim corridor as they set to work cutting the metal with zelfen-edged blades. Dake waited it out crouched by the wall, his blaster rifle cradled in the crook of his arm as he rubbed a panting Merkury between the ears. The thin air had affected the dog as it did him. Val hunkered down next to the dog, careful to keep ol' Merk between them, her focus intent on her skiff mate Reeve as he and Squib toiled. He, on the other hand, was too aware of the scent of her soap or perfume or whatever it was she'd used on her skin or hair. No raider that capable should smell that good. Well, if the plot to break into the bridge failed and all looked grim, he just might try Merkury's technique and steal his own kiss. A taste of those sweet lips, aye.

He scrutinized the unfinished design on her arm plate. As in his clan, Blue raiders used armor etchings to define themselves. "What's your design to be?" he asked, seeming to surprise her with his interest.

"I'm etching the wind."

"What does wind look like?"

She traced a finger around one of the swirls, then shrugged and dropped her hand. "I've got a long way to go until it's finished. When it's done, it'll look like wind."

"An unusual subject for a raider's armor."

"Not so a snake?" She gestured to his design.

"A sea snake. Graceful, quick, deadly," he said, patting an arm plate.

"And slimy, too," she pointed out.

"Caught in a net, aye, maybe, but not in the water. See, to appreciate a sea snake's true nature you have to risk meeting it in its element."

"The wind *is* an element. It's wild and free and can't be captured."

"That sounds like a challenge," he murmured.

Her golden-brown eyes rose to his, then one corner of her mouth lifted. "Take it how you like, Sureblood." Then she was back to checking on the progress of the hatch busters.

He couldn't pull his eyes from her. No woman had caught his interest in the year since his father had died. He'd thought his new immunity was a by-product of focusing on running his clan, but maybe there just wasn't anyone at home like this Blue girl in her armor. Wind had the power to destroy, or it could be as soft as a caress. Did he take it as a sign to stay away, or as a siren's call to do exactly the opposite?

"We're in!" The call went around the group.

The hatch busters had drilled through.

Curled like a gar-gar peel, the steaming edges of the new opening glowed. Through the clearing mist, twinkled the lights of a starship bridge. A man sitting in the pilot seat grabbed hold of a gun as he started to stand.

Dake hefted his blaster rifle and gave the silent signal to attack. Pirates stormed the bridge. "Weapon down!" he ordered.

The civvie froze. His uniform was soiled, faded black, the collar too tight. His eyes were half bugged out of his head with fear. "This ship is property of Rekkure Mining," he said, the gun still in his hand, his hand still on the nav table.

"The ship may be," Dake agreed, his focus never leaving that weapon. "The cargo's ours."

The civvie's arm tensed. That was all the invitation Dake needed. He squinted, fired and lasered the gun out of his grip. The man yelped, more from shock than pain, and the raiders took the bridge.

"We call that the Sureblood switch," Dake told the Blues. He touched Merkury's head next and pointed. "Go hunt." The dog streaked ahead as Yarmouth tackled the civvie. Dake swapped his rifle for a dozer handgun and grabbed the man by the collar, wrenching him to his knees as Yarmouth secured his arms behind him.

The civvie cargo hauler was Drakken and smelled like it. Tattooed with black ink, jewelry punched in all along the rims of both ears. Dake pressed the dozer to his stubbled jawbone. "Well, well. Looks like you're on the wrong end of my gun. You don't have to die. Answer my questions—and no lying. What's your position on the ship?"

"Security officer." The civvie swallowed. "Bridge officer, pilot, galley hand and cargo supervisor."

"Where is everyone else?" He held his gun against the sweating flesh under the man's jaw. His pulse looked ready to jump out of his skin. "You got thirty seconds to tell me everything you know, cargo hauler, or this dozer's going to scramble your brains."

"We're a skeleton crew." He stopped, realizing his mistake using the word *we*.

Merkury exploded into barking. He'd found someone. Then a dozer blast boomed in the confines of the bridge. The Drakken ducked as Dake jolted, spinning toward the noise as he swung his gun around.

Val stood with both gloves wrapped around her dozer. A thin stream of vapor floated above the muzzle. A second Drakken lay on the floor, Merk sniffing and snarling at him.

"I meant it's just him, the other pilot, and me," the civvie tried, panicked.

"Merkury found him behind those boxes—there," Val said. "He thought he could get a shot off." Her eyes were wild, though her voice was calm. "Stunned him, I did, but he won't be getting up anytime soon." As Squib secured the man's wrists and ankles, she cocked her lips into a smile Dake wouldn't soon forget. "I figured he might be worth more alive, depending on how much his company's willing to pay for ransom."

"Found another one!" Malizarr warned as the Blue raider Reeve bent over to talk to someone hidden beneath a table.

"We got civvies popping up like yar weeds after the rains!" Dake gave the Drakken a rough shake. "You said there was *two*."

"Cargo doesn't count."

Reeve helped an emaciated-looking woman up from where she'd been cowering under a navigation table. Long, black, unkempt hair, bare feet that looked practically blue, she trembled as he wrapped a thin blanket found on the floor around her overbony shoulders. Dake judged her to be as young as Squib, fifteen or so, perhaps once beautiful, now a walking skeleton with hollow, haunted eyes.

"Slave traders," Yarmouth said with contempt.

Lower than low. Scum of the galaxy. It was known that Drakken traded in human flesh, but he'd never run across the evidence himself. Slavers normally didn't traverse the Channels.

Merkury had lost that frantic, focused look, now sniffing here and there looking for tasty crumbs. Two civvies and a slave: the hostage was telling the truth about there being no more at least.

In two intense minutes, his cobbled-together team had taken over the ship. Light-headed from the lack of oxygen, Dake wanted to suck in what little air there was. He had no time to waste with uncooperative hostages. "My raider there—she kept your pilot alive for the ransom. Me, I'm thinking you're more trouble than you're worth. What do you say to that? Going to convince me I'm wrong?"

The Drakken was drenched in sweat, his superheated breath expelled as bursts of vapor. The black ink of his facial tattoos glistened as if freshly stamped.

"Any more slaves on this ship?"

"No! None."

"Why this one, then? What's so valuable about her?"

"I don't know. We get paid to haul what needs to be hauled, slaves or ore, it doesn't matter."

"Paid *to steal,* you mean."

The Drakken shook his head. "Stuff is uploaded onto our ship. We take it, the manifests and goods. No one asks where it's from, and I frankly don't care. It's not my job to care. It's my responsibility to get it where it needs to go."

By now Val was speaking gently with the slave girl who cast terrified glances at the Sureblood males, all of whom towered over her. "You okay? Are you hurt anywhere?"

The girl hid behind a veil of hair and shook her head.

"No one here will hurt you," Reeve assured her, the only male she seemed not to want to flee from. She even let him adjust the scrap of a blanket he'd draped over her thin shoulders. "I won't let them put a hand on you. You got my word on that."

All efforts to get her name or where she was from

failed. The girl was mute. Some slaves' vocal cords were cut to silence them, Dake had heard. Or maybe she was unwilling to talk. Her arms were covered in bruises, some old, some newer. Where her wrist cuffs chafed, the skin was scabbed. Gods knew what else had been done to her. And they called pirates barbarians? *Drakken animals*. "Take him." Dake pushed the civvie toward Yarmouth, disgust filling his chest. "Tie him up somewhere out of my freepin' way."

"We got trouble, boss!"

A pair of fighters streaked across the bow. Silver, wedge-shaped. "Coalition," Dake said with a snarl. So that was who had shot off the skiffs. Coalition and Horde trading blows over control of zelfen that was neither of theirs to claim—with the clans caught in the middle. Did Nezerihm know of the risk of an attack today? It was one thing, hiring pirates to chase down his property, but it was entirely another doing it with no regard for their lives. The clans were not disposable. "Seal the door," he ordered.

"Wait!" Val pushed through the crowd to the busted-open door and slipped through it. Merkury raced after her. Dake was there in seconds, grabbing her by the shoulder.

She whirled around, her fist cocked to smash in his nose, then froze mid-punch, seeing it was him. Her instincts were quick—and good; he'd give her that. "Where the hells are you going?" he said.

"What if the Blues are on the way? What if we shut them out?" She shook him off, taking a few steps away to peer down the deserted corridor, her expression intense as if she were willing her clansmen to appear out of the shadows. "I've been calling, but I don't know if they can hear anything with all that jamming. They're probably hunkered down somewhere to wait it out. Warrybrook's wife just gave birth—right before the raid. He's got to get home. What if we close the door too soon?" She dragged an arm over her forehead, looking as if she bore full responsibility for what had happened. "I can't screw this up. It's my first time out," she said. "As skiff commander."

Her first time out. Talk about a trial by fire. "Then I'll tell you something, leader to leader. There's no easing the pressure of feeling like you failed your fellow raiders when things go wrong. But you did all you could. It's all we can ever do."

Hells, he could be talking about himself. Grateful, she pondered him, as if she'd already figured that out. One last glance behind her, then she started back to the bridge—and stopped. Her gloves opened and closed, but she kept staring down the dark, foggy corridor. "I was told you Surebloods were no more than big brutes. That you couldn't string together a sentence let alone plan out a raid. And it's why you're always wanting to elbow in on ours." He felt he was seeing her for the first time when she lifted an unguarded, brown-eyed gaze to his. "I was told wrong."

Then, ducking her shoulder to pass by, she left him savoring the remains of her sweet scent and wondering if her words were an apology or a thank-you, or something in between.

"You heard him, raiders," she cried out. "Seal 'er up!"

The team went to work sealing up the door. Dake slid into the pilot seat and faced an array of antique controls. Grabbing the fly-stick, he pushed the throttles forward. Oxygen deprived, it was a struggle to stay sharp. Leaving masks behind on the skiffs was Sureblood tradition; it had always been that way, something about not being soft and not having to rely on nitrox, but they'd never raided a ship as large as this one. Never been trapped on a city-size vessel with someone deliberately aiming for their skiffs. He needed to get this bridge closed up, and soon. "How's that seal coming?" he bellowed to Squib.

"Workin' on it, boss. You gonna keep it smooth?"

Merkury whined and vocalized frantically. "What, boy, what?" Dake jerked his gaze higher. A fighter was diving in to attack. *Freep me.*

"Buckle up!" With a more immediate threat to his life to worry about than suffocation, Dake shoved the throttles forward and banked hard, nearly spilling everyone on the bridge. A powerful hit shook the freighter, knocking a chunk of insulation from the ceiling and making the control panel flicker. "That answer your question, Squib?"

"Here comes another one!" Yarmouth warned, taking his place by Dake and Merkury as if they were back in their skiff.

Blinding light, then a resounding thud. Squib called out, "Door's sealed, boss!" Oxygenated air, cool and sweet, flooded the bridge. The colors went from dull, almost black and white, to bright.

Dake filled his lungs with it. "Four fighters on-screen," he said.

"And those are only the four we can see," Val confirmed.

With each desperate maneuver, the freighter groaned and shuddered. "This old crate can hardly fly straight and level, let alone survive a dogfight."

Several more missiles hit, all at once. The impact was crushing. Dake grimly noted the alarms and flashing lights warning of pressure loss and catastrophic hull damage. It seemed the Coalition bastards were done playing target practice with the skiffs. Now they were shooting to kill.

CHAPTER SIX

"THEY WON'T FOLLOW US into the Channels," the Sureblood told them.

Raid and vanish, Val thought, nodding. But at high speed in a pathetic, broken-down monster of a ship? She cinched her seat harness extratight as the Sureblood set course for the Channels with fighters in pursuit, missiles pounding, and the old freighter barely holding together.

"Buckle up," he said. "We're going in."

The freighter soared into the field of broken worlds. Warning alarms rang out and lights appeared on the antique scopes. Yarmouth warned, "Fighters in our Six!"

"They followed us?" Reeve said. The slave girl sidled closer to him, her hands knotted in two white-knuckled fists.

"These are our Channels," Dake said firmly. "Our lands. If they come after us, they'll die."

The fighters screamed in pursuit as rocks whirled by in all quarters. The Sureblood wove through the canyons and caves—the Channels—as if he knew exactly where to go.

"Missiles unlocked!" Yarmouth yelled, then he swore. "They fired, boss, they fired!"

"Aye…"

So calm he was, Val thought, only the tendons in his jaw showing any tension as the missiles closed on them. They could do a lot of damage now, the impact sending them crashing into the rocks. She was sweating, gripping her harnesses, fighting the fear that wanted to blow apart her crumbling composure.

The nerve-racking seconds from missile launch to impact were almost physically painful. The Sureblood waited until the last possible second…then jinked hard left. The missiles sheered past. Ahead, an asteroid exploded in a show of celestial pyrotechnics, hurling a million pieces in all directions.

"Blast it, they're still on our ass," she said and swore.

The Sureblood was grim. "We've got to lose them before we're out of the Channels or we'll put the mother ships in danger," he said. "I'll not bring the enemy home."

Nothing was worse than bringing the danger home. She thought of Grizz and Malta. Aye, and even Ayl. They'd have to take a crazy chance to lose the fighters. She knew just the one. "Do to the fighters what you did with their missiles," she cried. "You have the Sureblood switch. We Blues have something just like it—except with ships."

"You mean, make them eat rocks, Val?" Hervor stared at her as if she were crazy, then he shook his head. "Aye, why not? We're out of options."

Val hoped the Sureblood had the resolve she saw in him. "It isn't for the faint-hearted," she warned.

"You've done this before, then."

"In skiffs."

Would it work with a ship this large? She saw the question in his face. "Brief me," he said.

"While the outsiders are aiming for us, we aim for one of those rocks. You wait, wait until you're real close, then keep going until you can't stand it. That'll happen before the time's right, so you'll have to force yourself to keep going. Then, when you absolutely can't stand it anymore, when everything inside you is screaming to pull up, you count to three and yank up and out of the way. Their fighters won't be able to follow in time. Instead of eating us for lunch, our Coalition friends are going to eat rocks."

"Aye." His smile turned to a scowl, and his laugh was just as cold. "I hope they like the taste."

He banked toward an asteroid that looked like a huge, moldy melon, then set his course and locked it. "Buckle up." The sounds of tightening straps and everyone grabbing hold and anchoring their bodies to something sturdy filled the silence.

"All four fighters on our ass, boss," Yarmouth confirmed.

Val grinned. "Right where we want them."

The asteroid loomed large. Details began to appear on the bleak, cratered surface. *Keep going.* The Sureblood held the stick with both hands, his jeweled eyes intense. His senses would start screaming for him to pull back on the stick.

"Keep going," she said. "Until you can't stand it."

Onward he flew, the asteroid centered in the view screen. Every cell in his body and soul was roaring, *Pull the hells up!*

"Boss?" Yarmouth ventured, sounding nervous.

A few of the raiders called out to the gods, even though pirates were notoriously lax in their beliefs. But the leader's concentration was on that asteroid.

"Not yet," she murmured.

Gritting his teeth, he forced himself to hold off.

"Keep going until you can't stand it. Don't stop." Val clenched her fists, tightened her thigh muscles, almost unable to watch the plummeting scene in front of them.

The Sureblood made a sound deep in his throat, but held the course. Sweat trickled down his temples. His lips compressed.

One…two…three seconds more.

Finally, he yanked back on the fly-stick, having to wrap both hands around it to get the control and force he needed to complete the maneuver. Too hard and the freighter would tear apart. Too soft and they'd crash onto the surface of the asteroid.

"Fighters still on our ass," Yarmouth yelled.

"Freep me," both Val and the Sureblood swore. She fought the urge to grab the stick with him to help, forced herself to trust him with her life, and with all their lives as acceleration built, pressing them into their seats. Violent shaking jarred equipment loose. They ducked as a chunk peeled off from the overhead comm board and bounced across the floor. The jolting was so hard now that she could barely see the instruments.

Useless to the Sureblood anyway—she knew he was going on instinct now. Aye, and swears and prayers, too.

She could see every crater, every pebble on the surface. They were dangerously low, dust flying, the freighter roaring and rumbling. At any minute, she expected to hear the horrific grating of the hull scraping a protruding rock. Then it would all be over.

"Come on, come on," she murmured to the freighter. "That's it, baby. That's it. Keep it coming. A little more. Don't stop."

At Dake's small private smile, she clamped her mouth shut. Blast it. It sounded as if she were in bed with him, coaxing him on. He didn't seem to mind at all, but she did. His dog observed her with a panting open mouth that seemed to form an approving smile, pink tongue waving.

"They're firing up their missiles! Aye, locked on."

"What?" Val cried, turning to Yarmouth. One good hit could send them careening into the asteroid that was now passing under the freighter.

The Sureblood didn't let up on the pullout. The asteroid dropped fully out of view. In the next breath they'd know if they cleared it.

And then, finally, they were climbing, the stars above, spinning as they escaped the pull of the asteroid.

She swerved her gaze to the display. Empty. "Gone," she whispered. Then, louder, "They're gone! Those outsider fools."

Cheers swept over the bridge. The slave girl cowered, but her eyes were wide with wonder.

Yarmouth let out a raucous war cry that defined everything Val felt in that moment. "We freepin' did it!" He bumped forearms with Hervor in a traditional post-raid victory gesture. There were a few distrustful expressions amongst the group, but most were celebrating, uncaring of who belonged to what clan.

Looking relieved, the Sureblood wiped a hand over his perspiring face as if he were staving off the aftereffects of breathing depleted air.

She feared the man would drop dead. She feared, too, that she actually cared. "All right, why don't you use breathers? Tell me."

He looked over an armor-clad shoulder at her. "We leave them on the skiffs."

"For all the good they'll do you there."

"You have your ways, we have ours. We Surebloods take our chances as we are."

She waved a hand at his intricately etched body armor and thick leather protectors crisscrossed with weapon belts and rugged knee-high boots. "If that were true, you'd leave your armor behind, too, and raid naked."

He choked out a surprised laugh.

"Going a-raiding with no breathers is just as stupid," she argued, unapologetic.

With the grumbles of his men in the background, the Sureblood was the picture of calm authority. "First you called us dogs. Nezzie's *pets*. Now you accuse us of being stupid. You seem to have a lot to say about my clan. Well, do you know what I hear? I hear you Blues are so desperate to fill the skiffs that your clan leader sends his own daughter out to raid."

As his men laughed and cheered, she blurted out, "Nothing wrong with that. She's just as capable as any man." Then she cursed herself for the defensive reaction. If she wasn't careful, she'd give her identity away.

If she hadn't already...

The Sureblood's eyes were newly intense as they scanned her face. "Capable she may be," he said, "but for her sake I hope she's more careful with her tongue than you are."

"Why should she be, when it comes to her enemies?"

"I wonder if Conn Blue would agree the clans should stay at odds."

"I know he doesn't agree with violating the law of first come, first raid."

"A needless law if we weren't always fighting each other for the best targets."

"Like this old crate?" She laughed. "A nice right prize Nez gave you this time, eh?"

"*Gave?* Hells, woman. We pirates are doing Nezerihm the favor, going after his ore stealers. The more zelfen's worth, the more the outsiders are going to try to help themselves to it without paying, too. Nezzie's got himself a problem—he doesn't have the resources to stop them. He's got no navy, no enforcers. Except us. He thinks he's got us under his thumb, dependent on him, aye, but I say it's the other way around. He needs *us*. Back in the old days, the clans didn't fight over scraps. We raided as a pack. United, we were strong. Now, divided we're weak." He raked his compelling gaze across the group, as if acknowledging every one of them, as if all the individuals there mattered, Sureblood or not. "Dependency is dangerous," he warned with contempt. "Dependency is death. I say *we* decide how we want ships divvied up between us for now on, not Nezerihm. Starting with this one."

His raiders and even the Blues let out battle cries. Just like that he'd turned the zelfen issue from one or two clans' problem to everyone's problem. An orator in war paint, she thought. The Sureblood had fired everyone up with pirate pride, not just her. It was like one of Grizz's pre-raid rallies but with far greater scope. "Are you proposing that we share the booty?" she challenged.

"If our clans can agree to terms."

She searched his face for treachery. Blues raiding with Surebloods and sharing the haul: she should laugh at the idea, consider it nothing short of blasphemy, but as described by this startlingly confident and charismatic warrior, it seemed almost a possibility.

She couldn't forget that Grizz had almost yanked her off the raid. She was here on shaky terms, and lucky to be here at all. Ought she be wheeling and dealing with the leader of a rival clan, one she probably shouldn't trust?

"It's not my decision to make." Not even Warrybrook's, if he were here. Or Grizz's. Her father was the only one who could. "You and our clan leader will have to decide how we split the booty."

The Sureblood's grin was blinding white. His chuckle was deep and husky, and his manner brash. "If that's an invitation, I'll take it."

"Six, this is raid leader, how copy?"

The comm call burst in her ear. Warrybrook! She flew to her feet and slapped her hand over her ear, her joyous gaze meeting Reeve's and Hervor's. "This is Six—on the bridge! Go ahead!"

"Do you realize how many times you've thrown me on my ass? My frozen ass. It must be minus fifty back here. We had a passage port half busted through this pressure door when you decided to put ten Gs on this thing. Yelzen about cut Ennille in half with the zelfen blade. What the hells have you been doing up there, Val?"

She closed her eyes at the man's scolding, not minding a bit. It felt too good hearing his voice. "Been working on getting your frozen ass home, raid leader," she said, grinning. *Home.* Never had the word sounded better.

THE FREIGHTER WAS EVACUATED via shuttles that transported everyone to the Sureblood mother ship, which was the closer of the two. Giant, bristling Surebloods inhabited *Tomark's Pride* and towered over the Blues. While they pounded their returning captain on the back and cheered his return, they regarded the Blues with leery, suspicious eyes. Val blended back in with the others, letting Warrybrook, the true raid leader, take command after her hours in his role.

In contrast, Dake Sureblood resumed leadership of his entire clan. The gloves that had gently treated her wounds and cleverly drew plans for storming the bridge were tossed away. His hands were the only part of him not covered by angry slashes of black war paint, thick layers of leather or armor. Long, blunt, strong fingers and square capable palms, golden skin with a bit of brown hair… She caught herself staring at those bare hands with the same tingle of forbidden curiosity as she did an unexpected glimpse of a naked, well-made man between the slats in the baths at home on Artoom.

She forced her attention away. He was Dake Sureblood, the cocky upstart leader of the Surebloods, the troublemaker, the man everyone had warned her about. They were from different worlds. Her people didn't trust his people, and vice versa. After today, she'd likely never see him again.

"So, they're wanting to split the booty," Warrybrook remarked at her side. His voice had an undercurrent of blame, as if she'd somehow erred in not turning down the Sureblood offer outright. He hooked his thumbs in his belt. "For his flying skills alone, we'll have to give away something of the spoils, and for saving you, of course." His eyes veered to her, narrowing. "You sure he did the saving, Val? You were knocked out. You wouldn't remember it all."

"There were witnesses," Hervor butted in, his jaw tight.

Warrybrook shrugged. "We'll take eighty and leave them twenty."

"Don't think they'll go for that," she said. "Seeing that they were more than twenty-percent responsible for getting us out."

"Seventy for us, then," the raid leader conceded. "Thirty for them greedy bastards. That's as high as we should go."

Yarmouth overheard and howled. "He's a funny one," he told Val and Hervor, then moved on about his business.

Warrybrook threw them a disgusted look. "Skiff Six's new friends, eh?"

"We got out alive because of them Surebloods," Hervor said. "Both clans working together. United, we're strong. Divided we're weak."

"You don't know what the hells you're talking about, boy," Ragmarrk, one of the elders, scolded, shooting out the words with disdain, his eyes black-brown under a cloud of curly white brows. "No sense of history, either of you youngsters. The idea's been bounced about for years, long before your births. Girl, even your father, the great Conn, caught the fever once. Wanna know why it don't ever work out? Because *it can't*."

"Ragmarrk's right," Warrybrook said. "They may be our friends today, but they'll be our enemies tomorrow. We've got to follow the laws we've always known. First come, first raid. Aye, I know what you're saying, Val, that Nezerihm sent those Surebloods to fetch it for him, but are we going to throw away the basic laws of piracy at the whim of a clanless ore digger? Nezerihm can't call the shots."

"Exactly," she said. "Dake Sureblood wants to change that. He says we pirates should decide what ships go to what clan and how the booty's divvied up, not Nez."

"Good luck to him," Ragmarrk grumbled. "What do you say we ought to give them, Warrybrook, sixty-forty? An extra ten percent for saving our Val. That's generous enough."

Neither man had been there to see why they were wrong. They'd been trapped and fighting for their lives. Like most of the other Blues, they'd never agree about the circumstances that led both clans to the freighter. She hoped her father could strike a compromise with the Sureblood leader, something neither clan was used to doing.

"Boss, you got a priority message!" Yarmouth called out over the noise as the last of the stragglers from the freighter were brought aboard *Tomark's Pride*.

Val's surge of relief and affection upon seeing her father on the big screen chilled instantly. Conn's face was expressionless, the ultimate poker face, and his brown eyes as cool as winter wood, but as his daughter she was expert in deciphering his mood. *He doesn't look happy.* How badly had she screwed up, working in tandem with her clan's archrivals? She thought she did right in many things but couldn't be sure. She wasn't very far out of her space apprentice days. She was still a newbie. She gathered herself into a straight-up stance as if she were about to be called to answer for her actions all the while making sure she was well hidden behind a forest of much taller raiders.

Her father sat behind a meeting table, his posture erect. She wasn't used to seeing him look this formal. Not since her brother's wedding had Conn gone through the trouble. He'd scraped his hair back in a neat ponytail, his favorite gold and diamond earring glittering in one ear. Off-ship leathers covered his lean, still-powerful frame. The outfit of rich and soft brown leather with braided trim was one of his favorites and the most expensive, conveying both his status and the clan's relative wealth. No one had as much money as the old days, and the threat of hunger was very real, but as Conn had taught her, the art of negotiation was all about appearances. "Conn of the Blues," he said as if he needed an introduction.

Dake stepped front and center, shoulders squared, his armor and etched sea snake aglow and breathtaking in the bright lights. He looked every inch a leader but minus any of the swagger Warrybrook accused him of having. To make this work, Val thought, Dake Sureblood was going to have to strike a balance between confidence as a leader in his own right, despite his inexperience, and respect for an elder such as Conn. But, stars, Dake looked so young. She found herself holding her breath for him. It wouldn't be fun being in his boots right now. "Dake of the Surebloods," he said, hitting just the right tone.

Her father was silent for a moment, seeming to take in the sight of this clan captain with whom he'd never had dealings but had heard much, all of it negative.

Then he laid both arms on the table, the symbol of having nothing to hide. One couldn't help noticing the good left hand, and the missing right one—his weapons hand, and why he no longer raided. "My condolences to you and your family on the loss of your father," Conn said finally. "Tomark was a good man."

The Sureblood's hands, hanging palms forward in the equivalent stance of nothing to hide, gave the briefest of twitches. Again, those hands revealed something about the man she hadn't seen before, or wasn't supposed to: he still grieved. "Aye, he was," Dake said, quieter. "A very good man. Your sentiment is welcomed, Conn of the Blues." He walked forward. "As I told the captain of your mother ship, the *Varagon,* your clan suffered no losses. We Surebloods were less fortunate, having sacrificed two good raiders to the Ever After."

"Our deepest sorrows. Even a single casualty is felt hard. But considering the odds, it's a bloody miracle any of you got back, in or out of a bio-sack."

"Aye. It was the work of both our clans that got us back, Blues and Surebloods. That cooperation is something I hope won't end after today." Dake stood facing her father, his boots spaced confidently apart. "To start, we'll proceed with arrangements to transfer the Blues back to the *Varagon.* Then, a mixed team of our choosing is needed for escorting the freighter to Nezerihm's world to be scrapped, the ore off-loaded and our share of both split between our clans."

Split between our clans. Everyone went silent at his straightforward pitch. Dake Sureblood didn't ask. He *stated.*

"I hear there are two hostages," Conn said. "And a slave girl. The hostages we'll hold for ransom, if they'll bring us any, and the girl returned to her home."

A sudden ripple went through the crowd of giants as the slave girl pushed her way to the front. The spare all-clime suit someone had lent her hung like a sack. She was stumbling in a pair of borrowed, too-large boots. But her pride was the perfect fit and hard to ignore. Gasping, she shoved her wild mane of hair away from her face and shook her head at Conn. Reeve was right behind her, his handsome face hard with worry. When he tried to grab hold of her wrist to pull her back, she gave him a forbidding look that he obeyed, his hands going up in surrender. The girl pointed to her chest, then to Val, Hervor and Reeve. "I think she wants to stay with us," Reeve said.

She nodded vigorously.

Conn frowned. "You don't want to return to your home, to your people?"

She shook her head and clasped her hands together as if entreating the gods for extra help. Her wide, vivid blue eyes were heartbreaking, the bright light making her starved and bruised body appear even more fragile. She was mute, but it didn't matter; she'd more than made her wishes known.

"You wish to live with the Blues?" Dake asked.

She nodded passionately. Reeve's mouth quirked with surprise, then obvious anticipation.

"Well, then," Dake said, turning back to Conn. "We've something else of value to consider that we hadn't calculated."

"Aye. We'll have to assign an amount to her," Conn answered.

Dake folded his arms over his chest, then remembered protocol and dropped them. "I assign zero as the amount."

The grumbles died down as Dake spoke over them. "Zero, I say. Not one Channel cent for the girl. I'm not a slaver. I'll not have the profit from human flesh on my conscience."

"Nor I," Conn said in his resonant voice. "It is agreed—her price is zero, and she is welcomed into my clan."

The slave girl looked to Reeve for assurance that it was indeed true. He nodded and she made two, triumphant fists. Val smiled, thinking she'd make a good raider with that kind of heart and courage.

Then the two leaders were back to eyeing each other. A decision had yet to be made regarding splitting the spoils. Warrybrook, Reeve, Hervor and all the Blue raiders on *Tomark's Pride* waited to see what Conn would do. Their asses were the ones on the line if the decision wasn't one the Surebloods liked. Val's hand went instinctively to her weapons belt only to remember that they'd all been disarmed before boarding the mother ship.

"I hear you saved my daughter's life," Conn said.

Dake's hands gave an even bigger twitch. She thought she heard Dake swear under his breath as his gaze veered to hers. *"You Blues are so desperate to fill the skiffs that your clan leader sends his own daughter out to raid."* She saw the words turn over in his mind. He seemed more amused than he was surprised. His eyes dipped to her pursed lips, then he returned his attention to Conn, saying with the faintest hint of a drawl, "It seems that I did help your daughter, Conn of the Blues. But it was without the knowledge she was your daughter. To me, to my men, she was a raider—and a fine one, too. An asset to my or anyone else's team."

Val's spirit swelled with the praise. At times her dreams of being a raider had her feeling like a fish swimming upstream. Now she had another clan captain's validation besides her loving father's.

Conn tried to find Val in the crowd with a protective father's eyes, but she remained hidden on purpose. She still wasn't sure what was coming. "If it were only me, I'd give you the entire share for saving her life," he admitted. "But it is not only me. I have a clan to think of and so do you. We will share the booty, fifty-fifty. The sum will be calculated once we know the haul's total value. What do you say, young Sureblood, son of Tomark?"

Son of Tomark. The label wasn't impulsive or accidental. Conn wanted to remind Dake both of his roots and the sentiments of the men who preceded him before he answered. But little did he know that Dake felt much the same way about the clans working together.

Dake nodded. "Aye, fifty-fifty."

Conn's grin finalized the deal. "Done."

And with that, Val thought, history had been made.

CHAPTER SEVEN

VAL WAS USHERED TO THE Blue shuttle with the others. She turned, hoping to say farewell to Dake, but he was surrounded by his raiders, immersed in making plans for the handling of the damaged freighter and protecting the ore. He glanced up as she was hurried past the group. His gaze lingered, his body turning when he realized she was leaving. Then a hand landed on his big shoulder, urging him back to the task at hand, and he was lost to her, hunched over with his raiders.

He had his life and responsibilities, and she had hers. She mustn't forget it.

She found a seat aboard and strapped in. As the shuttle dropped away from *Tomark's Pride* she saw Dake stride to the hatch. A glimpse of his bleak, painted face as he peered out at the departing shuttle, his hand spread on the porthole glass in a gesture of farewell, had her wondering if he felt the same odd tug as she did, that feeling you got when you had to leave a conversation unfinished.

"Good riddance, eh?"

Val jerked her attention around to Ayl, who'd been assigned to the shuttle, apparently, tallying the head count and accounting for injuries. "Hells, Val," he said.

"I was worried sick. You in their custody. Gangsters. Cheats. Did they try anything? I swear, I—"

"They acted honorably in every way. No blood drinking or wenching. They're a lot like us Blues, actually. Well, they're a lot bigger—like giants, some of them—but they're not barbarians and they're definitely not stupid. I don't know why Nezerihm says that, but I saw the truth myself."

Ayl hung on her every word, his expression shifting between angry and anxious. "Is it true—the Sureblood clan captain saved you from going overboard?"

She nodded. "Aye, he did. Dake Sureblood."

"Dake…" He made a fist on his thigh, his expression going hard, his dark eyes ablaze. "*This* is why it's too dangerous for you to be a-raiding. This is why I want you at home."

Here we go again. She tried to control the boiling irritation his opinions caused, tried to tell herself that he was simply protective and concerned for her welfare. That he didn't really want her under his thumb; he just came across that way. "I'm a raider, Ayl. Accept it, or we'll never be able to be friends."

"I want more than friendship with you."

She chose her response carefully as plotting out a raid. It was no different from trying to escape the pull of the asteroid after shaking the pursuing Coalition fighters: too hard on Ayl and she'd make his competitiveness and jealousy boil over, too soft and he'd think they'd marry tomorrow. Somewhere in between was the sweet spot where he'd eventually lose interest in her. "If you want more than friendship, then you have to accept that raiding is all I've ever wanted to do. I've got my eyes on being a raid leader. And someday, I want to be a captain just like Grizz. Those are my dreams, Ayl. I can't see giving them up—for anyone." She held on to his gaze, willing him to understand even the smallest part of her—what made her heart beat, what fueled her spirit. "Don't you feel the same about your own dreams?"

"Dreams, bah. I have cold, hard, tangible goals that I will achieve. *I will* see our clan into the future, Val. I will ensure its survival. There are many, many threats in the way, at the top are those Surebloods. You tend to be an idealist, always seeing the best in people and situations, a lot like your father, if you want to know. Reality is cold, Valeeya. Merciless. To trust the Surebloods or any of the other clans is to doom our future. We can't, and I won't. Someday you'll understand why. Until then, go on and dream if it makes you happy, because I obviously can't."

He pushed to his feet and lurched back up to the cockpit to sit with the pilot. She wasn't sure what bothered her more about Ayl—his eagerness to be promoted, or his blind desire to compete against the other clans—and win.

Was she really an idealist? She thought of how her opinion of the Surebloods had changed. Was it naive to trust the clan that had cheated them out of so many raids and now claimed those incidents were misunderstandings and Nezerihm's fault? The idea seemed feasible when she was in the Sureblood's company, listening to his stirring speech, fighting the outsider bastards at his side. But now she wasn't as sure.

The rest of the trip passed in pensive silence, with Val not knowing if she should doubt her judgment or be thankful for it. The moment the shuttle docked, she grabbed her gear and climbed the ladder to the upper deck, feeling about ten years older than when she flew down it the day before. There was no chance to stow her gear before she was summoned.

"Val, get your ass in my office, front and center!" Grizz bellowed. "Your father's here."

Gods help me.

She dropped her gear where she stood, the inner flaps of her body armor hanging open over her wrinkled all-clime suit, her loosened boot seals clinking against her leggings.

"I'll stow your stuff for you, Val." Reeve rested a reassuring and pitying glove on her shoulder. Even the slave girl acted afraid for her. Ayl folded his arms over his chest, as if he were glad she was about to get her due.

Conn was busy conferring with Grizz over a star chart when Val paused in the doorway leading into the room. The two old friends were more like brothers. Every time Val saw them together, she was reminded of their special bond.

Scowling, Conn dug in his pocket for a smoke, reading the chart as he twiddled a squatter's-leaf cigarette between two sandpaper fingertips. He'd changed into a more casual outfit, she noticed. A comfortable, slate-gray shirt and trousers tucked in boots meant more for

Artoom's rains and mud than a starship's sleek quarters. He took a deep drag on the cigarette, nodding at something Grizz said. He seemed as sharp as always. How the slightly narcotic squatter's leaf didn't affect him more she didn't know. She'd heard the body built up a resistance. He'd started smoking to combat the pain of losing his hand, but never gave it up. Maybe the pain of not being able to go out on raids hurt worse.

She cleared her throat. "Valeeya Blue, reporting as ordered."

Both men glanced up. Her heart caught at the sight of her father's grin. His eyes, so much like hers, filled with love and every good memory she had. A little girl again for a moment, she forgot about protocol and hurried into his open arms, drinking in the scents of laundry soap, her papa and the squatter's leaf.

His embrace was crushing, his voice low and rumbling. "Ah, Valeeya." He moved her back, his hand on her cheek, and seemed to take all of her in. His brows drew together. "You've got micro-hemorrhages in your eyes. Some bruising. How's your hearing?"

"Some ringing is all. It's nothing."

"'It's nothing,'" he mimicked. He swore and shook his head. "What else would I expect you to say? You're a raider. You take your falls and pick yourself back up, no less than I'd expect from any other Blue raider. But you're not any Blue raider. You're my daughter."

His eyes were strangely moist as he dragged deeply on the cigarette, his gaze warm with love. "I remember you as a wee girl, a tiny thing, crawling under the table, weaving between the boots while I was busy briefing my raiders."

"I was never tiny, Papa." She was chubby until puberty, then she "stretched out like taffy," her mother liked to say. She'd never be as willowy and tall as Sashya, but she'd inherited her delicacy if not her fragility.

"But you're all grown up now," he said. "I have to keep telling myself that. You're not the babe I held in my arms only a few hours after you were born."

"Aye, he did." Grizz chuckled. "'Look what the gods brought us,' he told me that day, showing you off. 'A girl child,' he said. 'Ain't she a beauty? Looks just like my Sashya.' I told him he'd better watch out—that the gods may have given you your mother's looks but *his* personality, just to drive him mad. He simply laughed, saying he'd deserve it if you grew up to be the most notorious she-pirate of all time."

Notorious. The word lingered in the air like the smoke.

The glowing tip of the cigarette illuminated Conn's eyes as he inhaled again. "You took over as raid leader when Warrybrook was trapped," he said, turning serious.

"As I was trained to do," she reminded him.

"You then directed your team to win control of the bridge, and encountered the Surebloods, who disarmed you."

"Aye." She stood straighter even as her insides quaked. "We were outmanned and outgunned. I thought of my team's safety first. You always say, 'Live to raid another day.'"

"Is that an excuse I hear comin' out of that mouth?" He sucked in an angry drag on the cigarette. "Well, girl?"

She swallowed. *Yes or no, which was the right answer?* "No, sir. It isn't an excuse. They were blowing up the skiffs and we had to make our way to the bridge. We had a common enemy—*enemies, actually.* If we fought each other, we'd have weakened our offensive. We probably never would have made it out."

"Hmm." Smoke drifted in front of Conn's face, obscuring his features. "So you joined forces and went raidin' with the Surebloods."

"I was protecting the interests of my clan, hoping to salvage the raid, sir. The only chance at that was to be part of that raid. And help lead it, which I believe I did. To a successful conclusion." She took a steadying breath to quench her simmering anger at the interrogation. They hadn't been there. They couldn't understand. "With all due respect, sir and Cap'n, I'm hearing a lot of second-guessing over what me and my team did. I'd like to know what any of you would have done different in my boots that would have ended up better than no deaths and a huge bounty to share. Or is the sharing the part that no one likes? Well, I could have demanded we keep all the bounty, but that would have been arrogant. I know what you always say about arrogance, Papa. The only thing worse is doing nothing when action could have been taken. Well, I did take action, using my best judgment. However unconventional my choices were, I got us home—every last one. No losses." She stuck out her chin. Her loosened body armor chafed her damp neck. "If I'm going to be stripped of my raider's standing, then I'll take my punishment knowing I did the best I could."

There. Now her father and Grizz knew from her own lips what her decisions were and why she made them. She'd face the consequences soon enough.

It was dead silent as Conn crushed out his cigarette in a vento dish. Smoke and the leftover, sweet odor vanished. "I have but one thing to say about your actions, Valeeya." He looked up slowly, his gaze intense. "They bring honor to our clan."

Val's heart started pounding so hard that coupled with her healing eardrums she almost wasn't sure she heard him right. "You're…not disappointed in me?"

"Hells. I'm so damn proud of you, girl, I can hardly stand it."

The next thing she knew, she was fighting tears of relief, grinding her teeth together so she didn't shame herself by letting them fall. "Thank you," she whispered as Grizz looked on, his eyes squinted with approval.

"You took a potentially deadly scenario and turned it into a success," Conn said. "Because of your heroic actions, and those of your skiff team, I'm promoting all of you—you, Hervor and Reeve. And you've got yourself a permanent skiff commander slot."

She allowed herself a grin. "Aye, aye, sir."

"But blast it, girl, it took long enough to get you to stand up for yourself. The only second-guessing going on was you second-guessing yourself! Learn to trust your instincts. Ain't nothing more accurate. When skill can't carry you and your luck runs out, your gut keeps you alive." His expression darkened. "You'll also live longer if you don't let the Ayls of the world get under your skin."

Ayl. She squeezed her eyes shut for a second. Grizz must have told him about her argument with Ayl during the briefing, friend to friend. Grizz's love for her father and for her was obvious. He had no children of his own, having lost the love of his life early. He'd treated her and her elder brother as his own kin all their lives. But it was her he seemed to dote on the most. With doting also came tattling, it seemed. "No man will get under my skin again, I swear it," she assured them both.

"Oh, it'll happen," her father said, his gaze whiskey-warm. "There'll be a man, Val, and you'll want him there. But you won't let him keep you from doing your job. Nor will he want you to if he's the right one for you."

No man fell into that category.

No Blue clan man. With a pang she thought of Dake, then shut down the crazy thought.

Chuckling at her flustered state, Conn dismissed her. "Shower up, girl, we're heading home. We've a gathering to prepare for." He seemed to enjoy her shock and surprise at his news. "The Sureblood suggested it and I seconded it—and offered to host the event. All the clans will be there. It's going to take a true Blue clan effort to get Artoom ready in time."

A gathering! Days of negotiations, competitions, feasting. Dancing. *Dake.* He'd pushed for a gathering.

To work on clan cooperation. But still, he was coming to Artoom. A rush of adrenaline spread throughout her body. It was like what she felt before a raid but different. Better.

Grinning, Conn rubbed his bad arm with his good one, then dug in his pocket for a fresh cigarette. "See what you started, daughter? Because of what happened on that freighter, Tomark's son saving your life, we're holding the first gathering since I was a boy. A new era of clan cooperation will begin."

You're an idealist, always seeing the best in people and situations, a lot like your father, if you want to know. Reality is cold, Valeeya. Merciless. To trust the Surebloods or any of the clans is to doom our future. We can't, and I won't. Someday you'll understand why.

Haunted by Ayl's warning, she hoped that someday she'd be credited with the first gathering in a generation, and not blamed for it.

CHAPTER EIGHT

TOO LONG WITHOUT... Too long being what she was not...

Driven by need and ridden with guilt, Ferren sneaked out of the cottage she shared with Reeve and his family. It wasn't her intention to anger the kindly land folk who, unlike the slavers, sought to contain her out of worry and compassion, not cruelty and control. Or erotic curiosity, she thought, shuddering at the twisted hobbies of her past captors. Yet, nothing the slavers had done to her since the capture could match the painful, slow starvation of her soul away from the water.

Weakened by too many months of deprivation, she'd listened all day to the rain pouring down, drumming on the windows, the roof, making her pulse beat with yearning and homesickness for the world she'd lost and to which she might never be able to return to again.

You volunteered for this mission.

Yes, but it didn't make it any easier.

You're a warrior.

Yet she felt no stronger for it in that moment of weakness, a desperate escape for a few moments' peace. For her rescuers, she'd tried to last the entire day required between the baths they allowed her. For these kindly land folk, she'd stoically endured her sentence on dry land until her clenched teeth ached and her temples throbbed. They thought they were protecting her from the cold, seeing her so frail, but water was her succor, like the very blood that flowed in her veins!

Holding back a sob, she ran down the path. The air outside was dense and cold compared to the house's quaint rooms. Rain needled her skin. With no patience to find her way to the village baths, she followed the sound of falling water that had sung to her all day from inside the house, her bare feet sinking into spongy grass. But it wasn't a waterfall at all. Rainwater gushed from a drainpipe attached to the roof of the cottage and emptied into a wooden barrel. Big enough.

Ferren climbed in, her long hair whipping against the thin, drenched shift she wore. The water was waist-high and so icy it stole her breath before making her cry out. Blessed Heart of the Sea, it was cold! She knew the shivering was dangerous, but only a few moments more. Ducking down, she let her head slip lower, water up to her chin. With the rainwater pounding her head, she dared to try what she couldn't in the tub earlier with observant, caring eyes so near, and what she'd managed to do only once during her captivity. After that, they'd never allowed her to be alone.

She was too valuable a find to lose. Too precious a prize. For she and her kind were rarer than any other in all the known worlds, and more coveted.

Quaking with cold and an indescribable hunger, Ferren dunked her face in the shockingly cold water. Inhaling was no longer instinctive. She had to force it.

Desperate and with all her might, she sucked in the cold, gushing stream. Her lungs filled. Then, a horrible wanting replaced her hunger.

A desperate, primal wanting for air.

Something clamped around her shoulders. There was a gushing explosion of water, and then she was splashing, fighting, yanked up and out and thrown onto dry land.

Gut-wrenching convulsions, then pushing, hard pushing on her chest. A man's angry voice. "Breathe, blast it. *Breathe.*" And finally she was retching up lungfuls of rainwater into the mud, tears streaming as Reeve held her head and hair. His hand stroking her cheek, his gaze aglow. "Whatever they did to you can't be forgiven," Reeve was saying as he swaddled her in his coat. "But you're going to have to learn to forgive yourself. You'll not escape through suicide, girl, I won't let you."

It wasn't suicide. It never would be. Her people, her prince, needed her. She was sobbing then, wishing there was a way she could make this beautiful, patient man understand that she didn't need the water to die. She needed it *to live.*

THE MUD OF HOME CAKED Val's boots as she slogged along a path from the docks where she'd been sentenced the entire day. Aye, sentenced, she thought, rolling her aching shoulders. Her heroics during the freighter incident had made her the toast of the village—for about a week. Now it was back to training as a raider. Being dirt-bound at dock meant fixing balky equipment and mending armor, off-loading old supplies and getting the

Varagon ready for the next raid. Pirates lived in a constant state of alert—never knowing when the next opportunity would come. They always had to be ready.

The scent of cedar was sweet and strong. Ancient, rain-heavy branches sagged, hulking shadows in the fog already billowing in to replace the day's soaking rains: a typical Artoom springtime evening. The closer she walked to the village center, the louder the merry music and the more she could smell the savory scents coming from under huge tarps sheltering the revelers. The wet weather sure hadn't dampened the spirits of her people and the arriving clans. Val wondered what the big men from the vast and open plains of Parramanta would think of her snug, ever-damp planet. Mostly, she wondered all day what one particular man from the Parramanta would think, and what it would be like seeing him again, outside the freighter.

Hervor splashed along at her side. "I'm hungry."

"Aye, me, too." The scent of baking pies made her mouth water. She grabbed him by the arm and pulled him over to where a group of women took shelter under a dripping overhang to prepare the treats. Val called to them. "Hoy! Are you saving them all for the feast tonight?"

"We always got extra for our raiders," one of the women called back, sending one of the children darting across the street with two paper-wrapped hand-pies.

As the little boy watched in awe, Val and Hervor tore off the wrappers. Val lifted the pie to her mouth and inhaled before biting in. The crust was flaky and warm, the inside syrupy and sweet: slow-cooked lamb mixed with early berries picked by the village children from the shrubs on the sides of the dunes along the shore. There were fewer pies baked recently and more dried and stored foods to eat—conservation of resources, her father said, in light of the reduced profits coming in—but the gathering had changed all that for the moment, bringing back memories of her early childhood when there was plenty and the clan was prosperous.

Blue clan could not have hosted the event alone. Luckily, the guests arrived with almost every item imaginable to contribute. It was one more thing their people had in common: pirates loved a good party. Midwinter batches of moonshine had recently been decanted and were already flowing by the sounds of laughter and loud talk.

"Ayl!" Despa's voice tinkled through the fog like music as she spied the raider in a group also returning after a day's labor. Ayl's lover was a healer popular for her concoctions with a business right on Main Street.

"He'd better run." Hervor laughed. "Or he'll find himself helping her out in the shop. She'll be open late tonight I bet, making money hand over fist with all the clans in town. Selling rocket booster to the raiders."

"Rocket booster, aye." Val snickered. Sharken was mixed in food and drink to boost a man's sexual passion. Its side effect of giving extra energy made it popular during celebrations. Despa's private blend was the best and the most potent. "Not that you'd know anything about that, eh, Herv?"

"Hells, no," he denied with a curse. "I've no need for boosting."

Despa dropped the herbs she'd been rinsing, her smile joyful. Her rare blond hair fluttered like the lush hem of her long skirts as she ran to Ayl and lifted his arm, tucking herself underneath it. She fed him a treat she'd fished from her pocket. Homemade and delicious, Val was sure, thinking of the tasty pie she'd just eaten that also was made by a kitchen-capable female, something else Val bypassed learning to become a raider. Ayl seemed to resist Despa's attentions at first, then gave in, drawing her close and saying something that made her laugh. They veered away from the group. Ayl was kissing the girl, his hands squeezing her bottom, before they'd even disappeared behind the flap of the front door of the shop.

Awkward, Val glanced away. "I don't know why he keeps trying to bed me when its clear Despa loves him. He must feel something for her."

Hervor's grin was wry. "Aye, the flarg-wad probably does, but it isn't the L-word you're thinking. Lust, it is. He's just biding his time until you come to your senses."

"I hope he likes biding time because that's all he's ever going to do when it comes to me." She gave her skiff mate an affectionate push and headed home. In the distance the camp dogs barked at something beyond the wall of trees in the direction of the docks where starship thrusters echoed hollowly in the mist. Was Sethen finally home? Her parents seemed to expect her elder brother's return at any moment. As usual he hadn't passed along the status of his ship and crew, frustrating their father to no end. But it was Reeve and some strangers approaching.

As he walked closer, she saw her friend's mouth twisted in an expression of annoyance she knew well.

He was escorting Nezerihm.

Luxurious wraps swathed the mine owner's gaunt frame. His thick, steel-gray hair was brushed cleanly away from his forehead and knotted at the base of his neck with a zelfen and gemstone band that matched the heavy clip holding the wrap around his shoulders. That clip was worth more than some clans' fleet of ships. Flaunting his wealth to make the pirates hungry for it, she thought. History said that the mines used to belong to all in the Channels. Then Nezerihm's family moved in from somewhere unknown and took over running the operation. At the very least the pirates should have insisted on a share of the profits.

Her people might be crafty and resilient but they weren't known for their business sense, Val thought with a wry frown. And maybe they were fools to allow Nezerihm to come to Artoom to eavesdrop. "He's not one of us," she'd tried to persuade Conn, but he wouldn't listen, arguing that excluding the man would have made him suspicious and defensive: "Girl, I'm remaining hopeful Nezerihm will cooperate to ease tensions amongst us pirates. Best everyone sits down to figure out a way the clans can hunt for him without stepping all over each other's toes."

We wouldn't have to worry about that if we had

control of the mines, Val thought, watching him walk closer.

Nezerihm looked miserable. He hated Artoom's weather and never passed up the opportunity to complain about it. Dark circles made perpetual smudges under the man's pale eyes. He looked as if he lived in a cave. Aye, under the surface guarding all his precious ore.

Then the mine owner recognized her and waved. Val had to force away a small chill at the sudden eye contact.

"I see Artoom has welcomed me with another one of your lovely spring days, Valeeya Blue." His teasing tone sounded sprightly and friendly, and at odds with his effect on her. "Has your father saved any moonshine to warm my bones?"

"There's moonshine and food aplenty."

"I plan to partake—as soon as I'm refreshed from my journey."

She stepped aside to let Nezerihm and his cronies pass. Reeve hung back for a moment. He wore a look of distaste she didn't have to ask about to understand; then he sidled up to Val, his gaze softer. "She's doing better. The slave girl." No one knew what else to call the girl they'd rescued from the freighter, and she refused to answer to any names. "No more trying to kill herself. I don't think she ever intended to." He paused as if trying to sort it all out. "She just wanted to be in the water. Wanted to breathe it, or something. Crazy." A shrug gave the impression he thought the girl was silly, but his expression gave away his curiosity about her, and his caring. "She hasn't tried again."

Val nodded in relief. Reeve had taken on the girl as his personal project. Was it because he felt responsible for her, or because he was falling for her?

He brightened. "I take her every day to the cedar baths. She's been happy as a clam. Those hot springs seem her personal vision of the Ever After. She'd live full-time in the bathhouse if we let her. Mama's too busy trying to fatten her up to allow it."

"Lucky her. Your mama's cooking is my personal vision of the Ever After." Val laughed. Then their focus shifted back to Nezerihm and his cronies. Reeve lowered his voice. "He's angry. Nezerihm. He says the Surebloods want to push all the clans out of the way, and even him. I heard him talking. He even said it to me."

"He told you that?"

"Aye and more. He says the Surebloods are making him the scapegoat for their raid crashing. Citing 'misunderstandings' as their excuse for stealing everyone else's share. He said we Blues had better not trust them."

"What do *you* think?"

"I think Nez is an ass."

"And the Surebloods?"

Reeve seemed torn. "I want to trust them. I'll tell you that, Val."

Nezerihm's group now realized Reeve had lagged behind. They turned and looked at them, Nezerihm's expression tight, suspicious.

"Hey, I gotta go," Reeve said and jogged away

to catch up with his charges, leaving her pondering Nezerihm's accusation and Reeve's doubts. Blue clan was wary and justifiably so. They were inviting their enemies into their camp, notably the Surebloods. But who was the real enemy—the other clans or Nezerihm?

The group vanished in the foggy streets, leaving Val awash in uncertainty. Had Conn done the right thing by agreeing to this gathering?

No. Don't let yourself be swayed by Nezerihm's gossip. Mistrust and infighting, for all the years Val had been alive, the pirates had known no different. Now Dake Sureblood, young and blunt and sure of himself, had burst forth with his ideas of working together and swept her father along for the ride. It had given Conn new life. He hadn't been this happy and energized since before losing his hand.

She wouldn't let Nezerihm steal that away.

With a renewed sense of purpose, Val hurried home to get ready for the dance. Getting to know Dake Sureblood better had become more than simply a desire to socialize with an exciting, attractive man. It was a personal act of rebellion against a manipulator who wanted to quench her father's dreams.

DAKE STRODE THROUGH THE soggy streets of Artoom with his contingent of clansmen. He felt like a predator released from a cage after being poked with sticks all day. All the clan captains, senior raiders and elders had spent the day locked away in meetings. They'd argued more than they'd bargained, and he'd been the focus of much of the anger, but he'd not let anything push him off the path he'd come here to clear.

A group of Calders passed by, loud and boisterous. More pent-up energy, Dake thought. It was going to prove volatile once mixed with moonshine. As part of the rules of the gathering, no one bore arms except for security. Weapons or no, there'd be fighting later—there always was.

"Hoy, Sureblood!" Their leader, Kel Calder, cupped his hands around his mouth and roared across the street. "You may be bigger than me, but give me a few slugs of that famous Blue moonshine and I'll teach you a lesson or two for your little *misunderstandin'* last month at Forfeit Moons. Aye, a taste of my fists will do you."

"If you're still wanting to trade fists after you get drunk enough to get your courage up, Calder, come find me. If you can stagger in the right direction."

The Calder started toward him, but was held back by his men. He guffawed. "Boy, I could beat you hog-tied and hungover."

Boy. All the clan captains called him that. He was used to it by now. All of them were old enough to be his father, or even grandfather, but if they didn't respect him, they wouldn't have spoken to him at all. Stories of the freighter attack had spread far and wide. The tales had been exaggerated and embellished, already turning to legend. His rescue of Val and the gratitude Conn Blue showed him because of it, coupled with the general sense of tragedy surrounding Tomark's death, had boosted Dake to his rightful place amongst the pirate leaders. Except, he was still "the boy."

"Drink hearty, Sureblood," the Calder cried. "I'll be looking for you."

He'd best look elsewhere. Dake had different plans.

He glanced around for signs of Val. Holed up in her father's meeting tent all freepin' day, he was sure that at some point she'd appear. No trace of her.

Now he'd need to concoct an excuse to see her, he thought. Surely, he'd dropped enough hints of interest to her father. Val had been on his mind when his mind was best focused on clan matters and a fragile new truce. She'd given him the fever, that girl had. Why had his virtual monk-dom been fine a month ago, hells, a *week ago,* and now it chafed like uncured leather?

He was going to have to do something about it.

And about her.

Tonight.

Dake and his men rounded the corner. Yarmouth elbowed him. "Look. You've got a female admirer."

Dake whipped his gaze around, hoping to see Val. One of the Blue elders, the female raider named Malta, waved to him from under a sodden awning where a crowd was beginning to gather.

"Since you're all set for the night, boss," Yarmouth joked, "that leaves me free to hook up with the clan captain's daughter."

"Not if you don't want to be skinned alive—"

"Ah, you wouldn't do that, boss. You like me."

"—and fed to Merkury."

Yarmouth's mischievous grin grew wider. "So Val's hands-off, eh?"

"Everyone else's hands, aye, except mine." That was, if Dake didn't lose out competing for her attention. After all, she was a beautiful girl as well as the clan captain's daughter, with a hells of a lot more to her than even that. Aye, like a smart mind for planning and nerves of steel under pressure, and the guts to stand up to him. She was everything he valued in one hot little package, the perfect match for him. Dake would just have to win her over, that was all there was to it.

"Boss." Yarmouth's elbow jabbed him again. "She's getting upset."

"Huh? Who is?" Dake peered around. Impatient, Malta motioned him closer. *Oh, her.* What could she possibly want? The elder had been nothing but chilly to him, scowling at him nearly the entire day of talks with distrustful brown eyes.

"Well, we don't want to upset the lady, do we?" Dake sauntered up and leaned a hip against the edge of the bar.

"Moonshine," she said, shoving a glass of pink-tinged clear liquid at him. "Family recipe. Unlike other families, my folk brew only once a year—midwinter. Best stuff on the planet, and don't be letting anyone else tell you otherwise."

She poured another small glass for herself, held it up. And then paused. "Are you going to join me or not, Sureblood?"

"Aye, I'll join you." He was surprised at the thaw. One minute the old pirate was growling at him, the next she was purring. He emptied the contents of the glass into the cup hanging from a lanyard around his neck.

Malta's brow lifted. "Our glasses aren't good enough for you?"

"These cups are a Sureblood tradition. We use them wherever we go, even at home."

Malta's raptorlike eyes took in every detail. "Etched like your armor."

"Less chance of swapping someone else's spit that way. You always know your own cup." Dake tapped his cup against her little glass, carefully, so as not to spill any of the potent liquid.

"Strange traditions you Surebloods got," she complained and lifted the glass…then paused again, faking him out.

Dake had almost taken a swallow, his mouth coming close enough to inhale eye-watering fumes. "Are we going to have a drink or not, Elder?" he growled.

"I've got to make the toast first, boy." She observed him with a critical and yet mischievous expression. "To the new clan leader of the Surebloods—not quite as much of a cocky bastard as I thought."

Then she clinked her glass to his, drained it and slammed it down on the bar. Dake did the same seconds later, dragging the back of his hand across his lips as the liquor scorched down his throat. "Tasty," he said and winked. "Best on the planet, I hear."

"Finally!" Malta cried. "Truth uttered from the lips of a Sureblood." She cuffed him on the side of his upper arm and waded away through the gathering crowd.

Some of the women there sent him sassy glances full of promise. Others were too frightened to make eye contact. He searched their faces for the one he wanted to see. No sign of Val.

Well, hells. In days he'd be leaving, and who knew when he'd ever have the chance to cross paths with her again. If he missed her, he'd have to come up with an excuse for another gathering on the heels of this one. He sagged back against the wall, slightly numbed by the one swallow of moonshine. It was one freepin' strong brew, he had to admit.

Yarmouth matched him slouch for insolent slouch, his hand wrapped around a cup brimming with ale. "Are my ears still stuffed up or did Malta call us liars, boss?"

Dake shrugged. "She was looking to get a rise outta me. I decided not to give her the pleasure."

On the other hand, there was someone he'd like to give a little pleasure to, and she bloody wasn't there.

VAL BURST THROUGH THE front door. "You're bringing the storm in with you," her mother cried, a loving grin and affectionate eyes taking all bite out of the complaint.

Sashya was resplendent in a deep blue, curve-hugging dress and tall boots of the softest matching leather. Long tresses of dark brown hair so similar to Val's swung from a pretty clasp at the top of her head. Sashya's parents and Conn's mother sat on the sofa, waiting to leave for the feast. Jaym, Conn's father, had died long ago in a training accident right here at home on Artoom. Val dropped her dirty work boots by the front door, gave and accepted kisses from the beaming grandparents, then snatched Sashya's shoulder to give her a quick kiss on the cheek. "I have to hurry. I don't want the slango to start without me." There hadn't been a dance with all the clans there in more than a generation. Like hells if she'd be late.

Val hurried to the washroom to shower and then dried off in a heartbeat, pulling on clean underthings. Her mother smiled at her frantic preparations. "All those young handsome foreigners to ogle. I'd be excited, too. I never had the chance when I was your age. We had no gatherings then. The only thing we Blues did with other clansmen was try to shoot them."

"If you'd fallen in love with an out-clan boy, you wouldn't have married Papa."

"Oh, I'd have married him all the same. There wasn't any man I ever saw outside the clan who came close to him."

Val nearly confessed that there wasn't any man *inside* the clan who came close to one she'd met outside it. Instead, she opened a box of makeup so rarely used that the lid was dusty. "Help me look my best, Mama." Because of all the special guests in the village, she told herself. And because she represented her clan. *That* was why she got all prettied up, and dabbed a fragrance that reminded her of sultry summer evenings on all her body's hot spots. Not because of Dake.

"Should I wear my hair up?" Val lifted it off her shoulders, exposing a slender neck she rarely looked at in the normal course of raider training, turning her head side to side to decide. Then she let her freshly washed hair tumble over her shoulders, shaking it loose.

"Yes, that way. To see your natural waves." Sashya dusted Val's cheeks with color. "What will you wear?"

"I was thinking of the green dress." *Thinking?* She'd already decided on the dress early that morning while on her knees scrubbing the exhaust nacelles on the *Varagon.* The green dress was silky, clingy and flattered her lean curves. The boots she'd wear were rugged enough to withstand the mud and light enough to dance in. She flashed a smile at the mirror, tilting her head to find the best angle.

"I've never seen you fuss this much. Now, who are you hoping to impress?"

"I'm not trying to impress anyone, Mama."

"Seduce, then."

"Mama!" Val choked to her mother's amusement. And blushed, too, much to her personal dismay. The more she sat in her parents' house under maternal interrogation, the less like a raider she became.

"It's him, isn't it? Tomark's son. The man who saved you. Conn told me that he asked after you today. Numerous times."

"He did?" Then, blushing, Val cursed herself for giving away the secret. "Father's filling your head with raider gossip again."

"Daughter, you've got your father's cockiness and his smile, but you're going to have to work on your fibbing."

Someone pounded on the door. "Hoy, Sashya! It's Hawkk."

Her mother went to answer the door. Val pulled her robe closed before one of her father's men tromped in.

"Don't be bringing the storm in with you," Sashya scolded.

"Sorry, Sashya. Is Val here?"

Her mother stepped aside to let the raider in the doorway. Val saw Hawkk's double take as he caught the scent of perfume in the air. She knew she looked far different with artificial color accenting her eyes and lips, and her hair falling wavy and loose. "Val, I'm short guards tonight." He sounded almost apologetic now that he saw her all prettied up. "Sethen's late getting back from Gosmorn. I need you to take his place on security."

Sethen, late again. Nodding, Val shoved aside her immediate and crushing disappointment. It wasn't the first time she'd had to fill in for Sethen. But why did it have to be tonight?

She picked up a brush and scraped her hair away from her face, weaving it into a braid. "I'll be there in five."

It was harder than she thought to pretend she wasn't let down. After Hawkk departed, Val hung the green dress back in the wardrobe and replaced it with a simple pair of off-ship pants and a matching blouse in the same shade of soft, moss green—to keep with her intended theme, at least. Instead of the delicate chain waist belt she'd planned, she buckled a thick leather belt around her hips and loaded it with daggers, a dozer and extra ammo. She gave a little shimmy. Everything rattled. "You can't say many of the other girls will be wearing this kind of ornamentation." Or the boys. Only security could be armed at the gathering. "I'll be unique, right, Mama?"

Sashya lifted her hand to Val's cheek, her luminous brown eyes sad. "I'm sorry."

"I'm not. It's the life I chose." Val closed her fingers around her mother's slim wrist and moved her hand away to clasp it briefly in hers. "It's the life I love."

Val grabbed her jacket off a hook and strode out the door. Duty called.

CHAPTER NINE

UNDER AN ENORMOUS TARP, the music had started up in earnest, and so had the drinking. The atmosphere was edgy, aye, but so far calm.

Dake wondered what Tomark would have thought had he been here tonight, seeing Conn Blue sharing his best food and drink with his rivals *voluntarily*. He savored the moment for his sire's sake.

Conn saw him arrive and waved a hand. "Hoy, Sureblood. I saved you a seat, boy!"

Boy. Hells. With the other Surebloods surrounding him, Dake took his drink cup in hand and pushed his way to Conn's table at the edge of the dance pit. Conn sat next to a stunning woman who resembled an older, more sedate version of Val. Conn's wife, he thought. Grizz and the rest of Conn's senior raiders were there as well as the other clan captains. Dake nodded at Grizz and the others.

Conn reached for a smoldering cigarette. "Sashya, this is him. Tomark's boy."

"Ah." Val's mother gave Dake such a thorough, appraising inspection that he almost felt naked. Whatever he might have wanted to hide was a lost cause, including, he feared, his hopes to get to know her daughter better.

He greeted her with a dip of his head. "Dake of the Surebloods."

"The man who saved my child's life," she said softly so that he had to strain to hear her over the noise. "Do you know what it feels like to lose a child?"

"No, ma'am. I imagine there aren't too many kinds of pain that are greater than that."

"No, there aren't. Likewise, there's no equal to a mother's gratitude for someone who spared her that pain. And that is the gratitude I have for you, son of Tomark."

He nodded in appreciation at her thank-you, phrased so that a Sureblood could accept it properly. She must have been briefed by her husband, who had spent time with his people.

"Do *you* have any children yet, Dake Sureblood?" Her gaze nailed him to the chair like a piece of leather drying in the sun.

"No, ma'am." He was aware of the amused looks from the entertained leaders listening in, and especially Conn's. They kept quiet, happy to have him be cross-examined rather than them.

She nodded as if she approved, and smiled. If this was a test, he hoped it meant he passed. "Join us," she said. "Please, sit. Food, drink, anything you wish."

Your daughter will do. Dake cracked a private smile. It would probably be too forward—too *Sureblood*—if he spoke his mind.

Malta was the only other female sitting there, and

she wasn't holding her liquor very well. As soon as she passed out, only Sashya would be left. Val was a raider. Ought she not be here, too? Maybe she'd flown off somewhere.

He swung his attention back to Conn. "Got any ships out on raids?"

"Why?" Kel Calder bellowed. "Gone too long without crashing someone else's raid, Sureblood?"

The Lightlee clan captain sitting there spewed his ale as the Freebird leader threw his head back and laughed. Chuckling, Gorgan Feckwith folded his massive arms over his chest as his men clustered behind him. The other Calders and Lightlees waited as well, their eyes glinting with anticipation of a fight.

They expected one. The Calder all but said he was a raid crasher. Dake drummed his fingers on the table. To ignore such an insult in front of their host was to demonstrate weakness, Dake knew. Kage, his highest ranking captain, and Yarmouth made sounds of displeasure in their throats as the rest of the Surebloods standing at his back tensed for battle.

Conn observed it all from behind a cloud of squatter's weed smoke from the cigarette pinched between his stained fingers, frowning as he watched the interaction. Would he allow himself to be dragged into petty fighting? Or was he man enough to remain focused on the larger issues? All these questions could very well be going through Conn's mind, too, as he sat there, quietly smoking his squatter's weed, pondering the future of his people, and to whom he dared entrust it.

Once again Dake felt he was being tested. The man's

eyes might look friendly, but his scrutiny was intense. Never had Dake felt as much under a microscope as he did then. *You vowed to behave.* Aye. That meant no bashing heads and tossing chairs. If Dake gave in to every animal impulse, the pirates would be right back where they started—at each other's throats and under Nezerihm's thumb. It took extra effort to tamp down his urge to throw the smirking Calder across the room.

Drily, Dake told the Calder, "If there's any crashing to be done tonight, it'll be my clumsy ass on that dance floor."

The Calder roared with delight.

Conn Blue's eyes crinkled with humor.

"Look." Sashya touched Conn's sleeve as a group of children came to the table with bowls of glazed berries.

Artoom might feel as if it were closing in on him at times with its relentless clouds and drizzle, Dake thought, but somehow it produced fruit like this, a rare and tantalizing treat for the people of his dry world.

Then one little girl came forward to hand Conn a flower. As the entire Blue clan looked on, from the elderly to wide-eyed toddlers, all grinning warmly, Conn made a show of choosing a berry to taste, then rubbing his stomach with much enthusiasm after he did. Then he pulled each of the giggling children close for a quick kiss on the cheek and a ruffle of their hair before sending them away giggling. The merrymaking resumed.

And soon…slango, Dake thought. The dance was energetic and very specific in its moves. It required spot-on reactions and endurance, and grace under pressure when competing against other couples. Raiders were notoriously good at it. Most considered slango the dance equivalent of busting hulls. Men could dance with other men, women with women, but the favorite to watch was a well-matched couple. It had to be done right and quickly, or you were out of the running. When was the last time he'd danced? He seemed to remember a curvy redhead as a partner and he fueled by ale, but it was a fuzzy memory like everything else fun.

With a cigarette smoldering between his lips, Conn offered the berries to the table and slipped the flower into his wife's hair. Whatever she whispered to him had him grinning like a fool.

He's a happy man. Conn loved his people and was loved by them. Dake was sorry that the fate that had ended Tomark's life too soon had prevented him from enjoying the same.

"Back to your question, Sureblood. I've got but one ship out at the moment," Conn said. "My eldest, Sethen. Been out at Gosmorn, the trade route there. The boy's always late, and not too good with staying in comm contact, which I don't like either."

He leaned his weight on thick forearms, his missing hand a constant reminder of how a raid could go wrong. "So, I asked him, what's going to happen someday when I pass, off to hunt treasure in the Ever After? What kind of clan discipline will we Blues have if that's the example he sets? I keep threatening to appoint his little sister clan leader in his place when I die."

Dake sat up straighter. "Val," he said, eliciting a shadow of a smile from Conn. Dake had asked after his daughter enough times today for the man to see through all the supposedly casual queries about Val's well-being. If Conn hadn't guessed Dake was interested, well, then he was thicker than the Artoom mud plastered to his boot heels.

Maybe it was why the girl was nowhere to be seen. Conn had hidden her away for her own protection despite his wife's gratitude for her rescue.

"Sethen thinks it's an idle threat. Sometimes it is, sometimes it ain't." Conn pinched the cigarette as smoke exited his nose. The pungent sweet smell of the narcotic-laced weed hung over the table, trapped by the tarp. "As you've already found out, my girl's got the makings of a leader, if not the opportunity. Our tradition favors males in the position of clan leader, not women. Sethen will take my place when I'm gone."

"Val will marry a well-positioned raider in our clan," someone interrupted. "In case anything ever happened to Sethen, there will be a male in position to be clan captain."

The voice belonged to a young, lean raider taller than most of his clansmen and with the kind of pretty-boy looks the ladies adored. The man was part of a group of Blues—a mix of junior and grizzled lifelong raiders— who loitered in an outer ring of revelers as opposed to those invited to sit with Conn's inner circle.

Dake noted the subtle snub and stored away the fact.

"That raider will be me, of course," the man said. "Ayl of the Blues."

The raiders with him pushed at him and laughed, offering all kinds of encouragement as Ayl preened.

His attitude all at once broadcasted insecurity, inexperience and the desire to impress. It helped keep Dake from bristling at the man's claim of ownership. "You're engaged to marry Val?" he asked, aghast if he was indeed her choice.

"The decision's not final," Conn muttered.

Dake's focus remained on Ayl. "But you're confident it's you," he persisted drily. Who was this competitor for Val's affections and how serious was the threat?

"It's nothing you'd understand, Sureblood."

Dake snorted. "I understand women."

"Not *our* women." Ayl glared at him, his dark eyes threatening, his manner territorial. For the first time all evening, the atmosphere was truly tense.

Dake thanked the fates Ayl hadn't been on the freighter with Val. There was nothing worse than a green raider with a gun and a head full of glory. It would be easy to goad Ayl into losing his cool. Then he'd have the excuse to beat the flarg out of him. But Conn's visible irritation revealed Ayl wasn't the frontrunner he assumed he was.

"Ayl." One of the senior raiders sitting with them caught Ayl's eye and shook his head. Dake noticed a resemblance. Was he Ayl's father? *Enough,* his expression said.

Sulky, Ayl obeyed and poured the last dregs from a cask into his glass. "Alleene—more moonshine!"

A serving woman tossed her long, curly hair. "Come

and get yourself some, then. And bring your new friends." She winked at Dake.

The preening raiders with Ayl seemed to miss the girl's invitation, but Ayl hadn't. Ayl walked past the back of Dake's seat to his clansmen's dismay. "Our women are hands-off, Sureblood," Ayl warned, his voice low and threatening while the noise of the party swirled around them. "Do you hear me? *All* of them." Then he lurched away. "Alleene! Come back."

Ayl's friends snorted and swore as they followed, acting more like a bunch of rambunctious, barely trained pups than raiders. Had Dake been like that once? He must have been. Life without the huge weight of clan responsibilities seemed so long ago that he couldn't remember what it was like.

"There ain't much time for pleasure anymore, is there?"

Dake jerked his head around at the sound of Conn's voice. The older man was observing him. Dake wondered how much he'd guessed of his thoughts. "When you're leader, it's all about the clan," Conn said. "Your own needs take second place…if there's no one there to remind you of them."

It was true. The clan came first. From the alcohol he might imbibe to the fists he might throw to the women he might take to bed, his actions affected his people. Dake gave him a quick, wry and grateful smile. "This isn't the first time you figured what I'm thinking, Conn Blue. That isn't good, if we're rivals."

"It is if we're allies, though."

Conn's words hung between them. They shared a

look that did more to fortify their tentative truce than the entire day of talks had.

Then Conn's attention jerked away and his face lit up like it hadn't all evening. "It's about time you showed up, daughter!"

Daughter? A woman walked in out of the damp night, pink-cheeked from the cold. Her long dark braid gleamed like the polished shell of a maccam nut as she cast her gaze around the tent. Bright and sparkly and full of life she was. The girl shot light into the part of him that had been dark since the day he lost his father.

Val Blue, he thought, rising to his feet. Finally.

CHAPTER TEN

FRESH FROM PERIMETER PATROL in the dark and damp night, Val blinked away beads of mist clinging to her lashes and wiped them from the fine hairs at her temples. A tall and powerfully built stranger pushed to his feet as she approached her father's table. Recognition flared inside her. Hells be. She'd know those eyes anywhere. It was Dake Sureblood without a specken of war paint.

Be still her pirate heart. Tanned and clean-shaven, the brash, charismatic captain brimmed with energy and raw good looks. His off-ship outfit was rugged in brown-and-black wool and leather. Only his thick hair, twisted into silky braids tied at the base of his neck with a leather strap, and his eyes were as she remembered. Aye, like gems they were and focused intently on her.

His gaze dipped, taking in the sight of her from head to toe, and seemed to quite like what he saw. "Val Blue," he said. "It's about blasted time."

"About time?" She laughed and hooked a thumb in her weapons belt. Slinging her rifle over her shoulder, she swaggered as she circled the table. "I was out, busy protecting this camp—in case any of you visiting clansmen were up to no good."

The men at the table chuckled at her sauciness even as they feigned innocence with dramatic gestures.

"And you, Sureblood?" Val said, stopping in front of him. "Are you up to no good?"

"I haven't had the chance yet." The men laughed as the twinkle in Dake's eyes challenged her. Up close, he was even taller than she remembered. Bigger. If it were possible to feel a man's body heat through layers of clothing, she did. "I could use a little fresh air to clear my head of your moonshine, though." He leaned on his fists. "But you'd best escort me…just in case I feel like misbehaving." His tone took on a softer, inviting edge. It almost made her blush. *Let's get out of here.* His intent was clear.

She took a step toward the door when she deflated, remembering her duty. "Can't. I've got to work." She turned away before their interaction drew more speculation than it already had. And before her disappointment showed too bloody much.

Suddenly, Grizz roared over the noise. "Shut yer traps! Conn's gonna speak!"

The noise ebbed about as much as it could under the circumstances. Conn climbed to his feet and then to the top of his chair, helped by Grizz. His face glowing, his smile brilliant, he scanned the crowd with pride and a kind of conviction she hadn't seen from him in so very long. Dressed in his best clothes, he was a man enjoying every second of a party he'd long dreamed of hosting. Joy overtook her seeing him like this.

Val's heart pounded with growing excitement as Conn peered out at the crowd. There were children and elders, clansmen and strangers. He looked so proud to have the clans here, all their people, and even Nezerihm, glittering with zelfen and precious stones as accents on an outfit fit for a king. He acted like a king, too, sitting at her father's table, peering around as if he were the one in charge.

But Conn rose above them all. Val stored away the memory of his triumphant expression to make it last forever.

At last Blue clan's leader took a deep breath and began. "Ladies and gentlemen—and raiders, now that we've got everyone here, I'll make things official. It's my honor to welcome you to the first sanctioned gathering most of you have ever seen. A fine tradition with roots in our very beginnings as a people. It's about bloody time we started it up again!"

A hearty roar went up.

"Get yourselves out there if you're wantin' to dance. Drink if you're wantin' to drink. And whatever else you might be wantin' to do—do it. Remember, what goes on at the gathering stays at the gathering!"

The stomping of boots and pounding of fists on the tables was absolutely deafening. Nezerihm was quiet as he observed the pirates celebrating. His pretend smile was more a grimace than a grin.

Val whooped even louder. Hearing her father's speech was as exhilarating as coming off a successful raid. The same high floated her spirits. No trouble-making, gossip-spreading outsider like Nezerihm would take it from her.

Conn sat back down with Sashya's help. The band

started up a slow thumping beat. A slango beat! She unbuckled her weapons belt and hung it over Sashya's chair. Then she quirked a corner of her mouth into a wry smile as she sauntered over to Dake swaying her hips. "I've got time for a slango, if you think you can dance."

His eyes glittered like jewels as they settled on her. "Oh, I can dance. Question is, can you keep up?"

"Why don't you come find out?"

To the cheers of their respective clans, including Yarmouth, Hervor and Squib, Dake hooked her arm with his and swept her away from the table.

As they passed Ayl, he glared at her with a what-the-hells-are-you-doing frown. Val held her head high, not ashamed of being with the Sureblood. Like Conn said, this was a new era. No more would she be the stepping stone to Ayl's impossible ambitions. She was a raider, free as the wind. If Ayl was lonely, he should be helping Despa stock shelves, not drinking with his friends and ogling other women.

Nezerihm appeared as disgusted as Ayl.

"He isn't too happy about this party," Dake muttered.

"That man," she spat, whispering back, "he's been telling people you're using him as a scapegoat for stealing everyone else's share."

"Of course, he is. He wants to start a fight between your clan and mine. Between all the clans. He's got a vested interest in stirring up trouble at this gathering. If we all start getting along again, we might not be so dependent on his charity, hunting down his ore stealers.

As long as we're dependent, Nez is in control. He'll do what he can to keep it that way. View everything he does through that lens, Val."

"Dependency is dangerous. Dependency is death." She remembered how Dake's words held two different clans of raiders transfixed that day on the freighter.

"Then he can view us dancing," she said with a daring glance at the mine owner. "Aye, let him see us together and see his future."

The slango beat started up and drowned out hopes of more conversation. Her blood sang with anticipation. Dake didn't know if she'd be able to keep up? He'd see.

Arms moving from high to low, she and Dake circled their hands a hairsbreadth apart, then turned, each in opposite directions. Weight on the knees, hips loose, feet stepping in a precise pattern. As the beat increased in tempo, keeping two different rhythms for the hands and feet took increasing coordination and stamina.

She had both. Did Dake?

The beat drummed faster.

Hands up, almost touching, then down. Boots slapped the floor so fast they were a blur. With each slam of the musical beat, Val expelled a breath, her skin tingling with a light sheen of moisture. Her green shirt fluttered, her braid swung as she whirled, repeating the steps faster now.

A curse rang out. The male half of the couple dancing near them missed a step and stumbled out of the way.

It nearly stole her concentration. *Don't think, just*

dance. Dake must have had the same thought. Exertion wet his forehead, and his mouth was tight with concentration. His body heat radiated his scent, musky and male with a hint of the exotic that made him so fascinating. Despite his size, he was an athletic dancer, tireless. His expression was one of pure delight.

The beat sped up yet again.

A lock of her hair came loose and stuck to her cheek. She didn't pause to push it out of the way. They'd reached the point where the dancing was more instinct than conscious thought. Like busting through a hatch under threat of an attack, if you thought too hard about what your hands and feet were doing, you'd trip over yourself, or lose the beat.

More couples fell victim to the increasing tempo. There were bursts of laughter and curses. Soon they were one of only a few pairs left.

Val and Dake spun together like clockwork, almost in a trance until the last notes finally slowed and the slango ebbed away. Breathless, they left the floor to the sound of wild applause.

She wanted to grab Dake close, and saw her desire mirrored in his expression. Too many eyes were watching them, waiting for public affection, she knew. Many pirates in both clans wouldn't approve of a mixed couple. As the clan leader's daughter, she always had to think of more than herself. She couldn't forget the clan.

But that wasn't the real reason she couldn't leave with Dake. She was on duty. She'd already taken a longer break than she'd negotiated with Hawkk. She was needed outside.

A wave of frustration washed over her. "I've got to get back to work. My brother's late. I'm filling in." It about killed her to say it.

Dake searched her face, then his expression turned determined. "I'll take care of this." He called out to her father. "Conn Blue! I understand your daughter's on duty. I'm requesting your permission to borrow her to show me around."

She almost laughed aloud at his audacity. Then nearly turned red. The Sureblood hadn't even asked her first.

Does he need to? It's obvious you want to go. Anyone could see it, aye. Yet, she'd given her word she'd provide security. Conn bent sideways and nodded something. Sashya whispered to him. The woman finished up her private message with a kiss, pausing to applaud in Val's direction, then wrapped her coat over her shoulders and left. Conn sucked in an angry drag on his cigarette. "Valeeya, come here."

She approached obediently. "Aye, sir."

"You're off duty for the rest of the night."

Fates, yes! She couldn't believe her luck. Still, she'd been assigned to security and it felt flighty running off. "But, Papa. You'll be short one guard."

"Don't 'but Papa' me. You've got my protective streak, girl, and my stubbornness in always wanting to follow through. But this is different. I'm giving you the night off. My order overrules Hawkk's. No arguing, unless you want to be scrubbin' waste ducts all day tomorrow."

She shuddered at the thought.

"Your mother's gone off to bed, and I'm off to have a drink or two around the bonfire with my men. Aye, and not with my own daughter there to babysit me. Even your mother knows to leave me to my vices. Music, drinkin', singin' bawdy songs. A man can still do that, can't he? Go on now. Show our Sureblood guest a little of our famous Blue hospitality."

The man's gaze glowed with genuine fatherly affection as he winked at Dake. Then he crushed out his cigarette and called out for Grizz to join him.

Dake conferred briefly with his clansmen, sharing his plans, then escaped the crowded feasting tent with Val.

Cool, moist air flooded under the tarp. Their boots made sucking noises in the mud as they ducked outside the flap. The air was thick with the scents of wet earth and cedar, muting the sounds of music and laughter, even that of her father as he joined up with his friends unsteady on his feet.

Val watched them go. A sputter of guilt took away some of the fun of getting out of her guard duty. "Conn won't be careful. He's too drunk."

"The others will watch him."

"They're drunk, too."

"Everyone is," Dake reminded her.

"Everyone but us, you mean."

"Girl, I'd have a belly full of moonshine myself by now, if not for wanting to be with you."

His eyes glittered as he gazed down at her, a melding of blues and greens, flecks of gold and shades of gray. It should be illegal, a look like that. "Sureblood, you're going to charm the boots off me if you're not careful."

"Your boots, aye. And your socks, and…"

"And *what?*" She stepped backward, luring him away from the tent. They were grinning like fools, their boots squishing in the mud.

"I've got to keep some mystery as to my intentions, don't I?" His boldness made her skin tingle and her heart dance. "Let's get out of here, Val. Too many prying eyes and wagging tongues."

Her father, though, was nowhere to be seen. But with the sounds of drunken singing filling the night, she knew that wherever he was he was having a good time. The man deserved it. He deserved this night.

And so did she.

With no more thought to the duty she'd escaped, she took Dake by the arm, laughing as they splashed away through the mud to the mist-clogged paths she knew by heart.

The woods were hushed but for the distant barking of the camp dogs. Rain pattered against the highest leaves and didn't quite reach the ground. "I know just the place," she said as they hurried along. The perfect place. She could smell the cypress-scented steam from the baths already.

"Dake pulled his collar up. His breaths were gusts of vapor, his golden skin aglow with the cold. "It's dry, I hope."

"Not exactly…but it's warm."

"Good. I heartily want to get there."

"Why? Is the boy from the plains cold?" she teased.

"Hells. I'm burning up. And I don't mean from slango." He caught her hand and spun her close, grinning slyly as he slid his arms around her waist. He was taking wild liberties and it made her as dizzy with anticipation as she was before a raid. His lips were warm as they brushed over hers. The roar of the surf couldn't quite drown the rushing of her blood, or her sigh. She reached up to pull him down for more, but he caught her head in his big hands, holding her still.

"I met a man tonight who thinks he's your future husband." Dake made the remark sound casual but it was obvious he wanted information.

"Ayl," she snarled. Crowing about their supposed engagement in front of everyone at the gathering. It made her blood boil. "What he thinks and what's the truth are different things."

Dake searched her face, then the tension in his mouth eased. His lips curved, his gaze suddenly intense. Hungry. She could feel a tremble of impatience, of desire, that went through his body. "Now, where were we going?"

Grinning, she snatched his hand and soon the sounds of the village had all but faded behind them.

FERREN HID IN THE SHADOWS where she'd listened in wonder to the throb of the music and the dancing. Reeve had been away all night on duty. Luckily, his mother was even kinder and more trusting than he was, not suspecting it wasn't Ferren sleeping under the mound she'd made out of bedding. It had allowed her to sneak away to the clan's tubs to savor a long soak while most were distracted by the festivities. She'd stayed as long as she dared, even as her soul cried out for her to immerse all the way and fill her lungs. She'd already figured out the danger of that. She'd lost the ability to breathe underwater. Did the same eventually happen to all who left her world?

Even to Adrinn? What would his captors do to him once he could no longer live underwater?

Ferren fought to breathe, one hand clutching her coat around her thin frame. She tried to conjure the memory of the prince—golden, so vital; the way his hair swirled in the shallows like spilled dye, the light shattered by the sunshine at the surface, making his skin glitter like crystal, and hers, too. The golden disks he wore in each earlobe, stamped with the symbol that marked him as royalty. Three chevrons beneath a star: the waves and the sun. Home.

Blessed Heart of the Sea. Her soul seized with another spasm of grief. At times she thought the grief would kill her, and at times she might not mind. But as long as she was a soldier in an invisible army, sworn to fight in an invisible war to free those like her and return them to their birth world, the only place they could exist as nature intended, she'd stay alive, no matter what it took, even if it meant remaining with land folk until the time was right to complete her mission.

Like a night bug flitting around a light, Ferren

hovered around the land people, drawn to them yet unable to be part of them. She shrank back seeing the raider Val leaving with the strapping Sureblood man. She wanted to train as a raider like Val, but until she gained strength, Val and others would scoff at the idea. Intrigued by the female raider, one of the few in the clan, she followed the couple as they walked off into the night. Ferren hurried to match their pace and slipped on the slick path. It sent her stumbling into the bushes. It frustrated her to be so clumsy. Underwater she was graceful and sleek.

She was halfway to her feet when boots splashed on the path. She dropped into a crouch on the spongy turf, her heart in her throat.

A man walked hurriedly past, so intent on his destination that he didn't see or hear her in the darkness. She recognized him. He'd been in the group Reeve escorted that afternoon. One of Nezerihm's cronies.

Nezerihm. Her hair stood on end. Having been sold by her previous owner, she'd been under transport to a "wealthy mine owner" when the ship was attacked. It must be Nezerihm who'd bought her. From what she'd learned from her captors and these pirates, he was just the kind of man who'd consider one of her people a collector's item.

She pushed to her feet and followed the crony all the way to the shopping area, where he entered a healer's shop. Moments later he reappeared and cast a furtive glance up and down the street as he tucked a small sack in his cloak.

What did he buy? The store owner was a pretty

blonde healer whose presence seemed to make Val act ill at ease. And vice versa. Ferren wished she knew what had happened between the women. They both seemed competent, especially Val.

The wary man huddled deeper into his cloak and hurried away. Curious, Ferren followed.

FAR BELOW THE BLUFFS, waves crashed onto a rugged beach. Ahead, several low wooden buildings appeared out of the drizzle and fog. Val chose the one that belonged to her immediate family and unlocked it, grinning as she pulled Dake inside and shut the door against the foul night.

The air was warm and humid. The fragrance coming from the moist cedar planks surrounding the deep tub was powerful enough to make a person feel drunk on it, and Dake's expression of pleasure told her he thought so, too.

"The cypress tubs are my favorite thing about coming home," she said.

"More than a tub. A room-size tub." His teeth flashed in the warm light. "I like the way you think, Blue girl."

He followed her lead, stowing their boots, heavy with mud, then their socks. "The baths are fed by geothermal springs," she explained, placing her weapons belt out of reach of the door as every raider was taught. "There's an ingredient that's supposed to bring clarity to the soul. It's said the water's got no equal anywhere in the Channels."

She lit tiny lights along the benches and activated

the underfloor warmer. Then she grabbed hold of the hem of her blouse and lifted it over her head—and froze halfway through lowering her trousers, seeing that Dake's mouth had gone slack at the sight of her casually stripping. His surprise marked him as a stranger to her world. Blues were raised partaking in the baths. Mostly, unattached males bathed separate from the single women, but shyness about one's body wasn't bred into them. Out of respect, she turned around to give him his privacy. "Leave your clothes on the bench when you're finished. You don't need to rinse before getting in."

By now the floor under her bare feet had heated up, warming the air even more. She waited until she heard Dake slip into the water before turning around, pulling her bra wrap over her head as she did so, flinging it onto the bench.

Meeting his dark, suddenly keen eyes was a shock. It was clear he didn't think as little of her taking off that bra as she had. "It's our way," she explained quickly.

He snorted. "You won't find me complaining about your ways."

The air had become somehow charged. The atmosphere intensified as she walked to the tub, with Dake seeming to take in, and savor, every inch of her. No man had ever looked at her with such undisguised need. Dipping her toes in the tub didn't help quench the heat. "The water's nice," she said, sliding in.

"Aye. Very, very nice…" Dake's pulse throbbed visibly in his neck. Water lapped at him mid-chest. The rest of his six foot five inches was underwater, outside her line of sight, if not her imagination. He extended a dripping, muscled arm. "Come on, join me. Don't be shy."

She tossed her braid and laughed. "I'm not the shy one here."

"Well, it sure as hells isn't me."

"I don't believe it, Sureblood." She waded through tendrils of mist toward Dake until she stopped in front of him. Her breasts floated at the water line. "Because you sure got quiet, seeing me naked."

"You take my breath away, Val. That's why I got so quiet," he said, startling her into silence herself. "You're freepin' beautiful." Moisture beaded on his hard, shadowed jaw and desire roughened his voice. "You're right, too, that I don't know all your ways—your Blue clan ways. But you look too blasted good for me to be happy keeping my hands to myself. I hope your ways don't require me to."

She rose up out of the water and slid her palms up his chest. "They don't," she whispered. "*I* don't…"

His eyes were dark and hooded as he dragged his callused thumbs over her jaw, curving his fingers around the base of her skull to hold her still like he had in the woods when he first kissed her. Another few beats of her heart and he brought his lips to her throat. The barest touch…a wisp of warm breath. Sighing, she shivered, her eyes closing as his lips moved higher, lightly kissing their way to under her ear. Another sigh slipped out of her.

"From the minute I saw you on that freighter, Val, I was betting you tasted as good as you look." He pulled back and paused, cradling her upturned face. "Turns out I was right." Water surged as he hauled her up against his body and kissed her full on the mouth.

Desire scorched through her like a plasma blast. She'd thought she knew something about kissing. She didn't know squat. She'd never felt anything close to this embrace, *like him,* hard and raw, holding nothing back and demanding no less from her.

She clung to him, suckling his lips, his tongue, just as hungry, just as reckless as he was. When water sloshed over the tub's edge, she barely heard it. He carried her to the tub's deck, falling with her down to the cedar planks. Mist enveloped them, running in rivulets past their locked mouths as he trapped her between his strong body and the floor, their legs writhing and entwined. He bore his weight with his arms, and she felt him then, fully aroused, against her thigh. The strain of that self-control was apparent in the muscles bunching in his back. Why was he holding back? She wanted him like she'd never wanted anyone else. Couldn't he tell? Then there was hot breath and a voice, deep and gruff, in her ear. "We probably should stop right here if you don't want things to go any further."

"Like hells we're going to stop." Gasping, she shook her head at him, her lips tingling, her hands greedy. "If you can't tell I want more, Sureblood... If you can't tell I want *you*—"

His mouth silenced her—but not on her lips. He'd suckled a nipple into his mouth, teasing and hot. A sigh slipped out of her, her back arching with the gentle, erotic tugs of his lips, the rasp of his tongue, until he moved lower, tracing a trail of fire all the way to be-tween her legs.

She choked back a moan of surprise as he started pleasuring her. She wasn't a shy girl, but no one had ever done such a thing to her. Bloody hells. "Dake…" The skill of speech seemed to evaporate. She writhed at his touch, gasping as he found the places of highest sensation. Then suddenly his lips were back on hers, kissing her deeply, while his wicked hand remained at work.

He kept at it until her body went taut and convulsed, and she moaned his name into his mouth.

Only then did he break off the kiss to grin down at her. "It seemed you quite liked that, Blue girl."

"Aye, a little."

"Only a little, eh?"

"*A lot.* Oh, gods." She let her head fall back as she laughed breathlessly, throbbing with aftershocks of pleasure.

"Don't get too comfortable," he said. "I know some-thing else you're gonna like." He rolled onto his back, pulling her with him. Then, without missing a beat, he was inside her.

Pleasure coursed through her body, head to toe, as he thrust deep. Words were soon forgotten as he set his mind to making ever-so-sweet love to her. Before she knew it, that breathless feeling came over her yet again. Their hands clasped, fingers squeezing tight, they rocked together there by the side of the tub until at long last their passion was finally spent.

Their sated bodies melted together as one. Not

wanting to let him go, Val closed her fists in his wet hair. His braids were as thick as ropes in her hands. The thigh she'd thrown over his hips trembled as she lay there marveling at what just happened.

With Ayl, it all had been over so quickly. She'd secretly wondered if it was her fault he'd run off to Despa's bed. She wouldn't wonder anymore. It wasn't her; it *was him*.

"What was that about?" Dake asked, lifting his head. "You tensed up. What are you thinking about?"

She levered up on an elbow, her chin propped on her palm as she gazed down at him. "My first lover. And my only, until you."

"Hmmph. A lover shouldn't be on your mind when you're with me." Dark brows lowered over his eyes like storm clouds over the sea in August.

"Don't worry. He compares mightily unfavorably. He was nothing like you. Not then, not now. Not ever."

He wrapped the end of her dangling braid around his finger, bringing it to his lips, pausing to kiss her hair, then her mouth, before pulling away. "Ayl," he said. "The one whose thoughts you say are different from the truth."

"We're not engaged, but he wants to be, and not because he loves me. He's extremely ambitious. He knows my brother Sethen is weak. He sees me as a stepping stone to power in the clan." She bit off the rest, wondering if she should be revealing the intimacies of clan politics to a Sureblood.

"I know about social climbers, Val. Any woman who

comes around lately brings dreams of being the clan captain's wife."

"Are any of them raiders like me?" Despite hardly knowing Dake, and certainly having no claims on him, she couldn't help feeling a twinge of jealousy envisioning him with other women.

"None of them are anything like you." He drew the end of her braid across his upper lip, inhaling her scent. "They're just camp girls."

"Ayl thinks I'd transform into one somehow, if we married. But a clan captain's wife is supposed to be content staying home by the hearth fires, tending to his babes. Not me. I'm a raider. I won't be tied down like that."

"Until the day comes that you have no choice."

She peered down at his sudden seriousness. "There's always a choice."

"I used to think the same thing myself. There was a time I hadn't a care in the world." His tone turned wistful. "I'd go out a-raiding every chance I got, taking my pleasure wherever I could find it. Having the best bloody time of my life—like you are, Val. Then one day my father, Tomark, didn't return."

Everything changed that day; she could see it in those eyes that suddenly belonged to someone much older than Dake's actual years. Someone who saw her as still very innocent about life.

"But you do what you have to do, Val. You shoulder the responsibility. My life didn't turn out how I expected, but I'd never walk away from it. My people depend on me."

Sympathy swelled in her heart for the tragedy of Tomark's death. "I can't imagine going through what you have," she whispered.

He shrugged. "All I'm saying is that I never wanted to be tied down either, and it happened. You never know what life's going to hand out."

"A dark thought," she murmured.

"Not necessarily. Life hands out the good as well as the bad." His expression grew soft then. "No one says you can't end up happy even if life didn't give you what you expected. I sure never expected you, Blue girl."

"Or I *you,* Sureblood," she said, her smile just as tender.

"Dake," he corrected.

"Or, as some call you, the cocky upstart bastard."

He laughed. "I'm surprised I'm not called worse."

"Sometimes you are. But maybe you're the man who can finally stir things up enough to change them. For good. You and my father. The way it is between the clans isn't good. We need a change."

"Well, we're here, aren't we? Making love. That's a good start, and definitely a change."

Here, and not there—the village. She was playing in the baths only because she wasn't patrolling the perimeter on guard duty. Was her father asleep by now, or still out carousing? "I should go back," she said, suddenly guilty. "To check on things."

CHAPTER ELEVEN

VAL JOLTED AWAKE FROM an unintentional doze and found herself spooned by Dake's body. They lay curled up on their clothes they had used for a mattress. What woke her? Instinct or a sound?

Never argue with your gut. When skill can't carry you and your luck runs out, your gut keeps you alive.

She lay still, ears straining in the darkness trying to hear music or drunken laughter or even the barking and yipping of camp dogs. There was only the soft drumming of the rain and the steady sound of Dake's breathing.

He came half-awake and drew her to his chest. "Don't go yet," he murmured into her hair that held the scent of him and what they'd done. She cuddled closer, not wanting to leave the shelter of his arms.

Then—a shout, and the answering bark of the dogs. She flew upright. Dake jolted up next to her. Another shout, more voices. The dogs barked steadily and excitedly now.

"Something's wrong," she said and jumped to her feet, pulling on her clothes.

Dake threw open the door to the bathhouse to listen. Stark naked, his hair thrown around his neck and shoulders, his powerful muscles tensed into battle stance as he peered into the night. A woman's cry rang out. It was the kind of wail that signified someone had died.

Val swung her focus to Dake as dread chilled her to the core. For the fraction of a second that their gazes connected, she knew she'd transmitted her sense of urgency.

"I'll get dressed," he said simply.

Then they were off, racing along the same path on which they'd enjoyed a romantic stroll hours earlier. Val's braid streamed behind her as their boots splashed through the mud. The sky had gone soft: not yet dawn and yet not still night.

The camp dogs were howling now. People were yelling.

Dake's raiders intercepted him. With one last frantic glance between them, Val ran on ahead, alone.

Ayl found her first. He grabbed her by the shoulders. "Sethen's dead."

"What?"

"There was an accident in the Channels. He didn't make it out. The ship is a total loss."

"No...no..."

He gripped her shoulders. "It's been confirmed."

Shock, disbelief, then frozen acceptance. Many of her clansmen surrounded them. They looked horrified for the clan, and for her. "Where's Conn?" she gritted out. "Where's Sashya?"

"Conn's taken ill."

She wrenched out of Ayl's grip and ran home.

Reeking of moonshine, Grizz met her at the door. "It's not lookin' too good, girl."

"Is he injured? Is it his heart?" Conn had dismissed the symptoms for so long, refusing medical advice.

"The doctors are trying to figure it out. We haven't told him about Sethen yet. Let him think all's well."

"He'll be angry when he finds out."

"Aye, then let him," Grizz said. "I volunteer to be kicked from one end of this village to the other, as long as he gets out of bed to do it."

Val ran to her father's bedside. He lay prone on his back, red-faced and shaking, surrounded by his senior raiders and Artoom's doctors. Sashya sat on the edge of the mattress, rocking as she sobbed quietly, grasping Conn's hand in hers.

"Mama, oh, Mama," Val whispered, not knowing how to console her about Sethen when Conn lay in such a state.

Sashya turned. Val felt her heart clench when she met her mother's glazed, pleading eyes. She'd lost her son. Would she now lose the love of her life?

Val stood as Grizz came closer. "We'd all passed out by the fire," Grizz said, quiet in her ear, briefing her as if she were in charge. "Reeve found him on the ground near the toilets. Looks like he went off to take a leak and fell ill. He must have been lying there for some time."

There, in the cold and rain. There, because Val *wasn't.*

Yes, her father had been surrounded by his top raiders, men who'd protect him with their very lives, but when they got to partying, well, their good intentions wandered. She knew that, and should have been watching as another set of eyes. But no, she was too busy playing in the bathhouse with the captain of their rival clan.

If she'd been in Reeve's place, she'd have prevented this from happening and her father would be complaining to Sashya about a hangover instead of fighting for his life. Guilt wrenched her gut, making her almost queasy.

Val stood over the bed as the doctors fussed over him and Sashya wept, the entire scene ringed by Conn's senior raiders. The more junior raiders and the villagers looked on from the outer room and outside. Conn was sweating profusely. His clothes and hair were drenched. He was flushed bright red. His muscles twitched continuously, every single one in his body from the tiniest facial tic to the heaving bulges in his arms and legs. His skin looked like a horse's hide kicking off flies.

"He's having an allergic reaction to something he ate or drank," the doctor said. "Or smoked." She said it in a way that reminded Val she didn't approve of Conn's addiction. She leaned over the man, taking his vital signs. "Pulse weakening."

"Give him something then!"

"I have. He's not responding. I hesitate to give him more meds but…" She hesitated, then injected a serum into a swollen vein in Conn's arm.

His appearance didn't change. Alarm coiled inside Val, a chilly worm of dread working its way up her spine. She dropped to her knees and slid her hand over

Conn's cheek. He was burning up with fever that was surely outpacing the liquids they were pumping in him intravenously. Sashya continued to weep. Val felt numb, seeing her two parents in such a terrible state.

"Papa," she said. "This time I'm giving you orders. You blasted well listen. You're not going anywhere. You're not dying, so don't even think of it." *Live, please.* He'd been the center of all their lives for so long. Of *her life.* She couldn't imagine his being gone. "Do you hear me, Papa?"

He groaned and his eyelids fluttered, showing only the whites as he rolled his head toward her voice. His pupils tracked past her, then disappeared. But he saw her; she saw the flare of recognition. He knew she was there. His parched lips trembled as he tried to mumble something. His fingers squeezed hers.

Joyful, she gripped their clasped hands. Then he stiffened, wheezing out a groan and convulsed into stillness.

"No pulse!" The doctor pushed her out of the way. A hollowness of the magnitude Val never felt before swallowed her whole.

She stood, turned her back to the doctors swarming around Conn Blue, using their equipment to jolt his heart back to a normal rhythm. Trying again when the first and then the second attempts didn't work.

Somehow, she knew the way it would end. Within a few moments, all was silent. Then her mother's wail filled the room, an unearthly howl of utter despair.

"Mama. Mama, please." Val tried to calm her to no avail. Sashya's sobbing and crying were uncontrollable, and tore at Val's aching heart. "Help her, please," she told two nearby clanswomen, and they took the woman from her embrace.

Conn was gone. *Gone*. Disbelief boiled up. Allergic reaction? Hells. To what? Val turned to the doctor. "I want a blood test." She barked out the order. Her father was dead, her brother was dead and her grieving mother was all but useless. Val had to step into the void.

"You think it's foul play?" Grizz whispered, low and rumbling.

"He had a bad heart, aye. He had a lot to drink, aye. But did you see him? The way he was sweating? Shaking? That's not normal."

Was it poison? No one dared ask the question, but she knew they were all thinking it.

The doctor returned. "His blood tests positive for extremely high levels of alcohol, squatter's weed…and sharken."

"Sharken?" It didn't make sense. "Why the hells would my father be needing rocket booster?"

"It ain't only used for passion," Grizz reminded her. "It gives you energy to stay awake longer. To be able to drink more."

"Too much sharken mixed with too much squatter's weed can cause a severe autoimmune reaction," the doctor said.

Val frowned. "Didn't my father know the danger?"

"We never discussed sharken," she said nervously. "I didn't see the point if he wasn't using it. To my knowledge, he wasn't. But he wouldn't give up the squatter's. Your father long ignored my advice on that subject."

Val's need to find answers kept her moving despite a torrential rush of despair. Anger felt a whole lot better right now than misery. "Get Despa in here."

Grizz grabbed Ayl and sent him after the girl. Grizz was a quiet steadying presence, but not his usual alert self. He was still fighting the aftereffects of moonshine, like all the senior raiders in attendance were, and most of the crowd outside, too.

"Despa, did my father buy sharken from you?" Val asked when the girl showed up moments later.

Despa stood unusually close to Ayl as if staking her claim. "No." She seemed uncomfortable, shifting from foot to foot. Val didn't know what made Despa more nervous—her or the topic. "He always said he didn't need no boosting."

Appreciative chuckles went around the room at that.

"Then how'd it get in him?"

"Food, maybe. Drink. You can't taste it." Despa kept glancing at Ayl as if for reassurance.

Ragmarrk stepped forward. "Them Surebloods put it in him." The eternally cranky senior raider glared at everyone gathered there. "Them bastards were with Conn the last time he was seen alive. I saw them."

"Is this true?" Val asked Grizz.

Grizz shook his head. "Couldn't tell you, I'm afraid. We were dead to the world."

"Ask Ayl," Ragmarrk said. "He was with me, and saw them, too. Weren't you, Ayl?"

Ayl swallowed at Ragmarrk's pointed stare. "Aye. I was there." Then he cleared his throat and seemed to speak with more conviction. "I saw Surebloods with Conn."

The grumbling grew louder. "*Dake* Sureblood?" Val demanded, testing his honesty, wanting to rip the guts from the accusation she saw forming. Only a small group crowded into her father's bedroom, but once the rumors spread outside it would be chaos. She had to contain it before it did or put Dake and his contingent in danger.

"No. Just his men."

Ragmarrk jumped in. "Them Surebloods were at Despa's earlier, buying sharken, weren't they, Despa?"

The woman nodded after another searching glance at Ayl.

"They weren't the only clan buying from Despa," Reeve said, jumping in to help defend Dake, whose heroic actions he'd seen firsthand. "Everyone was."

"Reeve, did you see anyone with my father after he left the dance?" Val asked her friend.

"Only Blues. By the time I found him he was alone. Just Conn lyin' on the ground."

"Show them what you found there, Reeve," Ayl said quietly. "What was on the ground next to him."

Reeve's lips compressed. He seemed almost apologetic as he pulled a cup from his pocket and held it out. "He was clutching this."

"A Sureblood cup!" Ragmarrk yelled as all the raiders roared in anger and shock.

Val's heart dropped. It was damning. The cup was the same kind that Dake had used the night before—tall, cylindrical, with a leather lanyard used to hang it around the neck. But it wasn't etched like Dake's was and those of his men.

"The Surebloods poisoned Conn Blue!" someone yelled.

"Are we going to let them bastards get away with it?" another sneered.

"Shut your traps!" Grizz scowled at them all. "Have some respect for the dead at least." He grabbed the cup from Reeve. "This was a gift. I saw the Sureblood give it to him."

"See? The proof!" Ragmarrk cried.

"It's not proof any more than the Surebloods buying sharken is proof," Val argued wearily. "I want answers as much as you do, even more. But not gossip. Fact. The cup's a gift like the many other gifts exchanged the past two days. There are items from all the clans scattered around the village." But the Blues wanted vengeance for what had happened, and the Surebloods were the most convenient target. She could tell them all that she'd spent most of the night with Dake and that he couldn't have been behind any plans to hurt Conn, but instinct told her to keep that secret.

What the hells did any of it matter now? She should have been on duty guarding Conn. He was a great man and now he was lost.

Emotion surged—aching remorse, guilt and gut-wrenching grief—but she couldn't show it. Couldn't show weakness. With her brother gone and her mother incapacitated, she had to represent her family and lead, or someone else would step into the vacuum created by Conn's death. Someone who might not have the clan's best interest at heart.

Suddenly Grizz was by her side. She murmured, "I don't know what to do next." She'd never felt so isolated and alone. Did Dake feel this way the day he found out his father wasn't returning home?

"Val, girl, doubt comes with the territory. The weight of command will feel overwhelming at first, and less so as you learn to shoulder the burden." His tone was hushed to assure their privacy, but his manner was matter-of-fact and confident, bringing her back to the days in space apprentice school and her first raider missions, taking lessons from the master.

"What if I can't? What if I'm not cut out for the job?"

"You are. You already know what to do. It comes from somewhere deep inside you. The spirit of Conn lives on in your soul. You're Conn's girl. *Our* Conn." At that, Grizz's voice cracked, a show of emotion she'd never seen in the man. "Make him proud."

Val's stare was hard and straight ahead, her throat tight with emotion of her own. Grizz's words of encouragement fortified her. She faced the group of Blues crowded into her home and focused on Ayl, Ragmarrk and the rest of the troublemakers. "We all blasted well want answers. And we'll have them." She turned to the physician next and gave her the cup. "Analyze the contents and bring me the results personally." Then she shoved her dozer in her holster. "Because my mother is indisposed, I'll make the announcement of my father's passing." And she had to do it in a way that wouldn't cause a riot. Conn's dream was unity. He'd started them down that path, and she knew he'd want her to finish it. She bloody well would.

NEZERIHM HUNCHED HIS shoulders against the rain as he waited for the Blues to make the official announcement of the news. Pirates crowded into the street outside the home, jostling each other and trying to foist blame on one another. Soon enough they'd point fingers in the right direction.

Then he could leave this wretched, cloud-soaked rock with the satisfaction of having made the region much more unstable than it had been before. There was more work to be done, of course, but the prospect excited him rather than tired him. What good was one's destination if one couldn't enjoy the journey?

The front door opened and those gathered inside began to filter out. Grunting and pushing, the crowd expressed their impatience to hear the news.

Ayl emerged from the home and peered around. Spotting Nezerihm, he separated from his cohorts. He fairly smoldered with dark emotion as he strode close. His words were a gust of hot air against Nezerihm's ear. "It's done. I told them."

Ayl's eyes snapped with self-doubt, fear and anger. He was worried he'd be caught in the lie. "I hope you're right about what happened."

"You already know in your heart who's guilty of murder," Nezerihm reassured him patiently. "You didn't change the facts. Merely shortened the process. Someone had to. Someone not under Dake Sureblood's spell."

Ayl's upper lip curled. "Like Val. Maybe she'll listen to reason now and quit embarrassing herself and us by drooling over him."

"She'd be a fool not to."

Smug triumph overcame Ayl's doubts as he hunted for the Sureblood in the crowd, just as Nezerihm expected he would. The boy was as predictable as he was malleable. It reinforced his belief that he'd made the right choice in coaxing Valeeya Blue's spurned lover to give an eyewitness account he might not otherwise have communicated. Someone had to clarify the events of the night before after all. They were all drunk off their asses.

With all the distrust and quarreling between the Blues and the Surebloods, it was easy convincing one of them to bring the evidence into the spotlight. Ayl was jealous of Dake. It made him the perfect conduit for inciting more division amongst the pirates. As long as the boy's lust for power and for Valeeya could be manipulated, he'd be of use. When he was no longer, he'd be discarded like the others.

Nezerihm smiled, savoring the sound of Ayl and his faction angering the crowd with rumors. There'd be no hope for the silly gathering after this. After pitting the barbaric clans against each other for years, undermining them at every turn to keep the bandits from becoming stronger than he, it seemed he was finally getting somewhere.

CHAPTER TWELVE

VAL EMERGED THROUGH HER front door to address the crowd impatiently waiting outside for news. It felt like a hundred years since she'd last come through that door. In the short time since, everything had changed.

"You never know what life's going to hand out." It felt like even longer since Dake had shared that wisdom. No, you never did know what life had in store. Today was proof of that.

Grizz remained at her side. His presence was steadying as well as symbolic. He was respected by the clan, long seen as the missing hand of her father. His support at this critical time was a huge boost in her favor. One by one all the senior raiders gathered around, even sullen Ragmarrk. They would have done the same for Sashya had she been strong enough to make the official announcement confirming what everyone already knew: Conn was dead. There was a new leader, and it wasn't Sethen. It was Val.

She paused outside her home. There were shouts, some scuffles. A baby cried, and male voices argued. The roiling crowd had all the makings of a mob: Blues, Surebloods, Calders, Feckwiths, Lightlees and Freebirds milling about, twitchy, nervous and hungover. As

Grizz bellowed for silence, she caught herself searching for Dake with a horrid mix of emotions: the pang of guilt for fooling around with him when she should have had her eye on her father; dread that if he'd already fled, it would give weight to all the accusations.

When she spied him in the crowd, the knots inside her unwound. *He's still here.* His eyes were filled with acute understanding of her plight and the unexpected rise to clan leader. He'd lived it. Just as quickly, she hardened herself to his commiseration. If she let his concern seep into her composure right now, she'd crack.

"Today Blue clan suffers a broken heart." Her voice was somehow steady despite her wrenching grief. "Conn of the Blues is dead."

The wails of the women of the clan rose into a sky bloated with dark clouds. Children began to cry, fearful and sad. Many men dabbed at their eyes. The Blues had loved their leader, and now he was gone, stolen from them. *Maybe, if you were a better, less selfish raider, he'd still be alive.*

She forced herself to take a breath and finish. "Now we Blues must mourn. The gathering is over. In honor of Conn Blue and his hopes for all of us, go in peace." She started to turn away, intending to make her way to Dake.

"Is it true it was poison?" someone demanded loudly, stopping her.

"Them Surebloods did it!" someone else shouted to the sound of booing. "They found one of their cups in his hand."

How did that spread so fast? Who had the big mouth? She didn't know Dake well, but she knew enough to believe he wasn't guilty. Yet she still caught herself waiting to see his reaction.

He reared back at the charge, his face alive with burning pride and defiance. And hurt. Only a flicker, but it told her it gutted him that anyone, especially her, would consider even the remotest possibility that he was guilty of the crime. Then all vanished in the most outraged, wounded look of insult she'd ever seen. "Bull flarg! We Surebloods aren't responsible for harming Conn Blue."

His men roared their displeasure, and the other clans roared at the Surebloods, happy to have the blame falling on someone else.

"Poisoned!" a clansman cried out, picking up the call. "Found murdered! A Sureblood cup in his hand!"

The crowd grew angrier as rumors flared and spread.

"We Blues want blood, and we'll have it," others bellowed as the Surebloods fiercely defended their clan's honor, led by the furious Dake who seemed to have no fear as they ganged up on him.

The prospect of dozens of angry, shocked, hungover raiders turning violent chilled her. She had to get Dake out of here.

"The only blood spilled around here is what *I'll* be spilling if anyone takes clan law into their own hands! We Blues take care of our own business. We'll find who did it. Justice *will be* served but not by a mob lynching."

She cast her glare far and wide while purposely avoiding Dake's. Meeting his eyes now would be like tripping over a rock in the road. She couldn't afford to stumble, not with the crowd calling for his clan's blood.

She turned to Grizz. "If this turns ugly, they'll kill him, or at least try to."

"Aye, I know. Best if we expedite his leaving." He took a step toward Dake.

She caught his arm. "I'll do it." His eyes flashed with sudden understanding. Grim, she walked in Dake's direction.

Ayl appeared and blocked her path. "If you need to tell the Sureblood something, let me."

"It's my place to do it. I'm moving the clans out. The Surebloods first."

"You're letting him escape?" Ayl glanced from her to Grizz and back again. "After he poisoned your father?"

"Move aside, Ayl."

He hesitated, standing in her way.

It was defiance, plain and simple. Others were watching, listening, seeing what she'd do. As leader, if she wanted to speak with Dake Sureblood or anyone else she didn't owe Ayl an explanation. If she didn't stand up to Ayl now, she'd never be able to put him in his place and keep him there. "I said *move aside,* raider." Her hand went to her dozer. The noise ebbed as the clans watched.

Ayl's eyes were black-dark. Angry. His jaw twitched. Those were the longest seconds of her life before he gave in and let her pass.

Nezerihm lurked only paces behind him in the mist. She froze. Her instincts prickled at the two men's proximity. *They were talking before you interrupted. Plotting.*

She remembered what Dake had told her. Splintered, the clans were weak and dependent on the mine owner. Their dependency kept him in control. *"He'll do what he can to keep it that way. View everything he does through that lens, Val."*

Conn's death, too?

She shuddered in the falling rain. Was Nezerihm responsible in some way for her father's murder? The thought slugged her like a fist. She gave her head a single hard shake as if to empty it of the crazy, grief-stricken thoughts. Yet the unease persisted, and she'd better take heed. *Never argue with your gut.*

As Nezerihm observed her, clearly wary of her thoughts, she narrowed her eyes to blunt her distaste of the man. It was a struggle not to call for guards to lock up the mine owner, but if she acted on emotion and accused without facts, she'd be no better than this crowd's instigators: Ragmarrk, Ayl and their cronies. She'd get Nezerihm off Artoom, but nicely. If she learned he was responsible for murder? Well, she and her raiders knew where to find him.

"Reeve," she said to the raider who hovered nearby, "escort our guest Nezerihm to his ship. See that all his needs are met."

Nodding, Reeve seemed surprised by her cool control. He had no way of knowing that grief was hot on her heels. Rain pelted her, and she gladly let it soak her to the bone. The more pain she suffered, the less likely she'd give in to the anguish of her family being reduced by half. Yesterday she had all she wanted within her grasp. How could everything change in so short a time? How could she go forward when she wanted to lie down and weep? *You already know how. You're Conn's girl.*

Then she was with Dake. "Val," he said. How could one word convey so much? Sorrow. Tenderness. Absolute understanding of what she was suffering.

With a gargantuan effort, she refused the urge to fall into his comforting arms. To delay his departure was to put him at risk. She wanted no more murders on this turf today.

Nodding, she made fists behind her back and pressed them to her spine to hang on to emotions already strained to the limit, fearing that if they snapped she'd have to give in to his steadying strength. "It's going to get ugly," she warned under her breath. "It's true what they're saying. They found Conn out cold with a Sureblood drinking cup next to him. Grizz said he saw you give a cup as a gift."

"Not that cup. I took back the other before the end of dinner to have it etched with Conn's armor design. It's on my ship. I intended to return here and give it to him, fully engraved by our artisans." *And to see you again,* his eyes broadcast plainly. Then he narrowed his gaze. "Someone else gave him that drinking cup. Someone wanting to cause conflict."

Nezerihm, she read in his eyes. "And if he caused my father's death?" she whispered, her pulse drumming.

"Then we'll wreak revenge as one people, Blues and Surebloods, and all the clans. Unity was my father's dream, and yours. Now it's ours."

They were speaking words of upheaval and war. Nezerihm held the power in the region and commanded most of the wealth. He'd never relinquish either without a fight.

"Surebloods—murderers!" someone shouted to hearty jeers. "Hang them now!" All around them there was swearing and shouts. It was like one of Grizz's pre-raid rallies but with a dark twist.

"Dake, you got to get out of here. Grizz will make sure you and your men get to your ship and get the first slot out."

Dake looked disgusted. "Girl, I'm not leaving. Not like this."

"You're in danger here."

"Danger? Bring it on. I'm staying here to defend my honor."

"No. Get the hells out. Now. We've got a mob brewing. It could flare up and get deadly in a heartbeat." But Dake glared down at her. She'd have no more luck moving him than she would a deep-rooted river stump.

Unless she left him with no choice.

"My life debt," she said as the idea struck. "By leaving, you stay safe, and I pay off what I owe. You've got no choice now, Dake Sureblood. Go!"

He blinked as her proposal sank in. "You're freepin' kidding me."

"If you don't have the sense to save your hide, I will."

He glowered fiercely, and she glared back. Their passion was a tangible thing; the very air pulsed with it. Then she let the air out of her lungs. This wasn't how she wanted them to part. "Please, Dake. I gotta deal with this on my own."

For a few more heartbeats, he stood there, his jacket hanging open, his breaths exiting in gusts of vapor, a wrenching look of indecision in his eyes. His anguish was heart-rending and stole her breath. For a second, she feared she might change her mind and beg him to stay.

"I know you do, Blue girl," he said quietly. "And I'll abide by your wishes. Blues warring with Surebloods will make Nezerihm very happy. I'll kiss a war pig's ass before I'll stoop to making that conniving piece of flarg happy." He paused, his regard fearless, intense. "I *will* see you again."

"I bloody well hope so."

His mouth softened a fraction as that promise hung between them. Then he turned and walked away.

CHAPTER THIRTEEN

"ARE WE LEAVING, BOSS?"

"You heard her," Dake snarled at Yarmouth.

"I heard her, aye. I just didn't think you'd be obeying."

Caught out in a miserable, unrelenting downpour, Dake frowned at his first mate as water dribbled down his jaw and seeped between his collar and his skin. They made slow, trudging progress along the road to the docks. The ground was barely visible under the puddles. At any given moment over the past two days, the cozy, cloud-choked planet of Artoom had threatened to close in on him, but never more than now. The horror of what had occurred within the past few hours seemed unbelievable. Val wore the tragedy on her face, and the guilt. She didn't have to say the words: she blamed their tryst for what happened.

Hells, if there was any guilt to bear, it was his. At his urging, she'd left her post to be with him. In truth, neither of them was responsible, but they'd shoulder that guilt for the rest of their lives.

Dake swiped the back of his hand across his face. In the drenching rain he kept seeing the devastation in Val's golden eyes. The heartbreak. Hells, he'd barely gotten to know Conn himself and still felt the loss hard. It was easy to imagine her anguish; he knew what it was like. He knew better than most how swiftly life could change. She was younger than even he had been at the time he first took command. It put her in an even riskier position with both her brother and father dead. Despite Grizz's show of support, knowing the jackals snapping at her from the shadows, like Ayl, Dake feared hers would be a precarious position to keep. He would have stayed, had she not kicked his sorry ass off Artoom.

For his safety, she'd claimed, calling on her life debt to force his hand. Bah. He wasn't scared of the Blues, or any other clan. And when he'd saved her life, it was instinctive, and expecting nothing in return.

"Rumors are flying," he told Yarmouth. "But Val's got a cool head, and so does Grizz. It makes sense to clear out of Artoom until things calm down."

"Halt, Sureblood!"

A gang of Blues, eight strong and armed with dozers, approached through the drizzle. Instantly his raiders drew out guns they weren't supposed to be packing. What did he expect? The Surebloods never followed all the rules.

"Easy now," Dake told everyone. "No shooting."

"I don't need your permission to shoot, *Sureblood*," Ayl said as he and his group glared down the sight of their weapons.

"You poisoned Conn Blue," an older man growled, looking all too eager to fire. "We have the proof. Why don't you just admit it so we can get your punishment over with—one, two, three?"

The gang laughed hard at that. "Don't you know what that means?" Ayl queried. "That's what we Blues call shooting off your balls one by one, then your brains. One, two, *three shots*."

More guffaws. Dake's clansmen grumbled and swore, weapons ready but not about to fire. Their discipline was impressive and made him proud. "I didn't kill Conn Blue. My clan's not responsible for his death."

"I'm supposed to believe that?" The older man's eyes narrowed at Dake. "You're a Sureblood. Raid-crashing, lying sons of bitches—"

"Ragmarrk! Ayl! Warrybrook! Are you bloody insane? What did I *just say?*" Steaming mad, Val strode toward them followed by a sizable group of supporters. Completely unafraid, she slapped down the Blues' weapons as she passed between the two groups. "You don't have the right or the power to take clan law into your own hands. Put your weapons down." She frowned at the Surebloods as well as the Blues. "All of you!"

"You heard her," Dake told his men.

The weapons came down.

Val pulled the weapon away from a startled Ragmarrk, and for a moment Dake thought she might strike him with it. "If I find out that my father was poisoned, I'll spend every last waking moment hunting down the assassins. But I will not—I *will not*—allow a witch hunt based on prejudice and jealousy."

A pointed glance at Ayl, then she turned to Dake, her chest heaving. "Weren't you going somewhere, Sureblood?"

"Aye. To the docks."

"Reeve." She pointed at her clansman who was trudging up from the docks after delivering Nezerihm to his ship. "Escort the Surebloods to their vessel. Then grab a helper and get all the other clans out of here."

"Aye." Reeve signaled for them to follow.

As they walked away, Dake glanced over his shoulder as Val glanced over hers. Regret passed between them, sharp with the sense of leaving things unfinished. It had been complicated between them from the moment they first aimed guns at each other. It would be even more so now.

He wanted Val in his life. He'd figure out a way to make it work. *I will come back for you.*

She nodded, that promise lingering between them once more. Then she was walking away with a bit of a swagger, Ragmarrk's rifle gripped in one hand and her dozer in the other. If Dake even made a move to go after her, she'd probably blow him into so much space dust. And so, leaving her to address the needs of her grieving mother and her clan, he had the grace to disappear.

THE MOOD OF THE CREW manning *Tomark's Pride* was somber. Company was the last thing Dake expected reaching the outer limits of Artoom's planetary system and their calculated jump point back to Parramanta. "Boss, we got a Drakken vessel coming in!" Yarmouth called out.

"Drakken?" Here? Dake strode over to the nav screen to look over Yarmouth's shoulder. Merkury jumped up to trot at Dake's side, his claws making a familiar rat-tat-tat on the floor.

The Hordish vessel was dark and menacing as they all were. "Hunter class," Dake said. Merkury's cold wet nose pushed against his palm. He moved the dog out of the way. "She looks like a troop carrier."

"In the Channels." Kage, his second-in-command, seemed concerned, and for good reason. They'd all heard the stories of pirates captured and forced to fight. "They must be hard up for recruits to be coming here looking for bodies to fill a quota."

"She won't be getting ours. Accelerate to jump speed."

"You sure you don't want to shake them down first, boss?" Yarmouth coaxed. "May be something they have that we need."

"The only thing we need right now is to be getting home." In light of everything that had happened, he wanted to be where Val could comm him and he could comm her in privacy.

Merkury whined and thrust his muzzle in Dake's hand again. He paused to hold the dog's head still, looking his loyal friend in the eye. "It's okay, boy." A quick ruffle of soft fur, then he was back to monitoring the displays with his crew.

Suddenly, Yarmouth swore. "Boss! They fired! They fired a freepin' torpedo."

Hells. "Decoys—now. Arm all guns and bring 'er about—hard starboard."

Yarmouth turned so hard the ship shuddered. The torpedo kept coming, sailing right past the decoys. Useless, they soared off into space. The torpedo was coming in too hot to let go another salvo.

"Fire all guns," Dake ordered. "Everything we got."

The ship shook as booms echoed from the plasma cannons and the main guns. But trying to hit a torpedo that way was like shooting bullets at a fly. You needed a lucky shot. It wasn't their day.

Kage was next to Dake, their fists lined up on the forward console. "We're going to have to outmaneuver it," his second said.

"Aye. Do it, Yarmouth."

The man started flying like a madman. As they rocked from side to side, Merkury nudged Dake and tried to get his attention with a high-pitched whistle that signaled distress. "Merk, not now," Dake snapped. The dog made one more disgruntled whine and sat hard on his rump.

The torpedo stayed on their ass. He couldn't freepin' believe it. A troop ship fired on them, and was going to make the hit. They'd be blown apart at the most, and at the very least disabled. "Brace! Brace for impact," he roared. They took seats and buckled in.

The impact almost knocked him witless even though he was expecting it. The ship rocked violently. Alarms wailed.

"I about swallowed a toenail," Kage muttered.

"Hull breach in lower cargo bay, after section four," Yarmouth reported, his voice at a higher pitch. "Sealing it off. Pressure coming back up. Got a fuel leak at the number one nacelle tank. I…I can't stop it. The shutoff's busted. We're going to go empty in seven minutes."

Seven minutes. "Keep trying," Dake ordered. "Where's our Drakken friend?"

He looked even as he asked the question, finding out for himself the answer he didn't want to know. The Drakken was closing on them, fast.

"They're hailing us, boss. What do you want me to do?"

"Don't acknowledge. They're not going to fire any more torpedoes. Too expensive. They'll only want to board us."

Kage swore. "And if we let them, we're all but agreeing to new careers in the Imperial Navy."

A chill washed over him. "Doesn't matter if we agree or not, they're going to come aboard. Don't mean we're going to give them a friendly welcome." He patted his dozer. "We'll go down fighting if we go."

Kage grinned. "There's still a chance we'll shake them down and see what booty they might be willing to share."

"Aye." Dake wanted to rail against what was about to happen; he wanted to plant his fist on the wall in frustration. A Drakken troop ship, of all blasted things, and here in the Channels, the middle of pirate hunting grounds. It was as if they were waiting for them. *Or for you.*

"This is an ambush," Dake said, the horror dawning as all the pieces came together.

His father had supposedly died in an accident after advocating clan unity. Now Dake had taken up his cause and quite visibly. Was this ambush his punishment? His *accident?*

This is no accident. Nezerihm. Dake's instincts roared the warning. He had not one bloody fact on which to base his charge but his gut, which had never steered him wrong. If he was already willing to believe the mine owner had a role in the tragedies that had rocked Dake's clan and Val's, it wasn't that much more of a stretch to suspect Nez had tipped off the Drakken.

Not a stretch at all. Nez had no more loyalty to Dake's people than he did the Drakken. His roots weren't in the Channels. He was an outsider who had managed to dig in. Now he was poised to take over. Right or wrong, Dake had to let the clans know.

"Yarmouth," he growled. "Get yourself in the one-man skiff. Now. Keep the lights off and get the hells out."

Merkury fidgeted restlessly at Dake's side, trying to do as Dake had asked earlier and not bark or whine. The dog sensed his unease as well as the danger they were in.

"You going with me, right, boss?"

"No. None of us are." Kage and the others listened in, their expressions grim. The ominous hulk of the Drakken hunter ship was almost upon them. "Tell the clan what happened here. Work with my stepmother and the clan to choose a new captain to lead till I get home. Make sure they warn Valeeya Blue, too. Aye, tell her not to trust Nezerihm. He may have tipped off the Drakken."

At that, Kage's head jerked around. The man's eyes blazed with the realization that Dake might be right.

"Like when them fighters appeared out of nowhere when we raided that Drakken freighter Nez lured us to."

Dake swore. Kage's observation sealed the deal for him. They'd been set up.

Yarmouth's expression turned flustered. "But why send me to warn them?"

"Your lucky day." Dake looped a leash around Merkury's neck. "Take care of Merkury."

Merkury let out a sharp, distressed yip as Yarmouth pulled on the leash. The dog had been a fixture at his side. Their silent bond went beyond anything he could explain. Dake crouched down and accepted a frantic lick or two. Then he took his loyal friend's head in his hands, making contact with a pair of urgent brown eyes, his voice tighter than he'd have liked. "You were always a good boy. This doesn't change that."

Then Dake stood. It was the best way, he told himself. The only way. "Now get out while you can, Yarmouth."

Dake strode to the very bow of the ship. "Weapons ready," he ordered. There was a terrifying grinding of metal against metal as the troop ship lodged alongside in preparation for a forced dock.

"The skiff's launched," Kage shouted over the din.

Dake nodded. Somewhere out there in the dark, Yarmouth and Merk were on their way. Home, he hoped. Parramanta. As he would be after a bit of a delay.

The intruder alarm screeched. Dake gave a silent signal and they took defensive positions around the bridge. He'd be shooting himself some stinking Drakken today, and he couldn't say he was sorry.

Just as he thought the bridge was about to be boarded, a grenade spun over the floor, clattering up against the nav banks. Pinkish smoke billowed out from the grenade. *Bastards.* "Gas! Get your breathers on!"

Right away, dizziness unsteadied him. Holding his breath, he grabbed a ledge for balance, then went down on his knees, reduced to crawling to the spot where the masks hung. His head spun, his mouth was cottony. *To the masks,* he commanded himself. He tried to shake off the feeling of peace that urged him to lie down and take a nap. *Reach…the…breathers…*

He fought his fading body, struggling to think through a clouding mind. His ears rang, his lungs burned. His obligations as captain urged him forward. His determination not to fail his clan, or Val, wouldn't let him stop until he reached the masks. The thumping of boots climbing the ladder from the docking area came ever closer. Drakken were aboard.

Must defend the ship.

Onward he crawled, his heart ready to explode, inching…inching…never stop…never surrender…

He paused for a breath before he realized he'd taken one. Mistake. His hands seemed far away from his body and the floor all too close. He stared at them, wondering. Then the floor jumped up and hit him with a single knockout punch.

CHAPTER FOURTEEN

DEAR SWEET FATES. He'd descended into hells.

Consciousness found Dake sprawled on a filthy floor, chained by the wrists and ankles. The air was so dry and frigid he knew instantly he was on a hunter ship. And in a holding cell.

How long? Hours, days?

Weeks?

He swallowed hard, sensing that more time than what he was aware of had passed. They'd drugged him, kept him drugged, and brought him where? How far from the Channels?

He opened crusted eyes and peered around in the dark. The four walls threatened to close in on him. He sweated even though his gut was icy cold. Tight spaces. No air. No way out.

He grimaced, trying to pretend the cell wasn't as small as his skiff. "Isn't as small…isn't as small…" he whispered, his chant a faint croak. *Isn't as small.* He tried to believe it with everything he had.

The alternative was to go mad.

He sensed others nearby—but who? His clansmen, or Drakken soldiers? As silently as he could, he tested his restraints. Searing pain roared to life, burning from his wrists and ankles. He glanced at the clotted blood and torn skin where the metal rings had eaten into his flesh.

He must have been fighting like a madman to free himself but he couldn't remember it. Drugs had suppressed his memory and his common sense. In his right mind he'd never have fought to the point of weakening his ability to fight back. A pirate knew better than to ruin his flesh for the sake of trying to free himself. The cell was filthy. An infection could kill him. He could lose an arm, a leg.

A fetid stink filled his nose. He hoped it wasn't his body he smelled rotting. Panicked, he counted his appendages. All still there. Bones not broken, though a few of his ribs might qualify. He rolled his head back in relief, then sucked in a breath at the flare-up of pain. The beatings he didn't remember but whoever was in charge had been thorough. There wasn't a specken of his body left untouched, it seemed.

His stomach felt empty but hunger was far from his mind. His mouth was as dry as a Parramanta dust field in summer. His tongue was like old leather, his lips swollen and cracked. He could use a drink, a gallon of ice-cold water would do nicely to start, like the kind drawn from the deep wells reaching down to the depths of Parramanta's aquifers...

Suddenly he was home, diving into the crystal-blue reservoir, his unbound hair streaming, the cool pressure of the water enveloping his body as he plunged deeper and deeper...

He snapped his eyes open, shaking off the hallucination. Something, a noise, had roused him back to reality—darkness, pain, a nauseating stench. How long was he out? Was it from the drugs or dehydration? Dehydration would kill him before anything else did. Where were Kage and the others? Couldn't see; his night vision seemed worthless, filled with flashes of light. He almost blacked out again when a door slammed open. Floodlights blinded him.

Heavy boots hit the ground which sounded gritty, slushy.

"Wake up! Freepin' lazy ass! Vacation's over. Time to get to work."

Water hit him in the face and nearly threw him over. Instinctively, he tried to right himself, causing excruciating pain where the cuffs dug into his flesh. A groan slipped past his clenched teeth. *Don't show them pain.*

"Hit him again. I told you we shouldn't have taken on these Channels scum. They don't like to work, and then they die on you."

Drakken. He knew that accent. The cadence and the guttural twist of the language they both shared was unmistakable. It confirmed what he already suspected— he'd been conscripted into the Imperial Army.

"But they can carry a gun," another said, "and I need the warm bodies. We're losing them by the thousands at the front. These will have to do. But they stink like yar-offal. I'm not giving them to Battle-Lord Harekkeen smelling like this. Clean them up, war sergeant."

Them. Were his men alive? Gods above, had his crew survived? He couldn't fathom being here alone.

No pirate captured and conscripted ever walked free. They died in captivity not because they couldn't tolerate the cruelty and violence, but because they couldn't live caged and without their clans around them. Even now he couldn't wrap his mind around not seeing his people again. Or Val's. He knew that once she heard the message from Yarmouth, she'd want to search for him. Fates, he hoped not personally. She was young enough, inexperienced enough and cocky enough to risk any danger to do what was right. That was what he was afraid of. Imagining her in Drakken hands was a nightmare he blasted well couldn't touch.

More water and foamy soap flooded the holding cell. It got in his eyes and made them water and sting. He spat out the bitter taste. There was laughter, and Dake was hit with the full force of the water hose again. The agony nearly knocked him out. Part of him wished he could pass out and be done with it. The larger part of him wanted to show this Drakken what he was made of.

What his people were made of.

In between hose blasts, Dake squinted at the form of his tormentor—a sinewy soldier seeming to enjoy aiming where it would cause the most pain: the raw, torn flesh, the freshest bruises. He saw Dake's regard and smiled, revealing a jeweled tooth. One side of his face was tattooed in the Drakken way, and his ears glittered with Hordish jewelry. Was this his future? Monsters like this in control of his mind and body?

"Get up!"

The chains were yanked, gripped in the war

sergeant's tattooed hand as if he were controlling a vicious dog, a dog to be punished. Dake weaved, dripping with watered-down soap, hoping he didn't topple over in that moment of exquisite pain, of utter despair, that he and whoever of his crew who'd survived were going to be the exception. He owed it to the Surebloods. He owed it to Val. His future was with them, and Val, and not as a short-lived conscript in the Drakken Imperial Army. He'd figure a way out. A way back home.

"Get along now," the higher ranking soldier said. An officer, Dake guessed. "You're heading out to training. As an Imperial soldier."

The war sergeant broke in. "For once in your life you're going to work hard. You better like it because it's the last job you'll ever have." Laughing, he yanked on the chains attached to Dake's wrist cuffs to make him walk.

Gritting his teeth against the agony, Dake met the Drakken's dark, malevolent eyes. *I won't groan or swear. I won't give you the pleasure.*

The march from the holding cell to another troop carrier began. Others fell in step. Familiar faces. He saw his second-in-command, Kage, chained, hunched over and his face so swollen and bruised he was barely recognizable. And there was young Squib, shaking uncontrollably. Dake tried to meet his eyes, but the boy's gaze darted as if he saw everyone as an enemy, even Dake. Only now did Dake know true anguish. What he felt physically was nothing compared to the sight of his Sureblood clansmen herded like animals into the belly of a Drakken warship.

He saw no more of his men. Could it be they were all who survived? "Have you seen the others?" he whispered.

A fist in his jaw rewarded his attempt to find out the whereabouts of his raiders from *Tomark's Pride,* men he'd handpicked to attend the gathering because they were his best.

He staggered, tasting blood. It may only be him, Squib and Kage. But he was still their captain, and all of them top Sureblood raiders. He'd keep them going by reminding them of their reason to live: to get home again. As for himself, he had a mission to finish when he got there: uniting the clans and ending Nezerihm's reign of power over his people. That vow gave him the will to go on.

VAL DUCKED INSIDE THE *Varagon*'s cargo bay to escape a soaking downpour. It was the wettest spring in memory. It was as if the world of Artoom was crying for Blue clan's loss.

After two weeks of official mourning and clan meetings, and another two back to normal operations, she had found no clue as to how Conn Blue had ended up with an overdose of sharken, a substance everyone claimed he didn't use. And they were no closer to finding out why Sethen's ship had collided with one of the many rocks in the Channels either. Grizz and a team of raiders and mechanics were in the process of sifting through the wreckage collected. She held fast to the hope they'd find proof of Nezerihm's involvement. The elusive smoking dozer. If they didn't, a darker truth would have to be examined, one that tortured her day and night: the meaning of Dake Sureblood's disappearance.

"If it's got thrusters or testicles it's going to give you trouble," Grandmama Uhsula had assured her with a spirited cackle, trying to make her feel better, but trouble didn't fit her impression of Dake. Where was he? Why hadn't he called? She frowned as she clenched a fist, shaking water off her leather coat. Dake's pretty words filled her head still, like butterflies she couldn't catch. His vow that if Nezerihm assassinated Conn, they'd wreak vengeance as one people—Blues and Surebloods, and all the clans—had inspired her on the darkest day of her life. When Dake preached unity, radiating his passion for the subject, he gave her hope they could carry on the work of their fathers *together*. The mission would help her heal and find closure, as well as sweet revenge.

United. Bah. Fine show of unity on Dake's part, vanishing like he did!

Her stomach clenched. Sweat tickled her brow and she took deep breaths to stave off her queasiness and her misgivings. Surely by now Dake should have quietly contacted her to see how she was doing. The first week had passed by with no word. She hadn't really expected one, although she'd secretly hoped. After two weeks, she'd begun to wonder if clan duties of his own had him swamped. By week three, she'd bounced between hurt and annoyed. Had the slango and what they shared afterward meant that little to him? It brought back the humiliation she'd felt after Ayl had abandoned her in much the same way. By month's end, doubt had taken over.

Now with each day that passed, her dread that she'd misjudged him grew. What if Dake's warnings about Nezerihm were only to throw her off the truth? What if Dake meant to distract her with his charm to keep her from guard duty and busy in bed while his men poisoned Blue clan's leader? In sending him away from Artoom against many clansmen's wishes, had she allowed him to get away with the perfect crime?

Crazy thoughts. Unproven thoughts. She tried to ignore them as she climbed down the ladder where Grizz waited for her. She was exhausted but tried to hide it. No one must know that each night the nightmarish what-ifs robbed her of sleep and energy, or that each morning she bore the consequences of her actions with an upset stomach.

"Good morn to you, girl," Grizz said and somberly pulled a tarp off a pile of twisted and scorched metal parts so Val could inspect the remains of Sethen's ship fished out of space and carried back to Artoom. "We've been through it piece by piece. It was a high-velocity crash, head-on into the asteroid. It shattered the asteroid and spread the wreckage widely. This is it, I'm afraid."

All that was left of her brother, she thought. Who'd be in her place right now if he hadn't planted himself on an asteroid. Sethen wasn't the most reliable of raiders, but she'd thought him better than this. She picked up one of the long ribbons of zelfen, the only parts not distorted beyond recognition.

"There's just enough here to identify it was the *Hareen*," Grizz explained as she ran a finger along the metal strip.

"With Sethen in command and twenty raiders with him," she said quietly. "A hard loss for the clan. Able-bodied men aren't around in infinite numbers."

"Any luck with the recruiting call for females to serve as raiders?"

"Some interest, no takers." *Just like her and men,* she thought, studying her reflection in the strip of zelfen, seeing a girl who was a fool with men. Not once but twice, and this time with deadly consequences. Yet the memory of that wrenching look in Dake's eyes before he left still had the power to twist her heart. She'd believed that glance cemented the beginning of a relationship. A month and no word from him, not even a "it was nice but." When it came to men, it was clear she had no judgment.

And it cost her father his life.

A pang of guilt, her constant companion, made her wince.

Grizz paused to observe her. "You're looking pale."

She shrugged it off. "When was the last time any of us saw the sun?"

"It's more than that, Val. You're not the same, and it ain't only the grieving for your father."

She sighed wearily. "He should have called by now. Dake."

"Don't know why he hasn't. That boy was interested in you. Half in love, I'd say."

"Love. Bah. Lust, you mean."

Grizz's eyes took on a certain amused sparkle. "Lust has formed the roots of many a lasting relationship in this clan. Your parents, for one."

"Grizz," she protested.

"It was more than just that with that Sureblood boy, though. He respected you, admired you. I saw it, and so did Conn. He wouldn't have otherwise given his blessing to court you. That was a lot for your father, you know, trusting another man with his little girl. Not anything he'd do lightly. You were the light of his life, Val."

She couldn't watch Grizz's face as he said it. It magnified her own grief and turned it painful and fresh again. "If my father's instincts were as good as you say, then why haven't we heard from the Sureblood?"

"There's got to be a reason for it," he insisted. "Some logical explanation."

"Like what, Grizz? Like *what?* Doesn't he realize how guilty this makes him look?"

He exhaled, rubbing his jaw. For a moment she saw the doubts she struggled with reflected in his rugged face. So, he also wondered if the Sureblood fooled them all. Then he spread his raid-worn hands. "Wish I knew the answer, girl."

"So do I." She swallowed hard. "You don't think he did it…do you? We never found hard evidence—"

"Girl, I know what I see when I see a man! That one had honor and courage. He was a cocky young bastard, but I knew he'd outgrow it. They all do, eventually. If I question anything about him, it's his ways with a lady.

Didn't expect he'd show no real interest in you after going back home."

No real interest. The words stung.

Grizz shrugged. "But that's his loss, girl, and that's the way you gotta see it. As for his hurting Conn, no. It ain't him. I know it ain't."

"Who, then?"

"If we knew, we'd be spitting on his corpse right now, wouldn't we?"

Val turned her focus toward the bridge and the comm panel where she could call to Parramanta, tempted to go ahead and do it once and for all.

No. He knows where to find you. Pride had kept her from making the call for weeks. Was it time to give in?

Then her belt comm vibrated, nearly sending her through the roof. Crazily, she thought it was Dake. Her confused feelings about him scattered and vanished like a school of minnows in the shallows. All doubts would be put to rest once they spoke. She snatched the comm to answer.

"It's the *Farsider*," Grizz said.

Only then did she realize the transmission had come to both their comms simultaneously. *It's not Dake, you idiot. It's one of your ships.* Her hopes fell and shattered. "Go ahead, *Farsider.*"

"We're docking now, Val. I've got news."

"Well, I got an ear. What is it?"

"I think it's better said face-to-face."

Moments later several of the senior raiders tromped in led by Rellen, Ayl's father, an experienced, capable man who was as different from his son in actions and attitude as a father could be. Still wet from the rain, they turned to her with grim faces. Rellen reported, "We came upon a convoy hauling goods through Kormanna hollows. The lead ship went on alone. We stalked her through the Channels. We knew no one else had her in their sights. Quite a haul, she'd be, we thought, and none of it to be shared with Nezerihm. She was ours alone, the Blues. And as we moved in to take her, the Surebloods crashed our raid."

Val's stomach clenched like a fist at the news. *Surebloods*. Back to their old tricks. She fought harder than she had at anything in her life not to lose her breakfast. Her silly hopes that this would have a different ending had finally evaporated. Dake Sureblood had never stopped being her enemy. He'd merely set a trap, and she'd skipped right into it. Because of that, her father was dead and her clan in disarray. It proved her judgment wasn't worth anything. She intended to change that effective immediately.

She never felt so alone and full of hate as she was at that moment. So cold inside, and old before her time. "Grizz, gather the raiders. We're going to have ourselves a meeting, a war council." It was time for Dake Sureblood to pay for what he'd done.

CHAPTER FIFTEEN

THE PASSING OF CONN may have muted the clan's spirit the past month, but it wasn't apparent in the midst of the war council. The gathering was as loud and raucous as ever in the meeting house. Maybe even more so. More was at stake than ever before.

The senior raiders sat at the table. Reeve, Ayl and the other junior raiders filled benches along the walls of the chamber. The outer ring. It was where she'd have been sitting if her world hadn't changed a month ago almost to the day.

"They made fools of us!" Ragmarrk's fist landed on the table as he stood to make a point. "They made fools of us because we let them. We gotta stop it right now, right here, and hit them back hard." The senior raider's eyes were as brown as winter mud as they narrowed with suspicion at Val. "Unless you're still soft on them Surebloods."

Val exhaled and broke off eye contact, feeling the heat of the raiders' relentless regard, all of them trying to get a read on her loyalties. She, after all, had let Dake Sureblood escape, a decision Ragmarrk wanted to make others believe was a rogue one, and not made with Grizz's blessing. Getting others to question her loyalty was a brilliant strategy from an experienced old raider. If he eroded the clan's faith in her, their trust in her ability to lead, then he and his cronies would make a bid for power.

Ayl listened intently but silently. He was too smart to challenge her in front of the rest and risk alienating her—he still fancied her for himself—but everything in his expression said that he, too, thought her soft on the Surebloods. *"You're an idealist,"* his eyes projected. *"Always seeing the best in people and situations, a lot like your father, if you want to know. Reality is cold, Valeeya. Merciless. To trust the Surebloods or any of the clans is to doom our future. We can't, and I won't. Someday you'll understand why."*

She supposed that she deserved the doubts the men raised. She'd let Dake get away after all. But freepin' hells if she'd let Ragmarrk separate her from the herd and run her down like a weakening calf.

Tamping down another wave of sickness, perspiring, she stood. Her hands were spread on the table surface as she glared back at Ragmarrk. "We Blues aren't ever soft on our *enemies*," she said, low and threatening. "The Sureblood clan is our enemy. Them greedy bastards want to crash our raids? They want to take what by rights is ours? Then they'll be looking at our guns!" She slammed two fists on the table.

Cheers filled the room, punctuated by the pounding of hands and boots. She burned with the prospect of retribution, focusing her whole being on punishing Dake…for *her* weakness.

"We won't stop there," she promised. "Every time

they go out huntin' they'll have to get past us. Every prize they go after, no matter whose it is, they'll be running from our fire. And if they still won't stop taking what belongs to others, blood will rain on Parramanta!"

For a startling few seconds it was dead quiet, almost a collective gasp. What she'd proposed was not the pirate way. It was all-out war.

War. Val couldn't help thinking of Conn and what he'd say about it. He was no dove, but would he have supported war in the conventional sense—against a rival clan? *Where's your pirate honor, girl?*

She grimaced, hearing his voice gently asking. *Papa, pirate honor died the day your trusted guest, Dake Sureblood, put sharken in your cup. Our world has changed. We have to change with it.*

Then it was bedlam all over again. It made it impossible to tell who was for and who was against. "Your clan captain just declared war!" Grizz glared at the gathered raiders, bellowing, "Is it unanimous?"

The thunder of fists hitting the table tallied in the votes. Ragmarrk kept his hands in his lap and abstained.

"The council is over," Val snapped, thinking how odd it felt saying the words her father always did. Being in Conn's place as leader remained surreal—and disconcerting. Talk about big boots to fill. Some raiders stayed behind at the table in the meeting house to argue their chosen strategy. Others left for home or duty.

Grizz watched her worriedly. She was pale as a

ghost. She started for the door with the piece of Sethen's ship in her fist.

"You intendin' to hit someone over the head with that?" he asked.

She examined the strip, turning it over and over. "I'm going to go see Garrmin about starting construction on my own ship." She examined the hunk of metal, but she was seeing something else entirely. She saw a phoenix rising from the flames of her stupidity. She saw redemption in a future of punishing Surebloods for their treachery.

"You can call the *Varagon* your own, you know. You want her? She's yours."

"Ah, Grizz. I'm deeply honored by the offer, but the *Varagon*'s yours. I need my own ship." More than he knew. She gripped the strip of zelfen. "She'll be called the *Marauder,* and when I go out a-raidin'—" she lifted the shard of metal "—it'll be with Sethen along."

"That's a nice sentiment, girl."

She saw nothing "nice" about it. Nothing nice about war.

She saluted Grizz with the zelfen and left. The rain had lessened for the moment even as swollen clouds promised more. A sea falcon swooped in low from the nesting areas near the bathhouses she'd once loved. She'd not been able to use the baths without thinking of Dake Sureblood and the time they'd spent there.

How easily she'd believed his reluctance to leave Artoom that terrible day. Sucked right into his little game, she was. Hells, she practically had to force him to go! Or so it seemed.

More nausea hit. She paused in the drenching rain until it passed. Despite the chill, she'd broke out in a sweat. Bloody hells. It was the stress of the past month causing the condition, all the grief and troubling silence from Dake Sureblood. She'd kept it a secret. She had to. No one wanted to know a leader was weak, mentally *or* physically.

Splashing along the path startled her. She was no longer alone. She pressed her fist to her gut and somehow managed to quell the nausea as she stood straighter, pretending nothing was wrong.

It was the slave girl, hurrying toward her, her huge violet-blue eyes full of determination. She'd put on some weight but still looked thin. She was headed straight for Val, and Reeve was nowhere to be seen.

The girl stopped, arms at her sides, back stiff, as if striking a pose—a caricature of a soldier. She pointed to Val, then to the *Varagon* at the docks.

"You're wanting to go home?" Val asked.

She shook her head violently and gestured again to the ship. She thought for a moment, then pretended to aim a dozer. Then she poked a thumb at her chest.

"Ah," Val said, the realization dawning. "You heard the call for female raiders."

The girl nodded vigorously. Someone had been listening to her recruitment speeches, it seemed. "But you can't be a raider if you can't speak. If you're in visual contact, we can see your hand signals, but what if you have to use a comm? Sometimes we raid in the dark. We gotta be able to hear a voice, even a whisper. Sorry, girl. I have to turn you down."

The girl's eyes filled with despair and also indecision. She dropped her hands and turned, seeming to stare at the rain hitting the mud, but it was clear her mind was churning.

Val hated to crush someone's dreams. "You can't be a space apprentice, but you can help out during training exercises here on Artoom."

The girl shook her head at that. She looked angry.

Val shrugged. "I'm afraid that's all I can do for you, girl. If you can't speak, you can't raid."

The girl made bony fists, squeezed her eyes shut, then she let out a very soft whisper. "Ferren," she said.

Val's heart jumped. "You can speak."

"Ferren," the girl repeated again, a little stronger, tapping a thumb on her chest. "Ferren."

"You're called Ferren. That's your name."

Nodding, Ferren smiled and it was like the sun peaking up over the sea on a summer day. The girl was stunningly beautiful, exotically so. It was no surprise she'd been captured and would have been someone's slave if they hadn't rescued her. It also explained why Reeve seemed to be so smitten. Ferren seemed to shrug off any romantic interest from anyone, Reeve included. While she wasn't afraid of the many besotted clansmen, she didn't seem interested in any either. Val wasn't sure what she'd endured at the hands of men, but it couldn't have been good.

"Well, Ferren, that's a start. See me later, and we'll work on increasing your vocabulary." Val took the girl's thin arm between her fingers. "We'll also talk about ways to get some muscle. Exercise, eating better—you gotta be strong to be a raider. You're skin and bones. If we can make some improvement in both those areas, I see no reason why you can't start as a space apprentice."

Now that they were going on the offensive against the Surebloods, they'd need all the raiders they could get.

Ferren grabbed Val in a hug. It caused a new surge of nausea. Val stifled a moan of misery. She was going to be sick.

Ferren stepped back, her eyes enormous orbs of empathy.

"I'm fine," Val said quickly. "Just something I ate."

She left a worried Ferren behind and walked away to settle her stomach. At the door to her house, she paused with her hand on the entry knob. Her mind was filled with worry about her illness and about how Dake Sureblood had tricked them all. She had so much bottled up inside her now that she was fairly ready to explode for wanting to talk to someone.

Val pushed open the door, standing dripping wet on the entry pad as she carefully leaned the bow piece against the wall. The foyer was deathly quiet. Although her mother was inside, it was as if nobody was home. Like the unseasonal skies these days, her mother was a pale, gray ghost of her former self. She refused to leave the house, sitting for hours staring out the window. On the outside she was alive, but on the inside it was as if she were dead.

Heart slamming against her ribs, throbbing with fury, Val walked into the back room and to the chair where her mother always used to sit when she and Sethen were children awaiting Conn's return from a raid. Now silent and gray, Sashya was locked in that pose, eternally waiting for her husband to return.

It's your fault. All of it.

Val dashed to the bathroom to be sick. When she returned to the room, her mother was looking at her, more alert than she'd been in weeks. "Come here, child," she said hoarsely, as if her voice wasn't something she'd used in a very long time.

"Mama," Val whispered, kneeling down at her mother's feet.

"You've had the sickness for some time now."

"Aye," Val admitted. "It's the stress. It comes and goes."

"At night? Or only in the mornings?"

"Mornings, mostly."

Sashya gave her a searching look as she smoothed Val's hair. "That night with the Sureblood boy, did you make love?"

Her heart jumped with shame. "Aye," she mumbled. She'd slept with a murderer. An assassin. A betrayer. Yet at the time she'd thought he was wonderful and that their moments together were magic. She'd been so caught up with the magic of Dake that she hadn't thought any further than that moment. And neither had he. Unless he assumed she was using birth control like most girls her age were. "I did a stupid thing, Mama," she whispered.

Sashya shifted her focus outside. Despite the late-season rains, the trees were beginning to take bud and blossom. Almost too softly to hear, the woman murmured, "New life..."

"Mama?"

She turned her gaze back to Val. For the first time since Conn died, there was a specken of color in those gray cheeks, and a spark of life in her eyes, and of determination. "By midwinter's eve, you will have Dake Sureblood's baby." Her cool hand covered Val's. "And you will tell no one."

CHAPTER SIXTEEN

DAKE'S VOW TO RETURN HOME kept him sane as they were transported to what was described as a new battle-front in the "Great War." Bah. To the Coalition and Drakken it was, perhaps. Dake saw nothing great about it. *May they exterminate themselves and leave the rest of us bloody well alone.*

Cleaned up and patched up, and given only enough food and water to keep them going, they trained to exhaustion with weapons and basic tactics any fool could master. The war sergeant who'd so delighted in hosing down Dake's open wounds bullied Squib as much as he could. Dake worked just as hard deflecting that cruelty from the frightened boy. Over the days, other conscripts came and disappeared. Dake suspected the war sergeant's beatings was the reason behind the missing men. At every chance, Dake filled Kage and Squib with hope. It was often like filling two buckets full of holes with water, but he never gave up on them or himself. He whispered memories of Parramanta when no guards were listening. When they were, he suffered beatings for the crime of communicating.

As Drakken soldiers, they were dropped on desolate planets, transported across war-torn regions of space

Dake never dreamed he'd visit, or wanted to, forced to fight an enemy with whom he had no conflict. Then Kage was shot in the gut. Dake refused to leave him, taking even worse injuries pulling his raider to safety. When he woke, there was no sign of Kage. No one knew where the Sureblood raider had gone. Dake could only guess he'd died.

Dake himself nearly bled out from his wounds. In that bleak moment, he wished he had. He was done fighting in someone else's war. Done with death, except his own and, by the gods, he began to think it couldn't come fast enough. Returned to his unit, he descended into a walking death of sorts like so many of the others—breathing corpses drained of all humanity. Out of it, drunk with lost hope, Dake watched the war sergeant beat Squib and the others, viewing it all with a detached sense of inevitability. His life before—Parramanta, raiding, meeting Val and making love to her—seemed to belong to another man. Almost a fantasy, not even real.

One day, he glimpsed the war sergeant kicking young Squib for walking too slowly. Squib went down, too weak to fend off the boots thumping into his skinny body. He looked like a discarded doll, flopping with no more resistance left in him.

"Are you just going to watch, boy, useless and tame?" The taunt came in Tomark's voice, silenced ever since Dake had lost Kage. *"You're no Sureblood I recognize. Or son. You're a quitter, that's what."*

The war sergeant screamed at Squib to get up, picking him up and dropping him repeatedly as if annoyed the game had turned boring. A game of kickball with a Sureblood raider barely out of apprenticehood while his clan captain *watched*.

How dared he? Dake jerked his head up as self-loathing and failure slammed into him. He pushed away from the wall he'd been leaning against and stormed toward the war sergeant. Grabbing his shoulder, he spun him around and plowed his fist into his nose. It left his so-called leader lying on the ground, a sociopath abuser who in the space of a month had killed more conscripts than the Coalition. Then he lifted Squib, who was somehow still breathing, and walked him away to the dispensary to get him patched up.

He never saw Squib again. When the guns were aimed at his head, he thought it was the end. The Drakken guards could have killed him that day for his insubordination, and blasted near did, but somehow he ended up in a Drakken prison instead. He was no longer a conscript but an inmate. Maybe for the rest of his life.

"I'LL FIND THE BASTARD and deliver his head to you on a platter. I swear it, Val." Ayl had launched into raiding against Surebloods with exhausting gusto, crowing loudly to one and all his goal of being the one to capture Dake Sureblood. Their shared hatred of the fiend actually gave them something in common for once. Those first weeks of slugging it out with the Surebloods were immensely satisfying, distracting her from thinking about her unwanted pregnancy. Then Dake and his thugs figured out they were under direct attack. After that, it turned ugly.

Nezerihm emerged as a surprise source of aid. He was appalled by the Surebloods' aggression and complained loudly they were causing him to lose money. He proved unexpectedly useful in giving away the whereabouts of Sureblood vessels. It helped give the Blues an early edge. Val relented on her personal dislike of the man. He had been right, after all, about the Surebloods' bad intentions. He still left a bad taste in her mouth, raising her hackles and suspicions, but as she'd already learned, her instincts weren't to be trusted.

The endless rains of spring and summer gave way to a long, dry autumn. Fields of vegetables sprouted in nearly every available spot, pot and barrel. The looming harvest was a sign of how much of a toll war had taken on the clan. Val hoped their homegrown efforts were enough to get them through lean times ahead. How quickly the coffers emptied now that they were using raid profits for weapons and ammo, and fixing damaged ships and skiffs instead of essentials like food. A third of the fleet was stuck at the docks under repair. Val didn't dare show any wavering on her resolve to see the fighting to the end, knowing that Ragmarrk's faction waited for signs she was "soft" on their rivals. If it took until her dying breath, she'd prove to them that she could lead.

Val flew raids until her belly grew so enormous that Grizz and Sashya forbade her any more missions. "Rest, or you'll lose the baby," Sashya warned.

She feared no such consequences. Every twinge

reminded her of what she carried in her womb. Her enemy's child. A curse. She should have done something before it ever got to this point. Made arrangements.

But she couldn't, seeing Sashya's transformation from a heartbroken widow to a woman radiant with excitement. The life inside Val had brought Sashya back to life.

Her wings now clipped, Val turned her angry energy from raiding to the construction of her new ship. As the *Marauder* took form and grew, so did the child inside her.

"She'll be the largest, most impressive ship the clan's ever constructed," Val boasted as Ferren tagged along with her on an inspection of the ship's soaring hull beams. "Built for fighting as well as raiding. She'll be the Blue's flagship, a warning to anyone wanting to mess with us. Especially them gangster Surebloods."

Ferren nodded, her wide violet eyes taking in every detail of the emerging cannon bays. The girl's battered, secondhand apprentice gear reminded Val of the state of the clan's supplies. Could the clan afford to build such a project?

Could Val afford *not to?* She'd be left with nothing else to occupy her mind but guilt. As it was, she tossed and turned every night reliving her time with Dake, analyzing each moment. How could she have missed the treachery that was surely in his eyes? How could he have acted so believably that she'd actually wasted time worrying that something horrible had happened to him and he'd in fact never reached home? His relentless attacks on her clan's ships made it obvious his intent was to destroy the Blues. Killing her father had been only the first step.

Ferren turned her head, and Val followed her gaze. The young woman's sweet face gentled at the sight of Reeve. On the heels of that affection was also confusion, even fear. Her emotions seemed no less muddled than Val's. The brave girl shared few words with others, and even less about herself and her past. Val wondered if she'd ever reveal what she kept bottled up inside. Yet, their untold secrets seemed to give them a special bond.

Reeve waved as he walked by. Several too-young recruits tagged along behind him. Ferren smiled, then her expressive face darkened suddenly at Ayl approaching in the opposite direction with his apprentices. Even from this distance Ayl's smoldering jealousy of Reeve was obvious. He still considered Reeve a threat to his winning over Val. Not even Reeve's clear interest in Ferren had doused it.

"He's upset that this child is Reeve's," Val said, her hand curving under her belly.

Ferren whipped her attention back to her.

"It isn't," Val assured her, gruffly. "Everyone thinks I went to Reeve out of grief one night. I asked him to be vague when he's asked about it—but not vague enough to kill the rumor I got knocked up by a lower-ranking raider when I'm supposed to marry a clansman of status. I want that rumor alive. But there's nothing but friendship between me and Reeve. We never—"

Ferren squeezed her arm, stopping her from saying more. "I know." Being a girl of very few words, she

made each one count. In fact, Ferren knew much more
than she let on.

Untold secrets. As long as no one else in the clan
was as clever as Ferren, Val's terrible secret was safe.

THE DAYS PASSED AND grew ever shorter. Winter sunshine slanted through the trees as Val made her way
to the docks, her leather jacket flapping open, too snug
to close over her swollen middle. Her breath steamed
in the crisp air. With both hands she supported her
distended belly, annoyed that pregnancy slowed her
down. She refused to let it. If this child wanted to be
born, it had better be strong.

Her lower stomach cramped painfully.

The more pain I feel, the less it hurts. A different
kind of hurting…guilt. Val set her jaw, striding along
the road at full speed. The clenching pain settled in her
lower back. "Blast you, Dake Sureblood. Blast you to
hells."

What would he think if he found out what their one
night together had cost her? He'd probably laugh his
head off.

Ahead the *Marauder* glinted in the sunlight. She
narrowed her eyes at her unfinished hull, wishing it
were done already and she was at the helm overseeing
the destruction of Sureblood ships, purging Dake and
how he'd duped her from her mind with each salvo.

A sharper pain ripped through her middle, making
her gasp. She stopped to catch her breath, her hand
fisted in the baggy fabric of her maternity blouse that

she tried to conceal without much luck under her leather raider jacket.

"Val?"

Panting, she jerked her gaze around. She didn't want to be caught like this. Vulnerable. *Soft.*

Thank the stars it was only Reeve. "Is it time?" he asked quietly.

"I don't know." She didn't want it to be time. Another pain took her breath. Some clansmen at the docks glanced their way, and she welcomed those curious looks. Ever-cooperative Reeve loved feeding the gossip when asked about her, earning her adoration. By now everyone assumed she didn't marry him to make an appropriately high-status match someday. It was the perfect cover story. And she'd spent every sleepless moment since worrying what would happen if the truth ever came out.

Another painful cramp hit, front to back, and she nearly doubled over. "Help me home."

Reeve took her by the arm. Ferren spotted them and sprinted over. A wealth of information passed between the couple in a single wordless glance. As a raiding team, they were unbeatable. As lovers they'd have been just as good, had Ferren ever allowed the relationship to take that turn.

"Tell Grizz," Val gasped, "he's in charge until I'm through. Then both of you stand guard outside the house." She had the pair's unfailing loyalty. They'd watch over her while she was at her most vulnerable in the coming hours. "Don't let anyone inside but the doctor or people Sashya specifically requests," Val instructed outside her front door.

"Aye, Cap'n."

Wordlessly Sashya stood upon seeing Val enter the living room. The next moments were a flurry of activity with her mother getting the bed ready and myriad supplies being arranged on the tables nearby. Then she helped Val change clothes and lie down.

Sashya dazzled Val with her calm efficiency. On a skiff out raidin' or busting through a hatch, Val knew without question what to do. Here, her mother was the leader. This was a realm Val knew next to nothing about.

Another contraction had Val wincing and gritting her teeth. It was happening fast. Too fast. Blast it, she wasn't ready.

Would she ever be?

Sashya took over, making sure she was in the proper position, draping a cold compress over her forehead, stroking her arm with her fingertips the way she used to when Val was a child and not feeling well. The doctor joined them, and another woman Val recognized as a midwife. As the pains grew more intense and closer together, the doctor reached for her with a med injector. Val thrust out her arm, stopping her.

"It's your pain blocker."

"No... No blocker." Val gritted her teeth until she could squeeze out more words. The pain was her punishment. She'd take it like a raider and get it over with.

Not long after she wondered if it was the right

decision. The birth proved more difficult than she'd ever imagined. Bloody hells, it hurt. She'd never had more respect for the childbearing females in the clan than now. In the past she'd dismissed them as mere hearth huggers when in fact they'd apparently endured more pain than most of the raiders.

They yelled at her to push, female voices as demanding and confident as any of the raiders she flew with. She marveled at that, was thankful for it.

A few moments to gasp for air, then another hit. She didn't think she could bear another contraction, but she took it head-on. Like gripping the control stick in a hi-G turn, the ship ready to break apart, sweating and shaking to keep it from plummeting into an asteroid, you just didn't let go until you came out the other side.

The searing, cramping pain reached a crescendo. Gritting her teeth, she strained, welcoming the pain, crying out in anger. One…last…*push*.

"Here comes the babe!" the midwife cried out in joy that Val didn't quite share. And then, it was born.

It's over, she thought with relief. *Over.*

A loud, impossibly indignant wail pierced the silence.

Val lifted her head. The women huddled near her bent knees blocked her view. "Is it all right?"

Was it a boy or a girl? She could have learned the gender from the doctor months ago, but she didn't want to know. She didn't want to know anything about his baby.

"Is a *he* all right." Sashya stepped forward, her eyes brimming with pride and joyful tears. In her arms was a naked, squirming, red-faced infant heaving mightily with each raucous howl as if the birth was the most unwelcome event in its brief existence. "You have a healthy son."

A son.

Val let her head fall back on the pillow. *I have a son.*

It was the end of everything.

And the beginning.

Sashya offered her the babe to hold and soothe. Val made shaky fists in the bedsheets and turned her head away as the doctor tended to her birth wounds. Once, she'd been like the wind, wild and free. She thought nothing could trap her.

She had a son.

"Valeeya!" Her mother's voice was sharp and edged with anger. "That's not how Conn and I raised you to be. What are you afraid of? You're a braver girl than this. A brave *woman.*"

What was she afraid of?

"You need some fear." Conn's wise words floated back after being silent for so long. *"Some. Too much paralyzes you, and too little makes you reckless. Arrogant."*

Her son screeched. Screeched *for her.* Was that what she feared—this babe needing her?

Or her needing him?

Sashya waited for Val's response. Then, with a weary, disappointed sigh, she started to turn away. "We'll need milk," she told a midwife.

"No, we won't." Val opened her arms impatiently. "Let me see."

Sashya placed the angry infant in her arms. As Val stared down at the babe, her chest ached with a surge of powerful emotion. It swamped her and left her speechless. This baby, this new life, came from her.

And Dake.

She stiffened, hating that thoughts of the Sureblood intruded on this special, unexpectedly overwhelming moment.

Tentatively, she touched a finger to the baby's brow, stroking the damp, soft brown fuzz. Then she curved her entire hand around the swell of his tiny head. She'd never seen an ear so tiny or as perfect. Two equally tiny fists expressed a raider's worth of fury. Val soaked in every detail. A storm of conflicting emotions filled her: wonder, terror and fierce protectiveness.

"He has Conn's features," Sashya said, sitting on the edge of the bed.

"Aye, he does that." Val's touch seemed to calm the child. Or maybe it was her voice that did it. "Well, you've heard me ranting for nine months," she crooned to the babe. "You'd better know who I am."

The crying stopped suddenly as her son's eyes opened wide and found hers. Two smoky gems.

Val sucked in a breath. The babe may have her father's features, but gods help them all, he had Dake Sureblood's eyes.

CHAPTER SEVENTEEN

Four Years Later

"YOU. *HALT.*" VAL STORMED up the mining transport's boarding ramp. "You are not authorized to operate this vessel."

The captain bristled at her order. *From a female official, no less:* Val could almost hear that thought going through his mind. It amused her. "You are mistaken," he said. "This is my ship, and I'm her captain. Remove yourself and your people."

"Not so fast, sir. This dock is under the jurisdiction of customs authorities. All ships are subject to inspection."

So far, so good, she thought, tense in a way she never was while zero-G hatch busting. Some in the clan weren't in favor of raiding dirt-side, but desperate times called for desperate measures. Dirt-side raiding required face-to-face deception. Attitude was everything. Val flashed an ID the man barely glanced at as she paced confidently forward. Her stolen customs agent uniform chafed, a tight fit even with her thinnest armor underneath. But she didn't dare raid without protection. "You are in violation of Borderlands code," she said.

"Everything on this ship is up to code. Beyond code." A stiff jaw broadcast his annoyance. "Move aside. I've no time for administrative antics. I've got a load to move and a schedule to keep."

"I'm afraid you will indeed have to talk to me, sir." Calling any of Nezerihm's company lackeys "sir" left a sour taste in her mouth. She tried not to spit out the word as she pulled out a data pad and pretended to punch in data—she had no idea how a data pad worked, but she could make a good show of it. "We're cracking down on transporting cargo while intoxicated. We have reason to believe you and your crew are drunk."

"Drunk!" The captain's eyes shone bright blue.

"My agents observed you and your officers all night in the bar, and—"

"Bull flarg! I am not drunk in the least. Nor are my officers."

She made a show of sniffing the air, stinking of outpost-quality liquor wafting from the direction of the bars along the docks. Then she pretended to type in more data. "Rules forbid the command of a cargo vessel while under the influence. You'll be allowed to submit to a blood test. Until then, consider you, your crew and this vessel detained."

He sputtered. "Bull—"

"Flarg, yes," she finished for him. "But rules are rules, and if my fellow agents and I don't uphold them, no one will. So, Captain. Will you go aboard willingly for the blood test, or will I have to arrest you?"

The captain's eyes were fuming mad as they fixed on hers. His kind were usually so guilty of drinking too much that they'd surrender with little argument, happy to have the choice of an onboard test out of the spotlight and metabolizers to erase the evidence of alcohol, keeping their names off the books. This captain acted different than the usual ore hauler. Sharper. Not in the least guilty and a whole lot suspicious. He should have gone inside his ship as ordered already. He stayed where he was and studied her instead. The back of her neck prickled as the wariness in his gaze coalesced into recognition.

"Good gods, you're her, aren't you?" he said. "That she-pirate."

Val hooked her leg around his and dropped him hard to the floor. His comm skittered away over the hardtop. As he tried to get to his knees, she shoved her boot against his rear and pushed, spending him sprawling. With dozers set to stun those who tried to resist, her raiders had the cargo crew stuffed back on board their vessel and secured with shock cuffs in moments.

"Close 'er up," she said and found a seat to strap into. Procedures on outlying stations like this one were lax. Even her newest flight-qualified raider was able to negotiate a blastoff without a hitch. Excitement flushed Ferren's face and lit up her wide-set indigo-blue eyes. She still didn't speak much, but her expression said it all: she was having the time of her life.

As free as the wind.

With a sudden mournful ache, Val saw in Ferren

the girl she used to be, the girl she could hardly remember.

It had been almost five years since the gathering. Five hard years of bearing the responsibility of keeping the clan together and fed. Five years of honoring Conn Blue's name and of feeling responsible for his death. Every single successful raid since had been an emotional boot heel ground in the memory of Dake Sureblood.

A vision of his opalescent eyes came back to haunt her now as they did on many a sleepless night. She'd toss and turn, cursing herself for missing what she should have seen that long-ago day: his treachery. Instead, she was tricked by the anguish and longing of their final moments together. She'd pined for him for a month because of that last look, wanting him, needing him, half falling in love with him in absentia. What a young little fool she'd been then, all because of what she *thought* she saw in his gaze. Those opal eyes would be with her forever. She saw them every day in the face of her son. *Their* son. Jaym.

Val gripped the armrests and waited out the rocky departure off the outpost, wishing away the ache of exhaustion. Last night, like too many others, sleep eluded her. At times she was desperate enough to resort to drink and even occasionally to squatter's weed but feared an addiction to both. More often than not, she gutted it out, feeling like the walking dead when she absolutely couldn't afford to.

At least this raid had gone well. They'd caught themselves a sweet little prize filled with a tidy load of ore. Nezerihm's ore.

It wasn't stealing; it was self-help. What did Nezerihm expect she'd do? She had a clan to feed. After a thousand years of bloodshed, the Great War between the Drakken horde and the Coalition was over. They had united, along with a new world called Earth, under the banner of the Triad Alliance. With peace, hunting opportunities had dried up. There were no more ore stealers and nearly every ship was accompanied by an armed Triad escort. Their options had narrowed to starve or prey upon unsuspecting ore transporters and make thousands selling the haul on the black market. The choice had been easy. Her clan would survive feeding off Nezerihm's mines.

If he didn't like their new tactics, too bad. Desperate times called for desperate measures.

THE VILEST SHE-PIRATE in all the galaxy.

U.S. Air Force Colonel Franklin Johnson waited in the halls of Parliament for Prime-Admiral Zaafran, the top military leader of the new Triad Alliance, to address the galaxy's lawmakers and leaders, but his thoughts were on the private briefing Zaafran had just given him. After a thousand years of bloodshed, the Great War between the Drakken horde and the Coalition was over. Quelling piracy was to be Frank's first order of business in his new job bringing law and order to the Borderlands. But a *she*-pirate? Hmm. By the sound of her lengthy record the past four years, Val Blue could qualify as the vilest pirate period, she *or* he.

And now it was his job to convince her to behave.

The sound of applause shifted Frank's attention to the prime-admiral taking the stage. He had to admit that as an Earth-born country boy sitting amongst the most important individuals in the known galaxy he felt a bit starstruck. In the audience was the Goddess-Queen Keira and her Earth-born consort Prince Jared, both instrumental in the assassination of the Hordish warlord and the downfall of the dark empire two years prior. The eminence of those around him made him acutely aware of the Triad captain's rank attached to his shoulders. It had been only a week since it had replaced his colonel's silver eagles. He had a lot more than new rank riding on his forty-three-year-old shoulders, though. A helluva lot more. Like his career, his very hide, and Earth's place in a three-way alliance with two far older and more advanced societies.

No amount of Triad support could make him less of an outsider. He knew it, and Zaafran knew it. In fact, it was why Zaafran had chosen Frank to command the diplomatic ship *Unity*.

"If anyone can accomplish this legendary ship's new mission of dealing with rogue people like the pirates, an Earthling can," Zaafran explained. His choice angered traditionalists, who didn't like the prime-admiral placing Frank in such a tactically critical position. It was the first job Frank had ever taken on where the people on his side—well, theoretically his side—wanted to see him fail.

He damn well wouldn't fail. It would make his boss look bad. Of all the things Frank wanted to accomplish in life, tarnishing the reputation of the top military hero commander of the Triad wasn't one of them.

The applause finally died down enough for the prime-admiral to speak. Frank leaned forward, resting the weight of his upper body on his arms and thighs, ready to concentrate on every word. He didn't quite trust his fluency in the queen's tongue yet.

"Ladies and Gentlemen of Parliament," Zaafran began. "In celebrating the two-year anniversary of the end of the war, I join you in giving thanks for our continuing peace. It is a day to count blessings, a day to remember from where we have come, and to realize we have more work to do. Not long ago, some would have considered an agreement between sworn enemies and a new, unknown world to be an unattainable dream. Today, we enjoy the gift of peace that such an alliance has allowed us. But not all people of our great galaxy are able to live as we do. In the Channels region of the Borderlands, many have existed outside the law since before the Great Schism. The region remains dangerous and largely ungoverned to this day, loosely controlled by pirate clan chieftains who regularly commandeer our ships and strip them of their crew and cargo, most notably zelfen, which as you know is a new and militarily critical component in the construction of space-worthy vessels. In plain talk, the Channels area is infested, and we've got to clean it up."

Infested. Frank winced at the prime-admiral's word choice. Viewing another human as something "less than" represented a fundamental difference in opinion. Yet, Zaafran was far more liberal than some who advocated a full military campaign against the pirates. The galaxy's war-weary citizens had no stomach for more violence, and luckily the request had died in Parliament. In hope of finding a diplomatic solution to the piracy problem, Zaafran had ordered the *Unity* to the region, figuring its famously mixed crew would give the appearance of fairness in the dispute.

"Pirates get in the way and drive up costs, a major concern in a postwar economy," Zaafran briefed the audience. "It is, ladies and gentlemen, an unacceptable situation. None of us want the public relations nightmare of exterminating an entire people. Yet as your military commander I must ensure better, safer access to all regions, no matter now remote. As such, I present to you Operation Amnesty, a campaign to neutralize the pirates by encouraging them to relocate away from the trade routes and mines. They'll be pardoned and assimilated into mainstream life, so they can enjoy the same freedoms we do. This is a sweeping humanitarian effort. A kinder, gentler approach to ending piracy, if you will."

Kinder and gentler. Hmm. Frank directed a small smile at his clasped hands. Back in his Special Forces days, not too many would have called Franklin Johnson kind, and definitely not gentle. Yet, he had a real problem making others suffer what his Cherokee ancestors had when they were forcibly and traumatically torn from their land and homes in Georgia and marched a thousand miles west to Oklahoma. Over four thousand men, women and children died on the Trail of Tears. He'd do everything in his power to find a diplomatic solution to the pirate problem before resorting to removal by force. If Zaafran hadn't given him the freedom to act within those parameters, he wouldn't have taken the job.

"Our goal is for them to see this not as punishment but as an opportunity. We'll dispatch emissaries to meet with each clan and discuss our hopes for them. Now, ladies and gentlemen of Parliament, it is with great pleasure that I introduce to you the man in charge of this mission—Colonel Franklin Johnson, our newest commander of the *TAS Unity*."

Applause filled the vast hall as Frank stood. He couldn't quite stomach the genteel "queen's wave" Earth's cross-culture committee, the CCC, recommended he use, and instead acknowledged the welcome with a jaunty, modified salute. It felt truer to who he was, someone he hoped he wouldn't lose sight of in the execution of his duties, which in essence boiled down to making sure the supply of strategically important zelfen remained uninterrupted. For all the talk about humanitarianism, that was all that really mattered to the Triad. If Operation Amnesty failed, another solution to the piracy was inevitable. One he feared would be deadly.

THE BOX HOLDING DAKE was as dark and cramped as a coffin. He flattened his hands on the roof and pushed. They'd sealed him in! His mouth was as dry as a sun-baked rag. Dust caked his face. It was utterly dark. Suffocatingly dark. He tried to keep the panic from overtaking him, but it invaded, icy and hot at the same time, making his heart kick and his skin sweat. His breathing was too hard, too fast; he'd use up the air. Two tiny inlets allowed in oxygen, but he was outpacing even that. Then dirt hit the outside. It rained loudly, and he could smell dust coming through the air holes. They were burying him! Get up! Get out! His knees slammed into the top, his arms hit the sides. The need to scream built until he nearly wept fighting to hold it back. If he did, they'd know they were getting to him, breaking him, and that would encourage them even more. It was bad enough they'd learned he abhorred cramped spaces. Whenever he violated some infraction, or was the subject of entertainment for a bored guard, they threw him in the box. Today's sport was actually burying the box.

What if it wasn't sport today? What if they were really going to kill him? Another shovel full of dirt and another. Dake opened his mouth to scream—

"All righty! Rise and shine, big guy. This is your lucky day."

Hells be. Dake jolted awake. His heart still slammed and his breathing was uneven. Sweat drenched his prison yellows and his back and neck ached from where he'd fallen asleep on the floor in a slouch propped up against the wall. That same freepin' nightmare. Years after the Drakken had buried his ass as punishment, it still haunted him. He scrubbed a hand over his face and rolled his head toward the voice.

A guard and a uniformed Triad official stood outside the holobars of the cell. The guard rapped a shock stick on the outside wall to get his attention as the official typed on a data pad and told him, "You're moving out."

Out? Dake swung from a bored daze to hyperalertness in a half heartbeat. Every move no matter how small meant a disruption in routine. Disruptions meant an opportunity to escape might appear. Would this be the day?

How many times have you thought it would be freedom day and it wasn't? Standing, Dake braced himself against the doubts, against disappointment. Giving up wasn't an option, although at times the lure to close his eyes and be done with it was all-powerful. Aye, but that would have meant surrender, and he flat-out refused. He'd return to his people and reclaim the life stolen from him. He'd find Val and win the heart of the woman he never wanted to let go. He'd hang Nezerihm with his own hands if he had to. Then he'd finish his work uniting all the clans. Five years in prison gave a man a blasted long to-do list.

Dake sauntered over to the holobars, slowly, acting lazy. In truth, he was ready to spring. He'd never stopped being ready.

Big. Dake could read the observation in the official's gaze as it tracked up his body to his face. Size hadn't helped him much. Shock cuffs and holobars were the great equalizers. "Got a whole load of convicted war criminals that need the cells, so guys like you are moving out." He paused to observe Dake. "You don't look all that excited about it."

Dake shrugged. "I'm going somewhere new. It's not the first time, and I doubt it'll be the last." He'd been in prison longer than anyone he'd met, passing from Drakken custody to Coalition and now two years after the war ended to the Triad. After a while, it didn't matter who held you captive, or where, only that they did. Although, if he had to choose, he'd say the brutality of the Drakken Imperial Army toward their forced conscripts was the worst of the lot. The bio-stitches holding his torn flesh together were long gone, but the scars still tugged and ached on occasion. A memory of beating up the war sergeant for his vicious attack on Squib, and the arrest afterward, came back in too much detail. He'd never know why the officers threw him in prison rather than kill him for the insubordination. Maybe they didn't blame him for what he did, or secretly cheered the fact that he did what they'd wanted to do. He'd never know, but being sent from battlefield to prison was probably the reason he'd survived.

The years spent incarcerated by the Drakken in conditions too foul to describe were among the most miserable. But that misery kept him alive. As long as he still felt pain, as long as he still felt *anything,* he was human, and he had a chance to escape. While being transported from one stinking Hordish hells hole to the next, the ship was captured by Coalition forces. For a brief, giddy moment, he thought he'd be freed, but he soon knew better. To them, he was just another Drakken prisoner. In their jails he landed and served his custody in a variety of loathsome ways over the years, segueing from Coalition to Triad with nary a bump until one day last week during spring-cleaning someone punching in data behind a desk figured out he didn't belong there. Or anywhere.

After a few interviews, he'd wound up here. It was an out-and-out guesthouse compared to every other place he'd been. He'd taken his first *hot* shower in five years. Now that was something. They'd even let him shave. Nothing good ever lasted, though. Of course they wanted to move him now. He should have figured he wouldn't get to stay for long.

The guard pointed at his arm. "Show him your number."

Dake pulled up the sleeve of his newly issued prison yellows. Behind his ear was a brand the Drakken had burned there—his soldier ID with them. The involuntary Drakken eagle tattoo on the inside of his left bicep was another souvenir of those days, fighting in their army. The Coalition was a little more civilized with their identifying methods. They injected nano-ink that lit up when queried by one of their computers.

722261375121. Blue numbers glowed suddenly under the skin on his forearm. "Seven-two-two-two-six-one-three-seven-five-one-two-one," the guard read.

The Triad official nodded. "Ladies and gentlemen, we have a winner."

Dumbfounded, Dake lowered his arm. The official actually used humor.

The official handed him a small, flat rectangle. "Take this chit and hand it to the relocation agent."

A guard let him through the holobars and directed him to a desk set up in the hallway. The official seated there also checked a data pad. Disoriented from walking free with no guards escorting him, Dake stopped in front of the desk. He shook his head to clear it.

"So. Where are *you* from?" the man asked without looking up from his data pad.

"Regannon Labor Camp."

He focused on Dake, then, amused. "Not what prison. Before that. Where's home? That's where you're going."

Dake stood there, unable to comprehend. The man might as well have been speaking a foreign language. For all Dake's desire to be alert for opportunities to escape, he hadn't expected *this*. *Home*. It was hard to fathom the word, though he long dreamed of it. The sea…wide, white beaches…grassy plains rippling in nearly constant wind…a land of infinite vistas and endless sky, of fireflies and fire. The memories made him want to weep. Would Merkury recognize him when he walked through the gates, streaking across the field to met him? He'd missed that blasted dog. He'd missed everything.

"Or, anywhere you like," the official said. "The Triad's giving you a one-way, all-expenses-paid trip to the region of your choice. That's right. You're getting out. Not just out of this building. *Out* out."

Dake was instantly suspicious. Maybe it was a trick. Another mind game. "Did anyone tell you why?" he finally managed. "Why me?"

The official glanced up. "Not just you. We've got hundreds in your same situation. Triad high command came up with something called Operation Reboot to give guys like you a second chance, the ones we've got no criminal records for, and get you out of our cells. We need the room for the real monsters coming here out of the war crime tribunals. Well, the ones they're not executing outright, that is." He gave Dake a hard look. "Don't screw up out there. You'll be in for a real long time if you come back."

More time locked up in a cage? No freepin' thanks.

"So, like I asked, where are you from?"

Dake took a breath, his chest swelling with rusty pride. "My home is Parramanta." Hells. It had been so long since he'd actually said the name that it felt strange coming off his tongue. "It's in the Channels region."

"The Channels. Hmm." The official looked skeptical as he scrolled through maps. "That's out in the Borderlands where all the pirates are. Dangerous territory. Nothing's getting in or out of the Channels but military ships right now. Wait—I do have a ship heading in that direction, military ship on a diplomatic mission. I know they're not full. Hold on, let me ask to make sure." The official wore a device on his ear Dake learned was called a PCD, a personal comm device. He spoke into it. "Is the *Unity* taking any passengers?" He scribbled absently with a stylus as he waited for his answer. "Copy. I've got an Operation Reboot here. He's got a ticket home to the Channels. Do you have space? Send him over? Will do."

The official returned to his data pad. "They'll take you." He gave Dake a chit for the transport. "Board at Berth One." Then he handed him a folded overcoat and a small sack large enough to hold a change of clothing and supplies to get him through the days of travel ahead. "From the Triad to you. Gods speed, mate. You're going to need it." The official waved him on and called for another convict to come forward. "Next!"

His head spinning, Dake read the chit in his hand. *Inmate ID: 722261375121. RELEASED.*

"Released," he murmured. It was that simple. As suddenly as he had been captured, he'd been set free.

VAL NARROWED CYNICAL EYES at the two men sitting across the table from her and her senior raiders on the *Marauder.* Two cups of excellent moonshine sat in front of the pair, untouched. It was an insult not to have tasted the brew and complimented her on it, but what did these outsiders know of manners? Or their captain, Johnson of the *Unity,* for that matter? Peace had turned life in the Channels upside down, threatening the way her people had always done business. They'd thrived in the chaos of war for millennia. Profited by it. Now some gargantuan new alliance thought they had their best interests in mind, offering them a new home with free everything *forever*—if they agreed to move out.

The gall of these men, thinking she could be bribed into giving up her home. Everything that mattered was there. Everything she loved.

And had lost.

"Hear them out," Grizz had warned gently as they'd prepared for the men to arrive. "Don't forget we're living day to day and hand to mouth. Because they're going through the trouble and being nice about it, let's see what they have to say."

With ore stealers almost nonexistent now that peace had come, and fewer ships daring to ply the Channels space lanes without an armed Triad escort, she'd heeded Grizz's advice.

But she knew better than to let her desperation show as she sat at that table. While her raiders wore their meanest scowls, she'd remained outwardly pleasant until the word *relocation* came up.

"You mean you want to evict us," she said, drumming her fingertips on her holstered dozer, a warning not missed by the messengers.

"Not evict," the outsider insisted. "Relocate. To a new and bright future. In exchange, you'll receive full amnesty for your crimes."

"*Crimes*. Is that what you call our struggle to feed our families?"

"I mean no insult, Captain Blue. This isn't a punishment in any way. It truly is an opportunity. Once again, you'll be given a new home, a chance at a good life, a better life. There'll be comfortable lodging, plentiful food, education for your children—all at government expense. You'll never have to worry about feeding your people again. Other clans are already in talks to take advantage of our offer," the messenger confided.

"What?" She leaned forward. "Who?"

"The Calders and also the Surebloods."

"The Surebloods!" The raiders around her laughed. "Those stubborn bastards won't give up a ship, much less their planet," she argued.

"They thought differently after we showed them

what we could offer versus the hard times they've fallen upon."

"We've all had hard times. It doesn't mean you leave your home."

"The Surebloods seem to feel differently."

Val tried to envision Dake Sureblood permanently dirt-side in a nice, clean box-size house and came up empty. Instead of being cause for possible celebration, the idea of any clan, even their rivals, living that way was oddly sickening. Even Ayl appeared aghast.

"Safety, security and a bright tomorrow over the challenges you face here," the messenger said. "If you care about your clan's future, Captain, you'll make that choice."

"If I care?" Val choked out. *"If?"*

Equally indignant grumbles erupted from the raiders assembled there. Malta cracked her knuckles and Warrybrook growled. The pair of messengers seemed to sense the sudden uptick in tension—and the danger in it.

Oh, she cared. Aye, more than these messengers or anyone at the table could ever know. She didn't care how "easy" of a life awaited them on some unknown world, she'd never let Jaym grow up rootless, not knowing a real home. With a fierceness that burned in her heart, she was determined to hold on to her freedom and that of her people. It was her father's wish, his legacy and her gift to her son.

"You make your offer sound charitable, but greed fuels it," she gritted out. "Like hells if I'll allow my clan to be thrown out just so your Triad can have zelfen at cheap prices. The ore belongs to *my* people, not yours." She turned around. "Now get the hells off my ship."

"It's understandable you want time to consider everything we talked about today, Captain Blue—"

"I said, get off my ship. Or I'll blow you out."

On cue, Grizz walked to the nearest hatch. "Your choice," he told the men.

The messengers collected their belongings and stood.

"I have a message to take back with you," Val told them. "Tell your Captain Johnson not to waste his time playing word games. We Blues like straight-up talk. Tell him if it's eviction he's after, then have him come and say the word to my face. Then we'll talk."

One peek at their expressions and Val Blue knew that these two, at least, would be taking every precaution to make sure they weren't a part of that return mission.

BACK ON ARTOOM, VAL'S long strides made short work of the distance between the dock and the village. As she passed the practice fields, she stopped to watch new apprentices go through their drills. It embarrassed her that funds were so tight that she couldn't afford to outfit them with zelfen armor, but local livestock provided plenty of sturdy leather. She peeled off her shipboard jacket and hung it over her shoulder to enjoy some of the first sunshine of the season. She always needed these few solitary moments when first returning home. Body armor was shed on board the ship, but before she walked through her front door she had to let down her emotional armor. Her clan and crew needed Captain Val; her family needed *her*.

Captain Val, Mama Val. It was as if she were split in two with the halves constantly shifting and grating like continental plates on a fault line.

Birdsong drew her attention to the budding trees lining the path. Ebbe apples weren't native to Artoom. Conn had brought them home long ago. Fates knew where he'd found them. She'd helped him plant the seedlings when she was small, no more than Jaym was now. It remained a vivid memory—the summer sunshine, her father, such a hero to the clan, yet so doting with her. "Someday you'll walk along their path long after I'm gone, Valeeya," he'd said. "Look at these trees and think of me."

I do think of you, Papa. Always. The trees had gone to bud, and some were beginning to blossom, looking as they did that cold, rainy day she'd kneeled at Sashya's feet and listened to the woman compare the babe in her belly to the new life on the trees. Her mother had been right. Jaym had brought new life with his unexpected existence, pulling Sashya back from the brink of despair.

"Mama, Mama!"

Every nerve ending in Val's body strained toward that exuberant, high-pitched cry. She grinned as her son raced across the practice fields to meet her.

"Mama!" Sunlight glowed on Jaym's golden head. His face was alive with excitement. Pure joy filled her heart as he barreled into her full-bore, jumping high to cling to her body, uncaring of the leathers and thick weapons belt. He wanted his mother, and she wanted her boy.

"I have so much to tell you!"

She buried her face in his silky hair. *My baby*. He smelled like dirt and sunshine and buttered bread. It wouldn't be too long before he was too big to carry, and racing to meet his mother would be beneath his male dignity. "I love you, boy."

"I love you, too, Mama."

"How much?"

He arched back in her arms, his skinny thighs squeezing her waist as he flung his arms out wide. "This much!" He was getting a little old for their ritual but was still willing to play along.

The boy's as much of a charmer as his father was, she thought with an accompanying, familiar pang of guilt.

"What wrong, Mama?" His gemlike eyes probed deeply, the way his father's had, wanting to know even what she wasn't quite willing to reveal. "You look sad."

"Aye, a little. I was looking at the pretty trees and thinking of your grandfather. I miss him." He was too young to understand the rest. She gave him a squeeze. "And I missed you!"

He let her drop him back on his feet, holding her hand as they walked toward the house they shared with Sashya. "What's all this news you wanted to share?"

"Well, Ferren's teaching me to swim!"

"Is she now?"

"So I can go on sea raids. I don't want to just be a space pirate, but a dirt-side and sea-farin' one, too!"

She grinned at the little boy's admiration for Ferren. The raider could hold her breath longer than what seemed humanly possible, and once she was underwater, she was as agile as a fish. She'd all but confessed to Val that she'd once had the ability to breathe underwater. To this day, Ferren refused to reveal her origins, but if her people were anything like she was, her homeworld was a special place and Val could understand the secrecy.

"And," Jaym went on expansively, his brown-blond hair gleaming, "I'm going to be the best raider Blue clan's ever seen! I'll chase those greedy, lying Surebloods to the ends of the stars and beyond! Like *this.*" Out came his imaginary dozers from their holsters. He whirled with natural grace and fired his two sticks. "Got 'em, Mama!"

Her heart clenched with maternal worry. Like the romping of camp dog pups, the boy's play was the precursor to real battle. She had no qualms about sending clansmen into battle. Sending her child was another matter entirely.

Jaym ran off toward the practice fields, picking up another, longer stick as he went, swinging it like a plasma sword.

Slaying imaginary Surebloods.

Like his father. Hells. If only the boy knew the truth about his origins.

Jaym had kept Val's heart from growing hard; he'd brought her joy in so many unexpected ways. But as deeply as she loved him, he was a reminder of her failings the night her father was killed. Jaym's father was their clan's sworn enemy. To reveal his paternity to the rest of the clan would endanger his life and cast her loyalties into doubt. What would happen to her and to Jaym should someone ever figure out the truth?

"Throw them Surebloods back to hells—where they belong, Jaym!" a male voice bellowed across the field.

Jaym's distant ferocious roar echoed back as he whipped the stick crosswise through the tall weeds.

"You're encouraging him," she said, turning to find Ayl striding up the path to join her.

"At every opportunity, aye. The boy can't forget who our enemy is."

Her heart skipped a beat and she glanced protectively at Jaym. Ayl never knew what happened that night between her and Dake, but despite Reeve's subterfuge he had his suspicions. What would happen if he ever learned the truth?

His smile was pleasant. "You made it back from your dirt-side raid."

"Of course, I did. And it was a success. We'll make a pretty profit selling that ore on the black market."

"Dirt-side raiding isn't right, Val. It isn't the way we do things. We're hatch busters, not land scavengers."

"We've made more profit dirt-side in one week than we did in almost a year of fighting for the scraps Nez throws our way."

"Aye, and I told them that."

"Told who?"

"The doubters. The ones who think we're taking the wrong path. I told them to give you a chance in this."

Her neck prickled with a sense of danger as a sizzle of annoyance sparked in her belly. Always, Ayl presented himself as a man of considerable influence who was also generously her defender. "Give *me* a chance? As if it's your decision whether I get one or not?" Her captaincy hadn't been seriously challenged since Ragmarrk was killed on a raid years ago, but it was by no means secure. "You can tell the naysayers that if they have a problem, they come to me. Gossip does nothing but spread doubt. On any raid there's danger—on a dirt-side outpost or on a skiff in space."

Ayl frowned at the blossoms, his jaw muscles moving. "I don't want to argue. Look at these blossoms. More than last year." He reached out and shook a small branch, releasing a flurry of petals. They looked overly delicate landing on her scarred and rugged boots.

"We'll have a lot of ebbe apples come fall," he said, changing the subject. "Maybe it's a fruitful omen that pays heeding." He touched her shoulder as if to thaw her. She neither pulled away nor encouraged him and simply, neutrally accepted the caress of someone she'd known all her life. It was a delicate balancing act with Ayl. On one hand, she recoiled at the idea of taking him as her husband. It wasn't the embarrassment he'd caused her when they were teens anymore, or the knowledge he still shared Despa's bed on occasion; it was something else. But when asked to explain it to Sashya, she fell short, saying only that there was nothing in her heart for Ayl. It was as if she were still waiting. Waiting for…

She jerked her focus back to Ayl. If she were to give him no hope of ever marrying her, he might figure he had nothing to lose and organize a mutiny to achieve his latent dreams of power. Maybe it was time to give in and marry him. It would be one less thing to worry about. She was so very tired of worry, she thought, feeling a fresh urge to smoke.

"This is our year to start our life together," he went on hopefully. "We've waited a long time for the moment to be right. It's not ever going to be more right than now. You need the support." He paused. "You need me."

He moved closer, taking her continued silence as an invitation. His fingers lingered on her shoulder and, after a heartbeat of hesitation, he leaned over and pressed his lips to her cheek in a chaste kiss.

Instead of pulling away, she closed her eyes and refused to submit to the memory of a man who'd made her shiver when he'd kissed her there, and everywhere... lips so warm and softly firm, with a stubbly jaw that needled her in the most delicious way... Grinning lips that made her body sing. No man had affected her in the same way since.

As Ayl pulled away, she realized how she hungered for that kind of tender contact, and the passion it would lead to. She might not have the feelings for Ayl she'd like, but was being alone all the time really the best thing? Wouldn't she learn to accept and even care for Ayl over time?

"Let me stay with you tonight, Val," he said, his voice thick. "Let me prove how much I desire you."

With that, reality flooded back, painfully, like a

bright light switched on in a pitch-black room. It would keep her awake tonight, she thought wearily. "I need a little more time before we...do that," she said.

"How much more time do you need? It's been four years. First, you were in mourning. Then it was the war with the Surebloods needing your attention. After that, Jaym was taking too long to get over a bout of camp cough—like half the kids in this village were, and their parents still shared a bed. Now you're all wrapped up trying to make dirt-side raiding work. There will always be something in the way, if you let it. There's no more reason for us not to be together. To marry. To start a family of our own. It's not like you've got other suitors." He paused. "Unless, you still have feelin's for Jaym's father."

Her heart stopped before she realized he meant her son's pretend father. She shook her head. "I've got no feelings for that man." Outside violent, gut-wrenching hatred, that was.

Ayl sighed. "Sometimes I think you're planning to lead me on forever."

"I think of this daily, if you'll know the truth."

"Then say yes. With me at your side, we'll see our clan into the future. We'll ensure its survival." His eyes glowed bright with passion he didn't have for her, only for his ambitions.

But deep down, she knew he was right. Taking Ayl as her husband would strengthen the clan as well as remove the distraction of a dissenting faction. It was time she stopped procrastinating. As leader she had to ultimately do what was best for her people, and not for her personally. The time had come to decide.

"I'll give you my answer. Soon, I promise."

"By week's end?" he pushed.

She hesitated. *Desperate times called for desperate measures.* "Aye. By week's end."

DAKE'S OPERATION REBOOT overcoat flapped around the legs of his Triad-issued trousers as he left the detention facility behind. A sense of urgency quickened his strides now that the shock of his release had worn off. Once the emotional shielding he'd erected over the years came crashing down, sharp fear for the welfare of the people he'd left behind sliced through him, leaving his composure shredded. If his worst nightmares were right and Nezerihm was behind the assassinations, what more had the man done to the Surebloods and Blues in Dake's absence?

Joy at his sudden freedom turned into resentment that he'd been locked away, losing so many good years, all because a vicious, calculating, power-grabbing rat of a man thought him a threat. *If* his suspicions about the mine owner were right. He feared he'd be so wound up by the time he found Nezerihm that he couldn't trust himself not to murder the man while trying to find out the truth.

"Don't screw up out there. You'll be in for a real long time if you come back." The official's order reminded him of his precarious situation. If he wasn't careful he'd end up back in jail. This time there'd be

no accidental transfers, no second chances. If he got himself arrested, he'd be locked up for good.

He'd die before that ever happened. From the moment a Drakken gun was dropped in his cuffed hands and he was ordered to kill people with whom he had no fight, to seeing his men killed off a few at a time until he was the only one left, to the nightmarish succession of stifling jail cells where he constantly fought his mindless fear of enclosed spaces, his life had been under the control of others. He'd been treated as less than an animal, left to lie in his own filth, to suffer hunger and thirst and untreated wounds, and to plumb the depths of loneliness that nearly drove him mad. How did he get through it? How did he survive? Captivity was a death sentence for a pirate. Most died within a year. He'd lasted five.

Because you had more reasons to live than to die: a clan that needed your leadership, a woman you wanted to get to know a hells of a lot better, joining your life with hers if she'd have you. A dream to see through to the end.

A monster to punish for crimes horrible beyond belief.

First get home, he told himself. Then he was going to start working his way down that list.

Gripping the ticket in one hand and his government-issued travel bag in the other, he finally found himself at the docks. Nothing but stars and docked starships as far as the eye could see behind an almost invisible barrier between him and space. The sight of an enormous pristine white craft stopped him short.

He checked his ticket, then the enviable craft. *TAS Unity.* His ride home.

He stepped forward and into a strange new world: the galaxy beyond prison. Outsiders, hundreds of them, moved up and down the various loading ramps as the great ship prepared to depart. Dake had never seen so many acres of *clean.* Every surface sparkled. Even the people. Conversations seemed hushed, actions restrained. How dull. How the bloody hells did they live this way?

"Halloo." A woman in a Triad tricolor uniform strode forward to escort him aboard. "I bet you're the Reboot passenger." She scanned his ticket. "Come with me. I'll get you through security, then show you to your quarters."

"I've got another passenger—a Reboot," his escort told the three guards waiting at the security checkpoint. They were armed with technologically advanced weapons that would have made Dake's dozer look as primitive as a carved stick.

"Operation Reboot," one said. "Means you were locked up, and no records, then set free with a mumbled apology and a one-way ticket home. Am I right?"

"Aye. That's about right."

"How long?" Pity altered the guard's tone as he plugged in Dake's information.

Dake frowned. He refused to be any guard's object of pity, be he Triad, Coalition or Drakken. The only pity he cared to ponder from this moment on was the specken he'd have for Nezerihm, watching the worm beg for his life. "Five years," he drawled.

"Not as long as some. Well, you didn't miss much. War and more war." The guard cleared him through.

Dake took one last look back at the location of his last prison cell, then turned and tromped up the boarding ramp of the *Unity*.

CHAPTER EIGHTEEN

"VAL BLUE MUST BE STOPPED!" Nezerihm slammed his hand down on the meeting table. His chair adjusted to his increased stress levels, softening the cushion and providing a slight vibrating massage of his lower back. Still, his heart was thumping from too much adrenaline, too much rage. *Mara's Prize* wasn't a large or important ore transport, but it was the principle of the thing—it had been destined for the Triad's main ship-building facility, the ore bought and paid for.

It was refined zelfen of the highest quality. *Promised* to the Triad! It wasn't Val Blue's to take. The Triad would see he wasn't reliable to provide their zelfen and they'd take him out of that role. Peace may have come, but he wasn't stupid—the Triad would still fight to have the resources it needed. It needed zelfen. "How did those flargin' Blues get aboard a land-docked ship?"

As one, his staff turned to look at the captain responsible, obviously pitying the man. By rights they should. He'd never again set foot on the bridge of any ship transporting company ore.

The captain cleared his throat and did his best to stand up to Nezerihm's scrutiny. "They confronted my crew while we were boarding, my lord. They accused me of being drunk."

"And were you?"

"Absolutely not! They were disguised as customs officials. And quite convincingly. I saw through them, but by then it was too late. There were more of them than there were of us, and they had weapons out before we did."

"And why was that, Captain? How did they out-maneuver my company on every gods-be-damned level?"

"The element of surprise. We weren't expecting a land raid."

Nezerihm shoved a furious hand through his hair. The captain's excuse echoed around the table of mining executives and in his mind, taunting him. Val Blue hadn't listened to his advice to stop stirring up trouble. Instead she'd expanded her tactics. How long before the other clans picked up on the idea? In transit, his ore wouldn't be safe in space or on the ground. He'd have to do something about her, and very soon.

"From now on all crews will carry arms, and all will expect and defend against pirates. No one should ever again use surprise as an excuse." All the staffers and mine foremen furiously jotted down the order. It would get out to the transport crews by word of mouth. He employed no chief of security. Power mustn't ever be consolidated in such a sensitive position. He alone held it all. His was a family company and until such time he had an heir he'd run operations on his own. For the same reason he didn't maintain a defense force either.

He'd never needed one. Until the war ended, the pirates had been a tolerable nuisance and nothing more, eagerly hunting down his zelfen thieves. He'd saved money not having to maintain an army. He didn't want an army. Armies were greedy for power. The next thing he'd know, they'd be plotting to overthrow him and take over the company.

Everyone wanted what he had—his life, his riches, his power. Everyone was jealous. He had to preempt the strikes against him. So far he'd been one-hundred-percent successful in doing just that, sending his assassins out amongst the barbaric, greedy pirates to do his bidding. Undermining the clans was easy with so much distrust already in place. Unified, they would have less need for his advice, his protection, his generous help. They might think his zelfen was theirs, like Valeeya Blue did apparently.

He never dreamed the scrawny little Blue girl would turn out to be such an irritant. If he had, he'd have offed her the same day he got rid of her father. He knew exactly where she'd gone off to hide that night. He knew what she'd done.

And with whom.

Good thing she'd never ended up with the young Sureblood as her father had so foolishly hoped. Now *that* would have been a problem: Surebloods and Blues allied through marriage. Any child born to the couple would have been seen as the leader of both clans. Instant unification—the stuff of nightmares, he thought. Then the thugs would come after him, after his company, his riches, even invading his palace here on Aerokhtron.

No pirate had set foot on this turf since the clans met to sign an agreement giving his family joint control of the mines in the midst of the Great Zelfen Rush. His father had intended to extend the expiring agreement's term through negotiation. Nezerihm cringed, glad he never allowed that to happen, and wake up the pirates to the fact that the mines really belonged to them. He knew better than to open up that can of worms. He made sure his father passed on to the Ever After without ever revealing what the idiot pirates didn't realize and didn't deserve to. Then he was careful to destroy the original treaty, of course, just in case the worst ever happened. He felt no guilt whatsoever about the tactics he'd employed to save his family's legacy. It was the old man's time to pass on anyway.

The idea of losing the mines made him feel very, very ill. Thankfully there was no chance of that now—or of little Blue-Sureblood bastards running about. Dake Sureblood was long dead. A crisis preempted.

But now another one loomed. Val Blue was irritating him greatly. He needed to take immediate action against her or lose the Triad's trust and business. But first things first... "Captain, come take a walk with me."

The transport captain glanced around at the men sitting around the table. No one met his eyes. All knew and understood how unhappy Nezerihm was because of his ineptitude. Now he'd have to give the man the bad news in private.

Trailed by the despondent captain, Nezerihm walked across the room to the balcony, shoving open the doors.

The breeze rushed in, the warm, summery air laden with moisture from the surrounding lake, a nature-made moat. Silently, the captain stood next to him.

"I wanted the moat to be special," Nezerihm commented, "and it's so ordinary. I tried stocking it with mer-people, but they all died. One of the unneutered males hung on, though, longer than the others. He was part of my motivation for obtaining a rare young female, to start a pod of my own, but the one I imported at extraordinary expense from the water worlds went astray before I could bring her home."

The staffer in charge of that foul-up paid for his carelessness with his life. It wasn't the only thing that had gone horribly awry that month. Like when he sacrificed one of his oldest, ready-for-scrap freighters as a decoy to cause a Sureblood/Blue clash and Drakken fighters came out of nowhere to attack it, most of the pirates escaped alive. Who would have dreamed Surebloods and Blues would cooperate instead of killing each other?

But Nezerihm prided himself on his recovery from that disastrous day. It certainly couldn't have been swifter. The incident itself led to the gathering and from there, things went better than he'd ever hoped.

Now this.

As the captain continued to stand at attention, Nezerihm gripped the railing and looked out over his domain. "I feel so alone sometimes, Captain. So attacked. So…surrounded by people who make mistakes. If I'm not proactive, I risk losing all of this—my empire, everything my ancestors built from scratch.

Your little incident has convinced me that something's going to have to be done about Val Blue and her band of brigands. The end of the war has changed everything. The world, my dear Captain, has shifted. I need to shift with it. It's time I legitimized my power in the eyes of the rest of the galaxy." He threw a jovial glance at the captain. "I've long fancied the title governor."

The captain's gaze was trained straight ahead. His mouth was a firm line as he patiently awaited news of his fate.

Nezerihm sighed. "I suppose you're anxious to know the consequences of your failure."

The captain swallowed. "Yes, my lord."

Nezerihm made a complete circle around the man before he stopped in front of him. "Would you like a refreshment before we get started?"

The captain's gaze flashed with surprise as he focused on Nezerihm, then annoyance before he managed to bury it.

It didn't matter. Nezerihm saw it and shook his head. "I'm sure you've heard that Prime-Admiral Zaafran of the Triad wants all of us to be kinder and gentler in our approach to the piracy problem. That includes me. Kinder, gentler Lord Nezerihm."

The guard posted by the door snickered. Nezerihm in fact found the topic anything but funny. "The clans will never leave their homes voluntarily, Captain. They'll have to be *exterminated*, starting with that arrogant Blue bitch. The one you let fly away with my ore." Grunting, he swung the back of his hand across the man's face, snapping back his head.

The captain dabbed his knuckles at some bloody spittle, then resumed his at-attention stance. Why didn't he act afraid? Why wasn't he simpering like all the others before him, pleading for mercy?

It was all so disappointing. Fear in others excited Nezerihm. It aroused him—sexually, intellectually and emotionally, and made him feel powerful. Addicted, he fed on human terror like a drug.

This man so far gave him nothing to work with.

Nezerihm pulled out his pistol and pressed the muzzle to the very center of the captain's forehead. "Look at that. Not even a flinch from you. No fear at all."

"I'm not afraid," the captain agreed quietly.

Nezerihm's cheeks flushed hot with anger. He'd felt fear every day of his life. Fear and hate. That this worm of a man didn't show a whit himself enraged him. He refused to allow this man or a lowly pirate whore to make him feel inferior!

The flare of plasma fire and the sound of a skull coming apart startled Nezerihm as much as it did the guard posted at the door. And the dead captain, too, judging by the wide-eyed stare of surprise as the body fell backward.

Nezerihm let out a breath and almost immediately felt better. "Get someone to clean up this flargin' mess."

"Kinder and gentler, my lord?" The guard's eyes gleamed.

"I could have aimed for his testicles first." Nezerihm

pocketed the still-sizzling weapon and returned in a much-improved mood to the meeting room.

ON THE *UNITY,* DAKE threw his gear on the bunk in his assigned cabin. It was excruciatingly sanitized like everything thing else on the ship, and felt cramped when he wanted no reminders of any of the cells he'd lived in. He wasn't going to spend another second staring at four walls.

A drink…he was desperate for one. Five-years desperate. He went in search of the ship's bar.

Even the corridors of the ship were a wonder, longer and wider than any ship he'd flown in, and filled with happy, busy crew members dressed in perfect uniforms. *It would be something, having a ship like this.* He tried not to appear like a little boy in his amazement. It was so bright and *clean,* and that repelled and fascinated him. In spite of the sameness of the uniforms, the three civilizations that crewed the *Unity* were obvious if he looked hard enough at the differences: the Drakken had their body ink and ear jewelry; the Earthlings walked in groups, their body language foreign and speaking in their strange tongue; the Coalition stood out by not standing out.

Outsiders all, he reminded himself. Distrust of them was bred into his bones. Yet he'd never gotten a close look at them outside prison. Here they were, putting aside countless years of war to pursue the dream of peace. It began to give him hope that his dream of unity between the clans was attainable, too. If Val hadn't already accomplished it in his absence, he thought. But the prison official said the region was unstable, and it worried him.

It was noisier in the bar. Dozens milled around inside. Here the crew of the *Unity* could let loose. Once again his hand went for a dozer that wasn't there. No need, he thought, scanning the large, nicely lit space. It might be more chaotic in the bar than the rest of the ship proper, but it was far more civilized than any Borderlands haunt he knew. No dead bodies to trip over, no dock whores draping their perfumed arms around him, no filth under his boots.

He didn't exactly like it, but he'd have to make do.

The tempting scents of alcohol and food drew him farther inside. Savory scents made his stomach growl. He'd choked down one too many bowls of gruel in his recent past to ignore the aromas tantalizing him.

He waded through a sea of unfamiliar faces to the bar. They watched warily as he passed by. Word must have gotten around about his ex-con status. Or it may have been his size.

He slid a couple of the chits that served as money across the bar table. The last time he stood at a bar was with Malta, tasting her moonshine. "Whiskey." He'd heard the Coalition liked to drink the stuff. It was a likely beverage to try first, though he had no intention of getting drunk. He was too much in the habit of wanting to stay alert for opportunities to escape.

The bartender eyed him curiously as he gave him the drink. "Welcome back to real life, mister," he said.

"If that's what you call it." Dake sipped the liquor. It tasted like water compared to moonshine.

"I can get you a girl." The bartender motioned to several pretty female crew members casting interested peeks in Dake's direction as they huddled over their drinks. One was tall with curves like Val. She even had long, wavy brown hair. "I expect you haven't had any in a while. If you want an introduction, let me know. You won't have any problem getting takers."

"No, thanks." Dake turned his back to the women. He didn't want them. He wanted Val. His Blue girl. He wasn't nearly done getting to know her. They'd only first met when fate ripped them apart. Even now he could see her as she'd looked as they escaped the slango dance: her face flushed with excitement, her eyes twinkling with mischief, sharing his anticipation at their chance to be alone together. Poised on the threshold of the rest of their lives. Or so he'd thought.

You never know what life's going to hand out. Like everyone else, Val would assume he was dead. She'd have no reason to wait for him. The probability that she'd married by now was high. Yet she'd been determined to stay free, unhindered by marriage and children. Free as the wind. Had she stayed so? The need to find out burned in him.

A crewman joined them at the bar. "You're a Sureblood, aren't you?" As if Dake was a novelty, he sized him up knowingly. "You've got to be, mate. Look at you."

Dake stood a little taller. He had nothing to gain hiding his past, and not much to lose admitting to it. Piracy wasn't what had gotten him locked up in the first place. "Aye, I am."

"I thought so, given your size and the fact you're heading to the Channels. I heard you'd come aboard. Hitching a ride to the Borderlands." At Dake's surprise, he smiled and lifted the drink the bartender poured for him. "Rumors get around fast on this ship. You'll be getting home just in time to help them pack up and leave."

"Leaving? No one's leaving."

"You haven't heard?"

The man was beginning to irritate him. "I haven't heard much of anything in the two hours I've been out." Dake was in no mood for making small talk.

"Operation Amnesty. The Triad wants to turn you pirates into fine, upstanding citizens. And we on the *Unity* get to convince you what a good deal it is." Oblivious to Dake's deepening scowl, he clinked his glass against Dake's. "And it is, mate. In exchange for agreeing to relocate, you get free housing, education, food and clothing. Tax-free. Forever."

Relocate. Dake's hand clamped around his glass. "Is that what you meant by us leaving?"

"That's the catch. You've got to move out to get the full incentive package and the pardon."

Dake snarled, "My people didn't do anything to warrant a pardon."

"The hijackings, maybe? Or maybe it could be the zelfen stealing, black marketeering or kidnapping? There's a rap sheet a light-year long on you folks. Now it'll all be wiped clean—if pirates agree to the terms."

Dake blinked, trying to sort out the information

being thrown at him as if it weren't the most disturbing, confounding news he'd ever heard. Had he been given his freedom only to learn a different kind of imprisonment loomed?

Who was leading the Surebloods now who would agree to this? Weren't they healthy and prospering? Wasn't the alliance between his clan and the Blues strong? "We Surebloods will never leave Parramanta! We'll fight until the last man, woman and child." People looked up at Dake's shout. He didn't bloody care.

"The Surebloods were singing a different tune last I heard, my friend, after we showed them what we could offer versus the hard times they've fallen upon. What I don't get, Sureblood, is how come the little Blues were able to stand up to our mediators, and you big ol' Sureblood giants sound ready to leave your planet without a fight. You used to be the big bad asses of the Channels. Now you're the teddy bears."

The Blues. *Val.* He nearly grabbed the man by the neck to demand more information, but outsiders weren't like pirates, yelling and pounding fists. They spoke more…civilly. He clenched his jaw until his muscles ached, holding back. "Did they speak to the clan leader? Val Blue?"

"Yep. We sent two mediators to the Blues to introduce the program the other day, and she threatened to blow them out the airlock." The crewman slurped some whiskey. "Val Blue. The vilest she-captain in the Channels, mate. Beautiful, I hear, but mean. She'd rather bite off a man's head than kiss him."

The shock of hearing Val's name after all this time

and in those terms sent both relief and alarm careening through him. She was apparently alive and well, just as plucky as he remembered, and apparently temporarily safe from Nezerihm's claws.

But she was up against Triad pressure. The pirates would never win by force. He shelved the idea permanently. He had to warn Val what she was up against, that she couldn't fend off the Triad like they did their enemies of old. The Triad was smarter, and now the clans had to be, too. He'd find her and work out what they were going to do about it. *And she'll know you're alive.* With a wishful image of him stripping off all her clothes in a passionate reunion, he knew he'd have to rush back to Parramanta to help his clan before it was too late. But how to get to Artoom…? "Isn't the *Unity* sending out mediators for another try?"

"I heard we were. Captain's trying to decide what to do about it—"

"Take me. I can help you with the Blues."

The crewman laughed. "Like they'd let a Sureblood get anywhere near them after your clan assassinated their last leader."

Dake reared back. "We didn't murder Conn Blue."

"Ha. Tell that to the Blues. I don't think you'd get them to agree."

Dake's head was spinning. He'd left the two clans on the verge of unity. Now they were at war, not with Nezerihm but with each other. Yarmouth must not have made it back to tell the others about the ambush and to warn them to watch Nezerihm. How else could it have gone so bloody wrong?

The crewman took a sip of whiskey as Dake's alarm spiked. "I guess it got old being ostracized by all the clans. No one in the Borderlands will be sad to see you Surebloods go—"

Dake snatched the man by the collar. "There's an assassin, but it's not us! It's *not us!*"

A hand landed on his shoulder. "Easy," someone said.

Dake shoved him away. Others were grabbing for him now, trying to pull him off the man he'd pinned to the bar. He threw a punch at someone, not sure who. *"Your clan murdered Conn Blue."* The crewman's charges rang in his mind. Not his clan. Not the Surebloods. He had to set things straight and save his people from leaving.

A restraint slithered around his wrists, cinching tight. He fought to pull free. His very life depended on it. *His clan's lives. And Val's.* The cuffs only got tighter. He roared in outrage and had just about kicked the last person out of his way when the crack of a dozer and a hit in the back sent him sprawling over the whiskey-splattered floor.

FRANK JOHNSON WALKED across his office on the *Unity* with a cup of coffee and settled down at his desk.

"Sir, he's here," his first officer informed him. Facial tattoos and an ear rimmed with tiny black diamonds told of the lieutenant's Drakken origins. In his case, however, one couldn't judge the book by its cover. Gwarkk was as steady and quietly efficient as they came.

Frank nodded. "Send him in."

He used the intervening moments until Gwarkk returned with the mine owner who'd requested a meeting to scan his data pad. The Triad dossier revealed that Lord Viro Nezerihm oversaw the production of all the zelfen in the area and seemed eager to cooperate in keeping the supply lines open.

At least someone was willing to cooperate, Frank thought. For all his efforts trying to work with the pirates for their sakes, all he'd gained was a threat to blow his two best mediators out an airlock. He took full blame. The fault was in his method of approach. He'd have to work with the clans if he were to have any chance of achieving his goals here. It meant understanding them—the people, the culture, their age-old ways. So far he'd failed miserably.

Captain Valeeya Blue ran the most powerful of the six main families. It was imperative he gain her trust, at least enough to have meaningful talks. Maybe Lord Nezerihm would have some ideas.

Frank skimmed through the intelligence data gathered on the mine owner. The Nezerihms moved into the Channels region from parts unknown and started a mining company. Indigenous clans—the pirates—saw the Nezerihm family as thieves and trespassers. Attacks on the Nezerihm fleet and company headquarters on Aerokhtron were frequent and bloody. Then zelfen was discovered and sought after by both the Drakken and Coalition. At that point the clans and the Nezerihms joined forces to keep them from helping themselves to the ore. A treaty was signed regarding use of the mines, but details were sketchy. Frank transmitted a task note to Gwarkk to research it further, then wrapped up his review.

Wasn't much more to see—Viro Nezerihm took over company operations after his father died and relations between the individual clans spiraled drastically downward to where they were now: rock bottom. Coincidence or—?

"Sir," Gwarkk said. "Lord Nezerihm."

Gray was the word that popped into Frank's mind upon seeing Nezerihm: a pale gray cloak, silver hair and brows, matching eyes and deathly white skin. He crossed the office like fog rolling into San Francisco. "Captain Johnson. A pleasure to meet you finally."

"A pleasure likewise, Lord Nezerihm."

The man declined all offers of food and drink, wanting to get right to business. Frank poured a second cup of coffee and got comfortable at his desk, but Nezerihm perched with prim intensity on the edge of a smart seat and said, "Your Operation Amnesty plan is a humanitarian one, but you'll waste countless hours, money and manpower trying to negotiate with the pirates. Trust me, I know." The man punctuated his apparent frustration with a dramatic sigh. "Look at what happened to your mediators on Val Blue's *Marauder*. They barely made it out alive. She wanted to eject them out the hatch. Your mediators had to beg for their lives."

"How did you hear that?" A vague unease prickled Frank's neck. This man knew too much.

"I have trusted contacts in all the clans. They're men

like me who want peace. Men like you and me, Captain Johnson."

Frank doubted he and this Borderlands ore lord were anything alike but he'd leave it at that, reminding himself that he was a diplomat now, kinder and gentler. Or at least he was supposed to be.

"Captain, my company is the sole legitimate source of zelfen in the Channels, and your Triad is the sole consumer. But we're bombarded by barbarians on all sides who would rather keep the place the way it always was—lawless and dangerous. If we want any chance at assuring a legal, reliable supply of zelfen, we need to work together, you and me."

"I agree we need to work together." Frank wasn't as sure about Nezerihm Mining Company being the sole legitimate supplier, however, not without knowing what that treaty said. "That's why the *Unity* is here, finding a solution."

"You won't get the Blues to agree to anything without a fight. They'll convince the other clans to resist peace efforts, too. It will get ugly, and that's exactly what the Triad wants to avoid, yes? Bloodshed," he said. "Captain, I can get you the zelfen the Triad needs without the war nobody wants. And I can do it quickly." In his excitement, Nezerihm's cheeks finally showed a little color. So the man was alive after all.

"Really. To say you've captured my interest is an understatement." Frank stirred more sugar into his coffee although it had already cooled down more than he liked. If this eccentric could deliver peace, Frank was game. "How do you suggest we do it?"

"Reconstruction, from the top down."

Frank stopped stirring. "Meaning?"

"First, we eliminate the biggest instigator of disobedience—Val Blue, the Blue clan leader. She's unpredictable and irrational, a loose cannon." He looked from side to side and whispered, "Utterly mad. She's costing me millions. Millions. Robbing my transports on land!" Nezerihm seemed to catch himself and forced calm back into his voice. His hands stopped wringing and spread over his thighs. The right hand, though manicured, was a lacework of scratches up to the wrist that looked fresh, like work of fingernails. Signs of a struggle? Frank narrowed his eyes.

Nezerihm grasped at the fabric of his pants to keep his hands still. "Captain, I have nothing to gain by generating more unrest in the region, and everything to gain by creating stability. Val Blue has made it very difficult for me to get zelfen to your shipyards. She's the problem. The solution is simple. Remove her immediately and install a new, responsible leader in her place. Zelfen will flow free once again."

Frank's hopes for a constructive dialogue plummeted. "Assassination is against Triad directives, Lord Nezerihm."

"Oh, no. We don't kill her. We simply put someone… more accommodating in her position. It will be easier than you think." Nezerihm leaned forward. "I know just the man. Remember, I have allies inside the clans." He was back to rubbing his anxious hands over the thighs of his expensive trousers. "I'm not the only one upset about Val Blue's land raids, you see. Her own clan is

on the verge of rebellion over them. It won't take much
at all to fall over the edge. After the mutiny, she'll be
delivered to you alive and well. No one gets hurt. I give
you my word." Nezerihm sat back in his chair for the
first time, waiting for his response. One finger rapped
against the armrest. A foot tapped on the carpet. He
was always in motion.

Was it nerves, Frank wondered, or a physical issue?
Living this far out in the Borderlands, the hinterlands of
the settled galaxy, could make anyone a little crazy. The
backwoods of the United States sure had their share of
hermits and mountain men over the years, but for Frank
there was an undercurrent of malice in this individual
that leeched the humor from his eccentricities.

It warranted further investigation.

"You bring up an excellent point," he said at last. "It
might very well be beneficial to work on the situation
from the inside out."

"It will be. Trust me in this. So, do I have your blessing, Captain Johnson?"

"Lord Nezerihm, I want to give this some more
thought before I decide how we will proceed."

"Of course." Nezerihm's expression was a study in
impatience, disgust and then acceptance. It was clear
he'd wanted to get started immediately. "I completely
understand. I'll wait for your word, then."

"I'll be in touch soon," Frank promised.

They said their goodbyes and the mine owner
departed.

Frank swore as Gwarkk closed the door behind him.

They regarded each other, incredulous. Then Frank drove a hand through his hair. "Did you hear that?"

Gwarkk nodded. "He wants to force a coup."

"I could use a shower after listening to all that."

"I don't blame you, sir."

"The idea actually excited him. He wanted to get started on the overthrow *today,* and install his own puppet leader." Frank scrubbed a tired hand over his face. "It would certainly speed things along if we could pull it off, but no way am I going to try." He was an Earth officer in a position of potential historical significance for the entire galaxy. The temptation of the easy way wasn't how he got there. "I'm going to find a solution acceptable to the Triad where the pirates can keep their homes."

At the risk of failing in his mission.

And ending his career.

"As well as find a solution acceptable to you, sir," Gwarkk guessed correctly.

"Yeah." Turning away, Frank folded his hands behind his head and gazed at the plaque he'd mounted on the wall. The same plaque he'd hung above every desk in every office he'd ever occupied. He made himself pause to reread the quote attributed to Davey Crockett, seeing his budding political career destroyed because he supported the Cherokees' bid to keep their land. "'I'd rather be honestly and politically damned than hypocritically immortalized,'" Frank recited. *Amen to that.*

He dropped his hands and turned around. "Lieutenant Gwarkk, research the treaty signed between the

Nezerihm family and the clans. See if there are any records of what, exactly, they agreed to."

"I'll get right on it, sir."

"What's next on the schedule, Lieutenant Gwarkk?"

"You wanted to speak to the passenger about the fistfight in the bar. Dake Sureblood. He's on his way up from the brig now."

"Oh, yeah. That brawl. Send him in."

FREEDOM HADN'T LASTED long, Dake thought, his left cheekbone and right knuckles throbbing from punches thrown and received. Not even a half a day free before he'd wound up back behind holobars.

Don't screw up out there. You'll be in for a real long time if you come back....

Like hells if he'd ever let that happen. Handcuffed and escorted by a guard from the brig down below up to the bridge, Dake exited the lift. "The captain's office is this way," the guard said.

As they turned, a gaunt, pallid man in a gray overcoat strode past to board the elevator. His pale eyes lifted to Dake's and went wide. He almost tripped, his skin turning even more chalk white at the sight of him.

Dake stared back. *Bloody freepin' hells.* Nezerihm!

He'd long ago learned to keep his feelings hidden—in prison any reaction could lead to unhappy consequences—and he kept them hidden now. Nezerihm, on the other hand, had no such discipline. He gawked at Dake, utterly dumbfounded and shocked. No joy at the realization Dake survived, no relief, just fright.

As if seeing a ghost.

That reaction told Dake everything he needed to know. It was the proof that he never was supposed to have survived the Drakken ambush. Nez had wanted him dead.

CHAPTER NINETEEN

GWARKK OPENED THE DOOR to Frank's office. With his firearm drawn, he allowed the detainee to walk inside. A big, good-looking man, the Reboot passenger didn't appear cowed in the least despite his cuffed wrists. On the other hand, he didn't appear threatening either, as if he understood the odds against him if he tried anything violent.

The ex-con looked the part, sporting a day's growth of stubble and a prison haircut, and not an ounce of body fat on him. The cliché stopped at his eyes. They were a startling color, or more accurately a patchwork of colors, and they fell upon Frank with anguished purpose. "Cap'n," the man said. "I don't like the company you keep."

Now, that was some opening. Frank leaned back in his desk chair and tapped a pen against his chin. "Who—my first officer?"

"No. Nezerihm," he snarled quietly, pointing out to the corridor. "He almost didn't recognize me. When he did, he looked like he'd seen a ghost. Because I'm supposed to be dead, that's why. Dead because *of him.*" His eyes flashed with agony he either didn't try to conceal or couldn't. "Why the bloody hells is he on this ship?"

"He asked for my time the same as anyone else can. I keep an open office, Mr. Sureblood."

"*Cap'n* Sureblood," the big man corrected fervently but respectfully. "Dake Sureblood. I'm leader of the Surebloods. Or I was until the day I was ambushed by Drakken and conscripted into their army." His glance at Gwarkk revealed no blame for the atrocities the first officer's people had inflicted before the war's end. "I always suspected Nezerihm set it up, sicced them on my ship. Now seeing his face out there, I know I'm right." Sureblood's jaw pulsed, his bound hands clenched into fists. "I've been locked up ever since with no cause until someone finally figured out I belonged outside a cell, not inside one. I've been out less than a day. And what do I hear? That my clan is accused of murdering Conn Blue! Nezerihm did it—not us. Nezerihm took him out, and left us Surebloods to take the blame. He's a murderer. A bloody assassin. And he's running free on your ship. Hells, he's been free the entire five years I've been behind bars!"

As Frank absorbed the enormity of what had just been told to him, Sureblood fell silent, his chest heaving. The sheer intensity of his gaze coupled with his accusations raised the hackles on Frank's neck. The mine owner had been all too eager to dismantle Blue clan's leadership. It seemed he had prior experience tinkering in clan politics. Sureblood politics.

"Wait outside and don't let anyone in," Frank told

the guard blocking the office entrance. "Lieutenant Gwarkk, come in and shut the door."

Frank got up and walked around to the front of his desk and sat on the edge, his arms folded as he studied the big pirate. "Is the accusation against your clan what caused the brawl in my bar?"

"*I* caused it. Your crewman said the Surebloods were fixing to leave Parramanta because they couldn't live with the shame anymore. I overreacted hearing the news. Cap'n, my people don't know I'm alive. All these years and not a single word of me. The day we were ambushed, I sent my first mate home to tell them what happened. He got out in a skiff before the hunters boarded, but by the sound of it, I guess he never made it back."

The pirate's facial muscles contracted as he seemed to struggle to maintain some sense of dignity and control in light of his clear anguish. When he began again his voice was measured and even. "I've spent too long in other people's cages to stay in one of my own making. I'll bloody well prove we aren't responsible for Conn Blue's murder if it takes me the rest of my days." He pulled against the wrist restraints as if desperate to use his hands to express himself. "Give me the chance. I'll prove Nezerihm's the cold-blooded killer. And that he's been pitting the clans against each other to splinter any chance of unity."

"Disarm the cuffs," Frank told Gwarkk. His first officer hesitated for a moment, as if wondering if it were safe to do it, then did as Frank asked. Hands free, the pirate flexed his fingers to get the blood flowing again.

"Having freed you, I'm compelled to issue a disclaimer. Make no sudden, threatening moves. I'll kill you."

"Or I will," Gwarkk said quietly, his earrings and dark eyes glinting.

The pirate hardly reacted. "I'd expect no less," he said.

Frank folded his arms across his chest. "Do you know anything about a treaty your people have with Lord Nezerihm that allows him to mine the asteroids?"

Sureblood thought about it and shook his head. "For as long as anyone knows, the Nezerihms mined those rocks."

"And reap all the profit," Frank pointed out.

"Aye, but my people don't dig dirt to survive. We sail the stars. Now providing protection for the mines for pay is something we don't mind. If there be ore stealers, we hunt them down for him. Nezerihm sells the ore and gives us a cut of the profits as bounty."

"*Did* give you a cut," Frank corrected. "The Drakken and Triad aren't competing for zelfen anymore. There's only one consumer now—*us,* the Triad. Nezerihm Mining no longer needs to pay for protection. That leaves you out in the cold. The company's making money hand over fist, but the only avenue for the clans to share it is to steal it. And that's what's no longer going to be allowed, by pirates or by anyone else." Frank waited a moment for that to sink in, then said, "I respect the fact that your culture looks down on the dirty work of mining, but I didn't know it meant not sharing in the spoils. They're your rocks after all. Unless that treaty says they're not."

The Sureblood searched his face for a stunned moment, making it obvious he'd never heard the facts put to him that way. "No one's ever talked about it."

"Maybe someone should start."

Sureblood nodded slowly, dragging a hand over his shorn hair. "First thing, I need to meet with the other clan leaders, and tell them. We'll find out who knows what—and who owns what—if we have rights to those mines or not." Then his lips compressed. "In the bar I heard about your trouble with Val Blue. I can help. She'll listen to me."

"She thinks your clan assassinated her father," Frank warned.

"Once she hears what happened to me, she'll know my clan had nothing to do with the murder. Give me a chance to fix the situation. I have the means to end the feuding."

Nezerihm said the same thing, Frank thought, exhaling. But the mine owner suggested a coup, and this pirate offered dialogue. Or did he? Did he risk trusting the man? Or would he use the opportunity to take care of old grudges? "If you go out there and cause more fighting, the Triad will consider the zelfen mines at risk. We won't ask the clans to leave the Channels. We'll *tell you* and then back up the order with force. Am I clear? This ship may be tagged for a diplomatic mission, but don't let that fool you. The *Unity* has enough firepower to make your eyes water, and the permission to use it. I really don't want to see that happen."

"We're of like minds on that, Cap'n. Let me go to her. I'll talk to her."

"Perhaps easier said than done. I already know what Blue clan thinks of the Triad. I'm pretty sure they won't be too welcoming if the *Unity* shows up in orbit around Artoom. I'd rather not see torpedo damage added to the list you're racking up on my ship, starting with the broken barstool from your brawl…"

"I'll fly to the Blues, alone. I know where they hunt. I'll dangle myself in front of them and they'll pick me up."

"And kill you, if they consider you guilty of murder."

"Not right away." The Sureblood's eyes glinted with self-deprecating humor. "We pirates like to play with our prey before wolfing it down. If I know that woman, she'll want to punish me first—make me pay. I'll have time to set things right. Give me a shuttle. I'll go right now."

"A shuttle. One of *my* shuttles." Frank cracked a skeptical smile as he shook his head. "How the hell will I explain to Zaafran when you don't come back with it?"

Sureblood turned serious again. "I give you my word, pirate's honor, that I will. You already have my people and my world—Parramanta—as collateral. I want them back." His tone turned pleading. Whatever pride this man had, he'd left it at the door. "Give me this chance. It's all I ask. I promise you I won't fail."

Frank weighed his options. This former leader of the Surebloods offered a second, more moral solution to the Channels problem than Nezerihm had. A shuttle was a small price to pay for bringing peace to the region once and for all, wasn't it? A low-risk gamble. If the pirate chose to make off with the craft, the tracking device hidden inside wouldn't let him get far. It was an invisible leash.

"All right." He was game to see what this Sureblood could do before Nezerihm returned wanting to create a mutiny. "In exchange for your word, you have mine that I'll delay the evacuation of Parramanta. Your people stay put. For now."

The pirate's gaze reflected a far deeper gratitude than words could convey. They regarded each other for a moment longer. The Sureblood had put everything he cared about on the line to give Frank what he wanted. Frank was just as crazy, just as willing to risk it all and give the Sureblood what he wanted. It seemed they'd just gotten a crash course in each other's character.

And liked what they saw.

Frank turned to his first officer after the pirate left. "I have a suspicion things are about to get interesting around here, Lieutenant Gwarkk."

VAL WALKED WITH GRIZZ around the *Bull Dog* to survey damage from a recent raid. Scorch marks scarred the fuselage from front to back. Luranium had a distinctive odor when burned to a crisp. The air around the hull stank of it. They stopped at the aft engine pod and appraised the damage. The *Bull Dog* wasn't even attacking when it was hit, just moving close for a sniff. The damage was from a Triad warning shot. It could have been worse—they could have aimed to kill. Everything coming in and out of the Borderlands was under escort now. Worse, Nezerihm had tightened ore transport procedures, which threatened to put the skids on her dirt-side raids. All while the Triad kept up the pressure on her to move the Blues to a "better life."

"She'll fly again," Grizz said, "but she's gonna need downtime. We'll be one ship short for a while. One good ship."

Val hunched her shoulders and frowned. "Everything else is short around here—food, armor, fuel. We might as well add ships to the list." At least winter was months away. There was still time to preserve the fruits and vegetables flourishing in the expanded gardens. But with no money for weapons, armor or new zelfen blades for hatch busting, they'd eventually lose the ability to raid. And then she'd lose her position as leader. Her back was to the wall like no other time in memory. She closed her weary eyes for a moment, her entire body aching for the rest that wouldn't come.

"You can't go on like this much longer, Val," Grizz warned gently. "You need sleep."

"Sleep? Hells." She swore. "It's a waste of good thinkin' time."

"You need it to keep your edge."

"I'm fine." She avoided his warm, worried gaze. Grizz was right. She wasn't as sharp as she used to be. Her insomnia had become chronic. When the dirt-side raids started going well, she'd gotten a few hours sleep at night, but now with a decision to be made about marrying Ayl, she was back to lying awake. Not that he'd care if she wasn't a perky bride. She could grow a second head and he'd be just as eager to seal the deal. "I'm fine," she repeated for Grizz's benefit.

"Mama!"

At Jaym's enthusiastic yell, she tore her attention from Grizz's skeptical expression. She gave her tired eyes a quick rub and pinched her cheeks for color before Jaym came running up to them with Hervor's son in tow.

The boys had twigs in their hair and muddy knees and dozers made of sticks. A black camp-dog puppy with a white and pink roly-poly belly ambled after them. It wore a strip of leather around its neck with some scraps of zelfen tied to it. Jaym's loyal raider, Val thought, smiling. Everywhere he went, the puppy went, too. Ever since he could talk, he'd pleaded with her for his own dog. In light of her upcoming nuptials, an event she hadn't yet discussed with him but felt guilty about nonetheless, she'd relented and granted his wish.

"Mama, can me and Yanney go swimming?"

The morning chill lingered in the air. She hooked her thumbs in her weapons belt. "It's cold."

"Oh, Mama! I'm tougher than that."

"Me, too!" Hervor's small son declared, idolizing Jaym. It seemed her son collected followers like other children collected seashells.

"You used to say the same thing, girl," Grizz told Val. "Always telling us you were tough. Nothing was ever too cold or too hot, too high or too low. And look where you are now. Captain of our clan."

A bittersweet achievement, she thought, considering the circumstances that got her there. "You can thank

Grizz for convincing me, boys," she told the little ones. "I'll let you swim, but only if you find us some rock oysters for boiling up later at supper."

The boys whooped and scampered off toward the beach with the puppy. She was glad to know that the problems the clan faced were opaque to its youngest members at least. She'd give her eyeteeth to go back to the days of that kind of naïveté.

Like five years ago…when she thought she saw a happy ending in the rival clan leader's gaze?

Val turned her frown to the *Bull Dog*'s scorched hull when her comm alerted her to an incoming message: Reeve, calling from his way back from a salvage duty trolling the Channels for stragglers. "What have you got, Reeve?"

"Captain, you won't believe what turned up caught in our nets," he said. "A Triad shuttle craft. And guess who's driving it?" Reeve paused for dramatic effect. "Dake Sureblood."

CHAPTER TWENTY

VAL COULD HARDLY HEAR herself think above the furious pounding of her heart. No notice, Dake Sureblood had showed up, without his gangsters, and asked Reeve to tow him to Artoom. *Asked!*

Too many different reactions shook her to know what she was supposed to feel. Relief, rage, hurt—she careened from one emotion to the next like a skiff on an end run through the asteroids. In the back of her mind she'd always wondered if Dake might be dead. Hoped, actually. It would have explained away his disappearance. But he was alive and definitely well, and it gutted her heart.

This man, this betrayer, this thug, this *murderer* was the father of her child. *Ah, Jaym. I'm sorry for the genes he gave you.* How could such a sweet boy with such a giant heart be sired by a man who had none?

"Val. He's requesting to see you when he arrives," Grizz repeated for the third time, intent on driving the idea into her head once and for all as they strode along the path back to the village. "He keeps asking. For you. You heard Reeve. The Sureblood says we're in danger. He wants a meeting."

"The only meeting that man deserves is with the executioner."

"Hear him out." Grizz issued the advice in his mentor's voice that he hadn't needed to use with her in many years. "I'd like to kill him myself, girl, for what his clan's done to us, but don't forget he's come to us, not the other way around. He showed up unarmed and in a borrowed ship."

"Or stolen. We don't know. And he *is* a Sureblood. How do you know it's not a trick?" But Grizz had a point. It wasn't as if they'd tracked down Dake and caught him like a rabid dog. He'd come trotting to their front door, begging to be let in.

To bring them a warning. Bah. What did he really want from the Blues? From her? She was done feeding him pieces of her heart. Done! In all these years he'd never once made the attempt to speak to her. Of course by then she wanted to kill him. He'd never learned he had a son, but that was his own fault.

A sonic boom high in the sky signaled that the pair of ships would soon land. "Have an armed group of raiders meet the ship," she said. "Then run him through a gauntlet, all our clan lining the road." There hadn't been a full gauntlet used on Artoom in her lifetime, but she'd heard the old stories. Some didn't survive it. An image flared of Dake being kicked, rocks being thrown, him bleeding. Then she thought of Jaym watching the spectacle.

Hells.

"Don't hurt him," she mumbled. "At least not permanently. And not in front of the children. I don't want them watching this." She didn't want *Jaym* watching. "Bring him to the square and tie him up. Everyone can look at him there. Better yet, throw him in the chicken pen for display. It won't be for long, I aim to have him convicted by dinnertime."

Ignoring Grizz's astonished stare, she returned home to tell Sashya the news.

HANDS CUFFED BEHIND his back, Dake stepped off the ship and squinted in the bright sunshine. Artoom. So green under a fair-weather sky shot through with puffy clouds. The sea sparkled in the sunshine. The humidity was minimal and the air was warm. It was another world from the last time he was here.

Aye, and he was another man.

The breeze carried the smells of hearth fires and dirt, sweat and leather, and homemade soap. He inhaled deeply. How he'd missed the smells of a pirate village. Missed home. *Soon.* At least he was off that sterile spaceship and in a place and amongst people who seemed real.

And who very well might kill you where you stand.

Villagers swarmed close but Val's former skiff mate, Reeve, kept them controlled. Then Grizz, Conn's old friend, and some raiders took over from Reeve. The man's wary, questioning glance wounded him to the core. Like Reeve, he acted skeptical about Dake's honesty, given the war they'd waged with the Surebloods. From their view, he'd acted like a murderer, a warmaking coward who'd broken their Val's heart.

He searched for her in the crowd. No sign of her.

"This way, Sureblood." Grizz jerked his gloved hand to where a group of frowning clansmen decked out in raider gear waited for him, weapons ready to fire. It seemed his welcoming committee wasn't near as pleasant as the weather. In fact, it looked as if a squall was blowing in.

He recognized some of the sneering clansmen from the last time he walked this path. Ragmarrk was nowhere to be seen, but Ayl was there, looking older and somehow harder, his hatred for Dake vivid.

He'd been Val's lover once. Was he again? The thought set off a spark of jealousy he had no right having after all the years he'd been gone, especially in light of the warring between the clans. *So much for your hoped-for, rippin'-off-clothes reunion with Val,* he thought. Yet, if Ayl had indeed been successful in his pursuit of Val, confidence and possession would have muted the man's hatred.

Ayl drew his weapon and strode out from the protection of the group. "Welcome back," he said, and slammed the butt of his dozer across Dake's face, opening up a cut on his left cheekbone, the same place he'd been hit in the bar on the *Unity*.

Hands tied, Dake moved one foot behind him to keep his balance. Warm blood dribbled down his jaw. Pain radiated through his skull.

"That's for hurting Val." Ayl wound his arm back for another hit. "And this is for—"

"Ayl!" Grizz caught Ayl before he could strike him again. "It's not your place to do it. It's Val's."

Ayl hesitated, and for a moment Dake thought he

might defy Grizz, but he pocketed his dozer. His eyes smoldered as he sneered at Dake. "The next hit was going to be for leaving after the gathering, Sureblood. For running off like the murdering coward you are."

Dake had heard no different from the man in the bar. Or from Reeve on the trip back here. He saw it in Grizz's eyes. The entire clan might have been willing to believe he didn't kill Conn…if it hadn't been for the slugfest his people and theirs had had ever since.

He'd have his work cut out for him, proving it was Nezerihm's fault.

The raiders herded him toward town. Dake itched between the shoulder blades, half expecting Ayl or one of his hangers-on to lose patience and shoot him in the back. Always, Grizz remained near, overseeing as they paraded him past angry, jeering Blues lining the way up the hill.

"Assassin! Gangster!" the Blues called out, encouraged by Ayl's raiders. "You'll get your due, Sureblood."

Trash pelted him as he was propelled along the path in his silly, too-new Triad boots. Hells, he'd been hit with far worse than rotting fish and fruit, like whip lashes, armored fists, a wide variety of boots and even a piece of a broken starship wing once. He'd been aimed at, shot at and pistol-whipped by just about every known weapon in the galactic arsenal. The Blues would have to come back with a lot more than compost to make him flinch.

"Bully! Boar-blood drinker!"

"Spineless bastard! Killer!"

"We're going to cut you down to size. Then kill you!"

Their fury was wasted on him. The real criminal was hiding out in a faraway palace built with zelfen money—money that would be in pirate pockets had Nez's family not elbowed their way into their traditional homelands and took over what never belonged to them in the first place. At that very moment, Nez was safe behind his walls of luxury trying to figure out how the man he thought he'd killed was walking alive today. The man who knew what he'd wrought.

As the raiders took turns shoving him up the hill, a small boy scampered past and caught his attention. His hair was gold-streaked, his skinny arms and legs deeply tanned. He wore a stick shoved in his belt like a dozer and gripped another, longer one in his hand like a sword. A fat puppy raced after him as he dived from one tree trunk to another to peer at all the excitement.

A boy and his dog, Dake thought, feeling a smile come over him. It was like seeing himself at that age.

A hand slapped the back of his skull. "Eyes straight ahead."

Soon he was back to stealing sideways peeks in search of Val. Still no sign of her. She must have stayed away deliberately. It wouldn't surprise him. He knew how she was when angered. Now that anger was directed at him. Dake kept searching for her nonetheless. Just one look, one shared glance, that was all he asked. And he'd explain everything.

The boy reappeared. The puppy trotting with the child was black and white with floppy ears like his beloved Merkury. By now, Merk should have been enjoying a slower life as an aged dog, Dake realized with a pang. Napping in the sunshine, a little hard of hearing, a well-loved, graying, loyal old friend, while Dake's own children scampered nearby. But that was not how it turned out, for him or his dog.

You never know what life's going to hand out.

The full impact of what he'd lost slugged him in the gut, and what he wanted for his future came into sharp focus. He saw where he'd come from and exactly where he wanted to go. He'd settle for nothing less.

In that instant, the child's gaze connected with his. There was an instant jolt of recognition. Maybe they both felt it. Before Dake could make sense of it, the boy had vanished.

Another smack on the head dizzied him. "Eyes down, you piece of flarg!"

With new clarity aiding him, Dake was shoved and prodded to the center of the main market square that he remembered from the gathering. The same women as before sold hand-pies to the crowd, except this time he was the entertainment. Children ran every which way, and the camp dogs barked. The air smelled more like the sea than the forest from the constant breeze sweeping up the cliffs from the beach. He could hear the distant thunder of the waves, and remembered the salt limning the rocky jetties like frosted sugar the night Val showed him the baths.

An old gate used for a small poultry pen was thrown open with a rusted screech. A raider shooed the squawking chickens out and tested the cage rungs for strength.

"Get in, you cowardly prick," Ayl said.

The boy needed some attitudinal realignment, Dake decided. When the time was right, he'd bloody well deliver it.

Ayl closed and locked the gate behind him, then took a deep swig from a flask of moonshine another raider offered him.

"Hawkk!" Grizz called out. "Hervor!"

The raiders came forward at Grizz's call. Dake was relieved to see Val's other old skiff mate. He'd liked the man, though he doubted Hervor still felt the same about him. With Hervor ordered to stand guard, Grizz walked over to Dake with a blade in his hand. "Give me your hands, boy." He sliced through the leather straps.

"Where is Val?" Dake persisted. "I have to meet with her right away."

"She'll come when she's ready."

"I gotta set the facts straight, about the war, about Conn. And Val."

The older man pondered him. There was more gray hair in his ponytail, a few more lines crinkled near his eyes, but he was otherwise the same strong senior raider from five years earlier. "Son, that you came back is what matters. The rest will follow. But you have your work cut out for you. It ain't gonna be easy with her."

Dake nodded. "I had that feeling."

VAL SCRAPED HER HAIR INTO a severe ponytail pulled so tight that her scalp throbbed. She wanted nothing soft about her at the war trial.

It seemed an eternity before Grizz knocked and stomped through the door. He looked exhausted. Her mother greeted him dressed in a pretty shawl that matched the hem of her skirts. She'd dressed up for the first time in ages, as if she was going to a party. The lifelong bachelor took in her appearance with a sweetly gentle, almost boyish appreciation that caused her to smile coyly and dip her head. All of which was quickly hidden by the pair upon shifting their focus to Val.

By the heavens. Was there something going on between the two? Why hadn't she ever noticed before? They presented nothing but poker faces to her curiosity.

"Val, he took it like a raider, from start to end," Grizz reported.

She frowned at the note of respect in his voice. Dake had impressed Grizz. She didn't want Dake to impress Grizz or anyone. She wanted him to act weak and cowardly. She wanted him to act *guilty*. Then there'd be no other excuse for his actions.

Like his using you.

They moved toward the front door. Val paused on the porch to don her raider jacket. Like her mother's festive attire, the gorgeous sunshine seemed somehow wrong. Violent thunderstorms and torrential rain would have better suited the day, she thought as they embarked on their walk to the square.

"Just warning you," Grizz said. "Ayl got to the Sure-blood before I could stop him."

"I said I didn't want him hurt before the trial!"

"It was just a dozer whip in the face. Would have been more if I hadn't gotten there. He's okay, but if he's bleedin' when you see him, that's why."

"Ayl oughta be the one bleeding for not obeying my rules," she ranted. "Always taking clan law into his own hands, he is." *If his audacity knows no bounds now, what would he be like if we marry?*

"I reprimanded him, Val. Told him it was your place to mete out the punishment, not his."

"Good," she muttered. If anyone was going to exact vengeance on Dake Sureblood, it was her.

"Where is the Sureblood now?" Sashya asked. "Who's watching him?"

"He's waiting in the pen for us to start," Val said.

"In the chicken pen, Valeeya?" Sashya appeared aghast. "You brought a man many view as our enemy into our midst and put him in a flimsy cage in the middle of the square!"

Grizz's tone was reassuring. "I've posted raiders as guards, Sashya. Level-headed men."

"They are now, but moonshine's a-flowing. If you're not careful you'll never get your answers, Va-leeya. You'll have nothing to put on trial but a bloody corpse."

"It'll serve him right," Val muttered.

Sashya stopped in her tracks, propping her hands on her hips. "You don't mean that for a minute."

Val glared back, steaming. She wanted Dake to

suffer the way she'd suffered. She wanted him to taste the same loneliness, the fear and despair that she did. Then she thought of the irrepressible little boy who bore his looks and spirit, and the thought of killing Dake sickened her. She lashed out at Sashya. "Why are you defending him? You of all the people in the clan should be calling for his execution. He killed your husband. My father."

"He's *accused*. We never found proof."

"The Surebloods are our enemies, Mama. We are at war. If Dake's so innocent, then why did he want to destroy us?"

Sashya's shoulders sagged. "I don't know," she whispered.

They walked for a moment in silence. "You might want to believe he's an innocent man, Mama, but he sure hasn't acted like one."

Shouts in the direction of the square pulled Val's attention to where a tall stranger paced inside the enclosure like a trapped predator.

Dake Sureblood. Her heart stopped, then began to race.

The sight of him brought back every memory of that first nightmarish month after her father's death in excruciating detail. His abandonment had gutted her. Ayl had taken her actual virginity, aye, but Dake had taken something much more fundamental: her innocence. It had made her stronger and maybe even a better leader, but the learning process along the way had been agonizing. Five years of not knowing. Now he'd shown up out of the blue alone and unarmed with news of a "warning."

Sashya warned, "Don't make this personal, Valeeya."

Val turned to Grizz. "Go on ahead. I'll be right there. Mama and I need to talk."

Then she pulled Sashya close. Her voice was low and keen with intensity in her mother's ear. "All I ever wanted was to be a raider and sail the stars. But fate placed me in this position, Mama, as leader. Love for my family kept me here—my fear that something would happen to you and to Jaym."

Sashya started to argue, but Val stopped her. "It's not just the choices I make as leader that are important, but how they look in the eyes of our clan. Every day some look for reasons I shouldn't be captain. I'm not going to give them any—today or any day. I have a son to protect, Mama. Today I'm going to secure his future."

Her posture stiff with nerves and pride, she resumed the trek to the square. It would always be personal between her and Dake.

FERREN SPED AWAY FROM the docks as soon as she'd polished the last cargo door latch mechanism for the day. Dake Sureblood had returned, and Val was putting him on trial. She didn't want to miss it.

She ran hard up the path, slowing only as she passed the dirt path leading to the bathhouses and the lovely, deep, warm tubs there. *Be strong in the face of temptation.* As she turned to keep heading straight, she rammed into someone. She was always so clumsy on land. An instant later her arms were filled with a lean, fit body, her nose with a lovely male scent and her sight with a flash of a white smile.

"Reeve," she greeted breathlessly. She spoke only when she had to—on raids mostly—but she did like saying the names of her land-side friends, especially Reeve.

"Whoa, little water sprite," he said, laughing. "You nearly swept me off my feet."

His hands were slow to leave her back. As always he held on to her a little longer than she did him and, as always, thinking he'd hidden his disappointment that it was still so virtuous between them. He wanted them to be lovers. And more.

Her desire for him constantly collided with guilt, reminding her of her mission. Until she knew for certain Prince Adrinn was gone, she must not commit to another.

But there were times when Reeve regarded her with his sweet smile that her resolve wavered, like now.

"I was just coming to get you," he said. "Grizz ordered all raiders to report to the meeting house."

Hurry. She snatched his hand. The market square was crowded with the entire clan there. It had a carnival atmosphere at odds with what might happen later that night if the Sureblood was sentenced to death. A couple of raider apprentices rolled over the dirt, wrestling each other. A group of raiders stood nearby swearing and cheering them on as they passed a flask around. A group she knew well to avoid. Ayl bore a scar on the heel of his right palm from the night he got drunk and barreled into where she was soaking in a bath. In her element, the water, she was irresistibly alluring. It was the curse of her species. He'd wanted more than to share a soak with her, but she'd had a blade within reach. He was lucky she hadn't cut the whole hand off. Instead she'd made sure he'd think of her whenever he looked at the thin whitish line bisecting his palm.

She'd never told anyone about the incident, especially not Reeve. He would have wanted to kill Ayl. Ayl never bothered her again. If anything, he acted a little ashamed about the whole thing. She would have felt bad for Despa if anything ever were to be said in public about it anyway. The healer had been ever faithful to Ayl, and he'd been anything but.

She kept wary eyes on Ayl as he suddenly walked away from his group. At first, she thought his intent was to glare at the Sureblood in his flimsy cage. No leathers, no armor, the Sureblood wore a red, black and blue uniform without any personal markings to define it as his own. It was no uniform she recognized from any of the hunters who came to the water worlds in search of her people—and that was a good thing. It would not have helped Dake's cause if he'd aligned with her foes. This clan that had unwittingly provided her with cover all these years didn't know she was actively fighting in a war. Her people's war.

And that they shared an enemy.

Nezerihm.

Curiously, Ayl's narrowed suspicious eyes weren't on Dake at all, but on Val's son Jaym, who was fascinated

by the Sureblood. Ayl just as raptly observed the boy—
but not with affection or even protectiveness. His look
was lethal.

Why would he react that way to little Jaym, whom he
seemed at times to dote on? And then she noticed the
way the sunlight made Jaym's hair glow, turning it the
same shade of golden brown as…Dake Sureblood's.

Blessed Heart of the Sea. Ayl had just guessed the
identity of the boy's real father.

CHAPTER TWENTY-ONE

A CHEER WENT UP AS Val Blue entered the village square, accompanied by Grizz and her mother. Camp dogs barked and howled, joining the squeals of children excited by the ruckus. Voices called for his speedy execution. It seemed his trial was about to begin.

Pirate justice, Dake thought. He'd missed it, especially after seeing how the rest of the galaxy handled their versions of "justice."

Val turned to him, seeming to steel herself at the sight. The indefinable something between them that was there from the beginning hadn't faded. In their younger years it was a playful spark. Now it was more like the crackle in the air before an intense thunderstorm hit, leaving him wondering whether to take shelter or risk staying out to drink in the rain.

With the raucous shouts for his punishment filling the sunny square, she swaggered toward his cage, long-legged, her hips swaying, her expression chilly and hard but with a touch of smugness—like a hunter who'd bagged a particularly sweet prize and still needed to deliver the killing blow. The past five years had exacted a toll on her. Pale and thinner, she appeared almost fragile, a deceptive impression he was sure, remembering how she'd chased off Johnson's mediators only days ago. Inner strength aside, life had been hard on her. On both of them. He mourned the innocent young couple they once were, and for all that could have been. Maybe they'd find what they lost. Although at that moment he was quite sure she'd rather sink a blade into his heart than let him win hers.

"Mama!" The boy who had been spying on him from the crowd for hours darted out of hiding and tugged on Val's hand. "Mama, look!"

Surprise and disbelief shot through Dake. Mama? *Val?* The girl who wanted to be free as the wind had a child? So that was what he'd seen in the boy when they'd shared a glance. *Her.* The inexplicable rush of recognition he'd felt seeing the child made more sense now.

Hells be, Dake thought as he did the math. Val hadn't waited very long after sleeping with him to jump under the covers with someone else. Who was the father? Who'd usurped him in Val's world with so little delay? He hoped not Ayl. The thought made him downright surly as he examined faces in the crowd. The stinking chicken pen Val had stuck him in or the fact he'd been standing in brand-new Triad-issue boots for hours, impatient, tired, and with an empty belly wasn't helping.

"Come on and see, Mama. A real-life Sureblood, and we've got him in a cage for safekeeping!" The boy tried yanking her in Dake's direction. He clearly wanted to share his "prize."

Val had shed her hardness like a raider peeled off armor. The tender expression suffusing her face revealed how deeply she loved this child. It grabbed at Dake's heart. Kneeling down, she whispered something to him. The boy hung his head. She insisted, and then he nodded. He threw Dake a forlorn look before he pulled out his "dozer," firing at the sky as he scampered off with the puppy hot on his heels.

Then Val resumed her swaggering approach, circling the pen with the deadly patience of a sea buzzard on deathwatch. Her disdain was overly dramatic, engaging and enraging the crowd. It was all part of the act. She had to maintain an image for her people. It was the pirate way.

"Look at you," she muttered with disgust. "Showing up in a fancy Triad shuttle. Wearing Triad colors. And new boots." She shook her head. "A shame to see you in this condition, but it's not really a surprise. Did you think you'd convince us to leave our home, like their other messengers? Is that what you're after, Sureblood? Our eviction?"

Dake gnashed his teeth until his jaw ached and kept his composure. And it near killed him. "Your clan's in danger, Val. I'm here to warn you."

She laughed without a hint of amusement. "About what? The sorry state of our supplies to carry us through the winter? The lack of cargo ships to raid to fill the coffers back up? My own ships sitting grounded with battle damage that we can't afford to repair? There's nothing you can say that I don't already know. But whatever you've got to warn me about, say it, because I'm itching to get started on convicting you." She thrust a hand in the direction of the crowd. "And so are they."

"You already know the Triad wants zelfen. But if they don't think we'll let them have it, they're going to move us pirates out to get it. By force if they have to."

She snorted. "Let them try."

"I was on their ship, the *Unity*. Val, it's nothing like we've got. It could scorch Artoom in the blink of an eye. To survive this, we have to work together. We have to heal the divide between us. Here. *Tonight*."

Her gaze flicked to his at that, her fear revealed with her suddenly too-tight jaw.

"I swear to you, on the honor of my people and on my father's name, the Surebloods never declared war on your clan, and we didn't murder Conn Blue."

She turned, shouting over the hullabaloo, "The Sureblood claims he's innocent on all counts. If we find out he's lying, he'll pay with his worthless life!"

The Blues reacted enthusiastically, with the raiders' stomping boots pounding out a threatening undercurrent to the yelling and insults. Val turned back to him. "Hear that, Sureblood? It's blood they want. Yours."

"Are you going to give it to them?"

"That," she said, "is entirely up to you."

"Bull flarg. You control the proceedings here."

She grabbed the rungs of the pen, her voice lower and between them only. "If you think my power is secure, you are naive. I've got dissenters in the wings, waiting for me to screw up, no thanks to you."

He was suddenly aware of Ayl glaring at their new proximity, a hand resting on his dozer.

"I was abducted. Kidnapped and conscripted.

Drakken ambushed the *Tomark's Pride* leaving your system. We never made it home, Val. Everyone with me that day is dead. My entire crew. I sent Yarmouth to warn you."

She absorbed his words, horrified and dumbstruck. He tried to make sense of the darkness under her eyes, her obvious fatigue. What had happened to his spirited, fresh-faced Blue girl? Neither of them were the same people who met in that cold freighter's corridor so very long ago. Neither had weathered the years without damage. They'd suffered. But while his beatings had been mostly physical, hers had taken an emotional toll. He knew what had happened to him the past five years but what the hells had happened *to her?*

He was suddenly glad for that cage. He didn't trust his judgment if he were free in that moment to touch her. Denial and deprivation had toughened him, aye, but at the same time his pent-up longing for her would explode like a match to dry tinder if he were to take her into his arms. He scrubbed his face with a dust-caked hand. He was sweating in that stinking pen, trying to block out the chants calling for his death.

"No one warned us, no one said anything. I waited, Dake," she whispered. "I bloody well waited for word from you. I thought something happened to you." Her tone was low and raw, betraying vulnerability she clearly wanted to hide.

Yarmouth must have perished. And Merkury along with him. Fates, he'd sent them to their deaths. He slammed his open hand against the rungs. "Blast it, Val, you could have commed my clan and found out we never showed. It's too freepin' late now, but why didn't you?"

"If you wanted to contact me you knew where to find me. That's what I thought. Then you started crashing our raids. It was worse than anything we'd seen. Everywhere we went, a Sureblood ship was waiting. I didn't know how you'd know where to find us—every blasted time. It was almost is if you were intercepting our communication."

"Someone was, but not us."

Her golden eyes flashed like heat lightning over the plains before she narrowed them. "Who've we been fighting if it's not you Surebloods?" What little color she had in her face drained away. "Nezerihm," she hissed as the realization hit her. Then she scowled. "If you're lying," she warned. "If you're trying to make Nezerihm your scapegoat—"

"Nez isn't a scapegoat. He's a monster. Every day that goes by that you don't see it, you're one step closer to losing everything. He's got us by the throat. Unless we convince the Triad that he's the enemy—our enemy—we can kiss our homeworlds goodbye."

Her hand shook as she smoothed wispy strands of hair off her forehead. Then she flushed at his penetrating search of her eyes, lowering them before any of her secrets could be revealed. *She wants to believe you, but she's afraid.*

As chaos churned all around them, he brought his face closer. It was the only privacy they'd get. "What are you scared of, Val girl? That they'll find me innocent tonight? And then there'll be nothing more to stop us from being together and staying together? Conn himself gave his blessing to us going off alone that night. He knew what we'd be up to. We were young and innocent and taking our pleasure, aye, but it was more than that. I blasted well would have been your husband by now if not—"

"If not for the murder. If not for your leaving and never coming back. If not for your clan crashing every raid we Blues attempted. If not for a million things." Harshly, she whispered, "I hated you."

"You were falling for me. And I for you, Val Blue. Don't deny it, or it'll be my turn to call you a liar." He gripped the wires, leaning closer. "Go on," he dared. "Deny I'm not the one for you."

Sunshine spilled from the sky, forming a too-cheerful backdrop as they glared at each other. "Ayl and I are getting married."

"What?" he growled. *"When?"*

"I haven't set a date."

As he absorbed her casual tone, he couldn't help looking at her hands, reading the mixed signals they sent. Her fingers squeezed the cage wires hard enough to bend them. He remembered the precocious child, her son. "Is that boy his? Val, is he?"

He waited out her silence as sweat needled his face.

"No," she said almost too quiet to hear. "He's not Ayl's."

Whatever relief she read in his eyes, she hardened herself to it. Aching for her pain and feeling murderous rage toward Nezerihm at the same time for causing it, he cursed himself for not letting his suspicions run amok five years earlier. It would have made him more careful about watching his back that day he left Artoom. And Val's back. If he'd been more suspicious, more cautious, maybe he could have avoided conscription. Maybe, freepin' maybe, he could have married Val and that boy would be his son instead of some other man's.

No. He'd not cling to what might have been. He'd seize the day and move forward. "I swear, I will make things right. With your clan, and with you. If that's what it takes to get you to listen to me, then I'm asking you to start this trial. We don't have a lot of time."

She glanced to the sidelines where Grizz stood with Sashya and signaled with a nod. Then she took a few steps back and once more shouted above the hullaballoo. "The Sureblood claims he's innocent. He claims Nezerihm had Conn Blue assassinated and tricked the Sureblood into waging war with us Blues ever since! Let us see if he's right or wrong!"

It was pandemonium outside as the shocking accusation spread far and wide.

Breathless, she turned back to him. "I'll prove it," he said. "Everything."

In those golden eyes he thought he caught a glimmer of faith—in *him*—before the guards led him away. He hoped he was right about that, for he'd just dropped everything that mattered into this Blue girl's beleaguered hands.

CHAPTER TWENTY-TWO

RAIDERS HERDED DAKE BY gunpoint into the cool shade of the meeting house he remembered from the gathering.

They chained his ankle to a post in the floor but left his hands unbound. In front of him was a long rectangular table for the senior raiders, already filing in. Grizz, Val and her mother took the three center seats. Chairs for the junior raiders and stools for the apprentices were set up against the rear wall. It was going to be a full house.

Grizz took it from there, leaving Val to watch with her mother. He read off the charges against Dake, and they were many, causing an undercurrent of swearing and grumbles. He was certain it was about to get louder, a lot louder. Grizz lowered the sheet he held and leveled Dake with a piercing gaze. "So, you're saying that Nezerihm is to blame for the death of Conn?"

"And my father, Tomark Sureblood. Both men dreamed of unity, and were on the verge of making it happen when Nezerihm ended it. He had my father killed first and made it look like a ship accident. When Conn tried to keep that dream going, Nez made sure he died, too. Fearing Sethen and I would do the same, he knew he had to stop us, and any chance of our clans forging an alliance. We'd be too strong, stronger than him—his greatest fear. Sethen's crash was no accident." He met as many skeptical glares as he could, lingering on Sashya's. "He was murdered!"

The reaction was immediate. Squeezing her eyes closed, Sashya brought the tip of her shawl to her mouth and Val rubbed her back. The raiders' shouts soon drowned in the thunder of fists pounding on the table and, where there was no table within reach, of boots hitting the floor.

"Nezerihm went after me next," Dake bellowed. "He knew when I was due to leave Artoom, the day he killed Conn and set it up so I'd be blamed. The Drakken hunter ship he tipped off was waiting for me at the exact deep-space entry point we'd use to get back to Parramanta. Aye, *Tomark's Pride,* a nice, ripe ship of healthy males, ready for the picking. I was conscripted, locked up. And I stayed that way for more than five freepin' years." Saying the words, he finally felt the full impact of Nezerihm's evil. He tugged at the ankle chain, almost forgetting that because of that evil, he was still chained up like an animal. Boots thundered and murmurs of "he lived through it" and "caged and survived" and "no pirate ever has" were thrown from raider to appalled raider. There was nothing worse to a pirate than the thought of losing all freedom. Val turned her gaze downward, staring hard at her clenched fists. If he knew his Blue girl, it meant he'd gotten through to her playing the shock and sympathy card. Now he had to underscore his story with proof.

"Aye, you're looking at a man who's supposed to be dead. The only reason I'm standing here today is because the Triad needed to make room in their cells for war criminals. Nez decimated the leadership of our two clans, plowing through us one by one until Val was the only one left, and only because he grossly underestimated her abilities. Now he's going to come for her!"

And he'd never allow it.

"Nezerihm's the killer," many began to chant, adding to the cacophony as reactions to Dake's accusations spread like a Parramanta wildfire, consuming allies and skeptics alike. The mine owner wasn't popular, maybe even less so than Dake to some.

Ayl cupped his hands around his mouth. "You're lying, Sureblood!" He sat with the senior raiders now. Much had changed in the clan since Dake was last here. "No one gets conscripted and lives to tell about it."

Dake reached for the fasteners on his Triad uniform shirt and shrugged it off to his waist. The cuff and chain around his ankle jerked taut as he turned slowly with his arms held out to the side to display the gruesome evidence of torture and beatings. He wasn't ashamed by their gasps and curses. He considered the latticework of scars and burns across his torso a physical history of his years of captivity.

"He's not the only one with scars," Ayl declared, yanking up a sleeve to show a long puckered scar. "Look at this one. Got it when the hatch we busted blew too soon. There's more, but I don't feel the need for another striptease. Do you? All of us are banged up. In this clan only hearth huggers and children don't wear marks of glory. What that Sureblood showed us proves nothing."

Dake bent his right ear forward. "I got this, too."

Val sent Grizz to see. "It's a brand," Grizz confirmed. "Numbers burned into his flesh."

"It's how the Horde kept track of their conscripts," Dake explained. "Their soldier slaves." He extended his left arm. "The Horde gave me this, too." The Drakken eagle inked in black on the inside of his left bicep forever marked him as a soldier in the Imperial Army. Then he thrust out his other arm. "My Coalition prison ID. You need a nano-reader to see the numbers, but if you press down hard enough you can feel the ridges. Scar tissue from the implants." He swung his glare around the room, daring anyone to call him a liar now. Then he wheeled his focus around from Ayl to Grizz, then to Sashya and finally Val. She sat with her hands spread on the table. Her jaw was tight and her eyes a storm of emotions.

"But I saved the best proof for last," he said, and a fresh round of noise erupted. Pleased, he narrowed his eyes at his audience. He was no less a showman than any of these Blues.

His throat was scraped raw from the shouting, but he lifted his voice until it could be heard clearly above the ruckus. "I was on board the *Unity,* hitching a ride back home to Parramanta, to my people, and guess who I ran into coming out of the captain's office? Nezerihm himself. He was there, negotiating for our destruction."

The uproar he'd caused whirled around him like the vortex of an over-maxed thruster. Val was deep in talks with Grizz, her mother and a number of senior raiders. Their heads were close together, a huddle, their conversations muted. Several fights broke out around them. Others stood yelling their opinions, some siding with Ayl and others cursing Nezerihm and calling for Dake to be set free.

Free… He'd never be free until his people were released from the threat that was their future. Hells, all the clans. Their fates were irrevocably linked. Nezerihm had that figured out a long time ago.

A defiant yell tore through it all. "Don't believe the lying bastard! He's using Nez as a scapegoat." Ayl stormed to the center of the room with his posse and an awkward Despa. "All his scars and numbers prove was that he was captured. Even if he was gone for five years and he wasn't behind the raid crashing, it doesn't mean he didn't kill our beloved Conn Blue. What happened was he poisoned Conn and fled—and just so happened to run across a Drakken hunter ship. Bad luck, and the Surebloods deserved what they got. Nezerihm had nothing to do with it."

Ayl's mouth curved with pleasure at the new doubts he raised. "I'd like to remind you all that a Sureblood cup was found in Conn's hand that night, and what was in it? Poison…in the form of sharken he shouldn't have been taking considering his health concerns."

The crowd was starting to get worked up again. Ayl was convincing in his hatred of the Surebloods. He could very well shift favor away from Dake, even after he'd revealed the evidence of his imprisonment.

"The Surebloods bought sharken from Despa that

terrible night. Tell them," Ayl prodded the woman. "Did you sell sharken to the Surebloods?"

Despa tucked a curl behind her ear and spoke to her shoes. "Aye, I did."

"To whom?" Ayl pushed. "Which one?"

As she turned her eyes to Dake and opened her mouth to speak, rage boiled up in him. "I did not buy booster from that girl!" he bellowed.

But the ensuing boos told him there were few who believed him, even now. Just as he'd won many over with the atrocious evidence of his incarceration, Ayl had deftly coaxed them back to his side.

Pirate justice, Dake thought. Right or wrong, the verdict always depended on the last opinion taking precedence before judgment took place. Whoever was the best at convincing won the case for the accused or lost it. It was not, Dake thought, looking good for him. He'd already pulled out all his cards. No more aces in his pocket.

There was a sudden commotion as the slave girl they'd rescued from the freighter pushed her way to where Dake stood. She'd filled out and grown up since Dake had seen her last. Her hair was even wilder and longer, her eyes just as hypnotizing blue. But she wore raider gear, and her limbs were athletic and strong, reflecting hard training. Her expression was intense and determined despite her clear shyness. She'd never been meant for a pirate's life, he thought, but this was the life she'd adopted and in which she'd apparently thrived.

"Hells be," Grizz muttered to Val. "Ferren." Everyone else looked as shocked as Grizz was by her actions.

The girl clutched nervously at her trousers for a moment as she scanned the crowd. Then she clasped her hands together to stop the fidgeting. "I saw Nezerihm's aide at Despa's store that night."

It was the oddest thing, hearing that meeting house go silent with her bombshell. Pirates weren't quiet people. Only time would tell if that hush was a good thing or bad. Dake was glad for it; her breathy voice was difficult to hear as it was. And their silence spoke volumes about how curious they were about what Ferren had to say.

"I watched people that night. When I was new here, I did it often to learn about my new home." Her accent was as exotic as her appearance. Everyone strained to listen. She lifted her pretty chin. "I saw a man go to Despa's store. Nezerihm's man."

"How do you know he was Nezerihm's man?" Ayl demanded. "He could have been from any clan."

"Because I make observations *only* with what I see with my own eyes. Unlike some." Ferren cast a withering glare at Despa. "I recognized the man from those Reeve escorted that day. He called them Nezerihm's cronies."

Laughter went around, Reeve shrugging. "I was their assigned escort." Then he exchanged a look with Ferren that revealed love and concern. "I didn't know she was out wandering alone at night, though."

In answer to Reeve, Ferren smiled sweetly but without any apology.

"Despa," Val said. "Did you sell sharken to the crony that Ferren mentioned?"

Despa gnawed on a fingernail. *She wants to lie,* Dake thought, but this time she was struggling with it. Ayl acted completely disgusted, shaking his head and muttering something that caused her to blush. "No," she said in a small voice. "I did not sell him sharken."

Dake swallowed hard at her answer. He'd hoped she'd reveal something to help his cause, so he could get started on everything he'd come here to accomplish. They were spending time interrogating Ayl's little puppet when there was little of it to waste. How long before the Earthling Johnson started sniffing around for his shuttle? Dake promised he'd check in after a vague amount of time, but he could very well be dead by morning. Would Val let that happen? Could she keep rebellious raiders from defying her if she didn't?

It took many moments for the roaring to die down enough to hear Grizz shouting for everyone to shut up. "Ferren's got something else to say."

In her soft, accented voice, Ferren spoke to Despa directly. "Many purchased from Despa that night, this we know, but maybe she will tell us what Nezerihm's crony paid for if not sharken."

Despa clutched at her skirt as she and Ferren exchanged a glance. Ayl whispered sharply to the healer. She froze, her expression pained. Then, swallowing, she brought her chin up. "The man Ferren saw bought something else." Her chin came up. "And I told no one, not even Ayl."

The raider's furious gaze bored into her, but she seemed to gain strength as she went on, almost defiantly so. "He bought some pyro from me. It wasn't a strange request. Nez hated the cold. He's come for pyro before to raise his body temperature on visits here."

"Pyro," Val said. "It causes a fever, then."

Despa nodded. "Aye. A little goes a long way, too."

"Doctor," Val said to a woman sitting at the end of the table. "My father was running a high fever when he died. What was his temperature?"

"Why, I don't remember exactly, Cap'n."

"Ballpark," Val snapped.

"It was high, very high. Five degrees above normal or more."

"In the deadly range."

"With his medical condition, with the strain already on his heart with the alcohol, the squatter's and the sharken, aye." The doctor nodded. "It was easily deadly."

"Is pyro something you saw in his blood when you tested it?" Val demanded.

"You can't see it. Pyrogens are identical to what the body produces to fight an infection, or a poison. It's carried to the brain where it suppresses heat-sensing neurons and stimulates cold-sensing ones. If you're asking if Conn Blue could have been given the pyro as a poison, aye, he could have been and, aye, it would have killed him."

Val squeezed her eyes shut for a moment, hanging her head.

Ayl tried to argue but the man could barely be heard over the resulting commotion. The noise reverberated inside the meeting house, threatening to bring the entire structure tumbling down as swiftly as Despa's and Ferren's testimony had destroyed Ayl's case.

Val turned her head to Sashya. "Mama," she said, "do you have anything else you'd like to ask or add?"

"Aye, I do." Conn's widow dabbed the tip of her shawl to her eyes, drying tears she'd shed during the proceedings. "If the rest of you pirates don't grow some balls and kill that conniving, rat-faced, cave-dwelling monster Nezerihm, I will."

The biggest roar of all went up then. It was sheer anarchy, and it went on seemingly without end.

Val stood. Her eyes were moist, but her pale face rigid as she held her emotion, in check. Dake knew well how she felt. He'd rarely been as drained as this, and he'd been pushed to his limits countless times as the prisoner and slave of two civilizations. He thought the trial had gone in his favor, but he couldn't be sure. He thought about what Val had said about dissenters second-guessing her, and it ignited a flare of worry: would his innocence make her look guilty? Would his guilt solidify her standing in the clan?

Only with Ayl's group. The majority of the raiders in the meeting house were chanting, "Sureblood, Sureblood, Sureblood," and singing out death threats against Nezerihm. It was what he'd hoped to do here. A common enemy was the beginning of an alliance.

Dake waited out news of his fate, his adrenaline surging as Val hopped up on the table and ordered the raiders to shut up. It took a couple of shots fired from her dozer through the roof to clear a break in the bedlam resulting from the bombshells launched by the women.

"All right, Blues!" Val declared. "This trial is ended. Due to overwhelming evidence in his favor, I hereby spare Dake Sureblood's freepin' life."

Dake was mobbed. Reeve unlocked his ankle cuff. The rest of the clan swirled around him. He was bombarded with congratulations and offers of food and drink. Someone wanted to go for a spin in the shuttle and another thought Nezzie's skull would make a good waste bowl. But no apologies. It wasn't the pirate way. If he'd been run through a gauntlet, beaten up and put on trial, he deserved to be. It was that simple. Nothing more needed to be said.

He tried to make his way toward Val but was blocked by bodies. The doors had opened, letting in people from the square. Towering above most of the Blues, he used his height to search for her in the packed meeting house. He caught a glimpse of her braid swinging behind her as she maneuvered through the crowd like a skiff navigating the Channels at full speed.

Aiming for the exit.

Not so fast, Blue girl. Dake started after her, and then Malta appeared in his path, her grin crooked, her intent to get him drunk as obvious as the suspiciously uncorked bottle of moonshine in her hand.

CHAPTER TWENTY-THREE

VAL BURST OUT OF THE meeting house into the sunshine. One day five years ago, without warning her life was turned upside down. Now it had been righted just as violently and unexpectedly. It left her reeling, completely off balance.

"You've got to appear strong at all times, even when you feel weak. You already know how to do it, Val. It comes from somewhere deep inside you."

Grizz's words from long ago reverberated in her mind. Strength was more than fighting the enemy, she thought. It was recognizing the enemy.

Her enemy wasn't Dake. It never was.

Miraculously, impossibly, he'd survived conscription, imprisonment and stars knew what else. He'd aged more than the years away would warrant, but then maybe so had she. He'd lost weight, and his once-thick hair was cropped short. Stubble shaded the chiseled planes of his jaw. His nose had been broken, maybe more than once. A fresh cut and bruise covered his left cheekbone, thanks to Ayl, and his right brow was split by a thin, raised scar she knew wasn't there before. His entire torso was a showcase of man's cruelty to man, a far cry from the smooth, golden skin she'd caressed in the tub.

Then, he'd been a cocky young raider captain. Now he was a battle-scarred survivor of the worst imaginable hells.

Despite the battered surface he still looked so blasted good that she didn't trust her willpower around him any more today than she had five years ago, when the mere glint in his eyes lured her away from her duty and into the worst mistake of her life.

The square bustled in celebration and also with talk of war. "Don't you worry, Val, we'll pull that coward Nez apart, limb by limb," some clan folk called out to her as she strode past. "He'll pay."

He'll pay. Like they'd wanted Dake to pay. How easily they shifted their hostility to Nezerihm.

Nez killed Conn. He killed Sethen and Dake's father, too, and fates knew who else from other clans in his quest to squash them under his thumb. With Ferren's willingness to speak up and Despa's capitulation, Dake had convinced the Blues that the wily mine owner was in cahoots with the Triad and planned to pit the pirates against each other to exorcise them from the region. But the raiders who tended to side with Ayl would see Val's pardon as evidence she was soft on Dake. She'd let him escape once before. Now she had again, in their view. And it put Jaym at risk.

You knew that risk going into this trial.

Without Dake around, Jaym's resemblance hadn't been so obvious. Seeing the two together demolished that safety net. They were father and son. She was shocked that Dake hadn't noticed yet. He would soon enough. She'd escaped the meeting house before he had a chance to start asking questions. Or Ayl.

Especially Ayl. He hated Dake. What would happen when he found out Jaym was Dake's? Val's instinct to protect her offspring quickened her strides. She wanted to hunt down Jaym and drag him into the shelter of their home. But he wasn't in the empty fields or any of his usual haunts. Of course not. Everyone was back at the meeting house, exactly where she didn't want to return. It would cause too much curiosity if she were to force him to come inside. *He'll be okay. He's with the clan.* She held back from babying him. Sashya was there. If not her, then Reeve would be there, and Ferren, none of whom drank to excess. They'd be observant enough to spy any malice directed at her child. It gave her some time to think this over, and she needed it to consider her next steps.

"Val!" Despa caught up to her. "I have something to say."

"You said it in the meeting house."

"Not all of it." Despa had been crying, but her voice was steady. "I never said why."

"Why isn't important." Val wanted no delays with the healer who'd done nothing but make trouble at every turn. Who'd enticed Ayl into her bed the night Val gave up her virginity to the man. "You told the truth. That's all I care about."

"Please." She clutched Val's hand. "I can't keep it inside anymore. I'm sorry I let you think—that I let everyone think—that the Surebloods gave Conn sharken.

If it was clear the Surebloods were innocent, it would have made Ayl look bad. I loved him. I protected him. Wrongly, aye, but I was young and stupid."

"You redeemed yourself in my eyes for speaking up today about the pyro. I forgive you, Despa. Is that what you need to hear?"

She shook her head. "I'd rather you forgive Ayl, for going with me the night you were together. Back when we were young."

Val's face burned with embarrassment. The humiliation was so old, but hearing the woman remind her dredged it all up again. "Despa, I don't want to talk about this—"

Despa blocked her from leaving. Her expression was fervent. "I gave him sharken that night. A very potent batch. He was on his way to the springs to fetch you water. He meant to go back to your bed, but I got to him first." Despa's eyes filled. "I baked cookies laced with sharken. I told him to choose a few to bring back to you, but I made him taste one first. He couldn't fight the booster—or me. I seduced him, not the other way around."

Shocked, Val thought back to all the times Ayl had insisted that was the case, and how she'd laughed at him, accusing him of lying. He'd become the butt of clan jokes, until he finally gave up trying to set the record straight. He could no more explain his attraction to Despa over the years than he could his cheating on Val.

"The poor sot had no idea," Despa murmured. "Still doesn't."

"Why did you do it when you knew it would hurt me?"

"Because you had everything," the healer admitted. "You were the princess of our clan. Everything you attempted to get you got right. You were so perfect."

"I was never perfect, Despa…" If only the girl knew.

"But Conn loved you. And then Ayl loved you. I didn't think it was fair to always have everything you wanted, so I stole what *I* wanted." She pressed her pretty pink lips together and sighed. "I'll never live down my sins against this clan and you, Val, but I will spend the rest of my life making up for them. I hope I did a little of that today." Wiping her tears, she began to walk away.

"Wait," Val called out.

Despa turned.

"Why did you finally decide to confess all this?"

"You don't have everything. I finally saw that. You've lost more than I ever had. Instead of envying you, I realized I'd started to admire you. And I figured out you can't force a man to love you, no matter how much booster you bake in his cookies." She offered Val a small smile. "Ayl's free to be yours."

Val blinked as she watched Despa walk away. But she didn't want Ayl. She wanted Dake.

It left Ayl with no one.

An Ayl who was a different man than she'd thought,

driven to be insecure and defensive over something he hadn't intended to happen.

Fates above, what else would she learn this day? It didn't seem as if there were any secrets left. Val strode home at full speed, her brain spinning from the day of life-changing revelations.

She bypassed the house and went straight to the garden. Somehow it didn't surprise her to see Sashya waiting for her by the ebbe apple tree planted outside the back door, the same tree they'd looked at the day they learned Val was pregnant with Dake's child. The child he still knew nothing about.

"I knew you'd end up here," Sashya said.

"I'm glad I'm so predictable." Closing her eyes, Val leaned back against the smooth trunk to catch her breath.

A hand came to rest against her cheek, cool and soft. Not a hand that bore the calluses of busting hatches and wielding weapons, but one that was just as skilled and strong…with love. "I was so proud of you today. You're Conn's girl through and through. You've got his courage. His passion. His principles. Aye, and his stubbornness—in spades. His precious Valeeya, he loved you so."

Val smiled wanly as her mother searched her face. "Do you know what he told me the day you graduated from your raider apprenticeship?" Sashya asked. "That you deserved to be leader when he was gone. Tradition made him pick Sethen, but it was you he felt was most worthy."

"You never told me this," Val whispered.

"Had your brother lived, I never would have. A good mother doesn't play favorites." Sashya smiled with teary, tired eyes. "Dake Sureblood's busy trying to extricate himself from the celebration and find you. When he does, don't you run him off again."

"Oh, Mama—"

"Don't you 'Oh, Mama' me. Make it right between you. For the sake of your boy."

Jaym. Her heart stumbled as she realized their words would carry. "Where is he?"

"I walked him to Hervor's house and told him to play with Yanney. We'll both stay there overnight, so you two can have the house to yourselves."

Overnight. It was happening so fast. Way too fast. After so long holding on to hatred and guilt as an anchor, she was afraid she'd lose herself if she let go. Lose herself in Dake. "I need more time."

"Time for what? For *thinking?*" Sashya groaned when Val nodded. "Now you're sounding like the typical bachelor in this village. You were in love with that Sureblood boy, and probably still are. You surely hated him hard enough."

Val shoved her thumbs in her weapons belt. "At the gathering, I'd just met him. I hardly knew him."

"You knew enough. I was no more familiar with your father when we started our life together. Deep down, that's what you wanted with Dake. A future. But life didn't turn out how you wanted."

You never know what life's going to hand out. Dake told her more or less the same thing when relating how he'd lost his mother and sisters to a fire, and his father in an accident.

"Aye, I did want him, and it didn't turn out like I wanted," Val admitted, her heart full. "I wanted it to be different. Not like this."

"It hasn't always been easy for you, girl, I know. You've had to carry a lot on your young shoulders. But you gotta roll with the punches life throws you, not run from them. And throw your own while you can. Conn used to tell me that when times were hard."

Val's gaze flicked up. "You and Papa had hard times?"

"Plenty. Back when the clans first started fighting, when your father would be gone for months out raiding and me here minding the hearth fires, raising you and your brother, there were days I thought I'd die of loneliness. Then, when he did come home, Conn acted like a stranger, his head filled with what he'd seen out there and from what he had to do to make sure we Blues made it through another winter. I hated myself for feeling unhappy because of everything he was sacrificing for us. Aye, girl, times were hard."

Faced with her mother's frankness, Val burned with embarrassment. How naive and self-centered she was, sulking about her bad breaks, wallowing in them as if she were the only one to experience hardship. She'd always envisioned her parents' life together as a fairy tale. Apparently there were realities she could hardly fathom they'd shielded her from so well. Just as she'd shielded Jaym from the precariousness of his existence.

A day of revelations.

"But we loved," her mother said, softer. "We loved well, your papa and I. That and having you and Sethen made all the hardship worth it. Girl, you've got to stop blaming yourself for Conn's death. It's time to let it go, Valeeya. I was able to, and Conn was the love of my life."

"You weren't responsible for what happened to him, that's why."

"Neither were you. None of us were. No matter where any of us were that night, on duty or off, that no-good outsider bastard was aiming to murder our Conn and would have."

Accept it, Val's conscience willed her. *Make peace with it. No more indulging yourself with guilt, hanging on to it like it's the only thing you've got, when all you have to do is look around and see you already have what really matters. Your clan, your family.* And this man, she thought, as the garden gate opened and slammed closed, allowing Dake Sureblood into the yard. "I was looking everywhere for you, Val."

Val's heart melted. Then she glanced around as if looking for an excuse to escape.

Sashya frowned at her reaction to Dake. With a big sigh, she tossed her shawl around her shoulders and glided over to Dake. She was more than a foot shorter, but might as well be six feet taller the way he acknowledged her with a respectful nod. "You'd be a fool, boy, if you agree to any of her silly reasons why it won't work between you and let her slip out of your hands a second time. You've got the house to yourselves tonight. Use it." A moment later she was gone, sailing out through the garden gate.

Then they were alone, or as alone as two people could be on Artoom. The hush of the summertime woods surrounded them. In the distance, the sounds of a celebration in full swing could be heard.

He started across the yard, his boots sinking into the thick turf. She'd forgotten how tall he was up close, how big. He wasn't the brash and boyish young raider she knew, but his eyes were still as gorgeous as she remembered, still as able to steal her composure—and her wits. His grin was still as sly, his teeth white, his lips no doubt still capable of making her dizzy.

Sunlight filtered the tree's lush leaves and tiny ebbe apples. So pretty, she thought, taking in the sight for a moment to blunt her reaction to Dake's proximity. "My father planted this tree. I come here sometimes when I need to think. Maybe we need to…think about this first."

"Bah. Behind bars there's plenty of time for thinking. Too much. I'd say I'm pretty much all caught up." He brushed his knuckles over her cheek. "Blue girl." The look on his face made her shiver. "I want you."

She knew what she wanted, too. *Him.*

Then she remembered they had a son together that he didn't know about.

"Blast it, Val. Every time you frown like that it makes me want to kiss it right off your mouth."

Heat flared in her face and spread throughout her body. "Then what's stopping you?"

The soles of her boots skidded over the damp grass

as he hauled her close, his tongue sweeping into her mouth, making her head spin and her body melt. His scent filled her nostrils, spicy and exotic, and she sensed his desire for her on an elemental, almost animal level. She flattened her hands on his uniform shirt, stretched tight over his chest, and tried to hold on to some impression of control of the kiss—of *everything*.

But the embrace was too many years in the making. She was as ravenous for him as he was for her. She half thought he intended to take her right there under the tree when they managed to recover enough common sense to move inside to the cool silence of the house.

Kissing, they stumbled to her bedroom. His rough and scarred hands stroked her upturned face as he shoved the bedroom door closed with his boot. She unhooked her weapons belt as he tore open his uniform shirt, the breeze from the ceiling fan whispering against their locked mouths. Off came their boots and her jacket. Still, it felt as if the clothes weren't falling away fast enough. She reached for his pants. Her knuckles grazed over the huge bulge straining his fly. The pants were gone and he trapped her between his hard body and the cool wall.

She untied the binding around her braid; he combed it out with his fingers. Her lips found his throat and traced a scar; he quickly and tenderly slid the strap of her camisole off her shoulder. Together they yanked off her bra.

Hot skin to hot skin, the kissing grew frenzied, him pressing her up against the bedroom wall. It was as if they feared they'd never have enough time to be together, the clock ever ticking, and that they somehow had to draw enough from this encounter to last another five years.

"And Ayl?" he rasped in her ear, his breath hot. "He's not sharing that bed, is he?"

"Would it matter?" Ravenously, she kissed him all over his face.

"If you're here with me, then it means your heart's not his."

"It never was," she murmured fervently against his lips. "Nor was this bed. Ever."

Dake seized her mouth fully, lifting her, his fingers sinking into the flesh of her thighs to hold her close, as if he feared she'd disappear before he could take her. A harsh grunt and he sank himself home.

He caught her cry with his mouth as they grappled for each other, skin slick and mouths hungry. No time for talk, they let their caresses speak for them. An exquisite pressure began to build deep inside her as she clutched at his heaving shoulders, gripped in his arms, riding the tidal wave that was her response to him.

That had always been her response to him, she thought. *There's no stopping it.*

She was too hungry for him, too frantic, to worry about making it last. All too soon she was arching into his body, muting her cry of surprise against his shoulder as she came apart, her thighs trembling with exertion. He lowered his head and let himself go, lasting only a few more plunges, his body shuddering, his breaths hissing as he swore at the intensity of the moment.

Then, finally, quivering and incredulous, their bodies wrapped together, they sagged against the wall.

The fan whispered a breeze over their overheated skin. He stroked her hair and she held him. He didn't need to tell her it would be all right now that he was back. Every beat of his heart promised it was true.

Finally, Dake lifted his head and searched her face with opalescent eyes and a lazy grin. "Again, Blue girl?" he dared, falling with her onto the bed.

"You're *asking?*"

Laughing, he took her head in his hands and dragged her back to him.

THEY SAVORED EACH OTHER as the afternoon deepened into evening, and finally padded to the kitchen to eat when it was late. Val cast a glance outside, hoping Jaym was okay, then got busy foraging for the food Sashya had thoughtfully left for them. The simple act of ready-ing a meal seemed to bring Dake to his knees.

"It's been so long since I was in a home, eating a homemade supper." Harsh emotion cut off the rest of Dake's words. He'd slipped back to a dark place, a place she didn't want him being.

She slid a hand down his cheek and jaw, summoning him back to the moment. "I want to know everything that happened, what the hells those outsider bastards did to you."

He shook his head. "No, you don't."

"But how did you survive it? No pirates do. How did you escape the Drakken? How did the *Unity* come to find you? You've got too many stories to keep them all under lock and key. Besides, our raiders can learn from them."

He was quiet for some time before he spoke. "There were times I wanted to lie down and die and be done with it all," he began. "But it would have meant never seeing my clan again, never seeing you. Never achieving our fathers' dreams."

What details he left out his body revealed. And what those scars and brands didn't say, his eyes did.

He'd suffered. He'd survived. And now he was back.

"We've got work to do, Val, plans to make." He tore into a hunk of bread and cheese. "Meetings. Another gathering—but this time in secret."

"We can't pass the word around the usual way, Dake. Nezerihm's listening. Eavesdropping. He intercepts our comms on raids. I'm sure of it. How else does he always seem to know where we'll be?" Dread crept in. "How long before he knows where you are?"

"Johnson fooled him with a story to throw him off the trail, told him I was going back to prison. If we're careful, he'll stay fooled."

"If we're silent," she cautioned.

"Aye. There's always good old-fashioned note passing and talking face-to-face," he said as he dangled a morsel of meat for her to nibble right from his hand. "Starting tomorrow, no one touches any of the Nezerihm mining transports. And no more fighting between ourselves. The zelfen must remain free-flowing. We can't risk spooking the Triad, and that means Johnson, or we'll find ourselves sleeping in donated boxes someplace no one else wanted to live. Everything we do from here on out has got to inspire confidence. The better we look, the worse Nez does."

He used a blade to hack off more meat that he dredged in gravy and devoured. His appetite didn't abate a specken as he shared his vision. "From what I can figure from listening to Johnson, we can stay here in the Channels, as long as we quit fighting and keep the zelfen going where it needs to go."

"And live on what—air? Dake, we gotta be able to raid to eat."

"Not necessarily. We pirates signed a treaty with Nezzie's ancestors so long ago no one remembers anything about it."

"When zelfen was discovered," she said, nodding.

"More like when the Drakken and the Triad discovered we had it. Zelfen had no value to the Nezerihms until it had value to them. We signed that treaty to stop fighting each other so we could fight them. What does it say? Maybe we own those mines. We gotta find a copy."

Her heart beat faster as she saw what he was getting at. Independence. Freedom. Not having to leave. "We have to ask the grand-elders if any of them remember hearing about it from their grand-elders. But, Dake, we're not dirt scratchers. We're pirates."

"Hells. Let Nezerihm scratch the dirt for us. We'll just take the booty and sell it. Right now he's keeping it all, and that's not right, not when it's our rocks he's digging."

Pirates as legitimate, law-abiding business owners.

It was an idea so revolting that she instinctively recoiled, yet one so bold it shocked her that no one had ever proposed it before. Having a share in the mines would end worries of hunger and the pressure of the ever-increasing risk of raids she'd never have attempted if times were better. She could give Jaym a future he'd lose if the Triad made good on their threat to evict them.

Dake wolfed down huge quantities of food like a starving man as he relayed his dreams, his eyes glowing with his passion.

Not all that different from Ayl and his passion, she thought, pushing around the food on her plate with a crust of bread. Dake wanted unity, but Ayl wanted power. He expected to marry her to get it. Now Dake was back, and she wanted him. More than she could ever have imagined. What would happen now?

She'd have to do what was right.

And not necessarily popular.

Dake's voice trailed off as she got up from the table and walked to a window, moving aside the curtain to peer outside in the direction of Hervor's house.

"You miss your boy," Dake guessed, gentler. "If you need to go be with him, I understand."

She bent down to caress his cheek with a tender, appreciative hand. "I'll see him at first light. If he doesn't invade here first. He listens, but not always."

He pulled her onto his lap. "I noticed him right from the beginning. As soon as they shoved me into the gauntlet."

"What? He was there? I told him not to go. He disobeyed me."

"A boy with spirit, he is. A mind of his own. Just like his mother." He laughed. "Nothing less than you deserve, Blue girl. If it helps his case any, he stayed undercover and out of sight of the raiders."

"He saw you beaten." She touched his swollen cheek. It had been cleaned, but it might scar, joining all his others.

"Aw, they weren't too hard on me. He followed me the entire way, he and his pup, on an adventure, just the way I once was with my dogs. My favorite was Merkury. Ah, ol' Merk. I rescued him from a scientific breeding facility doing intelligence augmentation experiments."

Her brows lifted in surprise. "I knew he was smart, but not how smart."

"I don't now how advanced he was, really. I simply allowed him to be a dog. A real canine raider, he was. Brave, loyal and all heart." His mouth contracted with sadness he managed to fight off. "What did Jaym name the pup?"

"He hasn't yet. He says he's still thinking. That's the part he gets from me. The rest, well, he's his father through and through."

His mouth turned down at that. "How old is the boy? He must be five years old."

"Almost."

"I've got no right to complain, but, Val, you didn't wait very long taking up with someone else after me.

Aye, I know the reason—me disappearing and all—but it seems awfully quick."

She propped her hands on her hips and grinned at him. "You're jealous."

"Of course, I am!" Dake appeared more genuinely hurt than angry at the thought of her seeking solace from another man, even under the circumstances.

"His father's an incredible man," she said quieter. "As a raider, there are none braver. As a lover, he's got no equal."

Dake spilled her onto her feet and lunged up from the chair. "Why didn't you marry him if he's so great?" He reached for his glass of wine and downed it. "Well, why didn't you?"

"He wasn't available for marrying." Her voice thickened with emotion. "Neither was I. I never admitted it, and even denied it, but I was always waiting for him to come back to me."

Dake focused on her with Jaym's same probing, perceptive gaze. They even shared the same furrow of concentration between their brows.

"And you did come back." She whispered, "That man was you."

He froze, searching her face. "Jaym. He's mine..."

Eyes brimming, she nodded. "Aye, Dake. Your son."

CHAPTER TWENTY-FOUR

I HAVE A SON.

A son! He'd never envisioned this. Dake's heart slammed hard as he stared back at the *mother of his child*. His hand shook as he drove it through his too-short hair. "I have a son," he whispered. His voice was as raw as his shock. "*We* have a son." He blinked, trying to take it all in. Then he laughed out loud.

They drank wine as Val told him the story of the weeks and months after his capture. Everything she could recall, right up through the birth.

Listening, hatred gripped him again. Nezerihm took that experience from him. Stole that moment of joy forever. It was incomprehensible the true measure of his evil.

"By blood, Jaym's next in line for succession to be clan leader," Val said as the conversation turned more serious. At the table, by candlelight, the sounds of a party raging outside, they weighed the risks of their son's mixed heritage. "It was expected that whatever man I married would claim Jaym as his, too. He'd have the future clan leader, under his influence. To someone like Ayl that power is irresistible."

"You were going to marry him."

"For Jaym, I would have, aye. Better to be held in the

enemy's embrace than be his target, I thought. When I agreed to hold the trial, it wasn't so much to determine your innocence or guilt but to assure my child's future."

Suddenly everything Dake had dreamed of took on more meaning. He could see why his father had been so willing to risk his life and reputation meeting with a rival captain in a bid for unity. He did it for Dake, just as Dake would do the same for Jaym. "I want him to grow up free, Val, knowing both of us and in a life he can be proud of. Jaym will be the symbol of unity between our clans, the future leader of both the Surebloods and the Blues."

"Careful," she warned. "You're why I kept his paternity secret all these years. Ayl and the others already suspect I had feelings for you. Now I've gone and declared you innocent. By morning they'll know I've taken you into my bed. It raises the stakes. If it looks like surrender to any of the dissenters, I'm done. I'll lose my leadership position, my place in the clan and maybe even risk losing Jaym, if the clan decides to keep him and raise him as one of their own instead of exiling him with me."

"Never," Dake growled. "They'll have to take both of us out."

Outside the window, a pair of drunk raiders passed by and vanished in the twilight. A giggling girl ran hand in hand with her beau toward the square where the party was still going on. A popping noise erupted, sounding like gunfire, and sparks lit up the sky.

Val walked to the window and closed the curtains.

Jaym was safe with Sashya, she told herself, tucked into bed by now, fast asleep and dreaming of fishing and battles. And Ayl? Was he drunk on moonshine and hunkered down with his posse, plotting? Questioning her decision, Jaym's paternity and cooking up a way to remove Dake from her life?

She heard Dake's chair scrape backward. His big hands landed on her shoulders, giving her a reassuring squeeze as he kissed her neck.

She leaned back into his warm body. "It won't be easy being with me, Dake. I'm leader of my clan, not some timid girl content to stay by the hearth fires. I'm never going to be that kind of girl, the kind you're supposed to marry."

"You're exactly the girl I want to marry." He turned her, lifting her hands and setting them atop his broad shoulders. "Brave, beautiful, smarter than me. Makes me so crazy I want to howl at the moons. Makes me want to go out and slay all the evil in the galaxy just to keep her safe." His voice deepened with feeling. "Makes me want to be with you day...and night. Come on. Let's go back to bed."

He took her chin between callused fingers. The look of tenderness and determination in his handsome face as he searched hers turned her to mush. "I promise you'll like it," he crooned in his rumbling voice.

And she did.

"BRING ME A GIRL," Nezerihm said. "I don't care which one."

An aide bowed deeply and scurried off to do his

bidding. Nezerihm didn't really care which whore they chose. He'd been so overwrought since learning Dake Sureblood was alive that he needed some adrenaline to break the mood. The last girl he'd entertained was recovering in the company hospital. Her own fault. She shouldn't have jumped from the balcony. He was only having a little fun, and the game wouldn't have hurt much. She was better than most, so very frightened. He'd loved it. But the residual benefit wore off quickly. He needed another fix.

The door to his bedroom chimed. That was fast. Rubbing his hands in anticipation, his robe swirling around his bare, muscular legs, he strode inside from the balcony. "Enter, please."

"For you, my lord." Another aide hesitantly offered his ringing PCD on a platter and stepped backward. Nezerihm enjoyed the fear in the aide's eyes. He must ask for this one to serve him again. Few showed sufficient respect these days. Not so in his father's day when a Nezerihm was a true lord among men. He vowed to return to that. He was working on it.

Until that bastard Dake Sureblood came back from the dead.

"Who wants to speak to me?" he snapped.

"My lord, it's your contact on Artoom."

His brow lifted in pleasant surprise. Ayl of the Blues. Nezerihm couldn't help feeling sorry for him. The second-rate pirate actually believed he was going to be rewarded for his service. Had Nezerihm *ever* rewarded the boy? Not once that he could recall...unless one counted the praise he heaped upon him. Ayl thrived on it. Praise was easy, and it came cheap. As did men like Ayl. No harm in letting him continue to believe he'd be leader of the clan because before that ever happened the Blues would be gone. It just proved how brainless and gullible the entire race of them were. They'd be better off in zoos.

Which was, he thought, exactly what the Triad intended to do with them. Relocation. Nezerihm could hardly wait.

"Val Blue better not be up to more of her land-raiding antics," he muttered and hooked the PCD over his ear. "Greetings."

"I thought he was dead," Ayl blurted out, sounding distressed. "You said he wouldn't give us any more trouble."

Dake Sureblood. Nezerihm's stomach fluttered. He knew it without another word being said. The man escaped Triad custody and ran straight to Val Blue, drawn inexorably to the wench like a stray dog to a bitch in heat. He should have guessed it, knowing those Surebloods. Animals. "He escaped. He was in Triad custody."

"Well, he's not now. He showed up today in a Triad shuttle."

A fugitive with stolen property. Nezerihm's first instinct was to tell the *Unity* where they could retrieve both. Then he realized the benefits of keeping this secret between he and Ayl. They could accomplish a little vigilante justice that way.

"We put him on trial. I thought we'd convict him. All charges were dropped."

"Dropped!"

The aide flinched at his yell, treating Nezerihm to a lovely jolt of pleasure. He eyed the man with sudden interest. Aides were as dispensable as whores.

"Aye. He's got all of them under his spell. Val and the rest of the sympathizers are convinced you're the guilty one. She's with him now. She's going to marry him instead of me."

Nezerihm could visualize Ayl's lower jaw jutting out. "You have every reason to be upset. She's sharing his bunk instead of yours."

"It's not right."

"No, it isn't. She's with him when it's you who's the clan's top raider."

"Maybe not top, but close. They don't see it that way. Not even my father does. They're blind to everything but the Sureblood's charm and his speeches chock-full of nonsense."

"That's why you have to act—because they can't. He's a dangerous fugitive, the most wanted man in the Borderlands. We'll return him to the Triad, and be rewarded beyond our dreams. Lauded as heroes, Ayl. Everything you want will finally be yours, including your sweetheart Val. Every last upholder of law and order in this galaxy wants that man put away for good. *Every decent person,* Ayl. You must deliver Dake Sureblood to me. *Alive.*"

"I have a better idea. You know Val Blue's boy? Well, it wasn't until I saw them side to side that I realized he looks mightily like his father. Aye, he's Dake Sureblood's get."

A Sureblood-Blue heir. Speechless, Nezerihm peered out the windows open to his vast lands. The lights of his refineries twinkled like stars. More lights glowed in the sky crowded with ships coming and going, loaded with ore. He'd been so worried about losing it all. Now suddenly his destiny was lit up like a glorious sunrise when all had been looking so dim. He'd take control of the boy and in doing so neutralize his greatest threat.

It was all so perfect.

"I want that boy, Ayl. Bring him to me—and let no one know."

The weakling pirate started to protest, sputtering.

"Not to *harm* him, but to find another loving family to raise him. A family...far away. Then after you get rid of Dake Sureblood, Val will have nothing but you. No disgusting half-Sureblood bastards running underfoot."

"True," he mumbled. Paused. "You promise you won't hurt the boy?"

"Of course not." Nezerihm imagined the boy looking up at him with abject terror. Emotion overcame him and he let it be heard. "Fate has given you a singular opportunity to save us all. I'm depending on you, Ayl Blue."

With that he ended the call, exhaled and motioned to the quaking aide. "Come with me outside. It's a lovely night to take in some fresh air." He tossed the PCD aside and threw open the doors to the terrace.

"Y-yes, my lord." Swallowing audibly, the aide followed.

JUST BEFORE DAWN BROKE, Val rolled over in bed to watch Dake sleep. She didn't envy his being able to rest, but reveled in his obvious contentment. She traced the line of his mouth, so much like Jaym's, and felt a swelling of deep attachment for the man she'd never known before. What would Jaym be like when he grew up? Brave like this raider? As patient and caring and steadfast, too? With the power to charm a woman right off her feet, like Dake did with her?

With a start, she realized Dake's eyes were open, crinkled with laughter as he studied her. "That's cheating," she complained. "You didn't tell me you were watching."

"Neither did you." He drew his arms over his head and stretched, a bit stiffly as he groaned, playing like he had aches and pains. "You've ridden me hard, girl. No mercy."

"Nothing a nice long, hot bath couldn't remedy." She winked at him, and he laughed. "I missed that laugh," she said.

"I missed laughing."

It made her sick what had happened to him. What Nezerihm had caused. She pushed upright and swept her hair over one shoulder. Outside it was already first light. She squinted in the direction of Hervor's house.

"As soon as he wakes we'll see him, Val. In the meantime…" He grabbed her and pulled her down to the bed and into his arms. Then paused, seeing her exhaustion. "Didn't you sleep well?"

She shrugged. "I can't, most nights. An hour or two here and there, sometimes more."

"Since when? Since I left?"

"Aye," she whispered. "A long time. I've tried drinking myself unconscious, even nearly got myself addicted to squatter's for a time. The meds I get from the doc leave me too groggy, so I take them only when I absolutely have to. Most of the remedies blunt my edge."

"So does fatigue, Val." He rolled her onto her back and gazed down at her. "It's your worry for Jaym that's keeping you up nights now. You're not struggling with your own fear, but your fear *for him*."

"Aye," she whispered. He bore his scars on his skin; she revealed hers through her bouts of insomnia.

"You don't have to carry that fear alone anymore, I swear it, Blue girl. It's going to take guts to get through all this, which I know you've got. And it's going to take trust—in me. You're not alone anymore. You got me. I won't leave this time." He laced his fingers with hers and squeezed. "Am I clear enough? I won't ever leave."

"You'll want to go to Parramanta. To see your clan."

"We'll go together. Grizz can take care of things here. Jaym will come with us, and meet the rest of his family."

Real excitement sparked inside her. Then the front door slammed and a little boy's indignant voice cried out. *"Mama!"*

Val jammed her feet under the sheets and yanked them up to her neck. "Cover up," she ordered Dake, pulling the quilt up his legs.

Incensed footsteps marched down the hall. "Mama, are you here? Grandmama said you were."

"Aye, in bed, Jaym," Val called.

"She said you were busy and not to come, but I just had to." The bedroom door was flung open with a bang and Jaym swaggered into the bedroom with so much more presence than his tiny size would explain. Chest heaving, still in his pajamas, a stick "dozer" in his little hand, he looked from Val to Dake, his mouth opening in a circle of surprise. "Hoy!" he cried. "The Sureblood!" His delighted face swung to Val. "Are you friends now?"

Val laughed. "Aye. We are." She beckoned to him and he crawled up into bed and lay down on top of the quilt, looking as if he intended to snooze away the last hour before dawn between their sheet-swathed bodies.

She turned to Dake, whose expression of joy intensified her feelings for him and almost made her weep. "Do you want to break the news, or should I?" she whispered.

Dake gestured to them both, indicating that they'd share that duty. "But not yet." For all his insistence that there wasn't ever enough time, he seemed content to spend a little of it lost in the innocence of watching his boy drift off to sleep.

THE DAYS THAT FOLLOWED were the happiest of Val's life, marked by revelations, purpose and action: her love for Dake blossoming, their living as a family with Jaym and Sashya and planning for the clan's future. Jaym shadowed his "Papa" every waking moment. When he was too exhausted to keep his eyes open at the end of each long day, he'd fall asleep in Dake's lap at the meeting table where the senior members of the clan plotted and argued deep into the night, as he made good on his pledge to heal broken treaties and old wounds.

Then they took the campaign off-world. One by one the Calders, Feckwiths, Lightlees and Freebirds threw their support to Dake. And when at last he returned to his beloved Parramanta for a reunion with his family and clan, a sight both wondrous and wrenching to witness, the Surebloods sealed the final breach between the clans. For the first time in a generation the pirate clans were one people. And for the first time ever they'd agreed to official talks with outsiders.

On the *Unity*.

The *Marauder* sat outfitted and ready to depart in the morning for a historic trip to the *Unity* at Captain Johnson's request. Val made one last circuit of her ship, checking and rechecking the hull, thrusters and cannons, as if they hadn't already tweaked the craft to top form. As always, they'd taken every precaution to evade Nezerihm's detection that they knew how. Grizz would stay behind and keep alert for any trouble.

While Val hadn't yet managed to sleep an entire night, what rest she was able to get eased her exhaustion. She'd been eating better, too, and fates knew, loving better since Dake's return, and it had all made her stronger in the face of an uncertain future.

She crouched down to rub her finger over a repair on the inner leading edge of one stubby wing. The peace

Dake had promised Frank Johnson would open the door to winning their fair share of the profit generated by Nezerihm's mines.

Nezerihm must know by now they didn't intend to cooperate with him. Rumor had it that he'd put out the call for Dake's capture as well as hers, with huge bounties on their heads. She responded with a round-the-clock patrol circling Artoom. No one got on or off her world without her knowing.

First through the blockade were the Surebloods. As she rose to her feet she sniffed the air and grinned. The scent of the meat they'd brought with them being roasted over a fire drifted up from the beach. Music and laughter, too, as the rocky relationship between the two largest of the pirate clans took a new turn. Torchlight flickered in the strengthening breeze. The feast between the Blues and the Surebloods would formalize their clan leaders' intent to marry. Most raiders saw it as the celebration of an alliance between the people of the rains and the people of the plains. Sashya of course called it "my daughter's engagement party."

Val smiled, smoothing a hand over the lush green fabric of her best dress, the one she never got to wear for Dake the first time, and swished the skirt, testing its swirl for slango.

"Hoy, Val!"

The shout caught her mid-spin. Blushing, she threw her focus to Ayl entering the docks. He was dressed in raider gear for his shift on planetary patrol. Instinctively she tensed, but his handsome face was as calm as she'd seen it in a while. It hadn't been that way when she'd first taken him aside to break the news she and Dake would marry.

"You sure look pretty tonight, Val," he said.

"Thanks," she replied warily.

"I got something to say to you." He wedged his fingers into his pockets. She braced herself for a tantrum or a salvo of words designed to make her feel guilty. "My reaction the other day when you told me you were getting married was wrong. I want to say sorry for that."

She blinked, wondering if she'd heard him right.

His eyes were shadowed and dark, genuinely remorseful if she could believe it. "You got no choice marrying him the way I see it. You got a son. Dake's the father. Marrying him is the right thing to do, just like you said the other day. No, I'm still not happy about it, but I wish you well all the same. You gotta do what you think is best for the clan's future." He paused, clearing his throat. "We all do. Right?"

"Aye. We all do." She offered him a smile. "I'm glad you wanted to talk. I don't want you as an enemy, Ayl."

"I know that. Have fun at the party. I gotta finish some maintenance on my junk heap of a ship before my patrol starts."

As he walked away, she pondered him. Had they really had that conversation? Could it be they were both finally maturing, forged by their hardships instead of being hobbled by them?

Laughter alerted her to Dake approaching with Jaym on his shoulders. The faithful puppy bounded along behind them. Every time she saw the pup she thought of Dake's first moments back on the windswept plains of Parramanta. She wasn't one for crying, but how could anyone have kept a dry eye that day seeing Dake reunite with Yarmouth, the first mate he'd thought for sure was dead, or watching an aged Merkury's hesitant first steps accelerate into a full-bore run, and Dake's expression of sheer joy as dog and master collided in a storm of barking and laughter.

It had taken Yarmouth and the dog over a year to find their way back home in the little escape pod. By then the two clans were at war. When Yarmouth did finally convince the Surebloods to contact the Blues with the news that Dake Sureblood had been captured and suspected Nezerihm was behind it, the Blues were in no mood to listen. Val remembered that day. Ayl was manning the comm. He never gave details, only that "those Sureblood bastards are trying to feed us more lies." If only she'd been there to hear the call that day. Would knowing Dake was in Drakken hands have made the long years without him easier or harder? No amount of soul searching would ever give her that answer, she imagined.

"Mama, look!" Slung over Jaym's neck was a decorated cup on a string: his Sureblood "drink cup" that he never took off, even for sleeping. His arms were flung out to the sides as if he was flying as Dake lifted him over his head.

"Watch out—he's coming in for a landing! It's going to be a rough one…turbulence. Hold on!" Gripping the boy by the belt, Dake swung him around, while Jaym pretended to be a skiff. His giggles and "hard landing" had Val laughing.

Jaym picked himself up, dusted off and ran to her for a hug. "Bye, Mama."

"Where are you going?"

"Spying."

She propped her hands on her hips. "Spying on whom?"

"All the grown-ups at the party!" Jaym launched himself at Dake next and wrapped his skinny legs around his father's waist. Val paused to soak in the sight of the look of tenderness and gratitude in Dake's face, and her precious son held fast in his father's strong arms.

Then Dake crouched down to attach a knife to the boy's pretend weapons belt.

Val balked. "That's a real blade."

Dake was unapologetic. "The sooner he learns and respects real weapons the better. You can't win a war with sticks."

"I'll be responsible," Jaym assured her, firmly, as if he were ten years older. "And if I need protection, I know I've got it." He ran off with the puppy in trail, leaving Val disconcerted.

"Only five and he already knows he might have to fight for his life," she said.

Dake snatched her hand and pulled her into a re-sounding kiss. Stroking her hair, he kept her close. "He's got to understand what he is, and what it means."

"I want him to have a childhood." She thought of

her own carefree years being stolen and didn't want the same for Jaym.

"He will, Val. I promise you that. But leaving him free to play doesn't mean leaving him naive. He knows that already, I think."

Jaym was going to be the leader of their people. "King of the pirates," some were already calling him. Jaym took it all with his usual aplomb. As big as his personality was, he was innately humble.

"He's got the best of both of us in him," Dake mused as if guessing her thoughts.

"Aye, he does." Knowing the uncertainty of the future, she hoped it was enough.

CHAPTER TWENTY-FIVE

THE FEASTING WENT ON until the wee hours. Moonshine flowed, and there were always new platters of food being left out. They couldn't quite afford the splurge, but Sashya insisted, telling them that there was a time for belt-tightening, but an engagement party wasn't one of them.

"You'll eat bread tomorrow," she said with a sniff, looping her arm through Grizz's. The couple had stayed close all evening.

"We'll eat *Triad* bread tomorrow," Val boasted. To raucous whoops of approval, she raised a glass of moonshine. They'd take whatever the Triad was willing to give them. Not charity, Val pointed out, working hard to convince the skeptics in the clan, but booty of a different sort, reaped through a form of hatch busting they'd not yet tried: *diplomatic* hatch busting.

It wasn't the pirate way to kowtow to outsiders, but times were different now and they needed to adapt to them or die. In the end what mattered was survival with pride. It always would. They'd never be the Triad's pets, but they'd keep the ore flowing, so long as their new outsider allies kept their word they'd let them stay.

Val downed the tiny cup of moonshine. Dake's cup

was empty, and he seemed a bit tipsy as he hooked an arm around her waist. His stepmother and stepsisters had already gone to sleep, and Despa was teaching his handsome half brother how to dance slango. The healer and Ayl didn't seem to be on speaking terms any longer.

"Come here, Blue girl." Dake pulled Val into a shadowed corner and kissed her. He tasted like salt and moonshine. "Mmm. I've been waiting to do that all night."

"We *have* been doing that all night. No waiting about it." She kissed her way across his mouth. "Now what I'm *waiting* to do can't be done but at home in the bedroom."

He cupped her bottom with his hand and chuckled, his breath hot on her throat, his jaw rough but his lips tender. "What's stopping us from going there?"

Impulsively she hugged him and held him. "My heart is full," she said softly.

"My heart is *yours,* Blue girl."

Happiness, she thought. It had taken them under its blissful wing. After so much pain, they were both ready to rejoice in their new state. Gripping each other's hands, they returned to the revelers and said their goodbyes. Eventually they found their way up the path, picking their way home in the moonlight, carefully, being under the influence of the moonshine. Merkury padded ahead of them, but the old dog's eyesight wasn't what it used to be.

A few lights were on in Hervor's house where Jaym was sleeping with Yanney. Hervor and his wife, Julen, were relaxing on the porch. Dake indulged Val's need to make sure Jaym was all right.

Her former skiff mate put down a book at their approach. Val grinned. "If it's not a bother, we came to kiss our boy goodnight."

Hervor shook his head. "He's not here. I thought he was staying with Sashya."

Val's heart skipped a beat. "Sashya's at the feast." In the village it wasn't unusual for children to come and go, for it had always been safe. But she more than anyone should know that was no longer the case. She cast her gaze about in the darkness.

Dake gave her hand a squeeze. "Jaym's fine. He wanted to stay in his own house is all. He's fast asleep in our bed with his trusty guard pup."

They hurried home. The pup's barking didn't greet them at the front steps. Val swallowed a leaden ball of unease. Merkury sniffed around, tail wagging, but his little friend wasn't there.

Neither was their son. "Jaym!" she called. They tore through the house seeing only empty beds.

Dake cupped his hands around his mouth to yell out the back door. "Jaym!" No enthusiastic "Papa" answered the calls.

The old feelings of not being where she needed surfaced, of being reckless, of taking pleasure over duty. Dake took her by the shoulders, turning her to look her in the eye. "We'll go out and find him. Don't worry."

But there were plenty of hazards for a child, or anyone, out wandering after dark. "I'm going to teach that boy something about accountability," she grumbled. "Just in case he takes after his uncle Sethen."

Their calls alerted the others in the village and soon more joined the search.

"He said he was spying." Dake peered toward the beach. "He might still be down there, probably sound asleep under a tree."

That made sense. She clung to it. Word had already spread to the revelers on the beach. Grizz shoved his dozer in his holster. "I'll have a look around down by the cove."

"I'll go with him," Sashya said.

Ferren headed off in the direction of the lake as Malta bellowed to several nearby apprentices. "They're looking for Jaym. If you see him, send him to his folks."

The apprentices fanned out. At least two of them were drunk. Val winced, wishing she hadn't drunk moonshine, wishing the clan was sober. "Why wasn't I paying more attention?"

"There was no reason to. We thought he was with Hervor."

"I should have made sure. I should have—"

"We'll find him. It's not the first time a little boy's gone lost, and it won't be the last."

The camp dogs known to be good trackers had their muzzles rubbed in a piece of Jaym's clothing and were sent off to search. Merkury took off in a determined path, nose to the ground, jerking this way and that as he followed a scent trail Val hoped was Jaym's. Ferren dived in the lake tirelessly. With her bare hands she stirred up layers of muck on the bottom all while Val hoped with everything she had that the girl wouldn't be successful.

Where was he? Beyond the torchlight the night loomed. Jaym would be everywhere in any given day, never sitting still for long, and that got Val's stomach churning. It was difficult to figure out where he might have gone.

While you were drinking moonshine and dancing slango instead of making sure your son was safe.

Dake took her chin between his fingers. She could tell he was fighting letting his own alarm show. It would only resonate with hers and grow larger. They were pirates, but they were parents. It required a whole new method of operation. "You got me, Blue girl. You're not alone anymore."

She squeezed his arm. "I know."

The entire village plus Surebloods were engaged in the search now. All through the night they looked for Jaym. Then, finally relenting the feverish hunt at daybreak, Val sat down with Dake, leaning against him, utterly drained. She was offered hot soup, accepting only after Dake forced her, but she had no appetite for it. His family and hers stayed close while the drumbeat of dread boomed louder.

"Hoy!"

Val flew upright at an approaching raider. Ayl strode over to them, carrying an exhausted puppy. Val's heart sank at the sight of the dog that never parted from his master, and the terrible look in Ayl's eyes. She'd never seen him looking this bereft, not Ayl, and it drove home the reality she might have lost her baby. Inside, she started shaking. "Where did you find him? We called and called." She took the pup from Ayl. "Why didn't you come?" she murmured in its fur, burying her hands in the warmth to hide her trembling.

Dake rested a hand at the base of her neck to steady her and let her know he was there.

"I found him cowering in deep brush over by the docks," Ayl was saying. "He wouldn't come to me. I had to coax him out." He pulled something from his pocket next. "I found this, too."

Jaym's lanyard with the drink cup dangling.

Val's throat seemed to swell shut, the drumbeat of dread reaching a crescendo. She pushed to her feet; swaying, she pressed her hand to her forehead and scanned the woods around her as if she could some- how rip away the shadows of which she swore held the secret to finding Jaym. *Let him not be dead. Please.* It was impossible to imagine life without her boy.

"I'm sorry, Val." Ayl actually did appear sorry, his eyes dark and anxious.

Dake took the lanyard and gave it to her. "See? There's the pup and the drink cup. It means we're get- ting close."

Close to what—finding him dead or alive? She didn't ask; she couldn't bear to hear the answer. Jaym never left the pup, or vice versa. He never went to bed without his Sureblood drink cup either, since decorating it as Dake had taught him. She was mama-proud of Jaym's handiwork. In the torchlight she could see the tiny, primitive figures he'd etched: a boy, a dog, flowers and trees. Child's art.

Jaym was so self-assured for his age that it was easy to forget he was still just a baby. She couldn't bear the thought of him badly hurt. Or worse. She clutched it to her breasts, the noise of the clan swirling around her, her husband-to-be organizing the next steps in the search. The decision was made to scour the docks for the lost boy. It was crowded with ships. Jaym may have sneaked aboard one, and now he was either hiding or asleep. But an all-out search of every ship yielded no boy.

"Funny how the boy went missing when *they're* here," Warrybrook sneered, glowering at Yarmouth and the other Sureblood clansmen helping in the search. "Can you really ever trust a Sureblood?"

Dake stopped in his tracks, turning to the Blue raider as the clansmen started to grumble at the insinuation that the Surebloods were somehow responsible. Ayl's group was taking advantage of raw emotions. "What are you saying?" he demanded.

Warrybrook exchanged glances with Ayl. "I'm sayin' that we've got too many outsiders here for my liking. Now a missing boy."

"My *son*," Dake said hoarsely, white-hot anger bursting behind his eyes. Yarmouth lunged at the man. Dake's half brother caught him, pulling him back, as Grizz fought Warrybrook backward, too.

"We've got a boy to search for," Dake said, disgusted at them all. "This is no time for fightin'."

"Since when did you take over as my clan captain, telling us what to do?" Ayl snarled back.

It took everything Dake had in him not to swing his fist and level the raider right then and there. Keeping the fury and his dislike for the man out of his voice was almost as hard. To Warrybrook and to Ayl, he said, "I want to keep the focus on finding our son. If you haven't figured out how much that boy means to your clan captain, then you're to be pitied."

Ayl stiffened, setting his jaw. Dake wasn't sure if the intensity of his disappointment had rendered Ayl silent or only the despair behind his words, but the raider said nothing more.

Yet as the hours passed, rumors of the Sureblood's involvement continued to spring up. Insulted, Dake's clansmen just as vigorously denied them, blamed it all on the Blues' lack of security, and more fights broke out. There were heartening signs of teamwork, too. Grizz reminded him that many more clansmen got along than didn't.

Their unity was still fragile. Anything that stressed the bonds, like Jaym's disappearance, threatened to destroy it. His people would not run this time. They'd stay until things were set right.

Dake fought off a vision of Drakken hunter ships waiting to haul his entire clan away, should they decide to leave, then he scoured his hand over his face. No more Drakken. No more Coalition. Peace had come. Although there was little of it to be found in his own life, he thought bleakly. His son was missing, there was renewed friction and suspicion between the clans and now he and Val were officially no-shows for the historic meeting with Captain Johnson on the *Unity*, putting their one possible chance at a future in these Channels in jeopardy.

Johnson had thrown a rope across the raging river of conflict and hate, expecting Dake to yank it tight and bridge their differences. Instead it would look like Dake dropped his end. He'd think Nezerihm was right about the pirates: reliable only in their penchant for causing trouble.

On his exhausted return home, he stopped to watch the sun sink below the horizon. A second night beginning for a lost boy. As the last rays retreated, Val joined him, clutching Jaym's abandoned drink cup in a white-knuckled hand. She hadn't let go of it since he'd handed it to her. "He can't be dead. Dake, if he is…if Jaym's gone…I don't think I can survive it."

He swore. He'd been so focused on the search all day he'd forgotten about her. "You got through today. We'll get through the next hour." He slowly advanced, his arms out, his hands turned palm up. "That'll be our goal tonight. Hour by hour. Minute by minute if we have to." Dake snatched her wrist. "You'll survive this. *We* will."

She swung her tangled hair. "I've let down my clan. I've let down my son."

"Not true!" She swore at him when he dragged her close and wrapped her in his arms. "You can't control everything. I learned that a long time ago. Leader or no, there are times that fate will overrule you."

She was shaking her head.

"You can try your best, and we will, I swear it. But Blue girl, fate has the final word in good things and in bad. We can do no more than accept it. A raider knows when the battle is won or lost."

With a wrenching, despairing sound, she broke down. This, coming from a woman who the Blues bragged had never shed more than a tear or two in all the years they'd known her.

She wept, alternately pounding her fists against his chest and gripping him close for all she was worth. The only constant was her tears. With the same hands that were forced to fire Drakken rifles and grip sledgehammers to smash blocks of rock, he held her with all the tenderness he knew how. He could tell the moment she surrendered her fight when she let her head sag to his chest, without words, simply drawing on his soul to feed hers, exactly what he knew she'd do for him if the tables were turned.

This was what love was at its most basic, he realized. This was what you got when you stripped away infatuation and lust to uncover what was unconditional and true. This was what he'd lived for, and would fight for, for all the days of his life.

This, he thought, would get them through this crisis and all the ones to come.

Finally Val stirred in his arms and looked up. He took her sweet, pretty face in his hands, stroking her cheek with the back of his hand. But in her eyes he could see her broken heart and felt helpless to heal it.

HE LEFT VAL WITH ORDERS to get some sleep and to ignore clan business until she did so. He and a mixed team of clansmen did another sweep through the woods.

When he finally returned at sunrise, he caught up short seeing Val sitting with Ayl, her hand in his. The man had brought her flowers and a few hot pies, all still lying untouched on the table. As irrational as the feeling was, jealousy pricked. Why the hells was this trouble-maker here, pretending he was torn up about what had happened? And why was he holding his wife-to-be's hand?

Dake shoved open the door and stomped inside. "If you care so much about her, then you should be outside helping search. They need all the hands they can get. I didn't see you all night. Where were you? Here?"

Ayl stood, wary and for good reason. He was tall for a Blue, but Dake was still inches taller.

Sashya put down the cloth she'd used to blot her endless tears. "He'll go out and help. Right, Ayl?"

"He's been here only a short time, Dake," Val said, defending the man.

A ball of outrage swelled in his chest. "I don't want him here."

Val's eyes darkened. "I speak to anyone I want. I'm clan leader."

"I know you're clan leader. And I'm *protecting* her." He turned to Ayl. "I've been hearing things out there. Things I don't like that you're saying. Is it true you still think we're to blame for my son going missing?"

Ayl gathered his jacket and tossed it over his shoulder. "I'll talk to you later, Val. When he's not so tense."

Dake grabbed hold of Ayl, forced him outside to the front porch and swung him up against the side of the house, his knuckles wrapped in the fabric of Ayl's collar.

Ayl hit with an "oomph" sound and Dake ratcheted down his force a specken. He was fine with killing, just not accidental killing. "Tense, you say? I had five years of my life stolen from me. Five years fighting someone else's wars, being beaten and starved. Five years of waking up to someone poking me with a stick to see if I was breathing or another carcass. I watched my crewmates die, Ayl, good men all. I watched them die and I could do nothing to help them. I was forced to leave my future wife alone in her darkest hour, leaving her to give birth to a son whose father she believed betrayed her. All this, Ayl, all this because of your good friend Nezerihm." Dake fairly shuddered in rage at the idea and at the panic that flashed in Ayl's dark eyes. "I swear it, I'll block you at every step, if you're wanting closer clan ties with that monster."

"Then maybe you're as guilty of laying blame on others as much as anyone else around here. Maybe you can't get past what happened to you either. Maybe there isn't any hope for unity after all."

Dake paused, never expecting this turn in the conversation.

"You keep bringing up what you went through, Sureblood. I'm not saying it wasn't hells for you, but you can't let it go either."

Dake set his jaw. How did one let go of something like that, when the man who caused it still walked free?

"What I'm saying, Sureblood, is that I'm not the only

one clinging to old transgressions. You're as guilty as anyone else is around here, hanging on to the past. Aye, your heart's as filled with hate as mine is."

Hells be, he thought, scowling. It was like the man had held up a mirror with a reflection he didn't want to see. He loosed his grip and let Ayl slide lower until his weight was back on his feet. One hand spread on the wall, Dake hung his head. The frenetic pace and emotional toll of the past two days finally caught up to him. He was wrung-out and exhausted, sick with worry for Jaym and for Val. "Maybe you got a point there about the blaming, but I like to think the forces that be, the fates, the gods—whatever you want to call them—let me live so I could do some good. I thought I could start here, on Artoom. But everywhere I turn there's you and your posse causing trouble from the shadows 'cause you're too scared to fight fair and in the open, where we can debate the issues and even solve them like Conn would have wanted us to. Why won't you meet me halfway, or at all? *Why,* blast it? How can I get you to work with me, and not against me?"

Disgusted, Dake pushed away from the wall. He started to turn away when Ayl said, "I wanted her, that's why. Is that the answer you want to hear, Sureblood? I wanted the clan captain's daughter to love me. Everyone would look up to me, then. They'd think of me as a great man because she wanted me. Instead all she ever wanted was you." His chin jutted out. He seemed to struggle to compose himself. "It's all gone to hells now. Everyone hates me."

"I don't hate you, Ayl," Dake said quietly. "I freepin' feel like killing you sometimes, but I don't hate you."

Ayl's eyes were suddenly moist, and it didn't look fake or generated for pity. "That's why you can't blame forever. Sometimes people do things for reasons you don't know or even understand. Sometimes…they make mistakes." Ayl dabbed at his bleeding lip with the back of his hand. He seemed a man overcome with misery. "You were right about Nezerihm all long," he said softly. "It was me you couldn't plan for."

A terrible pounding started up in Dake's head.

"I made a mistake…a big mistake. But I'm gonna make it right. I promise."

Dake's heart hit his rib cage with a sickening lurch. *He hurt Jaym.*

"Not all mistakes can be made right." The men jolted at the sound of Val's voice. She sent Dake a warning glance to keep him at bay as she stepped onto the porch. "But they can be *mitigated*." Her quiet, measured voice accompanied the grit of her boots as she stepped closer. Her skin was still pale, but her jaw was hard and her eyes flinty. Captain Val was back.

She might as well be in full armor, dozers drawn, as she stopped in front of Ayl. "Where's my little boy?" she asked, cold enough to extract the information she needed, but not sharp enough to spook him.

Ayl broke down, sobbing into his shaking hands. "Nezerihm's got him. Fates save us all, I let him take Jaym."

CHAPTER TWENTY-SIX

"THROW THE DOUBLE-CROSSING mucker in the brig!" Grizz's orders echoed as Ayl was led away in cuffs.

"Traitor," Grizz growled, his haggard face flushed with hatred as Sashya stood close to him, hollow-eyed, her hand pressed over her mouth. "Outsider's whore."

Their horror and those in attendance made the very air in the meeting house tremble. Val had to hold Dake back from striking down the shamed raider as he was shoved out the door. Hells, she could barely hold back herself from murdering the man with her own hands. She'd thought she'd seen the utter depths of human behavior in what Nezerihm had done to Dake. Ayl's confession convinced her she was wrong. He'd believed his actions were necessary for the good of the clan. Only in the end did he realize his mistake.

"Let them take him, Dake," she urged. "He gave us what we need—times, dates, places, plans…" Even his supposed reward once Jaym was disposed of. The more he'd confessed, the sicker she had felt. It was hard to think clearly despite the horror of hearing how Ayl had lured Jaym away during the party with promises of a joyride on his patrol ship, only to hand him off to a man who was arguably the most wicked in all the Borderlands if not the galaxy, who now had her five-year-old son in his clutches, the child of the two pirates he hated most. "For now, he'll be more use to us alive than dead."

"Bah. I care less about his 'use' to me than how good strangling him will make me feel."

"We've got a raid to organize," she urged. "The most important raid of our lives."

He turned to her then. The sight of her broken heart reflected so clearly in his face nearly brought her to her knees.

But she was already cried out, and growing colder and more determined by the minute, a frightened, distraught mother who in the space of hours had become a merciless, relentless instrument of rescue and vengeance. She would find her son and then eradicate Nezerihm from the face of existence. Aye, she'd do it without hesitation and with no regard for her own life.

The stunned clansmen around her continued to ask themselves how such a thing could have been allowed to happen. It was a very good question. Outsiders had never been trusted. No pirate in that room had been shocked to learn Nezerihm aimed to destroy their people. Most already suspected him of tampering with their communications and raids, and of pitting the clans against each other. But Ayl's betrayal blindsided them. All of them. Not one soul could have fathomed one of their own would betray them so completely. The boggling treachery was so far removed from any pirate's cultural expectation that it simply could not have been predicted. Within that bubble of naïveté Ayl was able to act. It caught them with their pants down.

The goal now must be to do the same to Nezerihm.

Ayl claimed Nez intended to keep the boy imprisoned on Aerokhtron and not kill him, but Val didn't trust Nezerihm's promise any more than she did his fragile grip on his sanity. They had to get their boy out of his clutches before Nezerihm snapped, or found that keeping a five-year-old alive was more trouble than it was worth.

With Ayl gone from the room, Dake pushed a hand through his hair. "We've got to contact Frank Johnson. He expects me back with his shuttle. At the very least, he expects to hear from me. The longer we remain silent, the more suspicious he'll get, and then he'll send the Triad after us, which will complicate any rescue mission we launch."

"What will you tell him?" Val demanded.

"The truth."

That they knew Nezerihm kidnapped Jaym? "No." She pushed at Dake, and he grabbed her hands, pinning them to his chest so she couldn't use them. "He'll say something to Nezerihm," she pleaded. "We can't risk him feeling cornered while he's still got control of Jaym." She tried not to let thoughts of the monster torturing her son fracture her dwindling composure.

"Johnson won't say anything. We'll tell him not to—and why."

"But he's an outsider," she argued.

"Not like Nezerihm. A different kind." Skeptical

grumbling rose up around them. "He'll cooperate. I know what the Triad wants—and what Nezerihm doesn't—all of us sitting down at the negotiation table. That's what we'll give them if Johnson works with us."

Boots started thumping on the planked floor. No raiders liked the idea. "We pirates owe Nezerihm nothing!" some bellowed. "Or the Triad!"

"The meeting will be our forum to show what a monster Nezerihm really is! He's holding a five-year-old child hostage, for fate's sake. A baby. If we prove Nez is capable of that, we can prove just about everything else we say he's done." Dake glared around the bustling room. "And bring him down."

Protests about trusting outsiders shifted to chants of "Bring him down."

"Are you sure?" Val asked. "Do you trust him?"

Dake paused, squeezing her hands. "More than any man should be asked to wager rests on me making the right decision. Aye, Val. I trust Frank Johnson."

And was willing to balance their son's life on that impression.

Sashya pushed away the raiders crowding in on her, her shawl flowing. "And if Nezerihm denies he took the boy? What use is the forum, then? He'll sit there and lie if he thinks it'll save his hide."

Grizz nodded. "He's the main source of zelfen. Your Frank Johnson has more to lose believing us pirates than Nezerihm."

"We don't need to worry about that," Dake said. In the chaos of yelling and stomping boots, Val saw, and recognized, the telltale glint in his eyes. Dake Sure-blood was one step ahead of them all. "Because we'll rescue Jaym from Nez before the muck-rucker ever reaches the *Unity*—and Johnson."

As the raiders whooped their approval and boots thundered against the planks of the floor, Val saw in Dake a reflection of her deadly resolve to find their son. Together the clans would pull off the most important and daring raid ever undertaken. It would be done at the risk of angering their one ally, Frank Johnson, and alienating the entire Triad Alliance with their false change of heart to hold mediated negotiations with Nezerihm. But only with her son back safely in her arms would Val sit down at any table on the *Unity*, with or without Nezerihm. That was, if Johnson was still willing to talk after he found out what they were about to do.

STRIKING A POSE IN FRONT of his mirror, Nezerihm dressed in his most resplendent finery. The boy would know he'd met a king.

He went back to pacing, wringing his hands in his impatience to begin the final stage of his plans. Ayl had given him something better than his most fervent dreams, and without a hitch. How easily he'd fooled Ayl into believing he intended to use the child as a hostage to further their aims. Hostage? Please. Try casualty. So trusting and dim-witted the pirates were, even when it came to their own offspring. Didn't they know the consequences of not being constantly alert to threats to their realm?

Nezerihm knew all about such threats—and how to get rid of them. He'd exterminate the brat like a common housefly. It would gut the Blue-Sureblood resistance movement. They'd lose the will to fight.

And he'd win, just as he always knew he would. The pirates were simply no match for him.

His staffer Rolm commed him. "My lord, I have the child."

"Very good. Bring him to me."

Nezerihm trusted no one else with the task. R_ would have been his chief of staff if Nezerihm we assign such titles. But rank always went to men's h_ and so Rolm was no higher in status than any of the others.

Ever so impatiently, Nezerihm faced the doors they opened. He rubbed his hands together. He si_ couldn't stay still as a small boy stumbled throug_ doors. Anticipation shot Nezerihm so full of p_ that he trembled from head to toe. There was something so pure about a child's terror.

The disheveled youngster straightened and searched out Nezerihm. His eyes narrowed, appearing so much like his sire's eyes. "Let me go, you muck-rucking, dirt-digging outsider!"

The strength in that piping voice startled Nezerihm. He didn't like the way the boy stood there, boots placed sturdily apart, his clothing tattered and torn from struggling. He didn't like the way he showed no fear at all.

Just like the unrepentant transport captain he'd executed for allowing Val Blue to raid his ship. That man had been disrespectful, too, as disrespectful as this brat!

Nezerihm sauntered toward the boy in his glittering finery. He saw the child's eyes drawn to the zelfen and jeweled trim, undoubtedly nothing like he'd ever seen before. "Would you like a frozenade?"

"No!"

"A sweet cake, perhaps?"

"No!"

"You are being difficult, you know. It won't make it any easier."

"I want to go home," the boy demanded. "Take me now."

"I'm afraid that's impossible."

"You're lying. You just don't want to take me back." The boy's chin jutted out defiantly with confidence that belied his few years.

Nezerihm quaked with outrage, lifting his fist to strike the boy.

The brat didn't flinch. His fisted hands hung at his sides.

Nezerihm trembled now. He wanted to throw the little creature to the floor and beat him to within an inch of his life. He wanted to hear him sob and sputter for his mama.

And his papa, too. Maybe especially his papa.

Wait, he cautioned himself. *Wait until he shows his fear. It wouldn't take long.*

Shaking, Nezerihm held his rage in check. "Your mama and papa don't want you," Nezerihm said smoothly. The flicker of surprise in the boy's gaze heartened him. "They gave you away."

"That's a lie!"

"Is it? They let Ayl give you to me, yes? They were too busy at their party to watch you, caring more about each other, *loving each other* more than they do you."

The brat's little chest was heaving, his long dark lashes moist. No fear, but the little bit of uncertainty gave Nezerihm hope. He wasn't ready to be broken yet, no. He'd have to be worn down first like a too-spirited horse.

"With your parents, you'll always get the leftovers when it comes to love. The scraps."

The little boy's nostrils flared at that. "Scraps is all *you'll* get for now on, outsider! Because we pirates are back together. I'm gonna be the king of us all someday, too."

"Quiet!" Nezerihm screamed to cover up the flare of panic the boy's boast conjured.

"And if my mama and papa don't kill you, I will."

He swung his arm to cuff the boy.

"My lord…"

"What!" Lowering his fists, Nezerihm was shaking as he whirled on the intrusion.

Rolm was at the doors. "It's Captain Johnson with a priority message."

Nezerihm slowed his breathing. "Take the brat from my sight. Clean him up before you bring him back.

He stinks like a pirate. And dress him in some proper clothes."

Rolm scooped up the wriggling child and threw him over his shoulder, carrying him from the room. Wringing his hands, Nezerihm commanded his message screen open to take the incoming signal. Frank Johnson stood center screen, looking as friendly as always. The eye in the center of a storm.

"Lord Nezerihm," the captain said. "The pirates have agreed to mediation on the situation in the Channels. I don't want to proceed in talks without you."

"No," Nezerihm gasped. "Not without me."

"How soon can you be here?"

"Consider me on my way right now." With glee he pictured the pirates bellowing and jostling to argue their points, and he serene, not behaving like a barbarian. Now was his chance to shore up his dependability in contrast to them, with his calm and his utter qualification as leader of the Channels.

The boy...

Nezerihm spat and shivered. He reached for the comm to decline the invitation, so he could stay and work on softening up the child instead.

But he couldn't risk not being present for the talks, couldn't risk the pirates gaining any influence or taking his power. That meant not showing up with bruised knuckles or any signs of a struggle.

He couldn't forget the first time he'd met Johnson and the way the captain noticed the scratches on his hands from the little whore who had fought his attentions with such liveliness. No, he'd not finish off the little pirate brat just yet, but he'd keep him close by. The boy would come with him for the round-trip to the *Unity,* all while Nezerihm dreamed up his perfect, tortuous extermination.

LONG AFTER CLOSING THE transmissions with Dake Sureblood and Nezerihm, Frank remained at his desk. While Dake Sureblood had delivered on his promise to bring Val Blue on board the peace initiative, Nezerihm had done nothing but rock the boat—if what the pirate was telling him was true. Triad directives required him to treat all parties with neutrality, but he sure as hell would like to beat the crap out of the ingratiating zelfen merchant. Stealing a kid. Could the slimeball stoop any lower? Frank hadn't hesitated to agree to the terms of the pirates' request to use his ship as neutral ground for the hostage negotiations. He'd said nothing more to Nezerihm about it than invite him aboard, which the man accepted with nauseating eagerness.

"Sir!" Gwarkk burst into the office. Frank was about to vent about the mine owner when he noticed his first officer's disconcerted expression. "We've been getting signals from the shuttle. It seems to be stowed in the cargo hold of a larger ship."

"That makes sense, Lieutenant. They're bringing extra clansmen, too many to fit on a single shuttle. At least they're returning it."

"The tracking device says Captains Blue and Sureblood aren't headed here at all," Gwarkk said.

Frank pushed to his feet. "What does it say?"

"They're on a flight course dead set for Lord Nezerihm's ship."

WITH THE *MARAUDER* pegged at max velocity, Val stood silent and somber as Dake dragged his thumb across her cheek, leaving behind a bright slash of war paint to decorate her face Sureblood-style for battle. Everyone on their handpicked crew were the best of the best from both of their clans. All were hard at work donning their gear for the raid on Nezerihm's flagship that she hoped held her little boy, alive.

On board, it was loud, as it always was before a raid, but the moment between her and Dake stretched out, almost tender, the painting of each other's face taking on special significance. They were raiders and they were pirate captains, but they were also parents. They knew if the raid went wrong, Jaym could die, or if he was left behind on Aerokhtron with guards, he might die. Yet if they did nothing, he'd likely still perish. Nezerihm would never let a child of theirs grow up to threaten him.

"Jaym has the best of both of us in him," Dake said as if to reassure them both. "The boy is tough. If anyone can survive Nezerihm, he can."

"Aye. But Nezerihm will never survive me." She rubbed her finger in the colored paste and drew it across Dake's cheekbone. Soon she'd turned Dake into the Sureblood raider she first met on an old freighter years ago.

A lifetime ago.

Silence fell between them. He touched the center of her chest plate where the design was still blank and unfinished. "What will go here?"

"Our Jaym," she said. "His name, written in the wind. If we make it back to Artoom."

He took her hand and squeezed it, his opalescent eyes intense. "*When,* Val. Not *if.*"

She brushed her lips across his, and he crushed her to him for a kiss that quickly turned passionate.

"Let's go get our boy," she murmured as they pulled away.

Grabbing their weapons, they got ready for a raid like no other. This time the booty was her son, her flesh and blood, and Dake's.

Then, against a breathtaking backdrop of rocky worlds and shifting channels between them, still a haven for her people and a graveyard for everyone else, Nezerihm included, she and Dake addressed their raiders. "Blues!" she shouted as Dake bellowed, "Sure-bloods!" Together they roared, "Are you ready to go a-raidin'?"

Battle cries thundered in the confines of the ship.

She pumped a fist in the air. "Launch the skiffs!"

Thwump-thwump and the first skiffs were on their way.

Leaving Grizz in command, Val departed with Dake for the skiff they'd pilot as a team. Reeve and Ferren were already on board when they boarded. Painted fiercely, Dake hooked up his comm.

Val couldn't help marveling at the sight of such a mixed crew. Raiding with a Sureblood, the concept still boggled, yet she could no longer imagine doing it any other way.

Ferren pulled the hatch closed. The craft pressurized as Val quickly strapped into her seat and took the controls, just as she'd done for so many years. Only this time the consequences of failure were too great to think about. Losing Jaym because she wasn't good enough, or quick enough, or even brave enough, was something she simply couldn't, and wouldn't, entertain.

"Rescue One's ready," she told *Marauder*. The docking hooks retracted and the skiff floated free.

There was a time when the beginning of a raid made her heart race with excitement. The adrenaline rush now was no different. Only the goal.

"You need some fear. Too much paralyzes you, and too little makes you reckless. Arrogant."

I know, Papa. Tempered by time and tragedy, and steadied by love, she'd left arrogance behind. As well as recklessness, she hoped.

Once in striking range, she could see that Nezerihm's ship was large and sleek, reflecting his prosperity. Dake's eyes narrowed, his upper lip lifting in a faint snarl. She knew he was thinking how much of the money that went into that vessel belonged to their people. Everything would change after today. Everything.

Dake sat up straight. "Freepin' hells. Raid crashers."

"What?" Where? She spun around in her seat, her mouth falling open at the sight of myriad skiffs falling out of the stars—skiffs painted in the colors of every pirate clan she knew. "Calders, Feckwiths, Lightlees and Freebirds," she murmured. "They're all here."

Dake's expression reflected his surprise and pleasure at their appearance. And worry that she also shared. "I'm all for a show of unity," he said. "But there is such a concept as too much of a good thing."

Frightening Nezerihm would very likely put Jaym in mortal danger.

Her stomach flipped, her skin growing damp with nerves. But thankfully the other skiffs stayed back, there to support if they needed them, but not to disrupt the raid. Whatever happened today, it would be known that all the pirates were in support of it.

For the first time in a generation.

Val cut the power and they coasted into the ship from behind. Tension in the skiff grew as they descended in darkness and comm silence. Drifting up to a hatch, she brought the skiff into position.

Dake gave her a curt, approving nod, then flicked his gloved hand, launching the team into action. Soundlessly, they fastened masks and attached safety ropes, then made a seal between the ships. Hundreds of years of tradition guided their actions, with very few differences considering their different clan origins. It reminded her again of Dake's claim: they were one people.

"Pressure's good," Val said, watching data stream across on her cockpit display. "Holding steady."

Holding steady against the void. Her gaze spun outside to empty space, the utter vacuum. She remembered when the idea of being sucked out was the worst imaginable nightmare. She'd lived through far worse.

With the seal intact, they busted through the hatch. Then they were in. Rechecking her gear, she exchanged one last, lingering glance with Dake, then nodded to Reeve and Ferren in turn. *Let's go,* she mouthed and led the way into Nezerihm's ship.

CHAPTER TWENTY-SEVEN

THE BLUES AND SUREBLOODS flowed into the ship, tucking away into nooks and crannies and moving toward the bridge. It was as empty aboard this luxurious vessel as the freighter had been. Then she remembered Nezerihm's distrust of anyone on his staff. There would be few aboard.

They rounded a corner and almost collided with a tall, silver-haired man carrying a tray of food out of a hallway door.

Val's heart nearly fell out of her chest as her dozer came up, aiming between the man's eyes seconds after Dake's was already there. "That way," the staffer said, gesturing with his chin down the corridor. "The boy."

"And Nezerihm?"

"The bridge."

Dake had him pressed up against the wall in a heartbeat. "You seem awfully quick to sell out Nez—"

"Boss." Yarmouth showed up, pushing another frightened company man ahead of him. "Found this one folding towels. He says Nezzie's on the bridge."

"So, that's two of you making it easy to find what we came here for."

"We came here for Jaym," Val said quietly.

"Aye," Dake agreed, cooling his battle lust. "Him first. Vengeance second."

Val felt Jaym's lanyard under her armor, nestled between her breasts, right over her pounding heart. *Mama's going to get you free, boy. But you gotta stay calm and let me and your papa do it.* She willed the thought to reach Jaym, and herself to stay calm.

Everything depended on what happened today.

They cuffed the two staffers, leaving one with raiders and taking the other with them to show them the way. "Do it," Dake growled in the hostage's ear, shoving him forward to unlock the door.

The staffer unlocked it and they whooshed through. Dozer tracking, frantic eyes searching, Val fought to see into the room. Light from the corridor fell across the floor. The swathe illuminated a small form crouched in the corner, a broken piece of trim clutched in two small hands like a dozer. It clattered to the floor. Dake's jaw was tight with tension even as relief flooded his painted face. Val could only imagine what they must have looked like to Jaym, storming the room in their war paint, like savage wolves taking back their cub.

"Mama—" Jaym said as Val covered his mouth with her glove, her hard stare willing him into silence. His ankle was chained to the bunk. His eyes were bleary, telling her he'd been given drugs.

"Oh, my baby. My boy." It hit her hard, then, how lucky they were to have found him unharmed. "Hush. Mama's here now." She held him tight to her armored breast. His little-boy scent drifted to her along with his fear. A mother might have wept. A raider couldn't.

Dake vaporized the restraint and pulled Jaym's leg free. Then he tossed Jaym onto Reeve's back. "Get him to the skiff."

"But I want to fight, too," Jaym protested groggily.

"This time it's your mama and papa's job." Val showered his damp little cheek with thankful kisses in the seconds before Reeve sprinted away to the skiff with the precious treasure clinging to his back.

The urge to follow almost overwhelmed Val. But the drive to eliminate the threat to her family kept her going toward the goal—disabling the bridge of this ship. Chilling the core was standard operating procedure with a hostile target. Once the plasma drive was shut down it would take hours to bring back up—plenty of time to clear the area of vulnerable skiffs. Val had thought this would be the hardest part, but letting her son out of her reach after just getting him back was far tougher.

The raiders moved like shadows, pushing their hostages in front of them. They stormed the bridge as they'd done to so many others in the past, sealing off all other access points around them.

Nezerihm was there, a thin, gray ghost of a man. His gaunt, aristocratic face blazed outraged shock. "Pirates! Get them."

Two of Nezerihm's men grabbed his arms, pinning him. "For our amnesty, you can have him," one shouted.

Val had almost fired at him. Only her split-second reactions kept her from killing the staffer.

"Rolm, what are you doing!" Nezerihm gasped in shock at one of the men.

"No one else move!" Dake stood at Val's side, his dozer aimed. She wasn't so sure he wasn't about to let a few blasts fly. "I'd like to squeeze the life outta you with my bare hands," he gritted out. "But I promised Johnson I'd play nice. We're going to fly you and your ship, nice and slow, to the *Unity* and—"

"No!" Nezerihm wrenched free and reached inside his cloak.

Plasma fire exploded on the bridge.

Val's dozer steamed in her hands, matching the smoking hole she'd put between Nezerihm's eyes that seemed to gape at her accusingly for a few seconds more. Then his legs buckled. He fell, blood spilling from one corner of his mouth. Only then, when she finally remembered to breathe, did she notice the equally mortal wound Dake had blasted through his chest.

They stood over him. "Not a man," she whispered. "A monster." Dake pulled her hard against his side and pressed his lips to her hair.

But there was a third wound, Val saw, even lower still. They spun around to see Ferren, her eyes wild with hate, a dozer clutched in her tiny hands.

Fates alive, Val thought. She'd shot Nez between the legs.

Her lips had pulled back, baring her teeth. Then, blinking, Ferren transformed back to the girl they'd come to know—or as much as she'd allowed them to. "He knows what he did," she explained simply. Without a specken of remorse she lowered her weapon and walked away.

"Whatever he did to Ferren," Dake told Val quietly, "and to us, he won't be doing it anymore."

As the enormity of the Triad ship *Unity* grew to fill the shuttle's view screen, so did Val's awe and doubts. Dake was right—the ship was larger than anything she could have imagined. With an exhausted Jaym curled up in her lap asleep, she thought of the rescue raid they'd accomplished without Triad approval, and couldn't help ponder the consequences. By eliminating one enemy had they'd gained another?

But Dake had insisted on returning the shuttle. She hoped they weren't thrown in the brig when they boarded.

"You are cleared to dock," a female voice said over the comm.

Dake steered the shuttle into the enormous bay that alone could have fit Artoom's entire village. After passing through decontamination, they were given permission to board.

She lowered a sleepy Jaym to his feet and straightened his clothes, leading him by the hand inside. A pair of strapping outsiders greeted them, Captain Johnson and his Drakken first officer, wearing colors representing all the peoples in the galaxy, except hers. Johnson extended his arm, reaching across a void that had never been crossed to clasp her hand. "The most notorious, vilest she-pirate in the galaxy, I presume," he said with quiet humor that put her instantly at ease. *It would be all right.*

"Aye, Cap'n," she said and flashed her infamous grin. "At your service."

ON THE MINING WORLD Aerokhtron, one week later, Ferren escaped Reeve and everyone else gathered for a meeting at Nezerihm's former headquarters. Finally she'd found her way here. It had taken years, years of patience, to make it to this point. In the beginning this goal had kept her alive. Even after she'd found contentment and purpose with the land-folk she'd come to love, she never allowed herself to forget her true mission.

Would she find Adrinn today or closure? Anticipation and dread both filled her as she stripped down to her underclothes and dived into the sparkling body of water surrounding Nezerihm's former keep.

Shafts of sunlight speared the depths, making her chest tighten with regret. She was no longer of this world and mourned it still. Her stay down here would be limited. She could hold her breath longer than any land-folk, but not for an infinite length of time.

Following the faint strains of a song only her ears could hear, she found her way to the shadowy bottom. She stopped, her hair swirling around her, her lungs straining for the air she could no longer live without, searching for signs. She almost missed the symbol carved into the rocks below. A trio of chevrons below a star. Waves and the sun. *Adrinn.* Her heart slamming, she dived down, her hair swirling, her hand swishing over the pattern. The current dislodged what

she thought were scum-covered pebbles, until she saw
them glinting silver. She snatched them and pressed
her fist to her straining chest.

The prince was dead.

Blessed Heart of the Sea. Her chest convulsed,
squeezing what little air remained in her lungs. A few
bubbles escaped her lips. She followed the bubbles
upward, exploding through the surface. Gasping out
a sob, she floated on her back, gripping the earrings
to her breasts. Her tears were indistinguishable from
the water streaming off her upturned face. *Adrinn...
Adrinn...*

When she'd loosed the last of her tears, she climbed
out of the rippling moat. Reeve was waiting, his expression pensive. The sight of her nearly unclothed darkened his eyes, a look she'd seen many times before.
And just like those times, he fought his attraction to
her with clear frustration.

She shivered in his heated regard, then slowly closed
the distance between them. "Treasure hunting?" he
asked, confused by the earrings in her palm.

"It was my mission to find these," she said, no longer
afraid to let the lyrical accent of her people show. "They
belonged to my prince. It is the belief of my people that
with his earrings in possession of one of our own, his
soul can finally rest. And," she said softly, "I, too, have
found the closure I sought, allowing me to go on with
my life."

A flare of panic in Reeve's eyes told her he thought
she might mean without him. She pressed a hand to his
chest, stilling the question forming on his lips.

"His name was Adrinn. We are from the water worlds. There, we use a nano-particle that lines our lungs and allows us to breathe underwater. Once it wears off, we can no longer do so. I never knew how quickly, though."

His eyes narrowed, memories of her apparent suicide attempt going through his head as he realized what she meant. "The night I found you trying to drown yourself, you weren't," he murmured.

"That's right. I couldn't accept the fact that I couldn't fill my lungs with water and live. That I'd become land-folk."

"Is it so bad, being one of us?" There was an edge to his voice.

She whispered, "Not anymore. Adrinn was captured by slavers. I thought I would die when it happened, and I volunteered for a mission to rescue him, against everyone's wishes. They said I'd never return and they were right. Still, I had to try." She rested her other hand on his cheek. "He was the only man I ever loved."

A muscle in Reeve's jaw jumped under her palm.

"Until you," she whispered.

He went very still. "You love me?"

"I have for a very long time. But I had to know what happened to Adrinn first. I had to know in my heart. We were promised to each other. On my world, a promise to marry is not taken lightly."

"It's not on mine either." He removed her hand from his cheek and pressed it to his chest. "I've waited for you, Ferren. I know you never asked me to, but blast it, I wanted to. I love you, girl, and am asking you to be my wife."

"There isn't anything else I'd rather be," she said and answered his shining smile with a long and passionate kiss.

FRANK JOHNSON STRODE INTO the boardroom of the former Nezerihm Mining Headquarters and stopped at the sight of the table of men and one woman who glowered back at him like clouds poised to spit rain. It was a meeting of the clan captains. They'd invited him, but he couldn't tell by looking at them.

"Look at all those cheery faces," Frank muttered out the side of his mouth to Gwarkk.

The Drakken made a quiet snort.

"Well, we on the *Unity* aren't in the happiness business, I suppose. We're in the peace business. Let's see if we can get this done."

Six pairs of cool eyes watched Frank as he sat, waiting to see if he'd say anything about Nezerihm's death during the rescue operation. As far as he was concerned, Nezerihm was out of the equation. Even if he hadn't met a bad end, he would have been history after today.

"Well. Let's get started." Frank opened his data briefer. He felt Dake Sureblood's razor-sharp, multicolored gaze on him, and Val Blue's wary regard. She didn't want to trust him, but had begun to, and for that he was thankful. It was the beginning of a future few in the Borderlands, much less the Channels, had ever imagined.

"It seems the treaty that Viro Nezerihm had held you to was as fresh as month-old milk." Grumbles erupted at his statement, accompanied by the pounding of fists. "In other words, it's expired. Twenty-seven years ago, to be exact. You own the mines. All the clans. Nezerihm Mining Company has no rights to them whatsoever."

The drum of boots on the floor joined the pounding of fists. He exchanged a glance with Gwarkk. "Damn," Frank muttered. He waited until the noise had died down and continued. "Based on this information, Prime-Admiral Zaafran has recommended that the Channels be considered sovereign, rendering Operation Amnesty invalid."

Frank found that he was shouting now to be heard, but he didn't mind a bit. It was a definite departure from the usual, mind-numbing meetings he was used it. "This will have to be ratified by Parliament, of course, but I see no barriers to that happening. Unless you find you can't hold up your end of the bargain."

"We sure as hells will hold it up!" one of the captains bellowed.

"Freepin' right we will."

"Aye, Cap'n. You'll have so much zelfen, you'll be buttering your toast with it."

They all roared with laughter at that.

The Lightlee captain snorted. "Buttering their toast with zelfen? Calder, are you mad? Operating the mines? You've never done it before."

"Neither have you!"

"Some of the Feckwith elders know how."

"Digging tuber roots, you mean, not zelfen ore!"

"We're going to rename company headquarters, too," the Calder leader snarled, spurring a new debate. "I ain't calling that planet Aerokhtron. It's like that sound you make when you're spitting."

Dake Sureblood laughed, grinning at it all. The father of unity, Frank thought and felt damn humbled to know him. "Come, Lieutenant Gwarkk. Our job's done here."

Frank doubted anyone noticed when they left.

SOMETIME LATER, VAL AND Dake ducked out of the boardroom to check on Jaym. The roar inside was so loud that the door they had closed behind them did little to mute the noise. The warmth of love and pride filled Dake seeing his son, his golden head bent in concentration, coloring with crayons scattered on the floor while he waited out his parents' return.

"The king of the pirates," Val said softly.

Dake nodded. "In time…"

Jaym looked up and ran to them, joyful as he was hoisted into his papa's arms. Standing with his wife-to-be and his son, Dake took time to savor the moment like he would after any successful raid. Every good pirate loved a prize, he thought. The prize for him and Val had been absolution. She'd come to accept that the blame for her father's death didn't rest on her shoulders, while he'd finally restored his clan's pride and honor. Together, they'd realized the dream of uniting the clans: Blues, Surebloods, Calders, Feckwiths, Lightlees and Freebirds, together as one people once more. So long as the Triad recognized, and respected, the autonomy of the Channels, there'd be no threat to their unification.

They were a legitimate territory now, and that would take getting used to, from not stealing their new allies blind to choosing the unlucky sot who'd be sent off to represent them in Parliament on the Triad's capitol in the central galaxy. Dake practically shuddered at the thought.

Behind them the din grew even louder as the details of the clans' new business were hammered out. Skiff drivers would train to be transport pilots, with armed-to-the-teeth pirate vessels providing protection just in case some in the Triad didn't respect the new company ownership. But would they hire outsider miners, or mine themselves, keep some of Nezerihm's workers, or not? Who would be forced to live in the Nezerihm palace, or would they ransack and demolish it? The raucous debating seemed to shake the very walls.

"Ah, the sound of freedom," Val said, her golden eyes sparkling with triumph as she took his hand in hers.

"Aye, Blue girl, freedom," Dake said, pulling her close. The pirates' future was by no means settled, but for now, it was theirs.

* * * * *

REQUEST YOUR
FREE BOOKS!

2 FREE NOVELS
FROM THE ROMANCE COLLECTION
PLUS 2 FREE GIFTS!

YES! Please send me 2 FREE novels from the Romance Collection and my 2 FREE gifts (gifts are worth about $10). After receiving them, if I don't wish to receive any more books, I can return the shipping statement marked "cancel." If I don't cancel, I will receive 4 brand-new novels every month and be billed just $5.74 per book in the U.S. or $6.24 per book in Canada. That's a saving of at least 28% off the cover price. It's quite a bargain! Shipping and handling is just 50¢ per book.* I understand that accepting the 2 free books and gifts places me under no obligation to buy anything. I can always return a shipment and cancel at any time. Even if I never buy another book, the two free books and gifts are mine to keep forever.

194/394 MDN E7NZ

Name	(PLEASE PRINT)

Address	Apt. #

City	State/Prov.	Zip/Postal Code

Signature (if under 18, a parent or guardian must sign)

Mail to **The Reader Service:**
IN U.S.A.: P.O. Box 1867, Buffalo, NY 14240-1867
IN CANADA: P.O. Box 609, Fort Erie, Ontario L2A 5X3

Not valid for current subscribers to the Romance Collection
or the Romance/Suspense Collection.

Want to try two free books from another line?
Call 1-800-873-8635 or visit www.morefreebooks.com.

* Terms and prices subject to change without notice. Prices do not include applicable taxes. N.Y. residents add applicable sales tax. Canadian residents will be charged applicable provincial taxes and GST. Offer not valid in Quebec. This offer is limited to one order per household. All orders subject to approval. Credit or debit balances in a customer's account(s) may be offset by any other outstanding balance owed by or to the customer. Please allow 4 to 6 weeks for delivery. Offer available while quantities last.

Your Privacy: Harlequin Books is committed to protecting your privacy. Our Privacy Policy is available online at www.eHarlequin.com or upon request from the Reader Service. From time to time we make our lists of customers available to reputable third parties who may have a product or service of interest to you. If you would prefer we not share your name and address, please check here. ☐

Help us get it right—We strive for accurate, respectful and relevant communications. To clarify or modify your communication preferences, visit us at www.ReaderService.com/consumerschoice.

SUSAN GRANT